The
Water Star

The
Water Star

PHILIP CASEY

PICADOR

First published 1999 by Picador

an imprint of Macmillan Publishers Ltd
25 Eccleston Place, London SW1W 9NF
and Basingstoke

Associated companies throughout the world

ISBN 0 330 37190 8

1 3 5 7 9 8 6 4 2

A CIP catalogue record for this book is available from
the British Library.

Typeset by SetSystems Ltd, Saffron Walden, Essex
Printed and bound in Great Britain by
Mackays of Chatham plc, Chatham, Kent

To Patrick Joseph Casey
and Annie Christina Cassidy
and their fellow exiles
London 1942–1957

Blue mountains are of themselves blue mountains
And white clouds are of themselves white clouds
And there is a blue mountain, Croghan Kinsella,
And around it there are often white clouds.

Whether all things are accurately themselves
Or modifications of each other I do not know,
But clear mornings from my bathroom window
I see white clouds and a blue mountain.

                    James Liddy, 'Blue Mountain'

PART ONE

One

HUGH

July 1950

They got off the trolleybus and Brendan headed straight to the newsagent's for cigarettes and a paper. Hugh crossed the road and waited for him. The rain had eased off, but in the distance the thunder still rolled away. It had forced them to stop work early, and they were drenched and tired. Brendan crossed through the traffic as if charmed, dragging on his cigarette, protecting his newspaper under his coat, and they walked by the low wall and railing of the flats in Wedmore Street, Hugh pushing himself to keep up. Brendan's cigarette never left his mouth, and his eyes were squinted against the smoke. Between drags he rolled it along his lips.

Shag this, Hugh thought, I'm not in the army. He slowed, but his father pushed on as if he hadn't noticed. The door was open when he reached number eighteen, and already Brendan was filling the tin bath upstairs.

Hugh covered the bedclothes with an army blanket and lay back in relief. His trousers were heavily smeared with mud, and every muscle in his body ached. The only sound in the room was the gas flame as the kettle boiled.

His father was slumped in the old armchair.

'They'll hardly have us work tomorrow.'

'Not worth the bother of getting up, so.'

'That would suit you fine, wouldn't it!'

On the street, Mrs Dempsey called Dennis as they arrived

home. He was forever running ahead, putting the heart cross-ways in his mother.

'More money lost,' Brendan muttered, adding the water he had boiled. Then he stripped and washed, standing in the bath.

Hugh took his turn, then emptied the bath into the porcelain sink, cursing quietly as some of it backwashed onto the lino. He glanced out the back window as he dried himself, and pulled on a dry shirt and trousers. Beyond the garden was a red-bricked office building. More often than not, there was a man sitting beside one of the windows on the third floor, and sure enough, there he was, looking down into the garden, watching young Dennis talking over the fence to the little girl next door. Hugh had never actually seen the man working. He was always either staring into space or looking out the window.

Brendan handed him a list, written with a carpenter's pencil, and read out each item deliberately. Hugh took money from a biscuit tin and went across the road to Sally's. Sally knew that he didn't speak very much, and he was comfortable with her. She respected a person.

Brendan set to frying the bread, eggs and sausages as the kettle boiled. The cooker, Hugh noticed with a vague disgust as he washed the dishes from the night before, was covered in grease. As he'd promised himself many a time, he'd give it a clean the coming Sunday, but right now he was starving and his mouth watered as the food spluttered in the pan.

'Are you going to Sarah's on Sunday?' Brendan asked as he finished his meal and pushed the plate away.

'I suppose so.'

'You better do your lessons, so,' Brendan laughed. He found the idea of anyone in long trousers doing lessons embarrassing.

'I'll do them tomorrow. Are you coming?'

'Ah,' he said, making a face. 'I'm past it.'

'She has me bothered asking about you.'

'She's a good woman,' Brendan said, lighting a cigarette, 'but Lord Jesus, she can be a fierce tyrant, and I'm too old for that kind of carry on. But you keep it up. You're young enough.'

Brendan took out his glasses and read his paper, but after a killer of a week, Hugh was too tired for anything but sleep.

He had deluded himself that he could lie in for once, and was baffled when Brendan called him early for work. It was a beautiful morning, but he carried the bricks on his hod with a grudge, especially as the oul' fella was in a good mood at the recovered day, and laid the bricks fluently, a cigarette rolling around his mouth.

By evening Hugh was exhausted, but after supper Brendan insisted on going for a drink to the Good Intent, an old pub a few doors down on Wedmore Street.

'Here,' he said, placing a pint before him. 'You earned it.'

'How come you wouldn't have a pint with the lads?' Hugh asked. 'I was dying with the drought when we finished.'

Brendan drank from his pint.

'Ah, the less you drink with them fellas, the better,' he said. 'You'd end up pissing all your wages against a wall, like the rest of them.'

Hugh drank in silence while Brendan read the paper. He couldn't bring himself to accuse his father of meanness, but that's what it was. Brendan couldn't bear to pay for a round of drinks, seeing as he had lost a half day's wages the day before, even though they had worked an extra few hours to make up for it. Shag it, it was the one bit of crack he had all week, those few drinks with the lads, when Seán was always good for a laugh, and the mean old whore couldn't even leave him with that.

'I think I'll go for Galcador,' Brendan said, folding his paper with satisfaction. 'He's only a miler but that French fella is lucky. Do you want to pick a winner?' He offered the paper to Hugh.

'Naw, I'm never lucky,' he said.

'Ah you're right. It's a mug's game. The Derby though, it's a big occasion.' He took another swig. 'Once a year.' He carefully folded the paper and put it away in his jacket pocket.

They had two drinks before going home to bed.

Brendan liked to listen to the radio in the dark. Hugh didn't like the posh voices, so unlike anything he had heard in England, but Brendan liked them.

When Brendan had been alone in England and Hugh had lived with his mother on the mountainside, he had missed his father so much that Máire, his mother, had often come across him trailing a saucepan along the bed of the stream, searching for gold. The thought of his mother cut through him. Why it had upset her, he had never discovered, but he persisted. Everyone said there had been gold on the mountain in the days of the landlord. He wasn't sure what gold looked like, but knew that if he could find one small nugget, or even grains, his father could return and stay.

Recently he had missed her a great deal. The pain of it struck him from nowhere, when he was working, or crossing the street, or buying groceries. Why had the hurt come now, he wondered, so long after she had died?

The hard week caught up with him, and the upper-class English voices drifted far away.

The next morning he woke at nine, confused. Brendan was snoring and would doubtless do so until the afternoon. That's how he managed to work like a horse all week, the old shagger. Hugh felt as if he hadn't slept all night, although it was a long time since he had slept so well, but he struggled out of bed and washed. He lay wearily back on the bed again for some time, but then he dressed in his Sunday suit, and struggled with his tie before he got it tolerably right. He could never remember the knack, and only got it out through luck.

The fine morning seemed to clear his head, and as he crossed Holloway Road at the zebra above the hospital, and turned into Tollington Way, he found himself whistling loudly. He waited until he had walked out of earshot of anyone who may have heard him, and began again, this time softly. He reached the T-junction at Hornsey Road, turned left and then right into Tollington Park, past Sarah's house. He looked to see if Deirdre, Sarah's daughter, was waiting for him at the window as she sometimes was. Sarah didn't go to Mass, so he assumed she was a Protestant, though Deirdre went to the Catholic school across the way.

He assumed this even though Brendan didn't bother any more either.

When he was a child, he had always thought that London had no hills. He remembered this as he walked up the incline of Tollington Park, past the large Protestant church and into Everleigh Street, where the Irish faithful were congregating. Hugh was perversely proud that his church had a corrugated iron roof, in contrast to its grand Protestant neighbour. No matter that Catholic churches in Ireland were of good stone and slate, the poverty of this one made him feel a cut above the Prods, morally speaking. As he dipped his fingers in the holy water font, he spied Mrs Dempsey with her husband and children.

After Mass, as they queued to get an Irish paper, they spotted him as he used his sweet ration at the hucksters, and waved, but small talk terrified him, so he smiled and moved on quickly. It meant he was too early for Sarah's class so he walked for a while into Upper Tollington Park, before doubling back. Along with the heat, his self-consciousness had made him sweat, and he thought with relish of the two bitters he had had the night before.

He arrived early at Sarah's, which he knew she didn't encourage, but he needed a drink of water. Deirdre greeted him as always.

'It's hot, Deirdre,' he said.

'Would you like a drink of water?'

'I'd kill for it.'

'Oh, there's no need to do that,' she said primly.

'Here's your sweets,' he whispered, following her inside.

'Thanks!' she said, her face lighting up, and she rushed in to hand them to Sarah, who was in the kitchen washing vegetables. Without a word, she took the sweets from Deirdre and put them away until after lunch.

'You're early,' she said.

'I'm sorry, Sarah. I had a terrible thirst.'

Deirdre squeezed in beside her mother to get the cup of water.

'Well, don't make a habit of it,' she said. 'The others'll think you're my favourite.'

'Oh. Right,' he said, not knowing what to make of that.

Hugh drank back the water and held out the cup to Deirdre for more. She filled it again and watched him as he drank a second time.

'I'll wait on the step,' he said, handing Deirdre the cup again. Sarah ignored him and continued preparing the salad.

She was only having him on, he knew that, but at the back of his mind he felt like a servant, dismissed until she was ready to call him. Sarah and her education often made him feel like that, but he put up with it because he knew that however high and mighty she pretended to be, at least she was sharing her education with those who needed it, and he thought a lot of her for that. For now he was grateful to sit on the steps, refreshed and lording it in the sun, alone. He didn't think – thinking was the last thing he wanted to do – and he drifted into an exquisite laziness.

The midday church bells rang. As they faded, the Pakistani woman climbed the steps with her daughter, and Hugh stood and nodded to them. Her mother's eyes remained cast down, but the girl, who was about sixteen, flashed him a quick smile. Kathleen Pilkinton, a young, stout Irish woman covered in spots, arrived as Hugh knocked on the door. She was flushed and out of breath.

Hugh didn't like Kathleen because her shyness threw him back on his own, but he felt obliged to greet her.

'How are you?' she replied, looking away. 'I thought I was late.'

Deirdre answered the door, and as they trooped in, she waited for Seán Burke who she spotted moseying along the street.

'Hello, Seán,' she called.

'Hello, flower!'

Deirdre was delighted. Sarah had remarked how Deirdre loved Sundays, when Hugh and Seán made a fuss of her. Hugh listened to her and was never impatient, and she loved Seán because he called her 'flower' and was always in good humour. Ah sure, everyone liked a bit of attention, not just small girls.

They gathered in Sarah's bright living room, on the left as

you went in the hall, with its big bookcase which never failed to impress Hugh. Sarah's West Indian tenant was already seated and smiled at everyone.

'Good man, Hugh,' Seán greeted. 'Hello, ladies.'

Hugh relaxed, grateful for Seán's presence. If he thought about it, he was his only friend. Deirdre wasn't the only one who loved him. Everyone did. The West Indian and the two younger women smiled at his every word, and even the Pakistani woman, although she'd probably die before she'd look him straight in the face, even she allowed herself a distant smile.

Sarah limped into the room, muttering hello, and sorted out the books on the table with her back to them.

'Right,' she said then, turning to them with a smile. 'Hello, everyone. I thought that maybe we've had enough of Kipling for a while, and that we'd like to read something mysterious and wonderful, so I found these little books about the Egyptians and their pyramids and how they were built. Deirdre, will you hand them out?'

Deirdre did so.

'Now, as usual, I will read them first, and then I will ask each of you to read. Everyone comfortable? There are some hard words, like "pyramid", but we can go over them a few times, and as you all have come on so well in the last few weeks, it will probably be easy for you. Right then. There are some nice pictures too, by the way.'

She began reading, slowly, distinctively. The Pakistani woman, who could not speak English, gazed at her daughter's absorbed face. Hugh was drawn to them, and Sarah's voice and the images of old Egypt it conveyed settled with the picture of the two women in his brain.

'Now,' Sarah said. 'What did you make of that?'

'They had great imagination,' Seán said.

'They had.'

'But they were tyrants,' Kathleen said.

'They were. And what do you think, Eriz?'

The girl thought for a while.

'Maybe tyrants with imagination make some good.'

Sarah smiled.

'Yes, I wonder about that myself, sometimes. Although a tyrant with an imagination is a rare beast, let me tell you. Have you any thoughts on the subject, Hugh?'

He cleared his throat and shifted in his chair.

'Ah . . . no. I think everything's been said.'

'All right then. Would you care to read? You have the page there, haven't you?'

He read slowly, unsteady over words which he had not the confidence to risk. Sarah was patient, helping him to pronounce them, and because the passage wasn't long, she asked him to read it again, and this time, taken by the story, he forgot himself and read it correctly. Then the others read, as Sarah took them over the difficult words. When everyone had read, they discussed these words until their pronunciation and what they meant were familiar.

Hugh saw that the class had gone well, and that Sarah was happy.

'You may keep the books,' she said, 'and I hope you get a lot of pleasure from them. As you know, this is the last class for a while. I'm sorry we're finishing a little earlier in the year than I expected, but you've all become so good that I think if you keep reading, you won't need me any more. If you think you do, come back in October – the first Sunday. If not, good luck to you all,' she said with emotion.

They grouped to thank her and say goodbye, and the women left quickly. The West Indian said she would see her later and flashed Sarah a smile, which she returned. That woman had fine teeth, that was for sure. On his way out, Seán stopped to give Deirdre a shilling, and Hugh intended to do the same, but Sarah held on to his hand.

'How's your father?'

'He's grand, Sarah.'

'He doesn't want to come any more, obviously – and he nearly the one who needs it most!'

'Ah, he's tired after the week's work, you know? And sure he's probably snoring his head off this minute.'

Sarah continued to hold his hand and look into his eyes.

Seán said goodbye again, and she replied and asked Deirdre to see him out, but she kept her grip on Hugh's hand. He was uncomfortable now.

'He says he's too old to learn.'

Sarah laughed.

'You're never too old to learn, Hugh, no matter what it is. Remember that. Stay for lunch.'

'Ah, it's all right, thanks,' he mumbled.

'Come on,' she said, squeezing his hand harder before letting it go. 'It'd be nice to have a man to lunch. Us women get fed up on our own, don't we, my darling?' she said as Deirdre came back, clutching her shilling. 'Away now and get plates for three – and knives and forks and spoons. And don't spend all that money in the one shop.'

Deirdre laughed and put her money in a piggy bank before doing as she was told. They went into the room across the hall which Sarah used as a dining room. The kitchen was off that. She dragged the table to the middle of the floor and he rushed to help her. She flashed him a quick smile, took a linen table-cloth from a drawer and he helped her to spread it.

Lunch. As far as he knew only Protestants had lunch. But now that she wasn't teaching, her voice and accent were more natural, and that was a relief.

Lunch turned out to be salad and crusty bread, what Brendan who had been to lunch with her called 'Sarah's sheep food', but although he found it strange, especially the oil, and although he wondered how a child could eat it with hunger, to his surprise he enjoyed it.

'Actually, Hugh, I have another book here for you,' she said, holding it up and flicking through its pages. '*The Bridge Over San Luis Rey*. Now there's a lot of difficult words in it, but if you feel like giving it a try, we could meet next Sunday in Finsbury Park, if it's fine – you know those three benches beside the lake, by the big tree?'

'God, that'd be great.' He was pleased, as he had come to rely on her classes for company other than his father's.

'And then Deirdre and I are off on holidays the following weekend, aren't we, pet?'

'Yeh,' Deirdre grinned. Her lips and chin were coated with the debris of her meal.

'Are you going to Ireland?'

'Oh no. We're going to France.'

'France? What would you be doing there?'

'We're going to get ourselves a Frenchman, aren't we, pet?' Deirdre giggled.

'We go every year, actually.'

'Oh.'

'Would you like some tea and biscuits?'

He nodded, yet again aware of the distance between them. As she left with the dishes, Deirdre came around the table and grinned.

'*Je suis une petite fille,*' she said deliberately.

'Is that French?' he whispered in her ear.

'*Oui,*' she said. 'Do you speak French?' she whispered back.

He shook his head, ashamed that even a child was better than him. 'But I speak Egyptian,' he rallied.

'Really?' Her eyes were as round as pennies.

'Ummm.' He nodded solemnly.

'Speak some!'

'Nahirz ish yo bujum nairy-o,' he said without hesitation.

'Ooooh.' She stared at him. And then curiosity replaced her wonder. 'What does it say?'

'It says ... it says, "The white clouds will carry me to a distant mountain".'

'Sarah!' she shouted, running off to the kitchen. 'Hugh speaks Egyptian!'

'I'm sure he does, Deirdre.' Sarah appeared at the door with a laden tray. 'I'm sure he does.' She poured the tea. 'You must have that book on Egypt off by heart already.'

'Every word.' He sipped his tea, unable to look at her.

'Here,' she laughed. 'Have a Marietta.'

Two

ELIZABETH

July 1950

'Hello, Beth,' Millie greeted her sister.

Elizabeth winced but then squeezed her hand and walked past her into the hall. She left her straw bag down, took off her hat and checked herself in the hallstand mirror. There was a comedy on the wireless.

'Is he here?'

'He's in the front room, choking the place with smoke,' Millie said, closing the front door. Elizabeth could smell it drifting into the hall. She hesitated, nervous, then kissed Millie on the cheek.

'Is he all right?' she whispered.

'Oh, he's full of himself. You'd never think he had a day's hardship in his life!' Millie smiled and nodded in encouragement towards the open front room door. They could hear him laughing.

Elizabeth stood at the door, leaning against the jamb, and watched him, a cigarette between stained fingers, another one behind his ear. He looked so young, much younger than when she had seen him last, but then his own clothes would make a difference, and his hair had grown a little. He laughed again, and it was nice to see he was so absorbed in a silly programme.

'Hello, Sam.'

'Wotcha, sis!' he said as he turned and rose to embrace her. 'You look fantastic.'

'Well, I went and did myself up, didn't I?'

'For your *bruvvah*?'

'For my *brother*.'

'You was always posh, Beth.'

They laughed and hugged. He had mortified her so many times, but he was her only living brother, and she always forgave him.

'Fancy some lemonade? Harry didn't come with the cider yet.'

'I'm not sure it's right to take strong drink on Sunday, Sam,' Millie said.

'Special occasion, Millie darling,' he said, giving her a sideways squeeze. 'Won't do no harm.'

'Tst!'

'I'm toasted,' Elizabeth said. 'I'll have some lemonade.'

He turned off the radio and got her the lemonade and she drank it back. As she was drinking, she saw that his face darkened, and he looked older and dangerous, as she had seen him in prison.

'Millie tells me you're shacked up with a Jerry,' he said as she handed him the empty glass.

'He's my lodger, Sam,' she said, turning away and seating herself in the old armchair. She looked him in the eye. 'He pays me good money every week.'

'What about it, Millie?' he shouted. 'Our two brothers at the bottom of the fucking Atlantic and she's shacking up with a bleeding Jerry.'

'Cork it, Sam.' Elizabeth feared him like this, but knew that she mustn't show it. 'The war's over. He lost all his family, and besides, he was in prison here for the war. All of it. He never fired a shot.'

'But he's a stinking Jerry!' he screamed.

'I said cork it!' She rose to her feet, angry.

'Bob's your uncle, Beth.' The storm was over as suddenly as it had begun, and he was meek and young again. Millie looked from one to the other.

'How do you think,' Elizabeth said quietly, 'how do you think I got you those extra rations when you were in the nick?'

'The boys . . .' He trailed off in disbelief.

'The boys? The boys?' Her voice shook. 'The *boys* didn't lift a finger for you, Sam. You could have rotted for all they cared. Out of sight, out of mind. Stay away from them. They're no good, and you go inside once more and you'll never see me again. Go back to sea, anything.'

'I'll go back to sea, Beth.'

'You see you do that. Earn some money, find a good woman. Our Betty, now, she's still fancy-free. There's lots of them!'

'Old Betty. Fancy-free . . .'

He switched on the wireless, but the comedy was over, so he switched it off again.

'Harry's late,' Millie said.

'Myra's making him clean behind his ears,' Sam guffawed. 'That's what Beth wants for me, Millie. Under a woman's thumb.'

'Someone has to keep you in line, Sam,' Millie said.

'Yeh,' he said, dejected. 'Suppose so.'

There was a knock on the door.

'That'll be Harry.' Millie jumped to her feet to let him in.

'About bleeding time,' Sam muttered. 'I'm gasping.'

'Come in, Harry,' Millie said.

'Well, well, Millie Burton. You get better looking every time I see you.'

'Away with you, Harry. What would Myra say if she heard you!'

Elizabeth made a face and Sam grinned at her. He was sitting on the table, but when Millie, carrying a large white porcelain jug of cider, led in Harry, he stood, hand outstretched.

'Wotcha, old cock!' he said, looking at him sideways.

'Sam! You ain't changed thruppence worth!'

'They fed me well, Harry. They fed me well.'

They had a good laugh at that. Beaming, Millie placed the tall glasses on the table before Harry, and he poured elaborately. Millie handed them out, and Harry raised his to the company.

'Go on – you too, Millie,' Sam said, looking as if he might flare.

'Oh, all right then,' she said, and poured herself a glass.

'To freedom.'

'Yeh, fuck it, to bleeding freedom,' Sam agreed.

'What are we doing inside on a day like this?' Elizabeth demanded.

'Well then,' said Millie, 'come on, into the yard. Come on, Harry.'

But it was Sam and Millie who were first out with their chairs. Harry took off his jacket and turned to look directly at Elizabeth for the first time, and winked.

'On with you, Harry,' she said. 'The sun only lasts a tick in that yard.'

He reached for her, but she evaded him, pretending not to notice.

They sat in the small, whitewashed yard. The green paint was peeling from the corrugated iron shed. It had been peeling as long as they had been there, since the middle of the war. Elizabeth recalled her mother sitting against it, arthritic, and looking old although she was little past forty-five, in mourning weeds for her two sons. And to think she died in such a disgusting way herself. She drank back half her glass at once.

'A penny for them,' Harry said as he filled her glass again.

'Oh, nothing. Nothing at all ... I was just thinking of Mother', she conceded, 'sitting beside that shed on a day like this. Do you remember that day, Millie – was it '44? She got all cross because she didn't want her photo taken.'

Sam stopped just as he was about to drink, put his glass on a slab, and went inside.

'She was cross in the first place, as I recall,' Millie said, looking skyward, 'because you brought home that American airman without telling her, and her hair was in a mess.'

'Airman? Which airman was this, Beth?' Harry frowned.

'Oh, some airman, Harry. I met him at a dance and he wanted to see how the English lived.'

'So you brought him here.'

'Yes, I brought him here. I wanted him to take a photo of us before we were all killed. But he never sent it.'

'Fucking Yanks,' Harry said. 'Stealing our women while we were dying like flies.'

'I was never your woman,' Elizabeth said sharply.

Harry's glass froze at his lips. Millie was electrified.

'I reckon,' she said then in an even voice, 'I reckon the poor fool got blown to smithereens over Germany.'

'Yeh, Beth,' said Harry, chastened. 'I reckon so.'

'Funny how we never talk about the war,' Elizabeth said.

'Best forgotten,' Millie said, twisting her fingers.

Maybe it was. But she would never forget how her mother died. Nor little Georgina, neither. She chided herself then. She wasn't the only one who would never forget.

'I get some geezers down the pub, never talks about nothing else,' Harry said.

'OK, folksy-wolksy! Get ready to smiiillle!' Sam, marching into the yard, held aloft a Kodak, and planted his feet apart, finding the right balance, ready to snap.

'O Sam!' Millie groaned. 'Not now.'

'Come on, Millie,' Harry insisted. 'I want my mug taken with two beautiful gals,' and he sat between them, which mollified Millie, who arranged her hair; but Elizabeth was unmoved.

'Where did you get that Kodak, Sam?'

Sam lowered the camera and grinned.

'Where did I get it, Beth? From a mate, that's where. Come on now, say cheesey-wheezy.'

Millie laughed, and leaned her head towards Harry, but Elizabeth saw out of the corner of her eye that at the last moment he glanced at her.

'Harry, now you do the honours, mate,' Sam said.

'Eh? Oh, all right.'

Sam sat erect and solemn between his two sisters. They gazed into the lens, following it as Harry checked the position of the button. He squinted, tensed, and with appropriate effort recorded them for posterity.

They felt easy after that. When the sun moved out of the yard, Millie served a roast, a rare treat. Sam wolfed it down, remembering his fierce hunger, quelling it with a deep concentration. Elizabeth postponed her own meal as she watched him eat, realizing for the first time how the bones stood out in his pale face. She promised herself that she would encourage Betty Hindley. Betty's husband had been a merchant sailor too, lost in the Atlantic like Elizabeth's brothers. She wouldn't mind him being away months on end, and she had kept a flame for Sam since they were children. The irony of it. Sam had been on a bloody warship, and yet he was the one who survived.

Harry loosened his tie and paused, trying to think of something. Then his face brightened and he went to his jacket and brought back a box of cheroots, opening the box to Sam.

'You know how to celebrate, mate,' Sam said, sniffing the cigar.

'Ladies?' Harry offered in that way which Elizabeth had constantly to forgive.

They declined, but Millie opened a fresh packet of Woodbines, and the room filled with smoke. Sam sprawled in his chair, and reaching back, switched on the radio, full volume.

'Turn it down, Sam,' Elizabeth said wearily.

'Yeh, it's too loud.' He yawned, then standing and stretching, he turned it down low. He sat in the armchair by the fireplace, and stubbed out the cheroot in the empty grate. Then he sprawled back and closed his eyes, his chin dropping onto his collarbone. Harry pushed back his chair and dropped his bulk onto the settee. He smiled at Elizabeth, but it was Millie who sat beside him, placing the ashtray between them.

'Oh, I'm so sleepy,' she yawned. 'It must have been the cider.'

Elizabeth was sleepy too, but her corset was hurting her, a garter button was digging into the back of her thigh, and sweat was trickling across her groin. She could go to Millie's bedroom and arrange herself, but she was too lazy. She exhaled a cloud of smoke and watched it rise. Millie finished her cigarette and stubbed it out and lay back, her eyes closed, her body tilting towards Harry, but even when she fell asleep, her head never quite reached his shoulder. He too was nodding off, his cheroot still smouldering between his fingers. Elizabeth smiled. Another fraction and it would burn a nice big hole in his trousers.

He had gone quite bald, she noticed, and grey hairs were gathering at the side. Lately she had found herself wondering what she really felt about him. He looked well in his starched white cotton shirt, which Myra had ironed perfectly, and his red, blue-speckled tie. He was a fine man, there was no denying that.

Anyway, it was time to go. She got up, adjusting her corset slightly beneath her dress, which she flapped to air herself, and extinguished her cigarette beside Sam's cheroot. He was snoring lightly. She leaned over him and turned off the radio. Children were playing on the street, and there were some cars about. She could hear the rise and fall of Millie's breath.

In front of the hallstand mirror, she gazed at her face. If Harry was losing hair, she was getting wrinkles around her eyes that her make-up didn't quite hide. And there, on her forehead, those thin, puckered lines seemed to be multiplying.

She had sunburn on her chest. As she put on her hat, Harry came and stood beside her. She glanced at him. His eyes were bloodshot but he was staring at her, his lips open.

'My word, you look a treat,' he whispered.

She smiled and continued to arrange her hat, but stopped as he put his arms around her waist and they both looked at the other in the mirror.

'I think of you all the time, Beth. All the time. The good times we had, remember?'

'That was a long time ago, Harry. Besides, you forgot all that when you married Myra.'

'You're the one to talk! What about Eddie?'

'Eddie is ten years dead, Harry. And I wasn't going to marry him.' She wanted to unclasp his arms, and yet his urgency made her hesitate, uncertain of what she wanted.

'What about Myra?'

His hands cupped her breasts, squeezing them hard.

'Beth, let's do it. The others are snoring their heads off.'

'Don't you and Myra do it any more?'

He turned her around roughly and buried his tongue in her mouth, his swollen business bruising against her. She turned her face away, gasping, and he lifted her onto the box of the hallstand, pulling up her dress and trying to spread her legs. A bit of flirting was one thing, but she didn't want this.

'Stop it, Harry,' she said. 'Have you lost your marbles?'

'Eh?'

She pulled down her dress and stood up, her hat askew. He could not meet her eyes.

'Harry,' she whispered. 'What's got into you, old chuck? I don't know about you, but I don't want to be caught like that.'

'Then bring me to your house, Beth!' he pleaded.

'No,' she said, 'no I can't do that.'

'Tell me where you live – I'll slip up there.'

'You're married, Harry. Remember that.' She turned to rearrange her hat.

'And you're a spinster. Don't you want it?'

A cloud darkened the hallway for a moment and she took a light cardigan from her bag and put it on, avoiding him.

'You think you're too good for me, don't you? You live up there – where is it? Camden? What's wrong with round here?'

'Go home to Myra, Harry. She loves you.'

He stopped as if he had been hit.

'How come you don't speak like us? How come you speak posh?'

'Be seeing you, Harry,' she said, clipping him under the chin with her fingernail.

She walked through Cheapside. There was no way she would let Harry know where she lived. Millie knew and Sam didn't care. And that was the way it would stay. Her two lives were separate. She looked around, suddenly wary that Harry might have followed her. But he hadn't dared, or bothered. She was sweating, so she took off her cardigan. Normally she took the bus, but this time, as a precaution, she got the tube at Aldgate to Holloway Road.

The rock of the train lulled her, and she thought back over the encounter. He had tried it on before, several times, but never with such fierceness – whether it was because of her summer dress and bare shoulders or what, she couldn't say. But whatever it was, now that she was safe she was flattered, in a way. She laughed to herself as she recalled what he had said about her being a spinster. So he didn't know, then? That she was married to the enemy, in all but name, since '48? Millie had been discreet, to all but Sam, and he wouldn't tell it for shame. She was safe, and that was why her lives would always be separate, why they would never know where she lived.

It was six o'clock when she got home to Citizen Road. Karl was upstairs in his room, playing one of his boring old records. She had bought him the ancient wind-up player, with its beautiful brass horn, in the market for his birthday. She had also bought him some popular records from the 40s, but he had never played them. She went into the kitchen and drank a cup of water.

'How was your visit?' he asked softly. She turned and saw that he was in his underwear and bare feet, and wondered again how such a big man could make so little noise.

'Hold me,' she said after a while.

She pressed her face against his hairless, moist chest as his arms took her in.

'Hold me,' she repeated.

This was why she spoke differently, absorbing his correct grammar and precise pronunciation. This was why she sounded posh to those she had grown up with and still loved. But he would never know them either, which in a way made her alone.

'Are you hungry?' she mumbled.

'No. I ate at four.'

She looked up at him, then led him to her room. He got into bed, keeping his drawers on. She took off everything, loosening in relief her imprinted flesh, and pulled off the bedclothes before lying beside him.

'Just hold me, Karl.'

They lay together, sweating in the evening heat.

Three

HUGH

July–August 1950

He was parched. With two other men, Hugh wheeled barrow after barrow of cement into the foundation of the floor, which his father and three others were smoothing with boards. Cement had got inside his right boot, but he kept going. Everyone was stripped to the waist, sweating like bad country butter. There was none of the usual raillery; they were all concentrating on getting the job in hand finished by knocking off time.

They finished the floor, and pointlessly the whistle blew. It was only then that Hugh let himself feel the discomfort in his boot. They went to the nearest pub, and although he was limping, once the bitter hit the back of his throat, he put it to the back of his mind. They had done a great day's work, and they felt good.

Brendan stuck rigidly to his two pints, and Hugh dutifully followed his father. In the beginning the other men, Irish and Poles, English and Scots, had mocked him for it, but not any more. Hugh could see they respected him for not pissing his wages away.

By the time they got to Wedmore Street, he found it so difficult to walk he was sweating, and he barely made it up the stairs. Brendan went ahead and had his bath, blind to anything out of the ordinary. When Hugh finally managed to get his boot off, he saw the skin was hanging off his heel.

'O Jesus,' he groaned.

'What? What's up?' Brendan demanded.

He twisted his ankle around for his father to see.

'Christ, that looks sore.'

Brendan knelt down to examine it closer.

'You got cement inside your boot, you eejit. The bloody lime did for you. You better get that trousers off or you'll make it worse.'

Brendan kept the trouser leg away from the wound as Hugh cautiously rolled it down his leg.

'What the fuck are we going to do now?' Brendan demanded, as if it was Hugh's fault. Then he brightened. 'Mrs Dempsey. I remember her saying she was a nurse.'

'No, don't . . .'

Hugh scrambled for his clean trousers as Brendan went off to find Mrs Dempsey, calling her from the top of the stairs. There was no reply but he heard the kitchen door open and Dennis scampering out in front of her.

'Mrs Dempsey,' Brendan said. 'Mrs Dempsey, sorry to bother you, but Hugh has scraped the skin off his ankle, and I was wondering if you would have a look at it.'

'O my God . . . Wait till I get a few things and I'll be right up.'

Hugh had his trousers on, his trouser leg rolled up and away from the wound when Brendan returned.

'She'll be up in a minute,' he said, frowning. Then he grinned. 'Oho, I see you wasted no time in covering up!'

'Shh!'

Mrs Dempsey came up with Dennis and her baby, disinfectant and bandages.

'Get some clean hot water,' she ordered Brendan. 'That looks sore.'

'Hello, Dennis,' Hugh said, unable to face her. 'Anything good in the *Beano* this week?'

'*Desperate Dan!*' Dennis's descriptions of the adventures of Desperate Dan filled the awkward gap until Brendan arrived back with the water. It hurt when she bathed it, but despite her warning, he recoiled back into the chair when she applied the iodine.

'I'm sorry,' she said. 'I know that's sore, but it has to be done.'

He clenched his teeth as she continued. Then she bandaged him.

'You should bring him down to casualty in the Northern,' she said to Brendan. She stood up and surveyed her work.

'Ah no,' he protested mildly. 'No, no, it'll be grand.'

'Are you sure?' Brendan was relieved.

'Sure Mrs Dempsey did a great job.'

'She's a professional,' Brendan concurred.

'Well, whatever you think,' Mrs Dempsey said.

'O God, aye,' Brendan said. 'How much do we owe you?' he asked in a confidential tone.

'Oh now, Mr Kinsella, I couldn't take money for helping out a neighbour.'

Brendan beamed at Hugh, and then back at Mrs Dempsey.

'It's easy knowing, ma'am, that you're from decent stock.'

'I wouldn't go hopping about on that for a week at least,' she said to Hugh.

Brendan looked sharply from Hugh to Mrs Dempsey.

'A week? You mean he'll be out of work for a week?'

'Oh, at least, Mr Kinsella. Don't worry, I'll come up every day and change the bandage and get him a cup of tea.'

'Thank you, ma'am . . .'

She smiled at them both, and left, shepherding her children away.

'Well, that beats the band,' Brendan said. 'A week . . .'

'Can you manage?'

'I suppose I'll have to.' He lit a cigarette, and drew on it angrily.

'I'll make up for it next week.'

'And how will you do that, you thick? Don't you know that you're paid the same wages no matter how hard you fucking work?'

'Then why do we work so hard?'

'Oh, you're smart, aren't you? I'll tell you why: because there's ten Paddies and twenty Poles waiting to take your job if you don't, or how many times do I have to tell you?'

'There's pucks of work,' Hugh said quietly.

'Well, I hope you can find some when they throw you out on your arse for not turning up.' Brendan drew so hard on his cigarette that he almost broke it. He grabbed his jacket and left, slamming the front door.

Hugh sat where he was for some time, unsure what to think or do. Then he examined his bandaged ankle, aware again of the strong smell of iodine. He looked around the bleak room and found it strange. Then he remembered he hadn't washed, and as much to distract himself as anything else, and hopping on one foot, he laboriously refilled the bath, exhausting himself in the process. His ankle throbbed, and the deep sting was gathering into serious pain. He had to rest on the bed before he could strip and wash. The cold water refreshed him, and he put his trousers back on, lay back on the bed, and despite his ankle, fell asleep.

Brendan shook him, and he woke, blinded by the naked bulb.

'Get into bed properly.'

'What time is it?'

'Past eleven.'

Brendan half stumbled as he sat on the bed to haul off his boots. Hugh could smell the whiskey.

'I went down to Camden', Brendan said as he continued to undress, 'to see what's the lie of the building trade these days.'

Hugh was very hungry.

'Is there any bread left?'

'No, there's nothing. You'll have to fast till morning.' Brendan turned and got into bed. He coughed and was silent and then he said, 'I got in with a fella from Mayo. He said he'd see us right if we were stuck.'

Within a minute he was snoring. Hugh got up and hopped to the sink and drank from the tap. He hated seeing his father drink whiskey. It brought back that awful time after Máire died, when Brendan had gone on the batter. It took a whole six months for him to stop and it had been hell.

He drank some more from the tap. There could have been a lead weight on his foot, and when he got back on the bed he cupped his ankle in his hands. The bandage was thick and protective, and he felt the pain was much further away from his fingers than it was, and that if only he could touch the flesh he could soothe it.

He thought of Mrs Dempsey and how she had bandaged his ankle, her son looking on. When Hugh was Dennis's age – no, he had been much older, nine or ten – he had cut his knee against some shale on the mountain, but by the time he reached home, the blood had congealed, and his mother had made little of it. Thinking about it now, his grief surprised him.

He remembered that she had not only made little of it, she had turned him away in contempt. Why? he almost shouted into the darkness. Why, if you brought me into the world, did you treat me like a trouble that had to be suffered?

She hadn't always been like that. It must have been the year before that she began to change, the way, he realized, his father had changed when Máire had died.

Something had gone out in her, and a cold feeling spread through him thinking of this, because he knew that somewhere he had seen its dark ghost, and it terrified him. He covered his head with the bedclothes, but as he squeezed his own eyes shut, a huge female eye stared out at him from his imagination, dark and without expression. He longed to turn the light on, but knew it would waken his father, and he feared his contempt, especially now, as his mother's had come back to him. But the dread of one had calmed the memory of the other, and exhausted, he fell asleep.

He woke an hour later. His ankle was throbbing, so he sat on the edge of the bed, hoping that putting his foot on the cool floor would relieve it. He tried raising it against the headboard, his reasoning being that if the blood flowed away, the pain would also flow away. He yawned, caught between exhaustion and his insistent ankle, and he stayed awake like that, his thoughts straying through random images until they were pulled back to his pain. There was no escape. The hours passed and dawn came, and the birds sang with it. He was past yawning now, his eyes as heavy as his ankle.

The alarm went off at six thirty and his father rose. Hugh

was sitting on the side of the bed, the sheet covering his middle, and Brendan stopped to look at him curiously, but said nothing. Hugh sat there while Brendan went to the toilet downstairs.

As he was waiting for the kettle to boil, his mug in his hand, without turning he spoke softly.

'So you can't make it today?'

'No.'

'Are you sure?'

'I am.'

'Do you want a mug of tea?'

Hugh didn't answer, but Brendan made him tea in a mug, the leaves rising to the top.

'Mrs Dempsey'll leave you in a sandwich. Will you last?'

'I will.'

Brendan lit a cigarette and smoked in silence, taking large draughts of tea in between. He stood, placed the mug on the table and held it there, lost in thought; then he left.

Hugh left his tea unfinished, as he heard his father speak to Mrs Dempsey. He put his foot on the ground again. It throbbed so heavily that his heart pounded, but he had to walk. Nature was calling. He stood, and almost immediately gave up. At first he tensed his body, trying to defeat the burning, but when that seemed only to magnify it, he tried with an equal will to relax, to become detached from it, to let it be. This worked up to a point, but needed concentration; yet he managed it, somehow, even as he dressed.

He hopped to the door on his good foot. He had to hop backwards to allow it to open, then he hopped out to the landing until he came to the stairs, and supported himself with the banister post. He had never given the stairs a thought before, but now they seemed as steep as a mountain, and as treacherous. If he hopped down, a step at a time, he would surely lose his balance and fall. He was tired already, and his only wish was to get back to bed, but his bowels were insisting powerfully, so he sat on the top step, and eased his way down, repressing thoughts of being unable to return.

When he got to the bottom, he was able to hop awkwardly along the hall, supported by the banisters, but when they ran out, he dropped to his hands and foot, hoping desperately that no one would see him like this. Then he farted and stopped. He was so tired, and had put so much concentration into getting this far and coping with his ankle, that he was almost past caring why he had set out in the first place. Suddenly the urge was all-consuming, and he was panic-stricken in case the slightest movement would make him soil himself. And what would happen now if Mrs Dempsey came out of the kitchen and found him like this? Or was she at work?

He squeezed his eyes tight until the urge eased, and carefully made the rest of the journey. The smell still hung in the air, but he didn't care about that any more. Once inside, the urge assailed him again, and in a frenzy, he awkwardly turned, leaning his shoulder against the wall and tearing at his thick leather belt. He sat on the bowl just as he could hold out no longer.

'Jesus,' he mumbled, dizzy with fatigue.

Eventually he recovered enough to clean himself and make his way back. He didn't care who saw him now. His only thought was to make it back to bed. Panting and sweating at the foot of the stairs, he sat on the step to recover. Yesterday, he had been pushing barrows of cement; now, and he grinned in spite of himself, now he was mortal. Why was this amusing and not terrifying?

He placed his hands on the step behind him and pushed, holding his injured foot out to protect it. That got him up one step, but the effort was tremendous. No matter. He rested and went again. Two steps, and so on until he reached the top, drained but elated. His elation carried him to bed, where he fell into a black sleep.

He woke briefly, to stare at a sandwich and mug of steaming tea, then fell back into the depths.

When he woke again, his father was washing. Brendan dried himself and emptied the water. Hugh's eyes fell shut again. He breathed shallowly and was motionless and heavy.

'Are you awake?' Brendan whispered. Hugh's eyes opened again, but he said nothing. 'Heh!' Brendan chuckled. 'You've slept all bloody day!'

Hugh smiled.

'Mrs Dempsey left you a mug of tea and a sandwich,' Brendan said. 'It was delicious!'

Hugh smiled again.

'Come on, now, shake yourself, sir. I'm going to make something to eat. You must be starving.'

Hugh still didn't move, but then the powerful smell of rashers and sausages made his mouth water and he took a deep breath and sat up. He felt dizzy, and his ankle hurt, but he forced himself to sit on the edge of the bed. He looked around for his clothes, and then realized that he was dressed. As he came to, he thought he had wet the bed, but it was sweat. He thought of the cloud on the mountain, how it blanked out everything and made him believe he had left his body and was floating through limbo. He got himself from the bed to the table and sat in. He was trying to waken fully but somehow he could not. The dampness of the cloud settled on him.

'There you are now, get that into you,' Brendan ordered.

His mouth watered, and he knew he had returned. Ravenous, he ate the rashers and sausages and fried bread. He drank back the mug of tea and stopped, out of breath.

'Ho ho, you were starving,' Brendan laughed. 'You'll be up and around in no time.' Satisfied, he launched into his own meal, and drank back the strong tea. Hugh watched his father's Adam's apple going up and down.

They both relaxed in silence, picking their teeth with their fingernails, and stretched out from the table. As an afterthought, Brendan reached back and took new slippers out of a bag. Without a word, he took off his boots and tried on the slippers, standing on each foot to gauge their comfort. Then he sat in the armchair and, putting on his glasses, opened a newspaper. Hugh stared at the slippers.

'Where'd you get them?' he asked after a while.

Brendan dropped his paper and looked at Hugh over his glasses. 'Oh, them!' he said, stretching out his feet to view the slippers. 'Up in Highgate.' He went back to his paper.

The evening was warm and bright, and Hugh felt revived. He was also restless, and wanted to shout or push against something, but he held back and lay on the bed, blinking at the ceiling as a mounted policeman clopped through Wedmore Street, and children's voices came from the back garden, sounding like a nest of mice.

A few evenings later, neither of them paid attention to the knock on the front door, or to Mrs Dempsey speaking to a woman, until they heard steps on the landing. Brendan closed his paper and looked at Hugh in alarm. Hugh sat up and checked his fly. Someone knocked on the door. Brendan still gawked at Hugh, then signalled with a jerk of his head that Hugh should answer it. Hugh pointed urgently at his injured ankle, at which Brendan angrily threw his paper to the floor and stood. For a moment, Hugh thought Brendan might climb out the window to escape, but suddenly he composed himself and answered the door.

'Sarah! Begob. And young Deirdre!'

Hugh jumped up and tidied his bed.

'Well, Brendan. Can we come in?'

'Jesus. Yes, Sarah, of course.'

'Hello, Hugh!' Deirdre was first in.

'Hello, Deirdre. How are you?'

'What happened to *you*?' Sarah demanded.

'A bit of an accident at work,' Brendan interjected, scratching an eyebrow. 'Ah . . . sit down in the armchair there, Sarah.'

'No, the chair will be perfectly fine, thank you,' and she sat, taking in the bleak room. 'What kind of *a bit of an accident*, Hugh?' she demanded, limping over to inspect his injury.

'Ah, a bit of lime got into my boot.'

'A bit.' She grinned.

Hugh glanced at his father, mortified for him that he was still in his slippers. Deirdre smiled at Hugh and he smiled back. Out of the corner of his eye, he noticed that Sarah was uneasy, and while this was unusual, it made him feel a lot better.

'How's the French?' he asked Deirdre.

'My mammy's teaching me lots,' she replied.

'But no Egyptian?' he smiled. This delighted her.

'Did you hear that Hugh speaks Egyptian now, Brendan?'

'Begob, Sarah, I didn't, but it wouldn't surprise me,' Brendan grinned.

'You learn all sorts of things in my class, you know.'

'There's no denying that.' He was on guard again, and turned to rinse the teapot.

'You missed a good few classes. Why don't you come down when I get back from France? I could give you special classes so you could catch up.'

'It pains me to have to tell you this, Sarah,' he replied, his back still turned to her, 'because you're such a nice and generous woman, but', and as he turned his eyes fell on her cleavage, 'I've lost interest in learning. I'm grateful to you, but I can read the paper and my wage packet and that's all I want.'

There was an awkward silence until Sarah turned away, with a dark face on her, and he saw why she had caught his father's attention. Her summer blouse opened in a V, and Hugh could see more than he had ever seen. He looked away immediately, hardly aware of the leap in his trousers, and smiled nervously at Deirdre, who had never taken her eyes off him.

'Well, if you read the paper, I suppose that's fine.'

'A drop of tea?' Brendan said, pouring the strong brew, and sitting in to the table. 'There's no biscuits or the like, I'm sorry to have to say.'

'Tea is fine, Brendan. A half cup for Deirdre . . .' Sarah trailed off as she noticed the stained, cracked cups he handed her. A stern but subtle nod to Deirdre ensured politeness from her.

'Deirdre and I are off to France on Monday,' Sarah addressed Brendan. 'Would you like us to bring you a bottle of wine?'

'I don't—' Brendan sniffed and lowered his eyes before facing her again, 'drink wine, Sarah.'

Hugh looked from his father to Sarah as they took in each other without a word. They looked very odd, as if they were about to break into tears over a secret between them.

'Oh yes. That's right,' she said quietly, looking away. She rose. 'Well, we didn't intend to stay this long.' Deirdre put her cup back on the table.

'Sure you haven't finished your tea,' Brendan said unhappily.

'No. Well, we'll be on our way, Deirdre. Stay where you are, Hugh. And mind yourself.'

'I'll leave you out,' Brendan said.

'Thank you. Goodbye, Hugh.'

'Goodbye, Hugh.' Deirdre waved, and he waved back.

He waited until he was sure they had descended and then hopped to the landing.

'Come again,' Brendan said.

'Are you sure you want me to?'

'Aye.'

'Well now, you know where I live too. We'll be in France for a fortnight from Monday.'

The door closed and Hugh rushed back to bed on his hands and good foot. He had to hide his breathlessness as Brendan returned, gathered up his paper and retreated behind it.

'Nice to see them,' Hugh said after a while.

'Aye.'

'You won't let her offer you a class, so.'

'No.' Brendan kept the newspaper to his face, and didn't turn a page until he threw the paper on the table and left without a word.

Now that his father was gone, the reality of Sarah's presence and its effect came back to him. There was something going on there, had been for a long time, since they had met when Sarah worked in the bookie's. He could see his father marrying Sarah. In the nature of things, this would mean that he would have to live alone, a prospect which attracted but terrified him. He lay back on the bed and thought of Sarah. She was old, at least forty, but her breasts were large and it was hard to keep his eyes off them. A warm feeling spread through him. He laid his hand lightly over his fork and his pleasure heightened exquisitely. He thought of his father, how he must have felt the same when he thought of Sarah, alone in the dark, and an anger took hold of him. But then he sat on the edge of the bed and laughed at his foolishness. Maybe it was only the young who had feelings like that, but in any case, Sarah was of an age with his father. If they gave each other pleasure, then well and good, but then he remembered his own loneliness, his lack of any comfort in a woman, and he twenty-two years of age already. On impulse, he pulled out the battered case from beneath the bed, but as he did so there was a knock on the door and he froze, before pushing it back.

'Yes?'

Mrs Dempsey came in with Dennis.

'Oh, hello.'

'I'll just do your bandage, Hugh,' Mrs Dempsey said.

Dennis handed him the *Beano*, and Mrs Dempsey beamed at her son in approval.

'Is it good this week, Dennis?'

'S'great. I'm Dennis the Menace.'

'He's not in the *Beano*, is he?'

Dennis shook with laughter, and Mrs Dempsey laughed too, and knelt to unravel the bandage. 'Oh, you're a menace, all right.'

Hugh pulled up his trouser leg and lifted his ankle. It only hurt a bit now, itching more than anything else, and it had developed a scab.

'It's looking much better,' she said.

'It feels better. Thanks to you.'

'That's all right, Hugh. I'll put a light bandage on, so you'll be able to walk and keep the circulation going. But be careful.'

'That's great,' he said as she finished. A bone in her knee creaked as she stood.

'I'll look at it again tomorrow, all right?'

Dennis skipped ahead and they were gone. His ankle felt so much better. He stood and it took his weight, although he limped as he walked across the floor. It would take another while. His eyes fell on his father's slippers and he tried them on, and to his surprise they were comfortable.

He lay on the bed again and read the *Beano*, chuckling, but his pleasure mingled with shame at reading a children's comic, and midway through he left it aside and picked up his father's abandoned paper.

Smoothing the pages, he forced himself to read, all the while wanting to return to the comic. He read on, forgetting the story as soon as he read it, but he read two pages before tiring. Bored, he went to the window and looked out on the street. There was nothing happening. There was a props warehouse, for some class of theatre, but its big shutter was closed. He thought of the man at the office window behind the house, and wondered if he felt like this every day. One or two people walked along the street, and it struck him that walking was a miracle all of its own.

'I'll tell you one thing,' he said out loud, 'I'll never take it for granted again. How do you do it, anyway, one foot in front of the other?'

He amused himself with such thoughts, and still his father wasn't back.

He lay on the bed and woke at dusk to Brendan stumbling against the table.

'Are you all right?'

'Fuck you!' Brendan shouted, and hurled the chair against the wall above Hugh's legs, which he pulled aside as the chair fell back on the bed. 'Leave me alone. Jesus. Is it too much to ask to have a bit of peace?'

Hugh knew better than to answer that, as Brendan stripped and got into bed and was snoring in a few minutes. He stared at the chair and bruised wallpaper and began to shake. He felt as if the room were closing in on him, pushing the air out of his lungs. He shook more and more as the knowledge of his loneliness, so long held at bay, slowly crushed him until, through a blur, he noticed a strangely normal thing. He was still wearing his father's slippers. Dazed, he stared at them, as if they were two clowns at which everyone was laughing except him. He laid them under his father's bed. Then he pulled out the suitcase and rummaged through it until he found the statue of the Blessed Virgin. He took off his clothes and got into bed, holding it against the fading light, his fingers tracing the chipped outline. It was the only thing he had taken from his mother's house after her funeral, and he took it because she loved it so much. She had prayed to it every night, in Irish, completely lost in the Virgin when she thought that Hugh was asleep in bed. ''Sé do bheatha a Mhuire, atá lán de ghrásta . . .' The words came back to him. He had learned them in school, and they had been etched on his soul by his mother's lips which he had watched through a barely open door. 'Hail Mary, full of grace . . .'

She had given all her love to the plaster statue. This was why he had taken it. He had prayed to it many times to allow his mother to give one sign that she loved him. One. And now he would pray one last time. It had become dark as he prayed.

''Sé do bheatha a Mhuire,' he whispered, 'atá lán de ghrásta . . .' He held the statue before him, his eyes closed, the repetition of the prayer in Gaelic drawing him into deep contemplation of his wish. Hardly aware of what he was doing, he knelt on the bed, holding the statue before him. His whisper became a drone. Hugh prayed so hard that the edges of the statue crumbled in his drenched hands until, exhausted, he laid it aside. He knew there would be no sign. He got back into bed and pulled the blankets over his face and tried to think how he would die. He was falling asleep. And then his eyes went cold. The coldness streamed into his forehead, over his scalp, down his neck and down to his spine and as it travelled down his spine he couldn't resist uncovering his head and sitting up as if a magnet were pulling his iron brain. A grey mist of female outline stood at the foot of the bed. His heart beat quickly as he knew by her appearance that she had not forgotten him; but as he reached out to her, a knee on the bed, his left toe on the floor, his concentration waned and as it did, she faded.

The light came on and he turned to see his father staring at him from under nervous eyebrows.

'What are you doing rigged up like that at this hour of the morning?'

'My mother appeared to me,' Hugh said quietly.

'Jesus . . .'

They stared at each other.

'I'm not cracked,' Hugh said then, his voice breaking.

'You're doubly cracked,' Brendan said, as if threatening him. 'Now get back to fucking bed, and not another mad word out of you.'

Brendan waited until he obeyed before switching off the light and returning to bed.

I'm not cracked! Hugh shouted in his head. *I saw her. I saw her! I'm not cracked. I'm not. Sarah's always going on about how intelligent I am. He's the one who's cracked, living away in that little world of his that doesn't exist for anyone else. There's cracked for you!*

His thoughts raged on as he tossed and turned, but then, remembering his vision, he calmed, and stared into the dark, intensely happy. She loved him after all.

After a while, he noticed something odd. There wasn't a stir out of his father, but he was still awake. Waiting in vain to hear his familiar breath, Hugh imagined he could smell his fear. Growing up on the mountain he had learned to be afraid of animals only when they are afraid, and lying still in the darkness, he remembered this.

He slept fitfully after he heard his father snore again, and in the morning, before Brendan woke, he gathered his things, took money that was his by right, and limped away to Tufnell Park tube, not daring to look back.

The gates were still closed when he got to the station, and he had to wait in a drizzle, his uneasiness about getting away staving off the reality of what lay ahead. Finally the gates were drawn back, and he entered the swirling breeze of the station, and bought a ticket to the end of the line. The train filled as they journeyed on, and he studied the advertisements for Austin Reed and Ibex, or studied the slatted floor. After a few stops he began to worry. He had no idea where he was going or what he would do. His ankle had not yet fully healed, which meant that work would be hard to find for a while, although he was surprised that he could walk so well. And if he went to the end of the line, where would he be? Out in the country, maybe, with no prospect of work. The stations passed: Kentish Town, Camden Town. As most of the passengers were getting off, he almost got off with them at Euston, but almost as many got on again, so he let Euston pass, then Angel and Old Street, and Moorgate, the unfamiliar names exciting but paralysing him. He looked at the map and wondered if those unfamiliar names might lead into open country, and he couldn't let that happen so he got off at London Bridge.

When he emerged from the station he realized that it had

been raining heavily. But the downpour had done its worst, and Hugh idly watched the water gushing into a drain. The cardboard suitcase that dangled from his callused fingers held all he possessed – oddments of clothes, a pair of shoes, his working duds and the books Sarah had given him. Also, wrapped in a stale shirt, the small plaster statue of the Virgin. That, he thought, was who he was.

All around him, thousands were pressing on to work, severe in bowlers or trilbys, or intent in glasses and gabardines, the women mostly with their eyes on the ground, and the swell carried him along, over London Bridge, the buses and vans and cars slowed almost to a halt. He walked for an hour, finding himself in a large street called Cheapside, as the crowd thinned, before he knew he was lost. Conscious of his ankle, he walked lightly and slowly. Then he saw a large church. He had to be careful; in England you couldn't always tell whether a church was Protestant or Catholic, but this one had a large dome, like the Pope's place he had seen in a picture, so he felt confident enough about it. It was a fine building, there was no doubt, and maybe he could rest there for a while. It was old, that was sure.

He sat in a pew at the back. One or two people were walking around, looking at tombs, and definitely not saying their prayers. He had never seen a building so big, at least not from the inside, and he too forgot his prayers and looked around him in wonder, feeling insignificant. He stayed for a long time, overcoming his alarm and then embarrassment at the whispers which swirled around the dome, and even slept, slumped forward on the pew. It was hunger which made him leave, but he could find no place to eat. All the buildings were big and impersonal, as if no human breathed and ached in any one of them. He jumped on a bus, on which at least he could sit beside a person, smell her damp clothing, and hope his future would be revealed. He glimpsed a bomb-site down a side street, its rubble piled high, and knew from clearing them that they gave a shelter of sorts, so if the worst came to the worst, he could rest a night there, and he tried to remember where it was. They stopped alongside a large van at traffic lights. ARTHUR BERTON LTD., read the legend on the side. SURGICAL DRESSINGS. He thought of Mrs Dempsey, who would by now have knocked on his door with her bandages. For the first time, he thought of what his father's reaction might be. He guessed that he wouldn't have told anyone yet, his pride wouldn't let him, and he'd be working as usual, throwing his anger into the cement, the cigarette smoke blinding him. Sarah and Deirdre wouldn't know, at least not until they returned from France. He couldn't go back to the tin church, see all the familiar faces which he had always avoided. They were all emigrants, like himself, trying to find their way. Now he was cut off from them, and to his surprise, it made him feel nostalgic. He got off the bus, and found a café, almost empty. He ordered bread and marge and a mug of tea. He was very hungry but he forced himself to eat and to drink the scald slowly to prolong his comfort. No one took any notice of him. He stayed for an hour before trudging into the rain again. He thought he recognized some streets, and after a while it was obvious that he was going round in circles, and the same oppressive buildings loomed before him. As he rounded a corner he saw the dome of that church again and, confident now, he turned right and took another bus, and ended up in the same café. ALL DAY, it said. A fluorescent light lit the window. FISH & CHIPS was artistically painted on it, in white. TODAY FROM 1/$\frac{8}{-}$. The '1' was large and thick, the 8 half its size and an elegant wavy squiggle underlined it. He had hoped to see a familiar face, but the staff had changed. At least it was noisy and warm. He ordered fish and chips and tea, and asked the woman if she knew of any lodgings. She referred him to the pub around the corner. Of course. A pub. That's where everything happens in a place. They'd surely know there.

It was a nice pub, half full of mature Cockneys, men and women. The barman was bald and thin, severe-looking in his waistcoat, but courteous. No, he didn't know of any lodgings. Hugh took his half bitter and sat on one of the benches, hoping to make conversation, but it was left to him and he didn't know what to say. He liked these people, laughing and singing, the women drinking port, some of the men with their hats on, drinking pints. He had another half, then a pint, as it seemed to be only women who drank halves in here, and then another pint. The singing was in full swing by closing time, and he longed to join in, but he didn't belong, so he just swayed to their songs. They sang, '*We'll meet again, don't know where, don't know when,*' and he almost sang with them, but some clamp on his mouth stopped him. As they left, a woman looked at him kindly, and without thinking he asked her if she knew of lodgings. She didn't, but she hesitated, and he thought that maybe she'd take him in herself, but then she bid him goodnight and he was out on the cold noisy street.

He took his bearings by making his way back to the café, then walking up the hill. He realized there had been a lot of bombing around here, but most of it was hidden behind hoarding. Then he found the side street he had spotted earlier in the day, and here there was no hoarding. He had to climb a hill of rubble, covered in wet grass and wild flowers, and when he got to the top, although it was dark by now, he could see that the destruction spread out before him. Acres and acres of it, and in the distance, the lights of the river. He supposed there had been dwellings and backyards and streets, totally destroyed, falling into one another. In between there were the shells of houses, where at least it was easy to imagine families of real people having once lived. Making for the nearest shell, he heard the crackle of a fire and stopped dead. There was a drunken shout, and then some hacking, spluttering merriment. There was a couple at the second one too. They seemed peaceable enough, drinking quietly, a man and a woman. He could just make out their faces in the firelight. He backed off, anxious, and in any case wanting to be alone. He needed time to think.

At his third attempt he found somewhere, a partially collapsed floor forming a lean-to with its wall. He scrambled over the rubble at its mouth and landed in near darkness. A step further in it was completely dark; it was damp and he could hear dripping, but it would do. He stumbled and fell headlong, grazing his wrist. He cursed and sat up on the damp rubble. Although in the centre of what had been the building, it was exposed, where the roof had collapsed through three floors. The rain had stopped and the sky was clearing, and a fresh star blinked at him as a cloud moved away. He blinked back at it, lost in its beauty. As he turned away, he realized that his face was a few inches from a pool of water. He glanced at the sky and then back, enchanted that it was starlight which danced fuzzily in the pool, and then gazed at the star again, losing himself in contemplation of its lonely station up there in the galaxy.

'O water star . . .' he whispered.

He made his way back to the black shelter of the ruin. He shuddered and wriggled in his overcoat as if to huddle deeper into its comfort, then leaned back carefully towards the ground, hoping to rest his aching shoulders. Through his coat he felt something pressing against the small of his back, and reached behind. It was a door handle.

Afraid he might dislodge something, he turned slowly and traced the outline of the door. The timber had split, but enough was intact to serve as a bed if he could get it flat. He pulled, and some bricks fell somewhere to the right above him. Then there was a trickle of mortar. It stopped, and sweating a little, he pulled again and the door came away. He held it above him, afraid to breathe, but nothing happened, and he managed to get it flat enough. There was no question of sleep, but he was out of the elements and alone, and he needed to be still and alone to think. He stretched himself out on his back.

There was a mountain and his mother had lived and died on it. That much was true. She was dead seven years. He had spent eight long years in London with his father. They had cleared ruins like what he was sheltering under now, and built in their place too, lugging bricks and cement with the best of them. Eight years in London, without time to be sad. Always working, or too tired from working too hard.

He was happy now, alone but feeling less alone than in many years. 'And to think', he said aloud, 'that last night I wanted to die.'

He reached out, fumbling around in the darkness until he found his case and rummaged for the statue.

It was hard to believe it had all happened only the night before. He concentrated, and remembered praying so hard that the edges of the statue had crumbled in his hands. Shifting on the door, he shuffled his shoulders and buttocks, and was still again.

'*What are you doing rigged up like that at this hour of the morning?*' Hugh heard the voice as if it had just spoken. '*What are you doing . . . what are you doing rigged up like that . . . what are you doing rigged up like that*' – what was it?

'My mother appeared to me.'

Thinking of it now, he marvelled at how calm he had been.

Sarah stood up for him, always went on about how intelligent he was. Only for her, he'd have crawled away into a hole long ago. But Brendan treated his own son like a simpleton. Now what would he think? It was as clear as water what he would think. When your son knelt in the middle of the night, talking to his mother's ghost, there was only one place for him, and Brendan was the man to put him there. There was no going back now. He could never go back to his father. Never.

He was tired to the marrow, but couldn't sleep. Tomorrow he would find a lodging house, off Brendan's beaten track, and he'd get his strength back, find his way in a new world.

*

He woke in complete darkness, but felt comforted. Perhaps he would stay like that, and he did for a few hours, daydreaming about the great things he would do, how he would not return until he was wealthy and had proved his father wrong. A faint light grew on three sides.

Having washed and shaved as best he could in a public convenience, he had breakfast in a café before he took to the streets, looking for a room or even a bed. He longed for a bed. He bought a newspaper but in his anxiety he couldn't read it, the print fuzzing about on the page. And like a foreigner without the language he was afraid to ask, hoping to stumble on a ROOM FOR RENT sign. He knew how to read the NO IRISH NEED APPLY signs. He had seen them at the age of fifteen, spelt out to him by his father, who, like him, could barely read in those days.

The rain began, a few drops at first, then very heavy, making him aware of the huge street and its coldness. There were few about, and they seemed to be scurrying, absorbed in their own business. He jumped on a bus, and settled by the fogged-up window.

He would miss Sarah.

And then, delighted, he realized that he could see her the coming Sunday, in the park.

He stayed on the bus, heading north and, when he recognized Holloway Road, he got off and walked again. He reckoned he was only a mile or so from Wedmore Street, but as it was out of Brendan's way, it probably didn't matter and he was glad to be back in an area which seemed human and manageable. His coat was heavy and he felt the damp touch his shoulders. It was still raining. He turned into a dingy café, bought a cup of thick brown tea and sat, huddled into himself. Rain streaked his face, and he plastered his hair back out of his eyes.

He was not only alone, he now had no job to go to. There were other building sites. He wouldn't starve as long as his strength lasted, and he had enough money for nearly two months' lodgings. He was recovering, he'd be all right, and he hadn't become lost like this because he was a pauper or because his mind was gone. There was nothing wrong with his mind, it just needed time to take stock. He was on his own, he needed to work things out, that was all.

Everything swamped him. He had lived in the moment and once passed, it might never have existed. The past was dead, but it still walked about, craving justification.

He supposed he had met people, known them however slightly, and fear and pain and lust and happiness, known them every day, maybe, and yet only a few things stood out: the apparition, the reality of his father, Sarah and her daughter Deirdre.

What about them? Nothing much. Sarah and her missionary need to improve his lot. Her heavy limp. Her reading glasses. He couldn't even remember the colour of her eyes or hair. He'd had dreams, vague dreams about a woman and her infant, had vaguely felt a sensation they had left him. That was all. And work. He'd almost forgotten work. Now that he had time to himself he remembered more. He saw himself, awkward in his

Sunday suit, the tie he could never knot properly, the thick Brylcreem, all so strange to him when he could have walked down the high street in his pelt, or in some loose robe like the Arabs, his hair pasted across his head by the rain.

Like it was now.

I'm closed in on myself. I back away from women, from everyone. Even children.

He stopped short, unsure if he had spoken aloud, feeling himself blush, but no, even if he had, it could only have been a whisper, no one could have heard.

When he looked up a woman was watching him, a table away, grinning as if she had heard everything. Her head was inclined to one side, and she laughed hoarsely as he blushed and looked away. He knew she knew he was a virgin and that he had just confirmed it.

'Are you a Paddy?'

He clutched his teacup, suspicious, aware of his awkwardness.

'I'd know you Paddies anywhere, with your pink cheeks . . . and shy blue eyes.'

'Is that so?'

'Yesh, dat is sho.' She laughed at her feeble attempt at an Irish accent, and rightly so. Then, making up her mind, she sat in front of him, dragging her shopping bags onto the seat with her.

'How long have you been away from your mother and the parish priest?'

He fought against the nerves which confused him, because, inexperienced as he was, he knew her words were full of sex, and in the rush of blood to his head, he couldn't remember which pocket his money was in. He'd been tricked before and had no intention of being tricked again. This woman wasn't a streetwalker. She was sheltering from the rain too, but having just come from the clutches of his father, he might as well have been fresh from the mountain and wasn't sure if an ordinary woman might approach a fella like him, knowing she had nothing to fear. He felt her power and experience, and his own ignorance and nerves, and he knew she knew it.

'Do you live alone?' Silence. 'Have you just arrived in the big bad city?'

He had lived alone, in spite of living with his father. He had lived apart from them all. He hated it, and he hated this café almost as much, its bad light and the fungus on the lattice-work. There was more condensation on the walls than rain on the window.

No, he hadn't just arrived.

'I bet your landlady doesn't feed you well.'

'Well, I didn't ... I don't have a landlady, as a matter of fact.'

He remembered landladies, though, before they went to Wedmore Street. Always moaning about rations. He knew they snooped in their room while they were at work, the statue of the Virgin and his children's books confirming their prejudices about the Irish. He knew all about landladies.

'Oh. You feed yourself then. Lots of good meat, I hope.'

He tried to stop himself as he blurted it out, but he couldn't as years of being on the edge of hunger overwhelmed him.

'Eggs, mostly. Watery eggs. And rashers as thin as wallpaper, and sausages like sawdust. And bread I wouldn't give to greyhounds.'

'I thought so.'

And the green paint of the woodwork in this café. Well, it had been a class of green, once, and there was a time when it had been woodwork. It all seemed of a piece, somehow. His tongue was loosening. Food was not sex. He knew something about food, the lack of it, the craving for a floury potato which he thought he remembered, but perhaps imagined.

Her head inclined to one side again, amused.

'Come home with me, Paddy, and I'll make you something decent to eat.'

He hesitated as she rose, and by the time he made to follow her, she was already out the door. Begod, he thought, excited, begod, I've landed on my feet.

The rain had stopped.

They crossed Holloway Road and continued up Hornsey Road. She was walking briskly, ahead of him.

'Do you always walk so fast?' he called after her. She turned her head over her shoulder and without stopping flashed him a smile.

'Don't you see it's going to rain again?' and she continued as quickly as before.

He lengthened his stride to catch up, excited now for a different reason. He had never seen such a smile. She stopped and waited for him under the railway bridge. He heard the clatter of his boots echoing as he approached her.

'You're limping,' she said. 'Is there something wrong with your foot?'

'I've a bit of grit in my boot. It's nothing.' He'd hardly noticed, but he couldn't tell her the truth in case she thought it was really a blister from walking the streets, looking for a place to live. They looked at each other for a few seconds as a goods train rumbled overhead.

'It isn't far now,' she said, raising her voice and turning, 'it's just around the corner.' He walked beside her as they turned into the cul-de-sac and looked up at the train, a big plume of steam flowing over the leading wagons.

'What's the name of this place?' he asked softly, but she didn't hear. He looked for a street sign and found it. 'Citizen Road,' he murmured, liking it. She had already gone ahead.

She dumped her shopping bag beside the hallstand and took off her coat and scarf, shaking out her brown hair.

'You're soaked through,' she said. 'It's best you have a hot bath, straight away.'

'It's all right,' he mumbled, blushing, and he hated her again.

'Come on, Paddy, do as I say or you'll have pneumonia. Don't want no coffins round this house, now do we?'

He followed her upstairs without a word. She lit the gas and ran the water. It gushed from a snub pipe.

'A real bath,' he muttered, looking down at the lion's paws of the tub. His eyes wandered up her legs as she leaned over the bathtub to regulate the water. She wore black nylons with the seam running up the back. An oval of white flesh peeped from her calf where the stocking had run.

'There we are,' she said. 'That should be nice. You just switch it off here when it's ready.'

'Thanks.'

'Now you take off all those wet clothes so I can dry them at the stove,' she said, partially closing the door behind her. 'Come on, then, hand them out. And don't forget your drawers.'

Miserable, he caught the dirty tone of her voice, but nevertheless began to strip, keeping his arse to the door in case she should peep.

'I don't have any drawers,' he said.

'What? No drawers?'

'Not in summer,' he whispered.

'What's that, Paddy?'

'Not in summer,' he repeated, raising his voice more than intended. Keeping his wallet, he handed out his clothes in a bundle, and when confident she was returning downstairs, he opened the door slightly and called after her.

'My name is Hugh, not Paddy.'

He knew by the silence she had stopped dead on the stairs, and he felt his heart pound as he waited for an answer.

'These will be dry before you can say Jack Robin, Hugh. I'll have a nice stew for you when you're ready.'

He bolted the door, grinning.

'That shook her. Begod that shook her.'

A cloud of steam had already formed and he opened the window to let it out. Taking a deep breath, he looked down on the backyard. It was small, but to one side there was a raised vegetable patch and, incorporated into the back wall, a shed. And some distance beyond that, the spire of a small church.

He unclipped the safety pin, took off the bandage, and carefully folded it. Even when his foot was fully healed, he might still need it for support, especially at work.

His nakedness in a strange place made him uneasy, and he turned off the water before the bath was half full, putting a foot down to the ankle before withdrawing it immediately.

'Jesuzzz!'

Drenching his scalded foot with cold water, while awkwardly suspending his body over the bath with his hands on both sides and his right foot behind the cold tap – forming a tripod to suspend his arched body – he wondered if that woman had heard him and, if she had, if she thought he was a lunatic.

When he finally eased himself into lukewarm water, he began to wonder if, really, he was mad. He talked to no one, and had nothing to say. He was only twenty-two, which meant he could remember only ten or twelve years of his life. Before that . . . a mist, cleared here and there, by a fall against a rock, a guard puffing up the slope. That's all he could remember. And his mother, dead when he was fifteen, and the man who lived farther up, near the peak. It was a sure sign of madness, the way he remembered a frozen picture of it, how it lived inside him, how he carried it everywhere he went, how it stopped him from opening his mouth if a man or a woman spoke to him. Ghosts only appeared to lunatics, and his mother had appeared to him. Small wonder his father had been afraid, and would have him locked up if he found him. But London was a big city and he was safe here. She was going to let him a room.

How would he talk to her? He sat up, gripped by panic for a moment. There was food, he remembered. He had talked to her about food – for a minute or two.

He was suspicious, of her and himself. Where was his father now that he needed him?

He lay back again and stared at his floating toes with great intensity, wanting to experience the luxury. It didn't occur to him that it might be repeated.

Profoundly content, he sighed as his muscles unwound. He was, he realized, at ease, and had only ever felt something like this when he slowly woke on a Sunday morning. Or sitting in the church, coughing and shuffling like everyone else, letting the flow of Latin drug him. He could sit back, no thought or action required other than his presence and to stand or kneel according to well-worn ritual.

'*Dominus vobiscum. Et cum spiritu tuo.*'

He whispered the prayer, not knowing what it meant, but loving its music. '*Dominus vobiscum,*' he repeated.

He closed his eyes, and felt the current of warmth flood

against his belly as his hand brushed past under water. A tin bath couldn't beat this. He opened one eye, then the other, looking at his body as he had never seen it before. A scrawny white torso, a few bleak hairs on the cove of his chest, a bony arse and a sad tool, and his feet were too bloody big.

'Size nine,' he added aloud. There was a scar like a dry whin bush on his right knee.

What would he look like to her? He imagined himself, clothed, striking a pose. She would see what he couldn't see now – a young scarecrow, of middle height in badly fitting clothes, brown hair plastered back to keep it in place behind big ears, pale blue eyes, thin lips, a few freckles on the ridge of his cheeks. He recalled the face, which he hated, from his shaving mirror. He was always nicking himself on the point of his Adam's apple, and on the right edge of the chin there was always a bunch of pimples. Blood through his stubble. Blood on a knee. Something did happen, before the gap of his twelfth year. To him. Were these arms and legs, bones, hairs, and marriage tackle belonging to him? Me. I. Mine. Strange words. He wasn't sure what they meant.

'Hugh?'

He sat upright, splashing water on the floor.

'Your clothes are dry. I'm leaving them outside the door. You haven't drowned, have you?'

He didn't answer, heard her go back downstairs, got out, rubbed himself hard with a towel, his senses sharp to the door, listening. But she was gone. He got his clothes and dried himself more thoroughly, noticing the little rolls of scum the towel left in its wake. He brushed them away, absorbed in his self-discovery again, and pulled the plug, watching the water gurgle away. Only then did he remember he had dry clothes in his case.

*

He ate the stew in silence, knowing she watched his every twitch. When he had taken a few spoonfuls, he said, 'This is great.'

'Do you like it?'

As he finished, he realized he had been hungry for years, perhaps all his life.

'It's the best I can do with the rations,' she said. 'Not like before the war.'

'No, no, it's fine. Powerful. What's your name?'

'Elizabeth. Elizabeth Frampton.'

'Hugh Kinsella,' he said, solemnly rising and stretching his hand down the table.

'Very pleased, I'm sure,' she laughed, bowing and raising the side of her skirt in mock curtsy.

'I can call you Miss Frampton.'

'I'm not that much older than you ... eh, Hugh. You can call me Elizabeth, like the Princess. Or Liz. Don't call me Beth.'

'I'll settle on Elizabeth,' he said firmly.

'Oh, you are formal, aren't you. Why don't you loosen up a bit? You can relax here, you know. You're staying, aren't you?'

'Well,' he stalled, looking away from her and scratching the back of his neck, 'I don't know.' He sniffed. 'What's the rent like?'

'Two pounds two and six, take it or leave it,' she said, and he saw that she was trying to hide a smile.

'I don't know,' he repeated, sniffing and looking around him. 'I'll have to think about it.'

'No more watery eggs, Hugh,' she countered. 'No more bread you wouldn't give to greyhounds.'

His mouth dropped open and he gawked at her, then he stood up and stretched his hand down the table once more.

'Done,' he said.

'Done,' she echoed, squeezing his hand. 'You've no job, have you, Hugh?'

'How did you know? I only left ...'

She shrugged.

'I know where I can get a start on Monday,' he lied. 'In any case, I'm not short. I have some stored.' He showed her his twenty-five pounds and asked how much she wanted. She wanted two weeks, but he gave her five pounds.

'I'm impressed,' she said, to his relief. 'Karl will get you a start on Monday – I can see you're used to hard work,' she said, rising to put the money behind the clock on the mantel.

'Who's Charles?' he asked warily.

'Karl,' she corrected him. 'He's the other lodger. He's German. You don't mind Germans, do you?'

'Why would I mind Germans?'

'I was only asking. A lot of people do, you know. Some Paddies I know, and all.'

Hugh looked into the backyard and noticed the sun had broken through. It was going to be a beautiful evening.

*

He met Karl at supper.

'Who is this, then?' he demanded of Elizabeth, in an accent part foreign, part English. Elizabeth dished out a variation of her stew.

'This is my new lodger. His name is Hugh ... Hugh what's it again?'

'Kinsella. Hugh Kinsella.'

'Hugh Kinsella. He's from Ireland, so I suppose he's Catholic. And this, Hugh, is Karl Bruckner. He's Lutheran, and he's from Hamburg or Berlin, I can never make out which. A League of Nations in this house, I have.' She grinned.

They shook hands, Karl's grip, Hugh noticed, being if anything stronger than his own. He was of an age with Elizabeth. Hugh sized up the tough, tall figure, wondering if he had moseyed into the more experienced path of Karl's plans.

'I was hoping to be the sole master of this hole in the wall,' Karl said, as if reading his fears. Hugh looked quickly from Karl to Elizabeth and back, and Karl stared, his high cheekbones drawing attention to his blue eyes, but then he threw back his head and laughed.

'There's no call for that,' Elizabeth snapped.

Hugh couldn't decide if he was joking or thought he was a gom, and so played sober, which made Karl laugh again.

'I said there's no call for that, Karl,' Elizabeth said again.

'Ah, Hugh ...' Karl said with a hint of lament, and laid a

hand on Hugh's shoulder. But Hugh drew back, feeling that Karl pitied his ignorance and softness in a hard world. He didn't want pity.

'Where exactly are you from?' he asked him in near panic, feeling some response was expected. 'In Germany, I mean.'

'Where is any German from after the Monster.'

'Yes, I've heard you mention that once or twice,' Elizabeth muttered, sitting in to her meal. She was furious. That much was obvious.

Jesus.

'In answer to your . . . pertinent question, Hugh, I was born in Erxleben in 1917. We left for Berlin when I was five and afterwards Hamburg, so I don't recall much about it, except the Rathaus – the Town Hall, you know – and the square. Yes. And the fields around the town were flat as far as the eye could see, like the American prairies, I think. Maybe I saw that in a picture book. Maybe I made big hills flat so cowboys could ride their plains, what would you say?'

Hugh sat up in complete attention at this.

'My father worked for a timber merchant and my mother was always crying in her room. Perhaps she knew what was coming.'

'Karl's family were all killed in the Hamburg bombings,' Elizabeth said, without looking up from her plate. 'That big one in '44. Except his brother. He copped it in Russia.'

Karl's mouth curled.

'While I saw what was coming and escaped to England to fight the *Monster*. But . . . they dumped me in jail. Hmm? As a German national. A "hostile alien" they called me. Can you imagine the irony of that? You may think that an alien is someone from Mars, but the English are a cautious race, Hugh, would you not say?'

'Huh. I'm English,' Elizabeth said, yawning. 'In case you'd forgotten.'

The sun was setting. Its hard light caught Hugh's face through the stained glass of the back door, and a dull ache seeped into his eyes as Karl talked. He was now talking to Elizabeth and although he had lost interest in Karl's story, he felt jealousy tightening his throat. They were mature, and they knew the secret signals while pretending not to be thinking about sex at all. He didn't know how or why, but he was sure of that.

Eventually, his anger left him and his attention wandered. Although it was summer, the black stove was warm. He noticed how smooth and clean it was, as if worn by wind and rain, with the porcelain teapot in its cosy, to one side of the hotplate. The entire room was in a warm and polished glow. On the mantel was a clock in its walnut case which he heard for the first time as he stopped to listen. He doubted if Karl had ever heard it, he was so full of himself, although he was quiet now, as if he had made a big effort to be sociable and that was that.

One of the photos on either side of the clock was of three young men, the other of a couple who were dressed like Hugh's grandparents. Half the room was falling into shadow; the other half was caught in sunlight as wide as a row of hay, swarming with fine dust. The door, with its stained glass panels of a bird, was open, and he heard the whistle of a train.

Elizabeth glanced at him across the table. He had been watching a stray hair which had wandered from her well-brushed head. As their eyes met, she looked back again to Karl.

'Can you fix a start for Hugh on Monday?'

Karl sized him up.

'If he's willing to work hard. Brickie's mate, Hugh . . .'

'I've never done anything else.'

'I thought so. You have a strong hand.'

Hugh smiled, reassured and suddenly conscious of an affection for the big German.

'That's fixed then,' Karl said, and moving away from the table, found his pipe and newspaper on the mantelpiece, and brought his chair into the yard with an air, Hugh thought, of being master of this hole in the wall.

A faint despair entered him again, and he looked at Elizabeth for a clue or hope or something. But he could find no hint in her face as she noisily gathered the dishes and piled them into the porcelain sink.

'Are you going out?' she asked without turning.

'I might as well,' he said quietly. She dried her hands on her apron, reached behind the clock and retrieved a key.

'Here,' she said. 'Come in when you like, but don't make a racket. I've to think of the neighbours.'

He accepted it without a word and left, almost floating through the warm evening air on Citizen Road.

Four

SARAH

July–August 1950

'*Frère Jacques, frère Jacques . . .*' Sarah sang. She promised herself she would remember this soft image of her daughter drifting to sleep on a French song.

Or was it a lullaby?

Well, when you sang it softly it was, Deirdre mouthing the words as her eyes irresistibly closed. She had just shut the door behind her, but halfway along the landing she turned back for one more look at her sleeping face. All too often, she had left with relief, exhausted and craving time to herself. But not now, and it gave her peace both to gaze on this innocence and to know that her pleasure in doing so made her happy, in tune for once with what was right and true in her life.

The evening light still shone through a chink in the curtains, and fell on Deirdre's pillow, making her cheek seem like a billowing cloud. Fearing it would wake her, Sarah pulled the curtain tight. She took the golliwog and dolls, neatly arrayed on the bedside chair, and sat, clutching them to her. She listened for Deirdre's breath, as so often before; and as so often, she could not hear it, or see her chest rise and fall, and marvelled at how children can be so deeply at peace it seems that life has casually left them. Finally Deirdre breathed in, and Sarah waited for the next breath, becoming still, hardly breathing herself. Deirdre broke the spell by wrinkling her nose and stretching an arm, and Sarah smiled, still clutching the dolls.

Johnny thought you were the image of me when I was your age, in the last photo we sent him. I wonder are you still? Maybe now you're like your father. A child is like that, isn't she? Like her mother one minute, and then she looks up or laughs and there's no mistaking her father, or a great-grandmother dead before she was born.

Poor Mother. I suppose they said the shame would kill you. They all rallied around you, closing ranks against the slut who'd shamed you, didn't they? The wounded matriarch. How many women were banished from their homes because they'd brought shame on their families? And the same families went to Mass the following Sunday and prayed to Mary about the poor banished children of Eve without batting an eyelid.

She shook her head in bafflement. How could a woman, after all these years, not want to acknowledge her own flesh and blood? Was she not even curious about her own granddaughter? But you never knew how to love, Mother. You still don't.

And do I? Do I know how to love, I wonder?

An emotion she thought of as love spilled through her. How had she managed it, when her own mother and father were like fish washed onto the Clare shore? Their neighbours were kind people, and maybe they had saved her. She thought of her landscape, its stunted, skeletal trees rocked by the wind off the Atlantic. Sometimes, especially after she'd come home from hospital, she used to stare at the naked whitethorns, at their wizened branches, and startling shapes would emerge.

She was by halves amused and amazed. Those trees reminded her of the time she was sixteen, when her strange wild feelings for Mikey Crotty had no middle, until one afternoon in November she looked at the whitethorn behind the house and saw its branches take the shape of a woman, her legs apart, impaled on a big, gnarly branch, and it was all as clear as the air. It was like catching sight of a god, she supposed. Yes. It was surely something godly that drew her to the stables as if she had lost her will. In the heat given off by the horses, in the smell of straw and horsepiss, she had discovered pleasure. She had looked differently at men after that.

She stared at the dolls in her lap, and then replaced them on the chair, before gazing on her daughter again. Sometimes, Deirdre's existence baffled her, but then, so did her own. Its sole reason was this child who would suffer as surely as she had, as everyone did. She thought of the whitethorn again and, in a moment of grief that was also beautiful, knew that Deirdre could only truly learn by her own experience.

She kissed her and carefully closed the door. In the sitting room she took down Tom's letter again, and ran the English five pound note between her fingers. As usual the envelope bore a *Luimneach* postmark, and that, of course, was where he changed the currency. He never forgot, although it must have been harder with every passing year, with three children to support on a small, sodden farm. If only herself and Tom could have said to hell with shame, with what the neighbours thought, or what a priest might preach from the altar. But even though she had been thirty-three at the time, and Tom had been twenty-eight, even at that age they had been too young to stand their ground against class and custom. But maybe, after all, it had been for the best.

She put the letter and money back in the envelope and placed it on top of the cabinet, taking down the pattern and material with her needles and threads and settled into work by the window. Her life in Clare, with all its might-have-beens, annoyed her. What would have happened if she hadn't broken her hip at the age of thirteen? There was nothing surer – she'd be unhappily but respectably married to a large farmer, or a merchant in Kilrush. A primary teacher like her would have been snapped up. For a moment she indulged a fantasy of a gaggle of men with starched collars fighting for her hand. She wondered if there was a romantic soul to be found in that class of man. She doubted it. Not since the Famine, anyhow. What they wanted was good breeding stock and a dowry – or so her mother never tired of telling her.

Well, what they didn't want, she had decided early on, was a lame mare. Apart from the occasional teacher, the only men she had ever met there with life and music in them were working men, small farmers, and labourers. She had always been attracted to men like that, which is how she had met Tom. He loved books, music, nature. Every flower, every tree, every grass, every bird and wild animal – he knew their names and histories. She loved books, and music, especially when he was playing. He had been the only one to look past her withered leg, and didn't give a damn if he was seen with a lame woman on the main street of anywhere. That's why she loved him, that and his songs and tunes, and why she had given herself to him. She concentrated hard on the pattern and the ghosts gave way to the comfortable reality of a London street.

She picked up the pattern and cloth again, but after a few stitches she paused, and thought of Brendan. Six years she knew that man and the Lord knows why she put up with him. She remembered how they had met when she was working in a bookie's at the weekends to make extra money. He had asked to her to fill in the docket for him, and that was how she had got to know him, if she could ever say she knew him. His difficulty with writing his docket had given her the idea of the classes, although she didn't get around to it for a couple of years. In the end it was her one way to see him, hoping week after week that he would ask her out, week after week deluding herself that if she kept herself well he'd do something more than gawk at her. Now he didn't even want to come to the classes. Well, there would be no more classes. He could go and sing for himself.

Thank God she was going to France. The tickets and francs locked in her wardrobe kept her sane. They had gone every year since the war ended, to the same house and the same good people. Knowing there was another kind of life had helped her recover from Tom, from the shame of having a child out of wedlock. In France, her daughter was treated like a princess. She looked forward to a lazy time with Deirdre, doing the small things their usual lives did not allow. The previous holiday was memorable for that alone, and scenes came drifting back.

Like that time she returned from a walk with Deirdre, making their way through the orchard which had a carpet of light blue flowers. They must have returned from walks through that orchard many times, yet she remembered it as a unique moment. They weren't laughing, or fooling about. It was just – well, peaceful.

She could feel the French sun on her skin. The colours of the garden bathed her eyes, the sun drenching those orange and yellow flowers in front of the veranda. What did the *patron* call them?

She had often thought of packing up everything and living in that house outside St Lô, but it wasn't financially practical and maybe the idyll wouldn't last anyway. Maybe it was something perfect in her life she could hold on to, if she didn't overstay her welcome.

As much as anything else she drank wine to relive those glowing evenings on the veranda with Deirdre and the *patron* and his wife who often came from next door in the evenings – the table laden with food they had spent hours preparing, a moth circling the tilley lamp, the soft air and the wine going slowly, deliciously to her head.

She settled into cleaning the rooms, and was happy for a while, but the memories of Tom and Clare came back to worry her. Why couldn't she just look forward to France and to hell with everything else?

Eventually she finished her work and had nothing more to occupy her so she opened a bottle of wine. She drank back the first glass and, pouring the second, knew that she would finish the bottle. Instead of calm, relaxing thoughts of drinking wine on a French veranda, all she could think of were raindrops clinging to fuchsia, and the sound of water draining into a ditch in Clare.

It was terrible to be disowned by your own mother. To be called a slut and worse. And for what? For the crime of bringing a human being into the world.

She had to last out until she got to France. Everything would be all right then. After a few days she would think in French, about things French, and all of this would be far away.

After her fourth glass she felt safe and began to sing to herself. It was safe to think of Brendan again, and all through her song she held her image of the unsure, vulnerable man she had known him to be.

Ah! She had been codding herself for too long. Love had been useless to her, and the very thought of love made her laugh. The man was a total stranger, and there was no point, at her age, in acting like a girl, fooling herself into thinking she was in love.

'Oh dear oh dear oh dear oh dear,' she sighed, 'how foolish we are. How foolish.'

Pleased with herself, she drained the bottle and, amused by her clumsiness, put it away and rinsed out the glass. No, there would be no more foolishness. She'd enjoy herself in France. That was enough for now. And when she came back, if she found a steady, manageable companion, with enough *ready cash* to keep them in comfort, then well and good. Otherwise, she'd put up with the loneliness, instead of frittering away year after year of her life, hankering after a man who, deep in her heart, she knew would drag her down. She knocked back a glass of brandy to celebrate her decision, but she lay awake into the small hours, brooding, going though the possibilities and dead ends of her life over and over.

'Mammy,' someone was shaking her. 'Mammy, it's my birthday tomorrow!' The little fingers dug into the fat of her arms, and the strange, high English accent bore into her head.

'Oh don't, love, don't. Mammy's not well.' Deirdre pushed her again. 'Oh don't.'

'But Mammy, we're going to the shops, remember?'

'Stop it, Deirdre. I want to sleep.'

'But I've been waiting all morning—'

'Out. Out this minute.'

'But it's half eleven, and you said—'

'Stop it!' Sarah roared, sitting up and immediately regretting it. Hands on the bed, she steadied herself. When she focused on Deirdre, she saw that accusing look she had come to know well, only this time it was through tears.

'You've been drinking, haven't you?' Deirdre sniffled.

'No I haven't.'

'Yes you have. Don't deny it. I saw you last night.'

'Then why ...' Her anger was stillborn as she finished the question to herself. She held out her arms to her daughter, who ran into them, crying more freely now.

'That smelly old wine,' she sobbed into Sarah's breasts.

'Hush, pet,' she whispered, stroking her hair. 'I'm sorry. I'm really sorry.' She rocked her until she calmed.

'All right. I'm getting up now.'

Unable to hide a grin of triumph, Deirdre turned away and slipped out of the room.

'O God,' Sarah groaned.

Deirdre had prepared some toast for her and, although she almost gagged on it, she managed to keep it down. She drank back the tea, holding out her cup, and Deirdre poured carefully.

'Have you had your bath?'

'Yes.'

'And did you wash your hair?'

'Yes, and I dried it myself.'

'Oh. And who's an independent little miss, then?'

She was delighted with that, and hummed contentedly while Sarah finished her tea. Then she skipped upstairs to the bathroom and returned with a brush.

'All right then, come here,' Sarah said, and Deirdre stood patiently beside her while she took her time, brushing out her lovely hair. This was something she did regularly in France, and it was a lovely thing to do, taking her time with Deirdre, giving her all her attention.

'You're going to look gorgeous for your daddy,' Sarah said.

Deirdre turned, smiling beatifically.

Their first stop was the photographer's studio, and Deirdre was suddenly nervous and fussy, but once the photographer had settled her, her happiness shone through.

In his letter, Tom expressed the wish, as always, that his five pounds would buy Deirdre a winter coat and shoes, and his word was law to his daughter. She didn't care that it seemed strange to buy a winter coat in summer and in previous years they had tried several shops which had no winter stock. Now they knew exactly where to go, that big store on the Holloway Road, and Deirdre calmly accepted that she would have to grow into the coat.

Behind her calm exterior, Sarah's hangover was torture, with Deirdre taking advantage of her indulgence which she sustained only to prove to her daughter that alcohol was not her master. Somehow she made it through the day. It was funny how Deirdre didn't mind her drinking wine in France. But then the French were civilized, and ate good food when they were drinking, so she was never drunk in France. Not rolling-round-the-place, muttering-to herself drunk, at least.

Once home, Deirdre put her coat away carefully, looking at it from every angle as it hung in the wardrobe with its strange smell, before she settled down to write to her father with painstaking detail and care. The letter would be addressed to Mr John Considine, Sarah's brother, who would discreetly pass it on to Tom with the latest photo, both of which Johnny would keep. While Deirdre was engrossed in her letter, Sarah had a bath. Her hangover had mostly lifted, and she moaned with pleasure as she lay back in the water, the dull, deep ache in her leg easing. Peace at last. And France was only another day-and-a-bit away. Life was good after all.

After supper and assured that her mother would send the letter once the photo was ready on Monday morning, Deirdre went to bed without protest, and they sang their French songs together until she drifted off. She took down the pattern again, but hadn't the concentration and abandoned it in favour of a book she had been reading for some time, du Maurier's *The Hungry Hill*, which she wanted to finish before going to France. She could finish the dress in an hour if necessary. An hour passed before she looked up from the book, tempted to have just one glass of wine. Her leg was at her again, and the wine helped, sometimes.

She was making good headway when there was a knock on the front door. It was Brendan.

'Is he here?'

'Is who here?'

'The young fella.'

'Hugh?' He wasn't looking at her, but he nodded tensely. 'Why would he be here?'

'Well, he's gone, anyhow. Somewhere.'

'Come in, Brendan,' she said quietly, and led him into the front room. 'You don't drink wine so I won't offer it but can I make you a cup of tea?'

'No. Where is the mad fucker, Sarah?'

She was taken aback, his wild eyes accusing her, but she composed herself and outstared him.

'I have no idea, Brendan. But if he's left you, you have only yourself to blame.'

'What are you talking about?'

'Well, you allowed him no life. When he should have been enjoying his youth, you've kept a tight grip on him, that's for certain.'

She wasn't sure if he was listening but she persisted.

'Has he been to one dance? Has he as much as talked to a girl? A fine intelligent young man like that is afraid of looking a woman in the eye. I've seen it myself in this very room.'

'I worked every hour God sent, to get us back to Ireland.' His voice was breaking, and she bowed her head. She too had hoped to return, in her deepest sleep she had yearned for it, but the same yearning was a way of avoiding the hurt she had run from in the first place.

'Yes, Brendan. We all want to get home. Hmm?'

'Aye,' he said absently.

In the hush, she felt the old anguish of remembering Tom, his head thrown back in helpless laughter at his Sarah in dazzling flight. She had been the wittiest woman in Clare, but only with Tom.

'What was I dreaming of?' Brendan implored of the wall. He looked beaten, and she felt acquainted with every untold, broken illusion which had forced the question from him. Even if their lives had been so different in detail, essentially they had sprung from the same confusion. She took his hard yet limp hands and slowly he faced her.

'What age are you, Brendan?' she asked.

'I was born in nineteen hundred and a four.'

'That makes you forty-six, so. I'm forty-one,' she said, gripping his hand hard. It was like scratching the wall in a handball alley.

'Sit down, will you?' She let his hands go and he sat.

'Do you remember the year we met?'

'Aye. Nineteen hundred and a forty-four.'

'Your wife was just a year dead, remember?'

'Why wouldn't I?'

'And Deirdre was just a baby. Do you remember where we met?'

'What are you on about?'

'Don't you remember? You asked me if I'd write out the docket for you.'

'Ah, *fuck!*'

'Brendan, what's wrong?'

'I forgot to put a few bob on the Derby, all because I was worried about that mangy little blackguard.'

'Oh dear. What were you going to back?'

'That French horse. Galcador. You weren't listening to the radio, by any chance?'

'No,' she lied, 'I was out shopping with Deirdre and completely forgot about it.'

Oh dear, oh dear. She had managed to get home just in time for the commentary, and Galcador had won by a head at one hundred to nine.

'The one time I didn't back, and you can be bloody sure the damn thing won. The little bastard.'

'What's the next big one?' she asked, trying to distract him.

'What does it matter a fuck. You haven't seen him so I'm not going to waste your time any further.'

He got up roughly and left. So Hugh had done a bunk. Despite Brendan's gruffness, she was pleased. If Hugh wasn't around, maybe he'd rely on her more. She frowned, hating herself for this, but she couldn't help it. Maybe, just maybe, after all . . .

She slept it in, and Deirdre came and lay beside her. Sarah felt good after her long sleep, and put her arm around Deirdre.

'Happy birthday, pet.' Deirdre grinned and snuggled in under the bedclothes. 'I'll give you your present after breakfast, is that all right?'

'What is it?'

'It's a surprise, silly.'

'Oh. Can we have breakfast now?'

'In a minute. Were you awake when Brendan was here last night?'

Deirdre glanced at her, surprised, and rubbed her wrist across her nose.

'No, I was asleep. Was he here for a reading lesson?'

'No.' Sarah laughed. 'No, pet, he wasn't. He was looking for Hugh.'

Deirdre broke free and sat up straight, her eyes wide.

'Has Hugh run away?'

'No.' Sarah shook her head, smiling. 'Hugh's too big to run away.'

'But he's gone.'

'Yes.'

'But we'll see him in the park, won't we?'

'Maybe.'

'Did you say that to Brendan?'

'No.'

'Why?'

'Why? Because Hugh is a grown man, Deirdre. He's entitled to leave home if he wants to.'

Deirdre leaned towards her mother and whispered, 'It's our secret, then.'

'It's our secret.'

They rubbed noses, grinning, to seal their pact.

The meeting in Finsbury Park did not go well. Her hip was affected by the recent damp weather, and he seemed to have fallen already for his new landlady. She had never noticed it before, but Hugh was really very like his father. Most probably, when he filled out in a few years' time, he would be the image of him. She hadn't realized it until he had been grumpy with her, and she took a close look at him in his new, independent light. And then there was that nervous, vulnerable quality that they shared, which was only disguised in Brendan by the passage of years. Maybe it was her teacherly wont of seeing the parent in the child, but no, it was there all right. And as soon as he had revealed his erotic interest in his landlady, something had happened to her. She was jealous. This annoyed her greatly. It was bad enough being fobbed off by his father. She did not, definitely did not want an emotional complication with the son. Still, she had had the urge to run her fingernails through the hairs on the back of his neck sometimes, and could not deny a mild desire as she watched him give Deirdre money for her birthday.

She put it down to frustration, and the Lord knows she had known that for long enough. Women her age weren't supposed to feel desire, and if they did it was for their husbands of twenty years. All nice and neat and contained. She could tell him this much for nothing: she didn't think much of his landlady. But she didn't tell him anything of the sort.

On the way home, the thought crossed her mind that she should tell Brendan she had met Hugh. But no, that was silly.

'Now remember, Deirdre. If Brendan comes again, you're not to breathe a word about Hugh.'

'Why?'

'Why? I thought we agreed ... He has a right to his own life, that's why.'

'Will I have the right to my own life?'

'Of course ...' Not for the first time, Deirdre had stopped her in her tracks with her reasonable questions. This one had jerked her into a future she did not want to contemplate, and suddenly she had a great deal more sympathy for Brendan's grief at the disappearance of his son. It was getting very warm again, and she was sweating by the time they reached home.

They had some lunch and then Deirdre went off to play with Delly. Around four o'clock there was a knock on the door. She knew it was Brendan and she didn't move. He knocked again, this time louder, and she answered it.

'Any sign of him?' His eyes were still avoiding her.

'No, Brendan.'

'Maybe I should tell the police.'

'I think maybe you should come in.'

'Oh. Right,' he said, finally meeting her eye.

She led him into the front room, and he sat in to the table.

'Will you have a cup of tea?'

'Ah . . . no.'

'Well, take off that heavy jacket. It's tropical this evening.' He had no tie, but otherwise he was clean and neat in his Sunday best.

'It's all right.' He hesitated, then took it off.

'Brendan,' she said, sitting in to the table opposite him, 'you'll have to accept that he's gone. He's gone to make his own life. It's the natural way of things.'

'You'd say so?' He turned away from her again, his lips pursed. She reached over and put her hand on his. He tensed, muscles rippling along his jaw, but otherwise he did not respond and, feeling stupid yet again, she withdrew her hand. He struggled with himself for a while, before coming to an abrupt decision.

'You're a fine-looking woman, Sarah.'

'I accept that compliment at the speed of lightning.'

To her relief, he laughed, and she thought she saw something dawning in his face.

'Good!' he said. He concentrated on the table and it was obvious he was warring within himself again, and she knew that this time . . .

His hand moved slowly across the table and settled on hers.

'I know I'm not good-looking any more,' she whispered, afraid she was going to cry.

'Stop that talk,' he ordered. 'Things never turn out as you think,' he said then, quietly.

'Rarely.'

'I'm . . . I'm very lonely, Sarah.'

'That makes two of us.' She wanted to add that maybe he might have thought of that before now, but it wasn't the time. Nervous that she might frighten him off, she waited a decent interval before she got the courage to put her other hand over his, and squeezed it as hard as she could, though it dwarfed hers. He startled her by rising abruptly and coming around to her side of the table. He towered over her, hesitating, and she looked into his face, held by the grief she saw there.

He pulled her to her feet, tearing at her blouse and dragging it off. She stared at him as he wrenched off her brassiere and buried his head between her breasts. He pressed his face against her so hard that she struggled to breathe. His hands were crushing her shoulder blades, and she whimpered in pain, but didn't protest. His stubble scraped down her belly and he lost balance, somehow falling back onto the chair and dragging her with him. His eyes were clenched shut, his teeth bared, and she clutched at his hair as he pulled blindly at her skirt. For some reason she tried to stop him, though she didn't want him to stop, but he took no notice, and then something in her gave way, and she wrenched off the braces, and clutched at his shirt, and still he took no notice. She stepped out of her underclothing as he pulled them down, and he dragged her to the floor. As he balanced on one hand and knee between her legs and pulled his trousers down, she opened his shirt and pushed it back off his shoulders. She wanted his flesh against hers, not a cotton shirt, and he was forced to take it off.

She was shocked by the sudden pain of him pushing into her, but she braced herself and raised her legs over his back. The pain eased, but his violent thrusts winded her. As she concentrated on the ceiling, she didn't notice any more and her body was shaking as she felt deeper and deeper into herself. Below his rasping breath, as she took his pounding, he was trying to say something in the strangled tones of a mute trying desperately to speak.

'Why did you do it?' he shouted as he collapsed onto her.

She was appalled, and dug her fingers into his back.

She was still tense, spasms jerking in her muscles, but she ran a hand through his hair, and held him to her with the other, wondering if he knew at all, as he cried quietly, who was sweating beneath him now.

After a while he withdrew, rubbed at his eyes, pulled up his trousers and knelt away from her, putting on his shirt. Despite the ache in her belly and a vague dread of pregnancy, she had calmed.

'Maybe you should know that I don't make a habit of crying.'

'That's all right.'

'Well, it won't happen again.'

'You're not going, are you?' she asked quietly.

He stopped and looked at her. He seemed younger.

'Do you want me to stay?'

'Yes.'

'Do you mean for the night or for good?'

He had taken her by surprise. She had meant for a few hours, so that their parting would not be brutal, but now her mind raced, wondering what the implications were, how, most of all, it would affect Deirdre. She had daydreamed about this, but the reality sent a chill of resistance through her. Yet she could not stop what came to her lips.

'I meant for good, Brendan.'

'Right, so.' He stopped buttoning his shirt, as if there was no need, and handed her her scattered clothes.

Five

KARL

July–September 1950

Karl rose and stood in the bathwater as it drained away. It fascinated him to watch the water in its unfailing spiral, how it obeyed a natural law every time. In the southern hemisphere it spiralled in the opposite direction. To draw it from this angle, that would be an achievement. As he stepped out of the bath and dried himself, he wondered if, when his life reached its apex, he would descend again, passing through all the horrors he had found in its ascent.

There was a new lodger, a young Irishman apparently. Karl dressed himself with care. Something in Elizabeth's voice warned him that this man was of unusual significance to her. Women always seemed to know from the very beginning.

The Irishman was seated at the table when Karl went down to the kitchen.

Elizabeth introduced them.

To Karl's surprise, he seemed much younger than he had anticipated, especially when he spoke. And cowed, somehow. He looked at Elizabeth, surprised that she should be interested in a boy like this.

She was trying to be light, but irritated him by pretending to forget his birthplace. She found this most amusing, for some reason.

With great effort he concentrated on being sociable and shook Hugh's hand. Be jovial, Karl, he thought. Please be jovial.

He tried a joke, but Hugh seemed disconcerted by his efforts. 'There's no call for that,' Elizabeth chided him. She looked worried, and he knew why, but he couldn't help it. He found Hugh's bewilderment very funny.

'I said there's no call for that, Karl,' Elizabeth repeated, and this time her tone sobered him.

'Ah Hugh . . .' Karl said, melancholy replacing his humour; and in sympathy with all the Hughs of the world, in whose number he had been counted at one time, he touched him lightly on the shoulder, hardly noticing that Hugh recoiled.

'Where exactly are you from?' Hugh asked him earnestly. 'In Germany, I mean?'

'Where is any German from after the . . .'

Karl's mouth continued to form the words, but he didn't hear them. He had seen a vision of a medieval hell. Fire was spurting from cracks in a sheer rock face. Bodies were climbing over bodies. He knew he was speaking normally, that his face gave no clue to what he saw. He even knew that Elizabeth was angry, and why. She was afraid that he would go beyond her reach again, but there was nothing he could do. He was answering Hugh's question, and that was enough for now.

'Karl's family were all killed in Hamburg,' Elizabeth broke in again. 'That big one in '44. Except his brother. He copped it in Russia.'

He rambled on, justifying himself, blaming the English for his imprisonment.

The hellfire stopped, blanked out by white light. Elizabeth and Hugh were eating in silence, and he used it to break through to the present. It was a relief to concentrate on something as simple as eating. Elizabeth cooked well. Even when the rations were at their worst, she managed to make nourishing, pleasant meals. He was grateful for that. For so many things.

'Can you fix a start for Hugh on Monday?' she asked quietly.

Of course. Elizabeth had but to ask, no matter what complication or indebtedness to those he despised that it might entail. It was against his interests, he knew simply by the way she spoke of the young man; but Elizabeth had made a request. He pretended to consider.

'If he's willing to work hard. Brickie's mate, Hugh . . .'

'I've never done anything else.'

'I thought so. You have a strong hand.'

Hugh relaxed, and smiled for the first time and, despite himself, Karl found that he liked the Irishman. How little reassurance we need.

'That's fixed then,' he said. He found his pipe and newspaper and brought a chair into the yard. He carefully placed his paper and pipe on the chair and, sure he wasn't being watched, slipped into the shed and opened a large jute bag. He ran his hands across the expressionless faces and held them to his chest. They were still crude, but they would come to life in their own time, as his imagination reconstructed what he could not fully remember. He looked them over and caressed them once more before settling in the yard. He cut some slices of tobacco and slowly crumbled them. Yes, he felt better now. To keep in touch with his family, and yet, keep their reality at a distance. That was the way, he was sure. This moment, he thought as he puffed on his pipe, only this lovely moment. Elizabeth turned on the radio.

He read for a while, until he had finished his smoke, and found Elizabeth sitting at the kitchen table. She had cleaned and tidied everything away, but she was not reading or occupying herself, and he knew she wasn't listening to the radio. He leaned down and tenderly brushed his cheek against hers, but she pulled away. There was no point in insisting. He waited patiently for what she had to say.

'Why do you do it, Karl?'

'To what are you referring, Elizabeth?'

'You know well.'

Of course, but he did not reply. If he was to be blamed, then she would have to choose the words with which to blame him. He waited.

'Why did you have to go on about the *Monster* nonsense? He's only a boy.' He waited again before replying.

71

'You are right,' he said simply. She turned to him, her eyes bright with tears, then leapt to him, holding him tight.

'O Karl, I'm afraid. I don't want you to have one of those bloody things again. They scare me to death. Don't talk about all that again. It does no good. Please.'

'Yes, *Liebling*, I know.' She looked into his eyes and face, reading them for truth or evasion, her own eyes mad with need of assurance, and he felt as if he were breaking in two. He lifted her from the floor into his arms, as much to evade as to love her for this. His love for her was the single good and decent reality in his life.

'Karl . . . you're crushing me.'

My God . . . He let her down carefully and brushed back the hair from her face, but she shook her head and went to her room, leaving him stranded. He took a deep breath.

So be it.

*

He went to his room and with great effort, calmed himself sufficiently to browse through his book on mathematics. He cared only for one section: 'Geometrical Shapes in Nature'. The fine, silky quality of the illustrations and their heightened detail was in itself a joy. The shapes gave him a sense of essential order, and contemplating them allowed him to lose himself in their beauty. He turned the pages. On one, the cross-section of a semi-precious stone revealed its inner structure as a series of nestled triangles. Another illustrated a microscopic sea plant, and within an almost perfect circle, with ribbed radii, lay a magnificent stained-glass window, the equal of the Rose Window of Notre-Dame. That was not possible! he marvelled. But what fascinated him most of all was the chambered nautilus shell.

Its perfect spiral, its chambers perfectly equiangular, thrilled him. He closed his eyes and breathed deeply, transported by the precise beauty of nature. He had discovered that the most surprising objects took the shape of strictly logarithmic spirals: the curve of an elephant's tusk, the horns of a wild sheep, and nebulae. The daisy contained two opposite sets of rotating spirals, formed by the florets on its head: exactly twenty-one clockwise, and thirty-four anticlockwise. He closed the book and opened his eyes, consoled. How long had it been since he had seen a daisy, and had he ever looked closely at its head, ignorant of a code which constructed beauty and therefore peace, and yet charmed – he knew not why?

He found a pencil and some paper, and a compass and ruler which he kept in an old schoolchild's tin box which smelled of workshops, and began to copy the chambered nautilus shell. He made several drawings, each one more detailed and accurate than the last until, satisfied, he took down his only book on astronomy, *The Stars in Their Courses* by Jeans, and found again the Spiral Nebula. It didn't describe it as such, but there it was, the Nebula M 51, in Canes Venatici, its light probably taking over a million light years to reach Earth, although it was one of the nearest of the known nebulae. He chose his best drawing of the chambered nautilus, cut it out and placed it on the page opposite Nebula M 51. Content, he went to bed and slept peacefully.

It was bright and sunny when he woke. His first thought as he opened his eyes was that it was Sunday. Yes. It was. He closed his eyes again. Blessed Sunday. He knew by the quality of light that it was noon, or near it, but he lay on, thinking of the previous night as one of the happiest of his life.

He got up and, still absorbed by what he had seen and read the night before, he went to the kitchen and breakfasted alone. The stained-glass door threw a softly coloured light onto the floor. He absorbed it, the light, the silence, the weight of delft, the lightness of bread, the tannic satisfaction of tea. Now that he was calm he noticed everything in its being: the cool diamond pattern of the tiles which bordered the anaemically brown lino in the hall; the solidity of the banister and the nature of its grain hidden beneath the dark stain; the gradations of light as he ascended the stairs. He washed and shaved, every moment slow and conscious, and returned to his room. He looked out his window onto the street and watched some girls skipping on the pavement. A goods train passed, the leading wagons enveloped in steam. Slowly he became restless, as if this awareness had become too much. He placed the needle on Mahler's *Titan*, and wound up the gramophone, its great brass speaker suggesting to him, as always, a giant mushroom that one might come across in the forest.

He lay back on his bed and the music, as ever in being at one with him, calmed him. The front door opened and closed. It had to be – what was his name? Hugh. Yes, he had heard him greet Elizabeth, but heard no reply. A while later, she came upstairs. Ah, her Sunday afternoon bath. The music fell to a hush and stopped. He replaced the needle and lay back to listen again.

It lulled him to sleep and when he woke it was silent. He gazed at the ceiling, thinking how little the joy of the night before held for him now. From his experience, it would thrill him again, but it puzzled him how the deepest joy could mean nothing only a few hours later. What, he wondered, had been in him the previous night – and even that morning – which responded to what he saw as profound, and now meant no more than dust? He was falling into a hole, and in desperation he put on the music again, although he had had enough for one day.

'Karl?'

Her voice. Thank God. Thank God. He went to the door.

'Yes?'

'Karl, I'm off to Millie's.'

'Oh yes.' He opened the door and went to the top of the stairs. 'Yes. I'll see you later.'

She turned and smiled before leaving.

'Elizabeth . . .' he whispered, clutching the banister.

*

She returned at six in good spirits. To fill in time he had gone for a walk, and had enjoyed the beautiful weather, but his anxiety never left him. He had always depended on her, but this anxiety over a short absence was new.

She handed him his newspapers, and he took the hint and went into the yard. Although he didn't read, he had a smoke. He was at ease again, and refused to think beyond it.

Elizabeth called him, and he sat in to a hot meal.

'Where's that Paddy?' she demanded, but without irritation. It seemed that nothing would touch her mood this evening, and she went to call him. Was it just good humour in her voice as she told him that dinner was ready, or was it more? What was the word? *Flirting.* Yes. Was it flirting?

She returned, laughing to herself, and was soon followed by Hugh. He saw her look openly at Hugh, amused and admiring at once. This was no time for him to be present. He felt that dead weight in him, which, he sometimes thought, would allow him to kill, and he looked up at Hugh. Hugh was concentrating on his meal, still not alert, and Karl wondered if indeed one day he would kill him. He returned to his meal. Perhaps one day, but not today. Today Elizabeth wanted to be alone with him, that was clear. He rose and Hugh looked up.

'I'll call you at six a.m.,' he said, before leaving.

'Great. Great...' Hugh said, and despite himself, Karl smiled.

In his room, he quickly found Mahler's Third Symphony, cranked up the gramophone and played the fourth movement as loudly as possible. He did not want to hear soft, laughing voices, or anything, except this. He lay back on the bed and studied the ceiling.

She wanted to be alone with that boy and, because he loved her, it was his duty to make this possible. That was his role. Hugh was his nemesis, but in the depths of his soul he knew that if his life were to end, he would not care. You do not fight what you deserve. You embrace your doom. The song ended, and he got up to put it on again.

'*O Mench! Gib acht!*'

O man, she sang, *take heed!*

The next morning, he rose before six, joyless but unperturbed and looking forward to work. He avoided his eyes in the mirror as he shaved, and finished his ablutions quickly. At six o'clock precisely, he knocked on Hugh's door, went to the kitchen and had a light breakfast. He set the table, and made sandwiches for three.

To his credit, Hugh was ready sooner than he had anticipated.

'Is she up?'

'No, she goes out later. Help yourself. I'm making sandwiches for us all.'

Hugh poured himself tea. He gestured with the pot to Karl, who shook his head.

'What time do we leave?' Hugh yawned.

'Six forty-five.'

Hugh went upstairs for his bag, so Karl waited for him at the door. Unusually, Elizabeth wasn't up. He knocked, and she came out, full of sleep, and touched him on the arm as she passed to the kitchen.

It was a beautiful morning as they walked up Citizen Road and on to Hornsey Road. There was little traffic and he could hear the birds sing.

'Where do we get the bus?' Hugh asked.

'We walk. It is only one mile.'

They arrived at the site, and had to wait for the foreman. Karl hoped he would come early. He did not want to be seen to have influence in front of the other men. Two men arrived before Cooper, but sat behind a stack of bricks for a smoke. Karl met him, hidden from the others by a mixer, and made his request. Cooper asked him the usual questions, and when Karl answered in the affirmative he said, 'Right, Bruckner. It's up to you. If he can keep up with you, he's got the job of the first one who's late. I know who that'll be, so it suits me fine, as it happens.' He turned as other workers arrived and shouted at them. Karl gestured to Hugh to follow and went to the far side of the site. He mixed a bucket of cement while he waited and, as Hugh arrived, handed him a hod and proceeded up the ladder with his cement and began laying bricks he had left as starters at the weekend.

In moments, Hugh had laid a hodful of bricks conveniently beside him, and would never leave him waiting for either bricks or cement.

*

Karl found that he respected the young man, and felt easier about Elizabeth's interest in him, especially as his novelty faded, and it seemed she hardly noticed him as the week passed. Hugh also relaxed, and became normal, even pleasant. Karl wondered about Hugh, about what had made him so timid and passive. And then, the following Monday morning, he noticed that he had become nervous again, as if he had no centre. Karl said nothing for a few days, and then, with a sense of his own well-being, waited until the break. He poured the smoky tea from the billycan into Hugh's outstretched mug.

'What's wrong with you these days, Hugh? Have you bad news in your family?'

'No, it's nothing.' Hugh drank back his tea.

'You can't fool me, Hugh. I'm your friend.' That jarred as he said it. It was almost fifteen years since he had considered himself to be the friend of any man.

'It's the mountain,' Hugh said. 'The mountain's at me again.'

'The mountain?'

But why shouldn't a mountain influence a man's ease?

'I'm sorry, Hugh. Tell me. I'm interested, I promise you.'

Hugh said it was called Croghan and at one time there had been a goldmine there. Karl stopped feeling avuncular as the small shop in Berlin, smelling of metals, came back to him. But he could not stand the sight of gold any more, he told Hugh. He wanted to build. And then Hugh startled him with his notion of wanting to be the mountain.

*

The whistle blew. Karl laid as many bricks as he had cement for and washed his trowel. He did not want company. He was going into himself and needed to be alone. Hugh was animated, he could see that, but he did not respond. He needed desolation, empty of the living, peopled only by ghosts. On the way home, he forced himself to speak.

'Go ahead. Please excuse me.'

He turned and left Hugh, walking quickly down a side road. He knew and did not know where he was going. At a junction, he turned left, ignoring the occasional bombed house. At last he found what he was looking for.

To be it! God in heaven! Did he know what that meant?

Behind a bombed house was a ruinscape. He stumbled blindly across the loose rubble and thousands of bricks, intact, fallen into beautiful configurations, but tangled with weeds, until he came to a clearing, embedded with weeds and wild flowers, and lay down. He closed his eyes, stilled his mind, and raising his arms to the sky, waited for them.

The city was blacked out, but somewhere an accordion was playing. He could hear the waters of a canal lapping against its walls. Then the dogs started howling and the sirens wailed, and he heard the drone build louder and louder.

I am waiting, he thought. I am waiting patiently. The searchlights locked onto the sky, catching the terrified seagulls, which veered away. He was lying on a small bridge over a canal, tall buildings rising behind and in front of him. The curves of the canal's railing were visible as his eyes became accustomed to the darkness. There was a street lamp in a recess from which, if they never came, he could hang himself. The searchlights streamed into the night and the guns started, but still the bombs would not fall. The searchlights turned to a point above him and he was filled with hope, so that his body rose to meet the bombers; but still they would not come. The railings, he could now see, had fine lattice-work in continuous cruciform, and dimly he could perceive fire in the buildings further down the canal, their tall windows a beautiful series of rectangular frames for the conflagration. Even in horror there was beauty.

So the bombs must have fallen, but it was all too dim and he could no longer even hear the guns, and had felt no shock from any explosion. It was happening, but without him.

He opened his eyes to pacific daylight, and felt sick. It was gone. He stood with difficulty, and looked around him, puzzled. It was gone. It had never truly come. And where was he to go now? Home? He had a home in this enormous city, he knew, but he could only vaguely sense Elizabeth, as if he had not seen her for many years. Nevertheless, he went home, climbed the unfamiliar stairs to his room, and fell rapidly into a deep sleep.

*

The weeks passed, and he shared Elizabeth's bed several times, though they did not always make love. He had recovered, even if at the back of his mind there still floated ghosts engulfed in flames, unspeakably pressing him into inertia. She noticed, even when he had succeeded in making love to her. She stroked his face, gazing on him as if he were a newborn.

'My poor Karl,' she whispered. 'Where are you? Where have you been? Tell me.'

When he did not respond, as always her anxiety turned to anger, a more appropriate response.

'Why do you lock me out like this?'

If he could answer that, he would be a free man.

One Sunday evening while he was alone in the house, he went to the shed and took the effigies from the sack. He hadn't forgotten them, but had gone too far down to care. Now, like a convalescent, he was finding the strength to at least try to care. He took out his knife, and began to carve the effigy of his sister, and as her face, in its light and shadow, emerged, unconsciously, like fresh water on a parched shore, love touched him. He carved all afternoon, until he saw her before him. She was not finished, but she gave him peace, and he would finish her another time, when he most needed peace again.

When Elizabeth returned, she made dinner as usual, but only for two.

'Where's Hugh?

'At the cinema. Something called *The Actress*, but Jean Simmons is in it and he likes the look of her, as he says.' She laughed to herself.

So they were alone. There would be no Hugh in his room, perhaps listening. He touched her hand and she stopped laughing, and their eyes met.

'Finish your meal,' she whispered. They ate, and she did not look at him again, but her tranquillity moved him. It was good to feel this love, and not just gratitude, or a wanting to love. She cleaned the dishes and washed them, while he never moved. When she had finished, she stood behind him, put her arms around his neck, and kissed his head.

They went to her room and made love slowly, their fingers deliberating on the other's skin, their kisses unhurried, the blood in their lips exquisite. In this way they were together for hours, until they heard Hugh come in and go to his room. The outside world had returned, and with it his foolishness.

'I owe you so much,' he said.

'Stop that, Karl.'

'No, I have to say it. Without you I would be mad or probably dead.'

'Stop . . .'

She was uncomfortable now, and he knew she hated it, but he couldn't help himself.

'You took me in. You saw that I was a man before I was German. You fed me, brought me back to life, listened to me. And although I hardly dare to say it, you loved me. I want you to know that in my own crippled way, I love you in return.'

She smiled. 'That's the first time . . .'

'Yes. It is long overdue, but I want you to know that whatever happens, I always will.'

'What might happen, Karl?'

'You might love someone else, for example.'

For the first time since he had known her, she turned crimson, and did not reply. His finger played a circle around her nipple as she stared at him in silence. She pushed him away.

'Why do you have to ruin everything?' She threw back the blankets, dressed and left the room.

Yes, he knew that. As he lay there for some time, he knew he had ruined everything. It was his destiny.

On Saturday evening they were sitting in the yard together. They were all reading. Hugh, he noticed, read earnestly and took a long time to turn a page. Elizabeth was reading her usual diet of magazines. This one had a Hollywood actor on the cover. He put aside his papers and lit his pipe. There was nothing he would rather do than finish Gertrud's effigy. He supposed that Elizabeth must know, that she had been discreet. Perhaps one day, when she was angry, she would spit it into his face. *And what about those statues. Who do you think you are – Frankenstein?* Ah yes, Elizabeth, you were cruel if you were

80

hurt. She had not spoken more than a few words to him all week. Worse, she was polite, and even, in her actions, kind. She was playing the landlady, as if they had never been friends, much less lovers.

'Ooh,' she said out loud, but really to herself. 'It says here that Gene Kelly is happily married to film actress Betsy Blair. That rings a bell.'

Hugh looked up from his book and gazed at her. It was obvious that he was in love with her, although Karl doubted if he knew it.

A goods train rumbled along the embankment and Karl returned to his papers, at one point getting a pen to work out the crossword.

'Hugh, would you like to come with me to the market tomorrow?' She said it so quietly, that Karl wondered if he had imagined it. He glanced at Hugh, who looked like a startled calf.

'That'd be great,' Hugh said.

'Eleven o'clock?'

'Right.'

'Right,' she half-mimicked him, grinning.

Satisfied, she went indoors. Karl heard the bath running. Careless now as to whether he was seen or not, he folded his paper and went to the shed, took Gertrud from her sack and began carving in front of Hugh, who was curious to know if Elizabeth worked.

Hugh closed his magazine and went indoors. Karl pressed the knife too hard against Gertrud's cheek, and sliced away a deep groove. This stopped him. He ran his finger up and down the jagged groove and shook his head. 'My poor Gertrud,' he whispered. 'What have I done to you?'

It was time he stopped this. It was past time. If he could not bear to feel, he must not drag Elizabeth with him. It must stop. Say it, Karl, say it. They will be lovers and you, you Karl, will be happy for her. He fought to maintain an exterior calm, though his spirit felt like a blanket wrung between washer-women. It was the time. It was the time to know that Elizabeth needed vitality, a head on her pillow that was not a dead-weight.

He tried to smile. He didn't feel an appropriate emotion, but yes, he could smile. He would smile for Elizabeth. He practised it again. His jaw ached, and he wondered if his smile, being false, would be grotesque.

He went inside and paused at the foot of the stairs as Elizabeth descended, closing her robe. He smiled, but she cast down her eyes and went into her room.

He lay on his bed, smiling. Then he went into the bathroom, being careful to lock the door, and forced himself to look in the mirror, realizing that he had forgotten how he looked. His hair had receded, and the revealed pate was tanned but scaled by the elements. He smiled, and yes, his smile was grotesque. He had fine teeth, but his cheekbones rose to almost obliterate his eyes and the furrows on his forehead rose to his scalp in a pyramid of steps. He practised: jolly – no; broad – worse still. It seemed that a meagre smile suited him best. After a few tries he was satisfied with this, and he went to sleep wearing his new smile.

He woke in mid-afternoon. He had dreamt that he had been thrown to the ground by a demon and that he had bitten into its waxy jaw to fight him off. He emptied his bladder and went downstairs, still heavy with sleep. Elizabeth was sitting at the table. Without thinking, he smiled, and she smiled back.

'You are not at Millie's.'

'No. Not today.'

He stripped and washed at the sink as he had done in the old days, his braces hanging down his legs, and sang as he washed. '*O Mensch! O Mensch! Gib acht! Gib acht!*'

She had his Sunday newspapers and he read them over tea, a few hours later than usual. She was fidgety, sitting and standing. He lowered his paper.

'Elizabeth, *Liebchen*. You are thinking of Hugh.'

She did not answer for a while, then told him that she wanted to make Hugh her lover. He had been prepared for this, perhaps from the day Hugh had come to the house, and had made a bargain with himself that he would share her. She was amazed of course. It wasn't an everyday reaction, but even as they spoke he knew it was true that he only needed her to love him some of the time, whereas he could love her without condition. She asked him why she was doing it, and that touched him. It didn't matter if she was deferring to him to compensate by making him feel important, or if she was so driven by instinct that she could not fathom her motive. He told her why, with a calmness and tenderness which surprised him.

If she did not know why she was seducing the younger man, then also, he did not know why he was making it easier for her. She told him she loved him, and that was his reward, but he could not help but wonder where love ended and gratitude began.

'What? You talk such nonsense, sometimes,' she chided him.

They kissed, and to his surprise, he felt pleasure. Ludicrously, their conspiracy had brought them closer, if only for a while. He almost laughed. She sat into his lap and was still.

'Come to bed with me,' she said, her voice muffled against his chest.

'When are you going to seduce him?' His hands were on her waist, his fingers touching her rear, and making that slow journey upwards that he loved.

'Seduce him? Yes ... I suppose so. Tonight, I think. But I want you before him. To make me secure, Karl.'

His hand rested on her left breast. He too needed security, an armour against the protesting voices in his head.

'Can we stay like this, for just a few moments?' he asked her quietly.

'For as long as you like.'

'Are you afraid?'

'No. I was.'

Yes. That was how he felt also.

He was determined to lose himself in her as they made love. This was as it should always be, with nothing dragging them down. A great romance of bodies which had been through much together. He could not be like this with any other woman. With Elizabeth, there were no questions to be answered, she knew him perfectly. She was pulling his body into her, actively wanting him. To be wanted, that was the most erotic of all and, his pleasure reaching towards agony as his heart and head pounded, he lost himself to her writhing body, to her wonderful moans. Then she arched into him and cried out weirdly as he continued, unable to stop. And then, all his life flowed into her, everything, and he plunged ecstatically into death.

He stayed on top of her as he recovered, and could feel her heart, still beating heavily, not quite in time with his. That this might never happen again was unbearable. Even as he thought it, he was grateful that he could feel, and he let his tears flow. She worked her fingers through his hair, protesting softly that it wasn't just gratitude she felt, but love.

'You are much stronger than I,' he said. He knew at once that he had ruined these precious moments by saying that – by saying anything at all. It was an old story with him. How could it be, he thought as she babbled on, that in ordinary moments he could be strong, thoughtful, almost a dependable man; but as soon as he made love to her he was like a needful child, unable to hold his tongue? And then it was an opportunity for her to justify herself, by praising him, what he had done for her, and there was nothing he could tolerate less than justification of either of them at the present time. So they ended their brief intimacy in resentful silence, as more than once before.

Over dinner, Hugh made a vacuous remark about priests and hell. It was his chance to strike at Elizabeth, and Hugh also, to spew some nonsense about living in hell every day. But he didn't have to utter a word. Elizabeth knew what he was thinking, he could see that, and he enjoyed her anger. Yet as soon as he had left them alone, he wondered why he was hurting her, when it was the last thing he wanted to do. Or was that the truth? He did not know what he felt, and the battle to know wearied him.

In his room he took down his astronomy book and forced himself to read. Hugh came upstairs to his room. So. It seemed Elizabeth had delayed her seduction, had perhaps lost her nerve. Maybe she was still too angry. Anger was not the ideal emotion with which to begin an affair, that was clear. Elizabeth closed her bedroom door beneath him, and despite himself he listened hard. This was not like him. He had always respected her privacy.

Nothing. No opening or closing of drawers, no audible weeping, or swearing, and no awful music from her radio.

Nothing.

He went back to his book. Was the universe finite or infinite? He closed the book. His own feeling was that it was infinite and unknowable, unlike hell. It was immaterial to him what they did. It was crazy. It was madness, but he had said it all. He belonged in hell.

Hugh left. What was going on? Despite himself, his heart jumped in hope. He read on. It was immaterial, completely immaterial to him what they did. He was alone at last, his natural state.

It was a while before Hugh returned, and this time he knocked on Elizabeth's door. Karl's heart pounded. He tried not to, but as if hypnotized, he went to his door and opened it, listening intently. He could not hear what they were saying, but they were in her room. He grabbed his jacket and noisily descended the stairs. He closed the door normally, and left, blanking out the thoughts which drove him on. Only one thing mattered to him now.

He reached the bomb-site, and struggled through the darkness, stumbling and cutting his hand against something sharp, probably a jagged brick, but he blundered on. He found what he thought of as his bed as easily as if it had been daylight and lay down, suddenly exhausted. The glow of the city cast a pale reflection on the sky, but when he closed his eyes all was mercifully dark.

When he opened them again he was beside the inner Alster and the bombers had gone. He walked along the tree-lined Junfernstieg and a car passed at a leisurely speed. There were fires everywhere but nobody he could see was running or shouting; they just stood on the promenade, hands in pockets, gazing at the fires in silence. He recognized one building. The Alster Pavilion, even at this distance, burnt like a sun, so that it seemed its roof was suspended in flames. To the left, another large building, probably a church, was consumed. He could not remember what it was. There was so much he could not remember. The spectators did not move, as if they were exhausted yet still transfixed. It was terrible, yet beautiful. Water lapped against the pier. Another unhurried car passed.

He recalled the Pavilion from his youth, with its balconies and flag turret, on the leafy avenue, relaxed people taking the sun at the pavement tables. He had often wondered what meandered through their minds as they sat there, talking and laughing, or arguing; what lust or sorrow these poor bodies supported as they raised a glass to their lips. How many of them were dead, beyond all that forever? He was so tired, and lay down under a tree and slept.

When he woke, it was dawn and the shells of buildings were in silhouette. He was cold and stiff, but once he had walked a distance he felt good. He let himself in quietly, and checked the clock by his bed. 6.05. That was all right, then. He went to the bathroom and shaved. He had cut his hand somehow, and he examined the congealed blood mixed through the shaving soap before washing it. It was an irritation, no more. Then he remembered the Pavilion inferno. He washed and dried his face and, towel in hand, he looked into the mirror. It was true. He had been there. He had done it. It was no dream; he had been there, and at last he could relax. Whether it was a time for joy or peace, he did not know. Peace, certainly, because although he had not yet found them, he was on his way. Were Elizabeth and Hugh on their way? he wondered. A drama had occurred in his absence. A certain place, in a certain passage of time, a particular, unique drama, pregnant with consequence, unfolded. He smiled, wanting to play Mahler, his beloved Mahler, who seemed to know all about hell, and now by some miracle, the same music spoke of heaven too. But instead he dressed and called Hugh for work.

'What has you in good humour at this hour?' Hugh asked him as he helped himself to tea.

'Sometimes, Hugh, it is good to be alive.'

'Begod, Karl, you're right there.'

They fell into their normal silence while walking to the site, but he noticed that Hugh walked with a pronounced swagger. He was growing old. There was nothing more sure.

That evening, Elizabeth and Hugh had eyes only for each other, so he let them be as he ate. How could he be so calm? There was an explanation, perhaps: the peace he had found on the bomb-site as he witnessed the flames by the Alster. Somehow, it had replaced his need for her. Without looking at either of them, he rinsed his plate and utensils and retired to his room. No, it did not replace his need for her, he thought, as he lay on his bed. It distanced his need. He imagined his journey towards peace as an ellipse: on one end, his quest, his search for his past and peace of mind; on the other, Elizabeth, the twin of his outer self. He knew he would travel between the two many times, and across the desolate regions in between, when he would have the comfort of neither.

*

Karl thought about the Pavilion all week, playing Mahler as soon as he retired to his room. The calm of the Fifth Symphony's Adagio seemed oddly appropriate. Elizabeth looked at him curiously but did not press him. On Saturday evening she knocked on his door, and when he called to her to come in, she opened the door but stood there, her eyes averted. After a while, she said quietly, 'Can you forgive me, Karl?'

He stretched out his hand and, hesitantly, she crossed to him and accepted it, still unable to look at him. The music stopped, the record continuing its momentum, and finally she met his eyes.

He asked her if she still had a little room for him and, as if in great relief, she affirmed she had. All was good, then. Hugh had gone drinking.

A proper man now.

She laughed at his little joke and took his hand.

'Thank you, Karl.' She took away her hand and cupped his face, smiling at him tenderly.

As she closed the door, he took a deep breath and closed his eyes. He put the record on again and settled for the night.

He woke to a rumpus downstairs. Elizabeth was screaming at Hugh and a neighbour was banging on the wall. Their first row, he thought. That was quick. The door slammed, and Hugh shouted from the street, and an argument started further up. Take care, Hugh, or you'll be arrested.

When he got up the next morning, Elizabeth was washing the hall floor.

'O God, I can't get rid of this stench,' she said.

'Here, let me help.'

'No, Karl,' she said without looking up. 'It's my mess.'

Their row amused him. He knew she had thrown him out, but he would be back in a few days, there was nothing surer. What amused him less was that she would welcome him with open arms.

He slept for a while, then read and drew and, deciding it was too fine an afternoon to stay indoors, he brought a chair out to the yard and read there. Then he got an urge to carve. When he went to retrieve them, he discovered that someone had tampered with his effigies. They were lying on the ground, obtruding from the jute. It must have been Hugh. Elizabeth would never pry. It disturbed him for a while, then he put it out of his mind and brought them into the yard.

He was in the yard, still carving, when she returned from Millie's. She was subdued. He put away his carving. Sam had gone on a drunken spree with his old friends.

'*Liebchen* . . .' He went to her and held her, and she clung to him.

'Why are men such babies?'

'That . . . I do not know the answer to.' He looked down at her and smiled, and she laughed softly.

'Karl . . . I need you just to be with me, for now. Is that all right?'

He nodded, still smiling.

They went to bed, but she did not respond to his caresses.

'*Liebling*, your mind is elsewhere.'

She smiled at that, and he had to smile too. She touched his face.

He closed his eyes, electrified by her touch, and nodded in acknowledgement. They fell asleep in each other's arms. It was evening when they woke, and he slipped out of bed, intending to make dinner. He was buttoning his shirt with a finger and thumb as he eased himself out and almost collided with Hugh as he came in the front door. They stood, looking at the other until Hugh, alarmed, put a forefinger to his lips. Karl nodded and followed him into the kitchen. This was the last thing he wanted to happen.

'She's asleep,' was all he could think of to say.

'Good,' Hugh said.

At least Hugh was making an effort to compose himself. This was ridiculous and could not go on. He sat at the table, his head in his hands. 'I'm sorry,' he said. Hugh did not reply. He was beating eggs. The silence was unbearable and, to fill it, Karl said more than he intended.

'I'm sorry. I'm truly sorry. I didn't mean to hurt you, Hugh.'

Still the beating of those damned eggs.

'I love Elizabeth. We've been lovers, of a kind, for a long time, but she loves you and I accept that. I've never had much, so I don't need much, I only need her love, even if it is divided. Can you understand that?'

Hugh looked past him, and he turned to see Elizabeth in her flannel dressing gown, a cigarette dangling from fingers by her side.

'What are you doing here?' she said flatly. 'I thought I threw you out.' She sucked on her cigarette. Hugh opened his mouth but he didn't speak, and continued to beat for a moment. Then he looked up.

'I'm sorry,' he said.

'Just look at the state of you.'

Elizabeth turned and disappeared, leaving Karl and Hugh alone. Hugh's fork made a lot of noise against the bowl. Karl could not move or speak. Then, at last, she returned, fully dressed, with her hair brushed.

'I'll make us a decent meal,' she said.

'I'll just wash then,' Hugh said, and yes, that was a good idea in the circumstances, and he went upstairs. She turned on the radio, and Karl listened intently, never taking his eyes off her. As she reached for the salt, he could see that she was crying.

They ate in silence.

'I will leave tomorrow,' Karl said, as she cleared away the dishes.

'You're not leaving, Karl,' Elizabeth said.

'Then I'll leave,' Hugh said.

'No one is leaving,' she said.

*

They went to work the next morning, subdued and polite. Hugh was pale, and Karl supposed that he himself was pale also. How ironic that all three had slept alone, united by the same, three-sided grief. There was nothing to do but work brutally hard, and be kind, solicitous, delicate, whenever they had to face the other.

A week later she returned from Millie's in high good humour.

'Guess what?' she said, holding both his hands and grinning broadly. It was the first time she had touched him since they had been together in bed.

'What?'

'Sam and Betty Hindley went to the pictures last night.'

'Is that significant?'

She laughed and swirled away from him.

A problem with her wayward brother seemed to have solved itself. It lifted his heart to see her like this – vital, young, happy. She burbled on about how wonderful it was, and humour flowed between them.

'Well! Dinner! What do you say?'

'I would say "dinner",' he smiled, happy that she was happy. She could be passionate about many things, but as for him, he could only be passionate through her. As soon as Hugh returned, however, they reverted to their neutral formality.

It took some weeks, of loneliness and wondering, but then the episode seemed to be forgotten, and they began to relax with each other. The fine weather helped, the familiarity of being together in the yard, even if they did not speak, creating a gradual ease. Karl's only irritation, which he hid, was Elizabeth's dance music, which Hugh had taken to playing on her gramophone. And then Elizabeth persuaded them both to accompany her – or bring her, as she preferred to put it – to Southend on fine weekends, and it was good to take the sea air together. In fact it was a happy time, and his long, lone swims out to sea allowed him to think about them. It was absurd to think he could give Elizabeth everything she deserved. Hugh could give her what he lacked, he could give her what Hugh lacked, and she would be happy. That was reasonable, was it not? He could not bear the thought of her unhappiness. She had saved him, after all. She had drawn him back from madness more than once. As long as he knew she was present in the world and thoughtful of him, he could bear anything. He owed her everything, and she was his only friend.

He turned back around the buoy towards land. Yes, it was a good solution, the only one.

As the weather grew hotter, Elizabeth changed her mind about Southend, and they went to Brighton instead, on day trips out of the claustrophobic city. No one could have guessed that they weren't just friends, or even brothers and sister, out for a day's fun. He was the quiet one, of course, but that was not strange.

One evening he was sitting in the yard, reading his paper, when Elizabeth put her arms around his neck from behind, and kissed the top of his head.

'How are you?' she asked.

'Good. And you?' She tugged at his hair.

'Hugh has asked me to the pictures. Do you mind?' Without turning, he took her hand in his.

'No. I do not mind.'

'Are you sure?' He turned and smiled.

'Yes. I am sure.'

She was relieved, and so was he. At last there was something to accept and live within, no matter how difficult it might prove to be. And she had asked him, had made him feel significant to her.

'It doesn't mean anything,' she whispered, smiling, and looking at him so softly. He nodded, and smiled too. She meant to console him and, although he didn't believe it, he felt that she believed it, and in this she consoled him after all. She ran her forefinger down his nose, and he felt a small wave of love rise and bathe him, and this would sustain him for some time.

But he was not given time. That very night she slept with Hugh.

When his music ended, he could not believe what he heard downstairs, and he tried to convince himself that it was imagination. Why had he supposed that if she wanted to do this, she would tell him? '*It doesn't mean anything.*' Her light dismissal of her outing with Hugh rang through his head. If only she had said, *Karl, I want to sleep with him tonight*, he could have prepared himself, accepted it. But not this. Not this. Not this because if she could not bring herself to tell him, he knew that she had chosen Hugh exclusively. Whether she herself knew or not was another matter. He knew. Stunned, he turned out the light and went to bed, staring into the darkness, trying not to think of them together, drenched in each other's sweat.

At first he bargained with himself that Elizabeth would be even-handed, or at least come to him too, occasionally, and that would have been enough. Despite his hurt, he wasn't jealous of Hugh. Why should he wish to have Elizabeth exclusively to himself? He had no proprietorial sense. Not any more. All he yearned for was the occasional comfort of intimacy with his friend.

They tried to hide it from him, as if he lived in a different house and could not hear the bedsprings and their muffled couplings. And he colluded with them, acting as if nothing had changed.

When he took long swims at Brighton, the salt water scouring his eyes and maybe his brain, he was sure they were holding hands, even openly kissing. It would be so easy now to fall into the release of madness. Or simply end things once and for all, now that his last defences were collapsing. How easy it would have been, and pleasant also, under that summer sky, to let his arms and legs spread out as they might, and sink to the bottom for ever.

He turned for the shore, not out of cowardice, but out of

conviction that it was not yet time. An eccentric force demanded that he endure, beyond a previous line of endurance.

*

When he wasn't carving or listening to music, he took down his astronomy book and drew a series of spirals.

It kept him sane.

He wondered if perhaps she was waiting for him to reach out to her, but he could find no impatience in her eyes, and yet, her familiarity continued to give him hope, only to have hope dashed that night, or the next, or all too soon.

Despite the fact that she had asked him not to, he had to leave, that much was obvious. He wondered what detained him, until one Sunday in Brighton, he remembered. He was waiting for her to tell him the truth. She had always been forthright and honourable, but now it was obvious she was afraid of the truth, afraid of hurting him, no doubt, and he felt belittled. He knew he was less than truthful himself, about so many things, but he could not bear to leave with her diminished in his esteem; could not bear that they were not true friends; could not bear that, besotted, she had forgotten everything she had been.

It was still warm in late September, and Elizabeth insisted that they make the last trip of the year to Brighton. There were scatterings of day-trippers, mostly young and skittish, but with a few older couples too, well wrapped up and huddled in their candy-striped deckchairs, so it was not as mad as he had thought. He had always gone for a swim, on their previous visits, leaving the lovers alone, but now the water was too cold, so he did what he presumed was expected and went for a walk by the tideline.

He should leave before winter set in, and accept that all that was left to him was reclamation, he knew not how, of his family. Yes, he thought, there were the displaced of the world, as he was, for whom all past attachments had to fall away before they could face what they had to do.

A girl's screech was carried to him on the wind, and he stopped and looked over his shoulder. She was grasping a colourful beach ball, and a youth had caught her by the waist. In the distance beyond them, Elizabeth and Hugh were kissing. He turned and continued his walk.

After supper that evening, he went to his room, leaving the lovers alone. His jaw felt numb, and the numbness was spreading. He put on Mahler's Fifth, the Adagio, and sat in at his table, going through his drawings of spirals. *Within.* A voice suggested that word, 'within'. It was repeated. He had heard this siren before, and was unafraid. He knew where he had to go, and welcomed the journey. Down, down through the spiral, down to within, where his task lay. The record spun on the turntable, the music ended. He stopped it, and set the needle again. Yes. It was over. He would tell Elizabeth tonight. Now. He could wait no longer, the time for it had passed. He saw it now. His family, Elizabeth's too, the terrible end of her mother and niece, somewhere within the spiral. The loss of her brothers. His brother. Sister. That's where they lay, beyond his reach. He had to find them all, reconcile what had been done to them. The record ended again, but this time he let it be.

Karl stood at the top of the stairs watching Hugh leave. He knew he would have to speak to Elizabeth quickly or all thought and speech would be impossible for he cared not to think how long. Already his muscles were so tight it was an effort to move.

And Hugh wanted to be, he thought, making his way down the stairs. To live in the moment.

If only he knew what that meant, with time frozen, without movement, and the meaninglessness of hope. If only he knew.

'Elizabeth . . .'

The utterance released him and as he opened the kitchen door he felt he could cope.

Elizabeth put her magazine to one side as he came in.

'Are you all right, Karl?'

'I'm leaving.'

She stared at him. He knew she was trying to keep calm, and that he should help her; but they were beyond all help.

'Hush, Karl,' she whispered. 'Sit down.'

He sat and pressed his hands on the table to steady himself. He could see she was desperate.

'All of it has to be put aside.'

'Karl,' she said, her voice breaking, 'what are you talking about? What has to be put aside? It's nonsense and you know it. Come here.'

She came to him, behind him, and put her arms around his neck. He leaned his head back into her breasts in relief.

'But for you I'd go mad.'

She stepped away but only to push her cheek into his hair.

'I don't deserve you, Elizabeth.'

'Don't talk nonsense. Come on.'

'No, Elizabeth. I must be alone. I must stay alone. I realize that now.'

'The things you men think of. Eh? You'd rather insult a woman than go against any daft idea that pops into your head.'

'It's not an idea,' he said, turning to look into her eyes.

'Come on . . .' she whispered, taking his hand.

Karl followed but all he could see was a wall of flame, shutting him out. She closed the door behind him and laid him back on her bed. His body was heavy and stiff. They had been through this before, but not quite like this. He looked down as she loosened his clothes, as if he and Elizabeth were parts of the same body, each operating on behalf of the other. She laid her body across his, kissing his head, his brow, his face, his lips. His heart swelled with pity. He knew about fear. He wandered around Elizabeth's, finding it all so familiar. Dear Elizabeth. He thought he spoke to her, but it seemed that he was too far a distance for her to hear. He tried again, this time louder. But she was deaf to him. He tried one last time before he left.

This time, *meine Liebchen*, this time let me go.

Six

HUGH

July–September 1950

'Hello, Hugh – have you sweeties?'

He almost jumped, then smiled at Deirdre who was standing pertly before him, unable to contain herself, then laughed in relief that he was free for the day, far away from lugging a dirty hod. Sarah was still limping along the path towards them. Brendan had told him once that she'd broken her hip when she was young.

'The cow jumped over the moon!' he yelled, standing up suddenly, and Deirdre, startled, retreated a step.

'Oh, you are a silly old man,' she reprimanded, though her attention never wavered, her eyes bent on the bulge in his jacket pocket which meant that surely, as always, he had something for her. Then with a grin he took out the sweets and she grabbed them, skipping down the path to her mother, shouting, 'Sarah, Sarah, look what Hugh brought me!'

Sarah, as always, took one herself, and ordered Deirdre to offer one to Hugh. But as Sarah knew well, he didn't eat sweets, and kept his ration for the child.

'Hello, Hugh,' she said gruffly, settling herself on the bench. 'I hope you've done a bit of reading for me this week. I get the feeling you've been slackening, you know.'

She was a doctor's secretary, but she had been a teacher once, and reminded him not so much physically as in her manner of the mistress in his two-teacher rural school. He had always been in trouble with the local garda sergeant for poor attendance. 'Young Kinsella' he called him.

He began to read for her as Deirdre played beside the lake, still sucking her precious sweet, but Hugh's mind wasn't on it.

'What's wrong with you, Hugh? There's no point in wasting precious time if you aren't going to concentrate.'

That was her all over, he thought miserably. Always moaning about time wasted. What was wrong with him? There was always a reason, and no reason.

He could see she was upset and that something more than his time-wasting bothered her. She had problems too, he could appreciate that, but he needed to justify himself.

'I left my father,' he said before he had really decided to tell her. She looked him up and down.

'So you've left Brendan. About time.'

'I thought he was going to kill me.' As soon as he said this it seemed ridiculous and that puzzled him a bit because he knew it was true.

'I see. So he attacked you.'

'Not really.'

'Oh, for God's sake, Hugh, do I have to drag everything out of you?'

He wasn't sure if he should tell her. She was, after all, a Protestant, and they didn't believe in such things as far as he knew. In fact, he couldn't think off-hand of anything they believed in. But she was a most persistent woman sometimes.

'Well?'

'I saw my mother and it frightened the shit out of him,' he said, head bowed. That was it. He had made an ass of himself.

'But your mother's dead, Hugh. Isn't she?'

He nodded. It was too much to have hoped she might understand. She was rooted tooth, nail and toes in this world and he three-quarters belonged to the other, or another, but all the same he told her what had happened, not knowing what to make of her silence.

'You need a mother that much . . .'

'I miss my mother.' He hated her compassion. 'There's a difference.'

97

'Yes. Indeed.' She sighed, fidgeting with her bag. 'You're not the only one in the world who's lonely, Hugh.'

'What do you mean?'

She turned from him to check on Deirdre, and watched her playing happily by herself. In a way Hugh was relieved she wasn't taking him seriously.

'She's seven today. Imagine.' She shook her head in puzzlement.

'You should have told me – I'd have got her a little present.'

'She'll be very happy with the sweets. You shouldn't give her so much, Hugh. Her father, who's never seen her, sent her five pounds, as he's always done.'

'That's a lot of money for a birthday.'

She laughed, but kept fidgeting.

'Have you been on your own for seven years, Sarah?'

'Seven years and seven months. Where are you staying?' she asked all of a sudden.

'Off Holloway Road. I met a woman with a room to spare. Just by accident.'

'There are no accidents, Hugh,' she said, watching Deirdre again.

'Eh? Honestly, Sarah. I just met her in a caff, by accident.'

'You mention her as if you're undecided whether you're in love with her or not. Or maybe *lust* would be a better word,' she said, with relish.

Jesus. How could she know that? And suddenly, there it was, out in the open, as if a space had opened out in his mind and it was there in the middle of it, naked and without an excuse.

'So I'm right. What age is she?'

'I don't know. A lot older than me. I thought at first she wanted me and then all of a sudden she seemed to go cold,' he mumbled. 'So I don't know where I stand.'

He was taken aback again, this time at what he had said, letting the cat out of the bag. It yanked him from where he had a certain control to where a cat like that could do a lot of damage. It was the second time in minutes he had left himself open like that, he who was normally so careful. It made him nervous.

'Ah. You want it handed to you on a plate. You don't want to struggle for it, risk rejection. No responsibility.'

'What's so funny? Did you struggle for it?' he hit back. 'I never see you with a boyfriend. Unless you could count my father.'

'There's no call for that, Hugh!'

'No, it's all right when you're preaching to me. It's different, though, when the boot is on the other foot, isn't it?'

'That's the love I struggled for,' she said, waving at her daughter and smiling in spite of everything.

'I'm sorry.' He was embarrassed and wanted to be anywhere but where he was. 'She was worth it.' He closed his book and rose. 'Can you be here next Sunday if it's fine?'

'Yes. You're right. Neither of us is in the mood today. Come to my place if it's wet.' Then she caught his arm. 'No, wait. We'll be away in France.'

'Oh, right.'

'And ... Listen, Hugh, you're quite the scholar now, you don't need lessons, really. All you need to do is to keep reading. And sure you can do that yourself ...'

He was relieved, secretly delighted even, and turned without a word and walked over to Deirdre. Sarah called after him anxiously, and he looked over his shoulder.

'Hugh – you don't mind, do you?'

He smiled quickly, then hunkered down beside Deirdre, who was playing on the grass with imaginary creatures. You could hear the traffic on this side, without the buffer of the bushes and trees.

'I hear it's your birthday today, Deirdre,' he said tenderly. 'What age are you?'

'Seven,' she said without looking up. 'My daddy sent me five pounds. He sends me five pounds every year.'

'Really?' he gasped. 'That's an awful lot.'

'Yes. My daddy said I should get a coat and shoes for the winter, and we got them yesterday and I wrote to him last night, and Mammy is putting the rest in the Post Office for me for when I'm big.'

'Oh, she's a wise mammy.' He pulled out his wallet and opened it slowly and Deirdre forgot about her elves. Suddenly, he held a crisp ten shilling note and pressed it into her palm. 'Happy birthday, Deirdre. Ask Sarah to buy something nice for you.'

Her mouth fell open, but clutching the note she jumped up and clung to his neck in a childish hug. Then she stood back, radiant, to look at him.

She ran to her mother who was still watching from her seat.

'Sarah, Sarah, look what Hugh gave me!'

Hugh rose and without looking back, left the park.

*

Elizabeth was up when he got back, but still in her dressing gown. She was pale and had dark circles under her eyes. She went upstairs without a word, disappeared into the bathroom, and ran a bath. Karl was playing some music in his room, very sad music, something like Hugh had heard once or twice in the cinema. He went to his room and lay on the bed, staring at the ceiling.

'You're a lodger,' he whispered. 'You're a lodger, and don't forget that fact.'

He listened for what he might hear, and thought he heard the faint ripple of water. She's naked, he thought, and immediately he was hard. He shook his head in frustration and went to the window.

How could Karl listen to that stuff? You'd need the pictures to distract you from it.

Two wooden rods jutting out of the window and joined by four cords served as a washing line. He opened the window and leaned out. Something similar stuck out from the bathroom window, which was open, he knew, because he could clearly hear the splashes. He stared at the church spire. It occurred to him that she could see the same spire from the bathroom. Just then he heard her get out of the bath, and wondered if she was casually looking out now, while she dried herself. God! No matter which way he turned, he found her looking at him every time. He had got himself out of one trap, only to walk into another. He stayed at the window, and his thoughts drifted. He wondered what his father was doing. Snoring, most likely. Poor Brendan, he was all alone in the world now, no friends, no family except a few cousins back in Wexford, and he would never go back there, that was for sure, for all his saving, to that mountain. Hugh would never set foot on it again, either, of that he was certain, but it floated through his imagination. On a fine day like this, it would be blue from a distance. There'd be the smell of gorse around the house. He could see the butterflies, and maybe the odd ladybird, and the dog dreaming. He could see the Irish Sea in the distance, and the mountainside breaking up in the haze.

The bathwater drained, and he was at once alert. The bathroom door opened and closed, and he went to his door and pressed his ear against it, but could hear no more. He stayed like that, a voice in his head shouting that this was madness, but he couldn't help himself. How long he was like that he didn't know, but eventually he heard movement, and then she called to Karl that she was going.

Karl answered.

Where was she going? He went back to the bed, his head in his hands. He couldn't bear not knowing everything about her, where she was going, who she was going to see. He vowed that he would know every detail soon, and to hell with Karl.

'O God, I'm tired,' he whispered, and he lay back on the bed and slept.

He woke to a knock on the door. Half asleep, he opened it and his heart jumped. At moments like this when she took him unawares, she took away his soul.

'Dinner, sleepy-head,' she grinned.

'Oh, right . . .'

Karl was already eating, and Hugh fought to waken properly and show some interest in the food she put in front of him. He must have slept for hours. Karl finished.

'I'll call you at six a.m.,' he said to Hugh before leaving.

'Great. Great . . .'

He knew that she was watching him, and finally he looked at her. She seemed amused.

'Karl takes pride in his work, Hugh, and even if he's a foreigner, he's a valued man. So he'll have no problem getting you a start.'

'Right.'

'Do you have anything else to say for yourself, besides *grate* and *right*?'

'Not much,' he said, and continued eating. Now that he was awake, he was enjoying the grub, and he kept his eyes on the plate. In her presence, she seemed much further away than when he saw her in his mind's eye, and it was a comfort that this made him feel stronger. Karl was playing his music again.

'Is he always playing that stuff?'

'Not always. A few times a week.'

'What is it, anyway?'

'I don't know. Well, he told me several times, but I forget. It's German, I think.'

'Oh. Right.'

He finished his meal and brought his plate and cutlery to the sink.

'What are you doing?'

'Washing-up after me.'

'Not in my kitchen.'

He left them in the sink and scratched the back of his neck.

'You wash your clothes – and hang them out *your* window – but I look after things here.'

'Right.'

'Oh, go on with you!'

He fled to the awful sound of her laughter.

When Karl knocked on the door at six the next morning, Hugh was dreaming of the mountain, Croghan, which had turned to gold, but he was up immediately. The fear of not doing what was expected of him concentrated his attention, and he went down to the kitchen where Karl had set the table for three and was making sandwiches.

'Is she up?'

'No, she goes out later. Help yourself. I'm making sandwiches for us all.'

Hugh shook himself, trying to waken properly, and poured himself strong tea. Karl had already had breakfast. The tea did its work, and he had bread and marmalade.

'What time do we leave?'

'Six forty-five.'

Hugh looked at the clock above the mantel, and saw that already he had little time, so he hurried upstairs for his bag.

Karl was waiting for him at the door. From the top of the stairs he saw Elizabeth come out of her bedroom in her dressing gown, laden with sleep, her hair in a mess. She touched Karl on the arm without a word, and drifted into the kitchen. Hugh stalled as this was going on, struck by jealousy again, but he acted as if he had seen nothing and they walked up Citizen Road to the sound of birds on a fine summer morning. Instead of turning left for Holloway, they turned right along Hornsey Road. It was near enough, so they could walk.

After some time Hugh could see the destruction which provided them with a livelihood. They arrived at the site, and soon the foreman, a heavy man with a large belly, arrived. Karl asked Hugh to wait while he talked to him.

Karl gestured to him to follow, and disappeared behind a wall.

He noticed a wild flower, covered in dew, and plucked it. It had no scent, but it reminded him of Croghan, which in turn brought back his dream, and he put it in his pocket for luck. Karl was waiting for him beside a cement mixer and a stack of bricks and, handing him a hod, he took a bucket of fresh cement he had already mixed himself by hand, and climbed the scaffolding in silence.

His ankle niggled for a few days, but he used the bandage to support and protect it, and after a week, Hugh felt good. They did smaller jobs than he was used to, replacing rows of houses flattened by the Blitz, or finishing the jobs of bigger contractors, and now that he had proved he was a good worker, there seemed to be a different atmosphere in the house. He had been accepted, which made him feel easier in himself.

During the week he stayed in at night laboriously practising his reading which became easier as time went by. Having put his preoccupation with Elizabeth to the back of his mind there was still no woman in his life. He didn't know how to go about it, apart from drinking himself into a stupor before going to the Pride of Erin dance hall on Tottenham Court Road on Saturday night. Then, towards eleven o'clock as the dance drew to a close, the only option was to join in the rush for a partner, something he couldn't bring himself to do. Once or twice in the dance he'd picked a girl who hardly glanced at him as he dragged her round the floor, their image multiplying in the mirrors arranged along the walls and he was completely taken by this, staring at them over the girl's shoulder. Then, as the call came for the last dance, he saw Kathleen Pilkinton.

O Jesus, he thought.

He had several drinks on him, but he tried to avoid her. Unfortunately, she had seen him too, and now she looked at him with what he knew was much the same feeling as he had for her, and she stood up, accepting the inevitable. He took her onto the floor, and they waltzed awkwardly until the dance ended. They stood looking at each other, neither knowing what to say.

'Well?' she said finally.

'Well what?'

'Are you going to leave me home, or what?'

She was waiting for his answer in growing panic in case he refused. Her friends were already emerging from the cloakroom, joining partners at the door and still Hugh hadn't answered.

'Begod I will,' he said then, to her relief.

She had a sup taken too and once she had retrieved her coat and bag and they were on their way, she talked at speed, not waiting for him to answer her questions, some of which she answered herself. It suited him, but to gain some respite from the torrent of words, he discreetly shared his naggin of whiskey with her on the way to her digs. When they arrived at her door, she signalled him to be quiet and peered through the letter flap.

'What are you looking through there for?' he whispered.

'To see if there's a light on in the back kitchen,' she said. 'But it's all right. The landlady's in bed. Come on.'

He couldn't believe it, but allowed himself to be led inside by the hand. She put her finger to her lips as she closed the door, then jabbed it at a door in the hall. The landlady's bedroom. They made it upstairs to her room, despite the creaking stairs, and she made tea on a small stove. After the first cup, they ran out of things to say and, somehow ended up on her bed.

'Oh no,' she gasped, 'oh no.'

And then she greedily pressed her mouth to his. But the alcohol was catching up with her, and while he was fumbling with her clothes her eyes rolled and she groaned, less from passion than stupor. Hugh was too drunk and nervous to do anything anyway and eventually they both fell asleep.

They woke facing each other and smelling of cigarette smoke and stale alcohol. Her dress was around her waist, and he could see the flesh above her stockings for a second before she pushed the dress back down to her knees.

'Have you a hangover?' she asked weakly.

'I'm grand,' he lied. She sat up and smoothed out her rumpled clothes.

'It's a penance, I suppose,' she said.

After this, he went into a nervous gloom again. When the mood hadn't passed after a few days, Karl began to show concern. During a break, he spoke to him as he poured the smoky tea from a billycan into Hugh's outstretched mug.

'What's wrong with you these days, Hugh? Have you bad news in your family?'

'No, it's nothing.' Hugh gulped down his tea.

'You can't fool me, Hugh. I'm your friend.'

Hugh looked doubtfully into the big, sincere face. Just what did that mean and did it matter a damn?

'It's the mountain. The mountain's at me again.'

'The mountain?' Karl looked at him sideways, and Hugh looked away, his doubts about friendship confirmed.

But Karl repented and asked him about the mountain.

Hugh shrugged. It was a mountain like any other, not particularly high, and from it you could see the Irish Sea. He wondered what could be different about this mountain that would make it real for Karl.

'It's called Croghan. There used to be gold there. So they say.' He chomped on his sandwich.

'Ah. Gold. For a while I was apprenticed to a jeweller in Berlin. You can work gold as fine as a cobweb, did you know that? Yet it takes more than a thousand degrees to melt it. Hmm. But I can't stand the sight of gold any more. I prefer building.' He looked over his shoulder at the site. 'Brick over brick.'

'Sometimes I feel I'm helping to build a mountain,' Hugh said. 'That somehow or other it's flowing out from inside me into the bricks. Like the Egyptians.'

'Like the Egyptians?' Karl chuckled to himself, and poked at the embers. 'So this is your golden mountain. And you want to build it.'

'No. I want to be it.'

'To be it. How can you be it?'

'I don't know. By thinking about it, maybe. Maybe ...' He could feel himself blush. 'Maybe it's like when you need a person so much, you want to become her.'

Yet it was true. It was inside him, sometimes no more than a crystal, and spoke through him and in spite of him. This flashed through his mind before he had time to grasp it.

'We must speak about this again,' Karl said, throwing the dregs of his tea into the fire as the whistle blew.

'There isn't anything else to say.'

'Not now, perhaps. But I have a feeling there will be.'

Maybe he was his friend after all, Hugh thought as he loaded his hod. It was some man who'd listen to stuff like that, and not run a mile. But the queerest thing of all wasn't that he had that sort of thing in his head, but that he could tell someone and not hate himself for being stupid. Yes, maybe he was his friend after all.

On the way home, Karl kept his own counsel and, some way along the road, he excused himself, and took another road.

Hugh's insecurity came flooding back, and he wondered if he had said something to insult him. He stood where Karl had left him, baffled, but then curiosity got the better of him. Maybe he was going to meet a woman. He knew it was wrong to follow him, but he couldn't help it. Some of the houses along the road had been bombed, and he saw that he wouldn't be short of work for a long time. He came to a crossroads and, as he looked left, he saw Karl leave the road and climb into a bomb-site. He was nervous now, in case Karl would find him out. Behind the bombed house were acres of devastation and Karl walked into the middle of them. Forgetting himself, he followed him, using standing walls for cover. The weeds were thickly spread, hiding loose bricks and rubble, and it was difficult to walk quickly, but then Karl lay down. Hugh climbed to the top of a mound to see him better. He seemed to be asleep. Then he spread out his arms, and his body shook as if he had been hit. His head rolled, and his body shook again, rising a little off the ground. Hugh watched in fascination, until he realized that he was an intruder. Maybe he was praying, and Hugh had a great respect for the privacy of prayer, no matter what the religion.

*

Hugh became what he thought of as happy. He adopted the custom of taking a chair into the yard after work if the evening was fine, lazily enjoying the warm evenings, and usually Karl and Elizabeth would join him. Beneath his contentment was a suppressed longing for Elizabeth, but it seemed remote, betrayed only by his too sudden laughter at her dry wit, his too eager and nervous responses. Almost without realizing it, he loved the composure of her bare arms and calves, how still they looked, with a sensuous weight he had never before noticed in anyone. He admired her and didn't want to think of her in a sexual way, not in her presence at least. That would degrade her.

She was reading one of those entertainment magazines, with some film star out of Hollywood on the cover. She loved all that stuff. Karl was reading his papers. He read two every evening and Hugh was in awe of such intelligence. He never produced his books, fearing they would laugh at him and during the long evenings it was only in the half hour or so before he slept that he looked at them at all. But he consoled himself that it had become easier since he came to Citizen Road. The security he felt in a decent home, with decent food despite the rations, had seemed to open out his mind, giving it an agility which surprised him and made him happy. He was still reading *The Bridge of San Luis Rey*, and although he had difficulty with the foreign names and some words like 'precipitate', as Sarah had warned him, he loved it. Despite their bad humour before she went to France, he knew her effort and his had been rewarded, and this was enough to make a man feel good about himself.

The yard was silent apart from a few late birds until a goods train passed. You could tell it was a goods train by the way it rumbled on forever.

'Hugh, would you like to come with me to the market tomorrow?'

'That'd be great.' He nodded and she smiled.

Elizabeth went indoors, leaving her magazine, and he took it up, nervous at first, but thrilled he could read it because in some way it brought him into her mind. He read a short paragraph a few times until he could read it quickly, which was a habit he had picked up; then went on to another, caring little what the words meant, until he had finished the magazine. Jesus, he'd done it ... He looked through it again, realizing he didn't remember a word he'd read, but once he saw the story he remembered. What did they say in the comics? Well, blow me down! He'd read the damn thing from cover to cover.

He glanced at Karl, convinced he had his beady eye on him, but Karl still had his nose in his papers.

So this was the sort of thing Elizabeth liked. He felt he knew her better now, and that made him feel good, but he was only starting.

Karl put his papers on Elizabeth's chair and, taking a wooden stake from the shed, began to carve it slowly with his penknife.

'She works, does she?'

'Somewhere in the East End.'

'Oh. Right.'

Hugh went to the bathroom, pausing on the stairs. He opened the bathroom door. Elizabeth was naked, a fine steam rising from her body, with one foot on a chair as she dried between her toes, her hair wet and stringy. She looked up, her breasts hanging each side of her knee.

'Hello, Hugh,' she said, not a bother on her, and smiled. He backed out, closing the door carefully and without a word. He went to his room and stared out the window.

'Hello, Hugh,' he whispered, beside himself.

In the morning she acted as if nothing had happened, but Hugh couldn't bring himself to look at her at the breakfast table.

When she called him to go to the market, he had convinced himself that his pretended weariness was real. Karl was playing his awful, morbid music. As she checked herself in the hall mirror before they left, he was sure he saw Elizabeth grinning away to herself.

They walked quickly to the underground, and Elizabeth talked about the necessity of getting to the market early for the bargains and, with this in mind, the silence between them seemed natural, even essential. She bought tickets for both of them, and he felt like a small boy on an outing with his mother.

A young tramp was lying asleep on one of the benches, reminding him of himself only a short time before, and a young couple loitered mid-platform as they waited for the train. Although she spoke normally, her voice seemed to echo all over the station.

'Did you like my body last night?'

She almost laughed at his surprise, but then she was serious. She was taking him seriously.

'You're beautiful,' he said.

The train arrived, and they turned towards it in mutual relief, but in the train, Hugh, without looking at her, took her hand and crushed it in his. When he looked up she was smiling at him, in a way, he thought, that suggested an agreement had been sealed. He wasn't sure what this was meant to lead to, but he took courage from it. He leaned over to kiss her and felt the shock of a woman's tongue in his mouth for the first time.

The train stopped and the doors opened so they sat up and looked straight ahead. When no one got into their carriage she laughed and relaxed towards him again, their faces touching lightly. He drew back to look at her and she laughed and stretched herself like a contented cat. Then it was their stop, and they hurried up the steps into the sunlight.

In the market they held hands. Hugh was shy about it at first, but no one took any notice. It was one of the things he liked about London, he decided, although the indifference had borne in on him before. Elizabeth took her hand away to rummage amongst some old, broken jewellery.

He would escape his past, from his childhood, his mother, his father. Already, he missed her hand. Would her body be the same? He still wasn't sure if he could expect to see her like that again. It all seemed too easy, had happened too fast, with no effort on his part except to lean across a train seat to kiss her, and even this had been on impulse.

They came to a fruit stall, with pineapples and grapes hanging from hooks, and apples, oranges, pears and rhubarb stacked on the trays.

'Will we have a pound of Cox's Orange apples or a pound of Navel oranges?' She nudged Hugh, her lips revealing her upper gums in a grin, her accent exaggerated in the teeming market. The fruit seller had a right chortle for himself, pushing his glasses back up his nose.

'Ah sure we might as well have both,' Hugh decided with a grin. If you can't beat them, then join them, as his father used to say, and he produced a handful of change.

He noticed his Irish accent was more pronounced in a place like this.

'The man of the house has *spoken*,' the fruit seller said rapidly, pushing his glasses up again and plucking the fruit from the tray and weighing it up as if the bargain depended on his speed.

'That's my boy,' Elizabeth whispered into his ear, and Hugh

felt good as he handed over the money. Something to be proud of, eh? But he let Elizabeth buy the vegetables alone. They browsed among the clothes, second-hand and gaudily cheap and new, not conscious of each other, taken up in the business of uncovering a find.

He sifted through the junk piled up on several stalls, most of it, he knew, coming from bomb-sites. He had seen many such pathetic odds and pieces in the rubble clearances, mostly damaged, belonging to people like himself, now more than likely dead.

In the shade of a tarpaulin, an amputee was playing the smooth and bending tones of the saw. Not far from him, a man was blowing bubbles to advertise his wares.

The air had gradually thickened all morning and the sun disappeared. A sticky sweat broke out on Hugh's body. He stood by as Elizabeth hesitated over a drawing of a child. Then she turned to him.

'I'm starved – come on.'

They went to a café which opened onto the street beside the underground. He didn't like being exposed like that, not when he was eating. But like so much else that had happened to him in her company in such a short time, he was quickly accustomed to it, and when the hot mushy peas, sausages and chips were placed in front of him, he discovered that he was hungry too. He thought of Karl making sandwiches for the three of them.

'I . . . I hope you don't mind me asking, but would I be right in saying you go out to work as well as being a landlady?'

Just then it began to rain and the small café became crowded, a fog rising from damp clothes.

'A landlady?' Amused, she took a mouthful of chips. 'Yes, I suppose I am. And yes . . . I work in a factory down the East End.'

'A factory?'

'But never mind that. I've minded my business till now,' she said as she chewed, 'but now I think maybe I've a right to ask?' She swallowed and grinned. Her accent had reverted to what it normally was. 'About your family, I mean – you don't have a girl, do you?'

He looked at a chip on his fork, and shook his head lightly.

'Well, are your parents alive, how many brothers and sisters – that sort of thing.'

'My mother's dead.'

'Oh. I'm sorry.'

'I fell out with my father just before I met you in the caff. It was brewing for years. I've no brothers or sisters. What about you?' he asked quickly to shift attention from himself.

'So you're alone . . . Me? My father died before the war. My mother had dodgy lungs too, but Jerry put her out of her misery with a flying bomb. Two of my brothers went down in the Atlantic. Merchant Navy. Bloody fools were on the same ship.'

'Janey. That's tough. And you don't hate Germans?'

She shrugged.

'We did some nasty things to them too. Karl's a German. Anyway, it was a war. We lived in a basement, see. When we were kids, I mean. In a slum I suppose you might call it, although we didn't think of it like that. A hotbed for consumption, though. You name it. Poor Mum tried hard. When she wasn't cooking for seven mouths, she was cleaning. She was scared of bugs – and crumbs and things, she said, attracted bugs. And rats. She was really scared of rats – so was I, mind you.'

'Rats?' It was hard to think of Elizabeth knowing anything about rats.

'They didn't seem to be scared at all. Sometimes you'd come across one sitting on the kitchen floor, its front paws in the air, staring at you with its little devil eyes.'

'I suppose that must have given you nightmares . . .'

'I never remember dreaming of them, but I remember lying awake at night, terrified in case one of the blighters might crawl over my face when I was asleep. We moved to a two up two down before the war, but that basement hardly saw daylight, never mind sunlight.'

His mother had died of pneumonia, or so Brendan had told him. He could see that she was being so open that she'd be free to ask him questions, questions to which he probably had no answers.

'Hugh, you've gone all pale. You all right?'

'My mother. My father said it was . . . Eh, I'll be back in a minute.' More likely it was galloping consumption.

'Oh. Don't be long,' she called after him.

The alley he escaped to smelled of rubbish. A few dustbins, their lids just hanging on, were knocked over. A cat looked up in surprise and scarpered as he aimed his boot at it. He turned into an alley which crossed with several others. Two young boys pretended they were hardened smokers. He came into the open beside a children's park. There was a slide, a monkey-puzzle, a see-saw, a merry-go-round, a sandpit, but there were no children there. He had never had such a thing to play in as a child and he sneaked in, dragging his feet through the sand.

Why had he run off like that? She'd think he was an awful fool, and worse, he was lost. He hurried back through the alleys, but they all looked the same. The boys were gone and there seemed to be cats and dustbins and that same smell in every alley. He kept running, and then, without warning, he came out into the market. He paused, sweating and out of breath, to get his bearings. The market was much larger than he had thought, but finally he made his way back to the café. She was gone, of course. Why would she wait? Some old codger laughed at him and he looked down to check if there was sand on his shoes. She had gone home, obviously, and he made his way to the underground. It was difficult to hurry through the crowd, but from a distance he thought he spotted her head disappear into the entrance, but by the time he got to the platform she was on the train. He waved and shouted her name but he hardly knew what he was saying. Then he saw her, her hands pressed against the window, smiling happily as the train moved out.

A factory. She worked in a factory. How did she manage to work all day, and then get groceries and cook for them and look after the house? He thought of her hand again, and yes, now that he thought of it, it was a worker's hand. He imagined her sitting in front of a sewing machine, or maybe she worked in that rope factory he had heard of.

He took the next tube, which was crowded. He bowed his head, so that no one would notice his lips shape the name Elizabeth. And the image of her, pressed against the window of the train, that haunted him. He could hardly credit it now, but he had been angry with her, and angry with himself because he could think of no reason why he should be angry with her. He was afraid, he could see that now. He was afraid of her, of her body, of the happiness she could give him, he was afraid of everything and he hated everything and just wanted to be alone and miserable. What was wrong with him?

*

He had nowhere to go except back home but every step he took along Citizen Road made him dread seeing her more. He eased himself in as quietly as he could. Karl and Elizabeth were talking quietly in the kitchen, so he slipped upstairs, tense in case a creak in the stairs would betray him.

His book, that's what he'd do, he'd read his book. He gave it a go, but it was useless, he had worked himself into a terrible state, taking deep breaths to calm himself. There was nothing for it but to get out of the house, to anywhere at all. If he bumped into her he could say he was going for a walk. That was all right, wasn't it? Yes of course it was all right, but he made sure not to make a sound as he slipped out again. He was clear of the street when it occurred to him that he hadn't heard their voices on the way out. Maybe they had heard him after all, and were listening for every sound. Lord Jesus, that was embarrassing.

He wandered around the streets, hands in his pockets, and gradually he calmed, taking in the small happenings of a Sunday afternoon. What intrigued him was what was happening behind the respectable walls of the terraced houses. They weren't much different to Citizen Road in a way, and look what was happening there in number forty-two, for Christ's sake. If there was one young fella in any one of them houses as nervous as he was right now, for roughly the same reason, then maybe it was bearable. Maybe it was just something you had to go through.

After a few hours of this he was tired and hungry and had no alternative but to go back.

Elizabeth greeted him with a smile over her shoulder. She was nervous too, standing at the stove. A blind man could see that. Karl lowered his paper and grunted his usual hello. Hugh sat into the table, playing with his fingers. He was near to panic because he could think of nothing to say.

She gave them their dinner and he gratefully attacked the steak and kidney pie.

'Were you at Mass then, Hugh?' Elizabeth asked, her back still turned to him.

'No. No, I'm giving it up. They go on too much about hell.'

'I see.'

She sat in with them, and ate slowly. He caught a glimpse of her as he dislodged some meat from his teeth with his fingernail. He looked quickly from her to Karl. There was something afoot, even a gom like him could see that. It was best to keep the head down and keep eating.

Karl finished, made himself a cup of tea, and went to his room.

She left her plate in the sink and went into the yard, pottering around for a minute. He hardly dared look as the top of her head appeared and disappeared at the window. Then she went over to the yard wall, and he could just see her as she lay back against the shed, stretching her face to catch the last of the sun. There had been little enough of it that day. He leaned back a little to see her better, forgetting his fear that she might see him spying on her like this. All of a sudden she came back in and his heart pounded as he failed to make the decision to bolt upstairs. As she cleared the table she brushed his hand, startling him, and at the sink, she turned her head and smiled. When she smiled like that, over her shoulder, it always stunned him. He managed to smile back.

'Well, I better go upstairs.'

'Will I see you after your little rest?'

She raised her eyebrows as she was saying that. O Lord Jesus.

'All right.'

'All right? Oi, you Irish is romantic, there's no doubt about it.'

He couldn't wait to get away to his bedroom to think this out. She had looked at him in that way, and he was sure, or nearly sure, he would see her naked again. He lay on his bed as he thought how he could almost feel her body oozing from her eyes when she looked at him like that. Then he realized that without having been aware of it, he was the hardest he could recall.

When he went downstairs, it was plain that if Elizabeth was in the house, then she was in her bedroom. Shaking, he raised his knuckles to knock, but just as he was about to strike, he drew back. He left the house and walked quickly along Citizen Road. He was running again. What the fuck was he running from? Would he end up running like this for the rest of his life?

Why am I doing this? he thought desperately. Calm yourself, Hugh. Calm yourself. He was scared . . . he was scared because . . . he was terrified because there was one Elizabeth he knew every day, and another in his head. Yes, that was it. Great. He was getting somewhere. He needed to think of the woman he knew every day.

He remembered taking her hand. Yes. It was an ordinary woman's hand, comfortable in his. Flesh and blood. He remembered her in the bathroom. Yes, yes that was what he wanted, what he could approach, and he stopped dead just as he was about to cross Holloway Road to the underground, and turned back, much calmer, pleased with himself.

It was a pleasant walk back, and he took his time, because he knew there was all the time he might choose to take. The notion of some kind of priestess was still there, shadowy, but it was the physical woman that held his mind.

He knocked quietly, but firmly. She called him in, by name. 'Begod,' he whispered, 'I have her.'

But when he opened the door, his confidence disappeared. Elizabeth was in bed, leaning on her elbow in a white cotton nightdress and reading a love story. Odd bits of her clothes were scattered about the room, but that very ordinariness made her more remote than the priestess. He felt heavy.

'Where have you been? I thought you'd run off on me.'

'Sorry . . . I didn't realize you'd be in bed,' he said lamely.

'Oh come on, silly,' she said, pulling over the bedclothes.

'You shouldn't leave a woman waiting, you know. Come on. Get those clothes off and get in.'

He was shaking.

'Do you want me to look away while you undress?'

He nodded, and she turned away, and he steadied his shaking hands enough to undress, letting his clothes fall to the floor. He got in beside her, not daring to touch her.

'Is this your first time in bed with a woman?' she asked, turning to him.

'Yes.' He was making a difference between being on the bed and in the bed.

He lay beside her, rigid, and she turned to put an arm around him, pulling him against her.

'Don't worry,' she whispered. 'It happens to everyone sometime or another. Don't worry – you don't have to do anything. It's nice to have you here beside me. Why don't we just talk? Why don't you just tell me about growing up on that mountain in Ireland. It sounds wonderful.'

'The mountain?'

'Yes. Karl told me about it. Where you grew up. I want to hear everything about it.'

'Everything.'

'Yes. Everything.'

'There's nothing to tell, Elizabeth. It's all dead.'

He burrowed his head between her breasts and held her close. In her warmth, his dreams about her came back to him and joined, like two rivers meeting, his hands remembering as they explored the fabulous mystery of her body. Her sighs surprised him at first, and he wondered how he could give her such pleasure. Then he became lost in them and, with her guidance, he slid into her.

As he lay awake that night, Elizabeth's arms uncomfortably around him, he couldn't shake off his resentment. The more he tried the more remote the reality of her became, and he began to feel afraid as he realized how little he knew her.

Then she moaned in her sleep and began to untangle herself from him, until she turned, her rear pushing into his belly, and her leisurely wind spread out from under the clothes. He turned his face away in disgust, offended that a woman should do this.

Ah, have sense, Hugh, he thought then. Have some bloody sense. Aren't we the same class of a creature when it comes down to it? Aye. Aye, that's about the height of it.

*

Remembering that Karl called him for work, Hugh slipped out of bed and returned to his own room. He slept for a few hours before Karl knocked and was immediately awake and refreshed.

'What has you in good humour at this hour?' said Hugh as he poured the thick tea.

'Sometimes, Hugh, it is good to be alive.'

He was right there.

He didn't know what he could tell him, if he would resent his success with Elizabeth. And he didn't want to lose a friend. They fell into their normal morning silence while walking to the site.

With his next pay packet, Hugh went directly to a crowded, smoky bar in Camden Town. Elizabeth was pleased to see him go out and enjoy himself, to see a bit of life. He had been unsure about leaving her on her own, of a Saturday night, but she had encouraged him and he admired her for that.

He fell in with two Dublin men, hospital porters, and bought them drink all evening to celebrate his secret and, in turn, they regaled him with stories. Each time they tried to buy a drink he insisted on buying the round, and the stories seemed to get better, more hilarious. Beneath the laughter, Elizabeth had not left Hugh's thoughts all evening. He had fought the urge to mention her name, until even she seemed distant.

All was well until they were out of the pub and Hugh's head started to spin and he collapsed on the pavement. He felt himself being hauled to his feet and instinctively answering a muffled question. Everything spun. Everything spun as he found himself outside his door, it spun but was focusing a little. He was getting a grip on things, and found his keys. His wallet was gone. Gone. Ah well. Easy come, easy go. He swayed, then threw up on the pavement. It seemed like a long time before he got the key into the lock. Then as he entered Elizabeth's bedroom he got sick again, turning too late so that only part of the vomit landed in the hall. Once it was done, it was done, it didn't matter any more so he ignored it. He struggled out of his clothes and crawled onto the bed to paw her. She woke suddenly, confused, trying to push away his hands.

'Hugh, stop . . .'

Something in her voice got through to him, and made him stop, but he was still sure of his welcome and he stood back on the floor and waited while she got herself ready. She turned on the light, blinking, and she looked like a right hag, he thought.

'You dirty pig,' she screamed.

Hugh thought she was going to become hysterical, and thought it wise to put on his trousers again. He felt defenceless without his trousers.

'That's right,' she shouted, 'you've got the idea. Get out of my bedroom and out of my house!'

He was in a morally feeble position, and couldn't think of any argument against it. Maybe it was reasonable and in his best interests to leave the house until she cooled down. She stopped him at the bedroom door, her hand out.

'Where's the two weeks' rent you owe me? Come on, Hugh – four pounds five shillings – now.'

'It was stolen . . . My money was stolen.'

Elizabeth threw back her head and laughed like a jackass and, for the first time, he was ashamed. There was a pounding on the wall and a dull voice demanded some quiet. Without warning her expression changed and she pushed him towards the front door.

'You drank it, didn't you. I was fooled by someone like you before and I'm not going to be fooled again.'

She opened the door and gave him one final push onto the street.

'My jacket . . .' he said lamely.

'Your jacket. Right!'

She slammed the door. He still had his shirt in his hand when the door opened and his jacket landed at his feet. He put it on, burning with humiliation and self-hatred.

'You're nothing but a whore,' he shouted. 'You've no feel-ings. You're not Christian at all.'

Old Rosenberg a few doors away pulled up the window.

'If you don't shut up, I get the police after you!'

'Ah shut up, Judas,' Hugh shouted back, and Rosenberg slammed down the window.

It was cold, there was a fog and London seemed deserted. He heard a motor and then it faded away as if it belonged to another time and had come into his head for just a few moments. A policeman in a cape stopped him, but he was able to give an address and convince him that he was out for a walk to sober up.

Even with his jacket collar around his neck, he was cold and already feeling awful. He took a risk and at the end of the road climbed a wall into a back yard. As it turned out, it wasn't as difficult getting from one to the other as he had imagined, the large dog he expected never materialized and he managed to reach base and rest peacefully between jute sacks in Elizabeth's shed.

When he woke the sun was high and the morning warm. His head was splitting and his caked eyes were hard to open. As he looked up, he saw the face of a woman staring beyond him, tears cut into her cheeks. For a moment, he thought his mother had come to visit him again, this time to give out yards, but as he focused he saw it was a statue carved in wood.

He stood up, distracted by the carving despite the mess he was in. Lying on the shelf were two other blocks of wood, both of them chiselled and one taking on the features of a middle-aged man. He ran his hands over the carved woman and let his fingers feel the roughness of the grooves through which her tears flowed, all the time holding in his mind Karl's patient face.

Behind the house, everything was quiet apart from the chatter of birds. The back door was closed but a window was open and he climbed in without difficulty. He stood still for a moment, listening to the beat of the clock. The range was warm but the teapot was cold, so he knew Elizabeth was still in bed – especially as her sleep had been broken. It was only then he realized his stupidity in tramping through the neighbours' yards and risking pleurisy and prosecution. The keys to the front door were in his jacket pocket. A wonder she hadn't thought about the keys. Then he checked his other pockets, stopped dead and grinned. His wallet wasn't in his inside pocket, as usual. But it was in his left side pocket. He kissed it and counted his much-depleted wages. To his relief, he still had enough to pay Elizabeth and scrape by for the week.

Not daring to make tea, he wolfed down two raw eggs and some stale bread and curdled milk. His vomit had been cleared from the hall, but there was still a staleness there and not having the courage to face her, he left as quietly as he could and walked to Finsbury Park.

He watched the ducks and the strolling couples and families, and the Sunday fishermen who caught fish only to throw the fish back in again. His hangover was growing worse and he stank.

He walked for miles, coming across a local market, walking across bleak acres of bomb-sites, rummaging amongst the bricks and dust. A tube curled out of the ground and, clawing away the rubble, he pulled out a gas mask, shook the dust from it and tried it on, breathing in its acrid smell. Retching, he flung it away. In the shell of a house, he discovered a tribe of filthy, hungry cats. They stared at him and he returned their stare. He came back to the untouched streets again, and discovered he wasn't far from Citizen Road.

He longed for a drink; just one.

When he eased himself into the house that evening, Karl, buttoning his shirt, bumped into him as he came out of Elizabeth's bedroom. For a moment Hugh was shocked, in case the collision might alert Elizabeth and he pressed his finger to his lips. Karl was shocked too, but nodded and followed him into the kitchen.

'She's asleep,' he said.

'Good.'

Karl was miserable and sat at the table with his head in his hands. He looked like a countryman without his collar. His braces were slack.

'I'm sorry,' he mumbled through his fingers as Hugh beat some eggs.

Hugh's body was too heavy for him to answer, all his energy was concentrated in his wrist in order to keep the fork beating the eggs. The fork continued, as if with a will of its own, beating the eggs in a weak oval. It was strange: he thought he could feel Karl's pain, but not his own. He lifted his heavy arm and plucked a sprig of parsley from a green bowl, laboriously breaking it into the egg. He concentrated on each detail, carefully measuring a pinch of salt, seeing each individual grain, it seemed, strike the yellow surface and disappear.

'I'm sorry,' Karl said again. 'I'm truly sorry. I didn't mean to hurt you, Hugh. I love Elizabeth. We've been lovers, of a kind, for a long time, but she loves you and I accept that.'

He continued like this, but Hugh barely heard him, and then some irresistible force made him look up. Elizabeth stood there in her dressing gown. Her eyes looked black and heavy; her hair was straggled, coming to rest on her lovely, soft shoulders.

'What are you doing here? I thought I threw you out.'

He opened his mouth to deliver a prepared speech, about how practical it would be for him to stay – she would get her rent – but he couldn't speak, and so continued to beat. When he looked up, he saw she was still looking at him, and he thought he had never seen anyone look so sad.

'I'm sorry.'

He was sorry not just for his behaviour, but for the sadness which filled the room because of him, and which seemed at that moment to be also moving through the world. It seemed natural that Karl should be Elizabeth's lover, unnatural that he should be. His presence in their lives was a mistake.

'Just look at the state of you,' she said.

She turned on her heel and left the men to themselves. When she came back she was dressed.

'I'll make us a decent meal,' she said.

'I'll just wash then,' he said, glad of the chance to escape, and Karl nodded.

O God, he thought as he shaved. What am I going to do? What am I going to do?

When she put the meal before them, they ate without a word, the only sound being the cutlery scraping against the plates, and the bloody clock which he passionately wanted to destroy.

'I will leave tomorrow,' Karl said, as she cleared away the dishes.

'You're not leaving, Karl,' Elizabeth said.

'Then I'll leave,' Hugh said.

'No one is leaving,' she said.

Karl and Hugh went to work the next morning as usual. They were civil, and worked like horses.

*

It wasn't easy being in the house, but he calmed and stopped drinking. His old insecurities came back with a vengeance, but he could see that Elizabeth was making an effort to treat both men on equal terms, which he appreciated, even if it meant that she stayed away from both of them. She was suffering too, and his understanding of this helped him a lot.

The Sunday after those mad few days he went to Finsbury Park for a walk, feeling he needed a wide open space to do some thinking. It occurred to him that he might bump into Sarah and Deirdre, and he didn't want this. Not today, but then it was a big place. He liked that about London. A man could be on his own if he wanted to – but even if he met them, that would be all right. He had come a long way since he'd left his father. To be able to idle away your time with no one breathing down your neck calling you a waster – that was freedom.

There was a bench beside the pond and he sat, watching the ducks waddle by the edge. His sexual need for Elizabeth had gone. He thought it was something to do with the fact that she wouldn't let him leave. She was different, there was no doubt about that. Another woman would have kicked his arse and said bye-bye sonny, good riddance. But then, with both herself and Karl, their minds worked differently to the usual run of people. If he wanted to get closer to them, and he did, he'd have to try to understand not only their way of seeing the world, but accept, and maybe even adopt it. Maybe it was just Elizabeth he wanted to get close to, but he knew there was no way around it: if he wanted to understand Elizabeth, then he had to appreciate Karl for who he was.

There was another way and that was to leave, and to dump both his old way and their ways, and find his own, but that didn't bear thinking about, and anyway, he felt he belonged with her and therefore them.

The following evening, he was walking home along Hornsey Road with Karl. He stopped outside Rosenberg's shop.

'You go on,' he said. 'I'm just going in here.'

The old man took his money without looking at him.

'Sir, I . . . Mr Rosenberg, I want to apologize to you,' he said. 'I am most sorry and ashamed of myself. It will never happen again.'

The old man still would not look at him, but Hugh thought he saw him bow slightly, and left, chastened.

Elizabeth was coming along Hornsey Road, so he waited for her.

'Would you like a sweet?' he asked.

She looked at the bag, amused.

'Thank you,' she said. 'I don't know when I last saw a sweet.'

She rolled the sweet around in her mouth, grinning.

'Fancy you giving me sweets,' she said later, 'and me up to my fanny in sweets at work.'

'I thought you worked in a factory?'

'Yes!' she roared laughing. 'A bleeding *sweet* factory!'

'You're not serious.'

'I *hate* sweets.' She held her belly as she laughed.

Over the days, his desire returned. At first it was pleasant, like a welcome guest, and he hardly noticed that his eyes lingered on the shape of her hips. Or on her absent-mindedly scratching her breast in the yard, where the three of them sat as if they were ancients, if it was fine. He sat with them because he wanted to be with Elizabeth in any way he could. But before long, as these moments seeped into his blood, not being able to touch her was torture, and he would lie face down on his bed, pulling at his hair and shaking his head, trying to get her out of his seething brain.

The summer had become fiercely hot, and they took to going to the sea at Southend. He discovered that Elizabeth looked down on her own people because they ate eels and drank porter. He teased her over it, and she got in a huff, so they ended up going to Brighton instead.

Karl was quiet on those trips, but looked contented enough. He was a powerful swimmer, and he came back looking peaceful as a saint, dripping water after another crack at baptism. As for himself and Elizabeth, they laughed their heads off, but when she wasn't looking, he'd go half mad, staring at her soft flesh continuing out of each end of a black swimsuit. And then he'd look at the young women skitting about on the beach and see nothing in them beyond a nice shape. So why was it that he'd kill just to touch the inside of Elizabeth's thigh?

It was only a matter of time before he lost control, and one evening he stopped her in the hall and pulled up her blouse to cup her breasts. How she was so calm about it he didn't know, but she took away his hands, and looked at him as if she would overlook it, just this once.

So that was the end of it, and all his passion seemed cheap and shameful. In that moment, it was urgent to be normal and easy, to redeem himself as dignified, somehow, and all he could think of was to ask her to the pictures and to his surprise and relief, this seemed to please her a lot.

They went that night, and afterwards she brought him to bed again. It was a roundabout way of doing it, but she did. After that they went to the pictures often, sometimes once a week. They asked Karl to come too, but he just smiled and said no, films bored him, and secretly Hugh was relieved. This was their special time together, and free of their cares, and he had to admit it, free of Karl, they laughed a lot.

She spent some evenings with Karl, and he didn't want to think what they might be doing, so he persuaded himself that he needed to hear Irish voices and went to the Pride Of Erin. He found, for the first time, that he was popular with women and vaguely recognized it was something to do with his love for Elizabeth, and the confidence her love gave him, even if it was divided. He still wasn't used to it but he had learned a lot since he'd first come to this dance hall.

Karl was discreet too, and seemed to know when he was mad for Elizabeth, which was most of the time now.

The summer was well over when she insisted on one last trip to Brighton. He didn't feel like it, but himself and Karl went to humour her. Karl was off on one of his walks, and he was watching a fine young one playing with a beach ball when she stunned him with the news that she was pregnant. Oh fuck, he couldn't get his breath. Oh fuck.

It took a while to sink in that he was the father, and that his life had gone into another gear altogether. Karl didn't know, how would he? Although she didn't say anything about telling him, there was no fear of him spilling the beans. She could do that in her own sweet time. All he could think of saying was that he loved her, but even this came out as if he didn't believe it, so he leaned over and kissed her.

When Karl went to his room, his head was teeming with things he wanted to ask her, though there wasn't one sensible question he could think of. But she was in a queer mood, not in the least lovey-dovey, as he had expected.

'Hugh, why won't you tell me about your mountain?'

As soon as she mentioned the word, he was back in his old life, looking at her for the first time in a damp café.

'Ah, it's just a bloody rock.'

'But what about your family? Are they still there?'

'My father's here in London. My mother's dead.'

'Oh, I'm sorry. You told me that. Is she dead long?'

'Seven years.'

'Seven years? You were young, then.'

'I was here,' he said. He could hear his voice go back to its slow, suspicious tone.

'Am I going to meet your father?'

He laughed. Oh that was a good one, right enough.

'I don't think so.'

'You don't get on.'

'He thinks I'm cracked.'

There he was, kneeling on the bed in Wedmore Street, staring across the room in the middle of the night at his father, who was sure he was cracked.

'I see,' she said after a while.

As he asked her about her parents, he realized she had spoken about them in the café in the market too, which made it all the more surprising that she didn't want to talk about them now, either. That gave him some freedom, and he heard himself telling her what had happened to his mother. He couldn't believe he would tell anyone about anything so shameful. That opened her up too, and she started talking about her father, who had died of the same thing as his mother. He prompted her a bit, and then she talked about her mother, and his heart went out to her, because it was awful and the poor woman couldn't bear it and before he knew it she was blubbering away in his arms.

'It was terrible,' she whispered. He rocked her, and she recovered.

She found a hanky and blew her nose.

'I'm all right. Here,' and she got money out of her purse, 'fetch me cigarettes from Rosenberg's, will you?'

'Sure.'

It gave him a chance to get his bearings.

This changed everything. Karl would go crazy when he heard, and if there was one thing you couldn't hide for too long, it was a baby. Part of him felt like gloating. He had won out. The child was his. But Lord Jesus, it wasn't so simple. He couldn't shake off the notion that this brought them closer together, all three of them. Try as he might, he couldn't see it any other way.

All this thinking was doing damage to his head. He had spent weeks trying to think out what was happening between them, and had only just come to the conclusion that sharing Elizabeth with another man, his friend, had made him suffer enough to understand what love meant.

Was that still right?

Rather than settling on something, as he thought he had done when in Finsbury Park, his point of view was changing all the time, perhaps when a different side of love cropped up.

And if this wasn't a different side, then nothing was.

He had always thought that love must be an unfractured whole, a single overpowering emotion. Now he wasn't so sure.

He bought the cigarettes from Mr Rosenberg, who had never once looked at him since he had apologized. And he got a ration of sweets for himself. A celebration was a celebration.

A train was crossing the bridge, and he thought of the first time he had come to Citizen Road with Elizabeth. It wasn't so long before, and yet it seemed like a lifetime. His old life had died that day.

When he got back, Elizabeth wasn't in the kitchen. He put the cigarettes on the table, and had a sweet for himself. Maybe she was in the bathroom. He looked up at the mantel over the range, and took down her jug. She was always cleaning it, as if it was precious, but he could see nothing special about it, and put it back.

Where was she? He was hoping that maybe they could go for a walk before dark, be together at a time like this. It wasn't every day that you heard you were going to be a father.

Then he heard Elizabeth's scream. She was in her bedroom. He ran in to find her kneeling beside Karl on the bed. He looked like a shop dummy.

'Is he dead? Is he dead?' His heart and the back of his head pounded.

'O Jesus Christ, Hugh,' she sobbed. 'O Jesus Christ help me.'

'Is he dead?' he shouted, but she continued to sob. He ran to her and shook her. 'Is he dead? Tell me.'

'For God's sake, Hugh, get an ambulance.'

Seven

ELIZABETH

August–September 1950

Well then, what was all this rubbish about love at first sight? True, she'd liked the look of him as soon as she'd laid eyes on him, but she'd thought of it as a bit of a laugh, really. Nothing wrong with flirting, was there? Of course, if he'd been confident to begin with – who could tell?

Had she known that he'd open the door and see her like that? Elizabeth realized that she'd wanted, and willed it. She wanted this fresh Irish boy. What was in his mind, apart from his misty mountain? More than anything, she wanted to know. She wondered how she would tell Karl, although for the moment it didn't worry her unduly. Not really, she told herself. She checked her bags on the platform as the doors closed and the tube droned away.

The sun was breaking through the clouds as she crossed Holloway Road.

'*Did you like my body last night?*' She repeated the question to herself. She had lain awake, amazed, knowing that he did, but she needed to hear him say it. And yes, he had said it. He had said, '*You're beautiful*', and she recalled the to-do in him as he said it. She could not believe it. But then, then there was the kiss. That kiss on the tube. Imagine! Her! Kissing in public, a young bloke, like that! What had got into her? He had nearly broken her hand when he grabbed it, but no, she hadn't batted an eyelid. What did pain matter at a time like that? And then he leaned over to kiss her, and she couldn't help herself, her tongue, more or less . . . fell into his mouth.

She walked under the bridge and turned into Citizen Road.

In the market they had held hands. She had been ever so happy and natural. And then when they were buying the fruit . . . Those two old codgers knew what was going on all right, the buggers.

As she hauled her bags onto the kitchen table, and sorted the groceries, she wondered why he had gone off like that. Had he got cold feet? And what about her, getting her knickers in a twist when he'd done a bunk? What had she landed herself with this time? Had she imagined it all?

As the doors closed, she'd spotted him running along the platform, looking in each carriage, and she waved frantically. Then he saw her and, delighted, she opened her hands against the glass, laughing her heart out as the tube gathered speed.

She placed the fruit deliberately in a glass bowl. She'd thought of his face all the way home, of the way he had swerved and dodged like a boxer, or a dancer, avoiding the dawdlers on the platform as if he could see them with a spare eye, all the time searching the tube for her like one of them searchlights during the war.

And he had no girl . . .

Karl was sad, and too gracious. He treated her like delicate china. It had moved her, it still did, but she also needed something unpredictable, something with which to begin again, and as she thought this, she felt sad and mean.

The fruit stacked up in the bowl. The surplus fruit and the vegetables, she threw absently into the pantry box. Karl was still asleep in her bed. They had not made love. They rarely did, nowadays. He had lain beside her like a dead horse. She had seen a dead horse in Covent Garden once. Fell down there dead on the road, cart and all, the vegetables sprawled all over the place. The owner had kicked at it to get it up, but it was no use, the horse was stone dead.

She had woken during the night to go to the toilet and Karl had been awake and she knew he had not slept. Now he was asleep. She wanted to speak to him before Hugh returned, but could not wake him, or tell him while he was still in her bed. Luckily Hugh stayed out on Sunday afternoons. The memory of his pleading face on the platform kept returning, wrenching at her. She made some tea and sat drinking it, legs crossed away from the table, brooding.

'Have sense,' she whispered. 'He's no Cary Grant.'

Karl rose at three, stuck his bleary face around the door, and smiled at Elizabeth who had distracted herself with a magazine. She smiled back, nervously.

'You are not at Millie's.'

'No. Not today.'

He stripped to the waist and washed at the sink while she set tea. He was humming a tuneless song with odd words of German, and she took in the strong line of his back. She had tried to make him lose his seriousness, but somehow he was too massive. The sadness in him was too great. And it would only deepen when Hugh became her lover.

There, she'd thought it.

She didn't exactly want it to happen, it was happening with a will of its own and nothing could stop it. Now that she had the opportunity, she could not tell him. Over tea he read his Sunday newspapers. She took down her recipe book, the same wartime book she had used for years. She had filled it out with her own notes as food had become less scarce, and now she plotted out the meals for the week, knowing all the time that her lips were pursed, her body in a ball of tension. But it occupied her for a while.

The sunlight filled most of the yard, and the whitewash on the shed wall was dazzling. The stained glass on the back door glowed softly. Outwardly the world was peaceful. She rubbed her finger along the side of the table, pushing it harder and harder. Why didn't she just get up and leave, go for a walk, get away from him? But no, she wanted to stay, held in a soup of happiness and regret, excitement and fear, lust and compassion. He lowered his paper and looked at her.

'Elizabeth, *Liebchen*. You are thinking of Hugh.'

She didn't answer, or look at him for a while. He had known all the time, and she didn't know if that made it all right, or just terrible. Her mind wanted to go blank, but she clenched her jaw and held on to a clear head. So this was it, then. She turned slowly to him and said with an evenness which surprised her, 'I'm going to make him my lover, Karl. I've decided.'

He looked back at his paper again.

'You say that as if you will exclude me from your bed.'

She stared at him.

'Isn't that normal?'

'Normal, yes.'

'Are you saying . . . are you saying that you don't mind . . .?'

'I don't need your exclusive attention, Elizabeth. All I want is a little of your love, some of the time. To thaw me out, whenever you feel you want whatever it is I can give you.'

'Are you sure?' she asked, and as she did, she knew it sounded as if she was agreeing with him.

'I do not say things I am not sure of.'

'That's right. You don't. It's just . . . a little unusual, that's all.'

He shrugged.

'Tell me why I'm doing this?'

'I don't want children. We've agreed.'

'Yes.'

'But you look at this young man, who has no horror in his head, and you know you want a child. He reminds you.'

'Reminds me? Reminds me of what?'

'Of hope.'

'Of hope?'

'It is normal.'

'Karl . . .' She was barmy to throw him up, a diamond geezer that could shake her to the bone like this. She made her way around the table to him. 'Karl, I love you,' she whispered.

'*Ach, Liebchen.* You feel tender because you are grateful. But then I am grateful too.'

'What? You talk such nonsense, sometimes,' she said tenderly, and she took his face in her hands and kissed him, pulling at his lips with hers, enjoying him slowly. Even as she kissed him she felt the contradiction. Now that in the back of her mind she was leaving him aside, she wanted him more than ever, and the freedom of it was like a drug in her veins.

'Come to bed with me,' she said, her voice muffled against his chest.

'When are you going to seduce Hugh?' he asked, his hands moving up her body from her waist.

'Seduce him? Yes ... I suppose so. Tonight, I think. But I want you before him. To make me secure, Karl.'

His hand found her breast, and she held her breath.

'Can we stay like this, for just a few moments?' he asked her, his eyes closed.

'For as long as you like.'

'Are you afraid?'

'No. I was.'

They went to her room. Before she fully realized what was happening, he had unbuttoned her. His hands spread out across her breasts and as he removed her blouse she reached back to unclip her brassiere, so that their arms were in a tangle. They laughed, almost apologetically, at that, as if they were doing this for the first time, and she let him do the rest, lying back on the bed as he unclipped and unrolled her stockings and she raised her bum as he pulled off her knickers. She had always loved that bit, it made her feel wanton, but now she couldn't keep her eyes off him as he undressed, wanting to remember every detail. She forgot everything as the bed took Karl's weight and he hauled her into his arms. He too seemed to be aware that this was maybe the last time, and his kisses lingered over all her body, leaving blooms of pleasure after them, so that when he entered her, long after she wanted him, she pulled him in, impatient to feel him deep within her. O lumme, he wants me so much. She folded her legs over his back. Oh, she felt everything as he moved inside and above her, and unable to bear it she threw her head from side to side, her nails clinging to his back, her moans tumbling out of her with a will of their own until she arched out to him with a screech, losing her mind until he shouted and it was over.

It was bliss to recover slowly. This was maybe the best,

contented part of it. His weight made it difficult to breathe, but she was used to that. They were so sweaty that she didn't notice his tears for a while. She worked her fingers through his sparse hair. The poor, dear sod.

'Karl, I do love you, you know. I'm not just grateful. We've been through too much.'

'You are much stronger than I,' he said.

It didn't take a genius to know why he was like this, but she couldn't bear to face the truth, so she deflected it by bringing up the reasons why he had been like this so often before.

'Karl, Karl ... How many times have we gone over this? There was nothing you could do. And! And! If you had died with your family you would never have met me, made love to me, helped me put my life together again. They're all dead. We're alive. We have a chance, Karl.'

'Do you think so?'

'Yes!' she said, convincing herself. 'Let them rest in peace!'

'It sounds easy after making love, I know.'

'You're impossible,' she said, unable to face him. 'You can keep your old guilt.'

'You see what I mean?'

'But that's just because ... Get up!' She pushed at his shoulders as his eyes closed. 'Get up. I don't want you here when Hugh comes in.'

After a moment, he lifted himself away and sat on the edge of the bed.

'Ah yes. I forgot.' He looked around at her.

O Christ. Suddenly, everything was more complicated.

'Are you sure you don't mind?'

'Hugh mustn't know about me. He's too young.'

She looked him up and down but said nothing as he left. Too young for her, is that what he was saying? That he should be protected from women who got their claws into fresh young blokes? Was that it? She tugged on a strand of hair, brooding for a long time.

Could she really lie here planning to bring Hugh into this same bed, when Karl's stuff was still inside her and his sweat had barely dried into her skin?

She went for a walk up the Holloway Road. It was unlike her, to go somewhere without a purpose, but she needed to get out of the house, and this was as good as anywhere. She stopped at most shop windows, idly interested in goods she would never notice normally. In front of a drapery window, she bowed her head and allowed herself to think of Hugh, and of his misty mountain which seemed like a cool breeze in her head on a day like this. He had been so generous and happy in the market, and her light, mocking humour had been, she realized, the giddy expression of her own happiness. She was smiling now, thinking about it, and nodding, as if she had realized something after many years of knowing it. She looked up at the window again. It had men's clothes. The women's and children's clothes were in the other window, and she went over to that, examining them all, comparing the prices.

Karl was oiling the hinges on the shed door when she returned. It was a small thing, but he kept the outside in order. Last year he had fixed the drainpipe, and it was a pity that she hadn't more for him to do, as he was happy to be useful. She greeted him, surprised by the tenderness in her voice. He looked up and smiled, just a little, and went back to checking the door. She didn't want to be tender towards him, it made things too complicated, but she couldn't help it. She looked at the clock, sure that Hugh hadn't come in yet. If so, he was late. This thing would be best got over as soon as possible. She stayed by the cooker, wondering what would happen.

And then he put the key in the door. It was an odd feeling, being aware of him in this way. She coughed and beat her breast to ease the uncomfortable feeling there and, taking a deep breath, she greeted him with a nervous smile over her shoulder. Karl lowered his paper and grunted his usual hello. Hugh sat in, drumming the table with his fingers.

So he was nervous too, but she didn't know if that was better or worse.

'Were you at Mass then, Hugh?' Elizabeth asked, her back turned to him.

'No. No, I'm giving it up. They go on too much about hell.'

'I see.' Elizabeth and Karl exchanged glances.

They ate dinner more or less in silence.

Karl made some tea, and went to his room. She glanced after him anxiously, but he seemed all right. She went out to the yard for a moment for a breather, pretending to examine her plants. What was going on in that skull of hers? The sun had moved out of the yard, but there was just enough to lean back against the shed wall and bathe her face in it. The fact was, she had been happy in those few minutes at dinner with Karl and Hugh. With both of them. It would probably never happen again, but there was no denying it: it had been very special. She wanted to stay like this for ever, the sun on her face, full of memory and anticipation. It wasn't even urgent to get Hugh into bed any more, and she knew now why she felt so tender towards Karl. He had made her free, if only because he hadn't abandoned her. Then she realized that Hugh had stayed in the kitchen, no doubt wondering what was going to happen next, and she felt a nervous thrill. She went back in, and touched his hand lightly as she passed, and the poor boy smiled. She piled the dishes into the sink, waiting to see if he would move, or say something, but he didn't. She knew he had no experience, but had assumed that his male nature would drive him to touch her, however clumsily. She turned her head and smiled at him as warmly as she could. He smiled back, very shy, and mumbled something about going upstairs.

'Will I see you after your little rest?' she grinned. She was touched by how natural he was. No sophistication, but no pretence, either.

'All right.'

'All right? Oi, you Irish is romantic, there's no doubt about it!'

Her smile persisted as he left, but then it seemed as if it were all a dream and in her kitchen which now seemed painfully familiar, doubt began to return. She ran her finger along an old jug belonging to her mother. It was the one thing that had survived the near direct hit on their old house, apart from Millie's cutlery, safe and intact in its box, found not two feet from where it had always been. She went to her room and turned on the lamp, intending to read, but she couldn't settle and put her head in her hands.

'What am I doing?' she whispered. 'What am I doing?'

Music. She needed some music, but then decided she didn't. Night was falling. All she could think of was the war, the sirens wailing, her stranded on the south bank, crouched in a doorway as the bombs lit up the blacked-out docks, so brightly you could see the cranes. She remembered telling Karl about this, and how it had impressed him so. She shuddered, but the memories persisted, like cut-outs: mangled bodies, blood flowing in a stream along the street in broad daylight, children playing a game across rubble that was still smoking. They had come back from the country at the beginning, war or no war. They wanted their mammies and daddies, and their mammies and daddies wanted them.

And then the cruelty of it, after all their suffering, just when they thought the war was over for them, after they had suffered more than their share . . .

She still heard that doodlebug, heard it cutting out and falling on little Georgina's school in broad daylight. Poor Millie, how was she still sane, losing her only child like that? And then their mother, standing at a bus stop. Christ Almighty. She felt centuries old when she thought of that.

She stirred as she heard someone coming downstairs. It was Hugh. She could tell by the weight of his step. She sat up straight in the gloom, as he hesitated outside her door, before leaving.

So. The moment had passed. It was nothing more than a fancy. Part of her was relieved. She stretched, letting her head fall back, and held her breath for as long as she could before letting it go.

In her room she put on a record and got into bed. She left the light on and stared at the ceiling. The last thing she wanted was responsibility for any of this. Let it go which way it wanted, she didn't care, as long as she didn't have to decide. Her breast was itchy and she scratched it through her nightdress, but the itch was deep inside her flesh. It would not be touched and she shivered and shook her head in irritation. Damn. The back of her arm began to itch and she pursued that, again to no avail. 'O God!' she muttered. 'When will I have some rest from myself?'

The key turned in the door and she forgot her itches. The record stopped. He had closed the door, but had not gone upstairs. He was standing outside her room. She leaned over to her dressing table and retrieved a hand mirror, arranged her hair and made sure her nightdress kept her modest, then reached for a magazine, her eye on the door. Her heart was beating heavily, yet his knock gave her a start. Too late, she realized she had been careless about where she'd dropped her clothes. She leaned on an elbow and flicked through the magazine, trying to compose herself before answering.

'Hugh? Is that you? Come on in.'

He came in slowly, his mouth open, his face pale. He was petrified, poor kitten.

'Where have you been? I thought you'd run off on me.' She sat up, smiling as coyly as they did in Hollywood, her mask falling naturally into place after all.

'Sorry . . . I didn't realize you'd be in bed,' he said, looking at the floor.

'Oh, come on, silly,' she said, pulling over the bedclothes. 'You shouldn't leave a woman waiting, you know. Come on. Get those clothes off and get in.'

He was so obviously shaking that she immediately regretted her remark. That kind of thing usually encouraged men. Oh dear. She was at a loss, unable to think of anything to do or say to calm him.

'Do you want me to look away while you undress?'

He nodded, and she turned away, thinking that, maybe if she took off her nightdress it would encourage him, make them equal and, as she did so, sure enough she heard the rustle of his clothes.

'Is this your first time in bed with a woman?'

'Yes.'

He lay beside her like a lump of meat, and she turned to put an arm around him, pulling him against her breasts, confident that nature would take over from there and all would be well.

'Don't worry,' she whispered, caressing him.

He wasn't as beautiful as she had imagined. His bones protruded, but he would fill out into a fine man, with the right food. These bloody rations would be over soon, but even since he had come to live with her he had improved.

'It happens to everyone sometime or another. Don't worry – you don't have to do anything. It's nice to have you here beside me. Why don't we just talk? Why don't you just tell me about growing up on that mountain in Ireland. It sounds wonderful.'

'The mountain?'

'Yes! Karl told me about it. Where you grew up. I want to hear everything about it.'

'Everything.'

'Yes. Everything.'

'There's nothing to tell, Elizabeth. It's all dead.'

It was as if saying this released him, and he pressed his head between her titties and at last he held her, his body alive and supple. His eyes were closed, and he did not kiss her, but sucked at her nipples, his hands travelling over her body. The bed-springs were making a racket and it was all she could do not to laugh, but it wasn't so funny when she heard Karl coming down the stairs. She held Hugh as tightly as she could, to quieten the springs as much as anything, but his fingers were doing wild things between her legs. The door closed and she heard Karl walk up the street, but she was really too far gone to care. Oh yes, this was it. O God she was moaning. Moaning her head off. O Christ. He was wild. He didn't know where he was. Every bit of him was hers. Every pore of his hard body. She guided him into her. O God, what am I doing? O Jesus Christ.

*

She was woken by them leaving, and without thinking she leapt out of bed and discreetly pulled back the side of the curtain, but they were gone.

She smiled. It was very nice to be flattered like this. Then she tugged on her hair. It was strange that Hugh hadn't asked about Karl, how it had never occurred to him that Karl might have some feelings in the matter. But then, she hadn't given it the thought it deserved either.

She sat on the side of the bed. At her age, she had accepted what amounted to companionship as enough. It wasn't, though. It wasn't enough. For years, oh, since the war at least, she had been terrified at the thought of children. She didn't want to bring a child into the world to be shot or bombed or worse. Karl felt the same way. And they were half starved for years. It wasn't right to bring a child into a world like that. But now she resented Karl. Had he ever really loved her, or had she just been convenient for him? Men were like that. They liked their convenience.

As quickly, it gave way to pity and sadness. Absent-minded, she went to the kitchen and made breakfast. What was she on about? Eh? What the bloody hell was she on about? A full day hadn't passed since she would have gone to hell for him and back. He had loved her, poor sod, in his own way, and it was wrong to rubbish him. It was just that . . .

She was still brooding as her trolley arrived on the Holloway Road.

'What number is it?' an old lady asked.

'The six-six-seven,' she replied, and the spell was broken.

'That's me for Poplar then.'

Elizabeth smiled but went upstairs. She could see that the old dear was bursting to talk, probably about the war, and the first at that, and she was in no mood to listen. She wanted to settle into herself. How was it that things were so complicated? She wanted to enjoy the ease of her body, to think about Hugh, about what he had done to her, for her. She narrowed her eyes at the pleasure of it, and she felt like stretching, with a big grin on her face, but she managed the faintest of smiles.

Two men on the same day. Well, well, Lizzy Frampton. Whoever would have thought it! And what was wrong with it? Why, Lady Muck, nothing at all!

No, she thought in wonder, nothing at all. Here she was, pulling herself asunder trying to do the right thing, when the right thing was waiting for her, under her nose. The things she'd thought about Karl, poor duck, just to justify herself, when she didn't need any justifying. None. She'd have to be careful, that's all.

They arrived at Poplar all too soon, and she made her way to the factory, meeting Betty in the mostly female stream of workers. Betty had just taken a cigarette from another worker, and was lighting up before starting, as many of the women were. She wasn't fat, Betty, but she was heavier than Elizabeth and wore rimless glasses. A brooch kept her blouse closed at the neck.

'Oh, Monday,' she groaned, and then laughed. Elizabeth laughed too, dying to tell Betty why she was so happy, but she had spent so long keeping so much of her life a secret, she hadn't the words.

'See you in the canteen, Betty,' she said jauntily. 'I want a word with you about that brother of mine.' Betty blushed, but tried to hide it with a laugh.

'What's he up to now, then?'

'Nothing, Betty. That's the point.'

She clocked in, and put on her white coat and cap. She stopped as the women flowed past her. It wasn't easy, it was near slavery, this work, and she had often thought of giving it up, but she needed it badly, to help her forget herself as much as the few shillings. She took a deep breath, to make herself hard, when all she wanted was to feel soft, and walk on air.

She could never get used to the sickly aroma of boiling sugar. It was boiled to crack, then scattered along the conveyor. With other women, she turned the edges over, into the middle, and mixed in the powdered citric acid, working it like dough, but without pulling it. Women down the line rolled the mixture in oil and it continued on to the ovens. The conveyor rolled upstairs, where the mixture was cut into pieces and rolled into drops, drenched with powdered sugar and packed into jars by the piece-workers, including Betty.

They met in the canteen. Betty was sitting at a table, smoking a cigarette and looking weary.

'You all right then, love?' Elizabeth asked her, sitting in to the table with her tea and sandwich.

'I'm knackered, Liz. I always seem to be knackered these days.'

'What you need, Betty, is a man to keep you on your toes.'

Betty snorted, then laughed heartily, throwing back her head.

'Oh blimey. The worst of it is, you're right. Do Methodists have nuns? It's all that's left me now, to become a nun.'

'Rubbish. There's lots of men have an eye for you, Betty.'

'That's right, Liz. And they're all at the bottom of different oceans.'

'Yeh . . . Sam doesn't think you're half bad.'

'Sammy?' Betty just didn't believe it. 'Sammy hasn't looked at me since we were—Well, since the day before I got married, at least.'

'That was then, Betty. We've all been through a lot since then.'

'Are you trying to make a match, Lizzy Frampton?'

'I know he's been inside.'

'That doesn't matter,' Betty said quickly. She dragged on her cigarette as hard as she could, and looked away as she released the smoke deliberately. 'Well then!' She stubbed her cigarette and rose, smiling at Elizabeth until they both laughed, and then she was gone, making her way through the packed canteen to the toilets.

Elizabeth missed her in the crowd after work, and she knew that Betty had avoided her. Well, it had to be done. They had to stand by each other, and get the car on the road. And yes, she had her own motives too. He was useless, but it wasn't as if men were falling out of trees. Well, unless you counted forty-two Citizen Road . . .

It was an effort just to go home. Her body ached in all the wrong ways, from standing there all day, going like a machine. No wonder Betty was always tired. And there was that brother of hers, sitting on his arse all day like a gentleman. Well, she'd tell him what for.

She had a mind to go down to the house and kick him out of it, but she had to go home to make the dinner. It never ended, it was one long roundabout, day after bleeding day. She pushed herself on to catch the trolley, but halfway down the street she stopped. Why should he get away with it, when everyone else was slaving? Just because he sat on his arse in Holloway for five years didn't mean he could sponge off Millie and leave Betty on her own for another five.

The more she thought of it the more worked up she got. A bus came and she was there in five minutes, but couldn't find the key in her bag. She was on the point of throwing the contents on the ground when she found it, but she was so agitated that she couldn't open the door.

'Millie!' She pounded the knocker. 'Millie!'

'What is it, Beth?' Millie was pale and astonished. She was still in her working clothes.

'Where is he? Where is the scumbag?' She pushed past Millie.

'Who, Beth?'

'Who do you think? Little Lord fucking Fauntleroy, that's who.' He wasn't in the front room or kitchen.

'Sam?'

'He's in bed. The tosser's in bed.'

'Beth?' Millie called as Elizabeth ran upstairs. She flung open his door, and Sam was sitting up in bed, his eyes wide in fear, his hands pushed out to protect him.

'You!' she shouted. 'You get up off your fat arse and bring Betty Hindley to the pictures or I'll swing for you. Do you hear me? I'll swing for you!'

He stared at her, his hands still outstretched.

'Are you listening, you stupid git?' she screamed.

'Yeh! Yeh, sis.' He recovered. 'Sure I'll bring old Betsy to the flicks. Nothing surer. What's on . . .?'

Elizabeth was shaking. She turned and left, ignoring Millie who stood outside, but on her way downstairs she called back to her.

'Make sure he does. Just make sure he does.'

Her fury turned to depression on her way home. As the trolley hummed and clanked, she dreaded facing Karl, and wished she could go away somewhere, to a village in the country where no one knew her, maybe, where she could forget everyone, forget having to think of Karl, of Hugh, of Sam, of Mildred, of Betty. Just for a week, or two maybe, so she could rest and be able for them all again. Or maybe meet a man who was strong, and full enough of himself to distract her.

She knew by the dried clay in the hallway that they were home. Before taking off her coat she got a brush to sweep it away. It was like two horns, and must have wedged in where one of them lost a steel toecap. She examined the sculptured clay on the dustpan, and wondered to which of them it belonged, whose foot had fallen to gather it up. Karl started on his slow, sad music. Over the years she had accepted it, and had even grown to like some of it now and again, but at this moment it was grating on her nerves. She emptied the mud into the bin and began dinner.

When they came down she was surprised to find Karl content. Surely he couldn't be. Surely it was a front. She smiled at Hugh, trying to hide her bafflement. He smiled back, full of warmth and, dared she believe it, love, and this surprised and frightened her until she thought about it. She was his first woman, after all, and he would be dazzled for a while.

Karl ate peacefully, it seemed, as if he had accepted the situation without a moment's reflection. It couldn't be, she thought. It just couldn't be. She didn't know whether to be offended or relieved. She smiled again at Hugh, and he returned her smile. He was happy. She looked up as Karl left the table, and behind his quick smile she saw the sadness in his eyes, and then, with impressive dignity, he left.

She tugged at Hugh, and lightly drew him towards her to kiss her. He tried too roughly, and she withdrew. Distracted by the little game, she smiled, and mutely invited him again, inclining her head. He took his cue, and kissed her as softly as she had ever dreamt it.

As they made love that week, the faint melodies of Karl's music leaked from upstairs.

*

She was proud of the fact that Hugh had changed. His confidence gave him the beauty he had lacked. Her happiness was such that she only thought of Karl in the way she might think of Betty, for instance, a friend who every so often wandered into her thoughts. Oddly enough, the sadness in those deep blue eyes comforted her. It was right. Things were in their proper place, and she could feel what she was supposed to feel. She had never been like this before. Karl was different. She respected and loved him. She had put it into words, and it seemed right. There was no drama about it.

But on the Saturday evening when Hugh announced he was going drinking with men from work, she found herself thinking of Karl in all his reality for her.

I'm a bitch, she thought, as he started playing his blasted music yet again. She turned on the radio to escape the damn thing. A button had come loose in her work blouse and she was repairing it at the kitchen table.

'I'm more than a bitch, I'm stupid,' she said aloud. She needed, or a part of her needed this big, sad man. He was her friend, and whatever had possessed her, the first chance she got she had thrown him away like a paper bag. She knotted the thread and trimmed it with her teeth, which left it a bit ragged, but it was on the inside so no one would notice. She went to her room, threw the blouse on the bed and went upstairs. Although she was determined and ready for anything, her heart pounded as she knocked on his door. He called her to come in, and she opened the door slowly, and stood there, unable to look at him.

'Can you forgive me, Karl?' she said then.

He stretched out his hand. She crossed to him and took his hand in hers, but still she couldn't look into his face. The music stopped, the record continuing to rustle around, and she found the strength to look at him. So this was the man who had comforted her for so long, whom she had loved in her own, guarded, distant way. He looked so unfamiliar.

'Do you still have a little room for me?' he asked in a voice so soft and calm that she wondered at it.

'Of course!' she said with all her strength.

'Well then. All is good.'

All is good. O Karl, O Karl . . . How could all be good? All was not good. She pursed her lips and lowered her eyes again, her tenseness leaving her more from weariness than from relief.

'Where's Hugh?'

'He's gone drinking.'

'Ah. He's a proper man now.'

She laughed and took his hand again.

'Thank you, Karl.' She smiled weakly and cupped his head in her hands, wanting to kiss him, but afraid he might think of it as a Judas kiss. She wanted nothing more than to comfort him, but held back, hoping that all the tenderness she felt for him could be felt in her hands, in the way she breathed.

In her bedroom, she closed the door behind her and leaned against it. After a while, the tears came. Why was life so complicated? She took a deep breath and went to close the curtains, but as it was still bright, she changed her mind. Maybe she ought to go out. But where to, on her own? To Millie's? Or maybe Betty's? Certainly not to Millie's and, with any luck, Betty was on the town with her good-for-nothing brother. She felt guilty dumping him on Betty, who was avoiding her at work, but then, it was what Betty wanted after all. She'd have said nothing unless she'd known that much. It would be all right, she was sure of that. She lay back on the bed, very tired. And then she laughed.

Here she was, with two men at her feet, alone on a Saturday night. She shook her head in disbelief at how she had so casually accepted him going out with his mates, as if they had been married for years. All right, she'd thought that maybe she'd had enough for one week. A woman needed a breather. And maybe he had thought the same, but now she needed him so she could stop thinking of Karl's patient face. She turned on her stomach and struck her head into the pillow.

She forced herself to get up and close the curtains, and looked around the room before undressing and getting into bed. It was tidy for once, and she had done it for him, the bastard. She lay in bed, agitated. It was still bright and too damn early to go to sleep.

That was what Karl had done, she thought, looking at the ceiling, above which he was probably lying in bed like her, thinking much the same thing. He had filled the empty moment for her, had Karl.

Enough! She jumped out and went to the kitchen and found her rations recipes and jotter, and got back into bed with them. When she had made up the meals for the week, she amused herself by browsing, which sparked off memories of the war, and for an hour she was lost in these before she drifted to sleep.

In her dream she was a girl again, paddling along the shore at Brighton, splashing Millie who was screeching and laughing, and Sam was building sandcastles with his mates. Far out at sea, a wave as tall as Nelson's Column was coming slowly towards the shore; but Elizabeth didn't mind because it would take many years before it arrived and destroyed Sam's castle. Mam and Dad waved from the promenade, and she waved back, excited and happy. Then the tide was out, and she was underneath the buttresses of the promenade, struggling with a smelly, hairy stranger who was trying to push her onto the stinking sand.

She woke, confused and irritable, trying to push away his hands before realizing it was not a dream after all.

'Hugh, stop . . .'

He left her alone but he was still breathing heavily in the darkness. The overpowering smell woke her completely and she got out of bed and put on the light. She blinked, gradually taking in his sweaty grin, and then the vomit strewn across her floor.

'You dirty pig,' she screamed.

He stared at her as her rage mounted. The fucker was stark naked, and she looked him up and down in contempt. Imagine. Imagine! She could hardly bring herself to think what he had intended, and worse, what he had assumed. O Christ Almighty. O Christ Almighty! She'd strangle the worm, she'd chop his bollocks off. He got the message, and pulled on his trousers.

'That's right,' she shouted, released, 'you've got the idea. Get out of my bedroom and out of my house!'

He'd sobered. She had frightened the life out of him. He was pulling on his socks and shoes at a terrific rate. O God, the smell was warm and awful. He was pulling on his shirt when it occurred to her that he had probably drunk all his wages. She jumped to the door to block it, her hand out.

'Where's the two weeks' rent you owe me? Come on, Hugh – four pounds five shillings – now.'

'It was stolen ... My money was stolen.' He had one arm tangled in a sleeve, and she laughed. He looked so miserable, like a little boy caught out and dreading his punishment. That busybody from next door was pounding on the wall. You couldn't fart in this place. A surge of violence swept through her and she pushed him towards the front door.

'You drank it, didn't you. I was fooled by someone like you before and I'm not going to be fooled again.'

She opened the door and gave him one final push onto the street. He staggered, but regained his balance.

'My jacket ...'

'Your jacket. Right!'

She slammed the door on him. His jacket. She found his jacket on the floor and, avoiding the vomit, she opened the door and threw it at him, then slammed the door shut again, and leaned against it, running her hands through her hair. This was a nightmare. Why, oh why couldn't it, for once in her life —

'You're nothing but a whore,' he shouted. 'You've no feelings. You're not Christian at all.'

'Oh yes. There's your true colours,' she said to herself.

Old Rosenberg shouted at him, and Hugh shouted back.

She listened intently, half expecting a brick to come through the window, but a weird silence had come on the street. He was gone, but where on earth would he go to at this hour of the night? For a moment she was mad enough to run after him and bring him back, but no, that might be what women did in the pictures, but not her. A night in the open would do him good.

She sobbed, but put her hand to her mouth and held it back until she calmed. She went to the kitchen and got wet tea leaves and sprinkled them over the mess, and swept it up as best she could; but when she returned to bed the smell was worse. She grabbed the bedclothes and a pillow, and placed them on the floor in the kitchen. It was too hard for her, so she got some winter blankets and put them under her, and wriggled about until she was comfortable.

When she woke, she got up immediately, opened the window

and front door and got her mop and water. Karl came downstairs.

'O God, I can't get rid of this stench,' she said, moving the mop hard.

'Here, let me help.'

'No, Karl,' she said grimly. 'It's my mess.'

Water and fresh air cleared most of it, and she emptied the bucket and ran the backyard tap over the mop, then rinsed her hands under it. She was aware of Karl moving about in the kitchen as he made himself breakfast. She leaned back against the wall and dried her hands on her apron. She plucked a few weeds from the pots and watered the herbs, then passed through the kitchen without a word to Karl, and ran a bath. She lay back in the water in relief. Where was he now? she wondered. Charming another landlady, no doubt. He would come back, though – wouldn't he? She soaped and rinsed herself, and let the water drain away. He would come back. She knew it.

She was halfway down Citizen Road when she stopped, realizing that she had not told Karl she was going to Millie's, as was her custom. Once again he would be hurt, but she was so dispirited she didn't care, and walked on to the underground. In the tube, her thoughts drifted idly. She read all the advertisements, stared openly at passengers as they boarded or got off, even traced the line of the slats on the floor. This vacancy continued as she walked to Millie's. When she got there, Millie put a finger to her lips as she greeted her in the hall. Betty was in the front room, polishing the silver.

'Betty, what's wrong?'

Betty kept polishing, but said nothing.

Elizabeth looked at Millie.

'Sammy went drinking with his mates for three days.'

Elizabeth was quiet for a moment.

'I see.'

Betty looked around at Elizabeth, still polishing.

'Where is he now?' Elizabeth asked her directly.

'In bed.'

'Need I have asked . . .'

Elizabeth went quietly up to his room and opened the door,

silently cursing the war, which wasn't over yet. Not for women it wasn't. He was sprawled back on the bed, with just his drawers on him to keep him decent. He was snoring and very pale. The blankets were on the floor, but his clothes were neatly tidied away on a chair, which puzzled Elizabeth until she realized Millie had put him to bed. Poor old Millie. The poor cow got the wrong end of every stick. Millie got on her wick sometimes, because she couldn't pull herself together like everyone else, but every now and then, sympathy broke through her impatience, and you only had to look at Sam in the state he was in now, to know this was one of those times. She went downstairs.

'Come on, girls, we're going to the ice cream parlour.'

'What?' Betty grimaced in disbelief.

'But it's not open on Sunday,' Millie protested, alarmed.

'Damn. Well, we're going somewhere out of here.'

'But where?'

'Anywhere, Betty, anywhere!'

'But what about Sam?'

'Sam's doing all right, Millie. He's as happy as he's ever going to be. Come on. Up off your bots!'

'All right,' Millie said, and went upstairs, shaking her head but smiling all the same.

'Just let me put on a face, Liz,' Betty insisted. At the hallstand mirror, she powdered her face and put on lipstick, Elizabeth looking over her shoulder and doing the same.

'I reckon we'll pick up a few sailors, Liz. What do you reckon?'

'I was thinking of stockbrokers, myself,' Elizabeth said, shaking with laughter.

'Whoa!' Betty shouted, and they laughed so much they fell into each other's arms.

Millie descended the stairs in a hat laden with artificial cherries, a red net falling over the brim to mask her eyes. Elizabeth and Betty stared, sobered by the sight.

'You're not going out in *that*?' Elizabeth said, grinning.

'What? Don't you like it?'

'Of course you are, Mil,' Betty said.

'But it was belonging to *Mother*!'

'Right,' Millie said, nodding to Betty. 'There. And it wasn't Mother's.' She made room for herself in front of the mirror and made a final adjustment. 'Well, I'm ready.'

'Well then! Let's go!'

They followed Elizabeth onto the street.

'Where are we going?'

'We're already there, Millie. Look about you, for Christ's sake. Look at that lovely day! There's children playing in the street, people sunning themselves at their front doors. Eh? Can't you see that even the bricks of the houses are glowing. Eh? Get some sun on your mugs and fresh air in your lungs, you silly cows. You work all week in a factory, and then you sit in all weekend. What kind of twerps are you?'

They considered this as she marched them at full pace until they came to Aldgate. A bus to the West End arrived and she insisted they get on, and smiled fiercely at the woman conductor as she paid their fares. Then she remembered the Lyons' House on Tottenham Court Road, so they got off at Holborn and walked the rest of the way, a wind blowing at their dresses, their high heels clicking. Maybe the others thought she was out of her mind as she marched on, and maybe they were right.

'Here we are,' she said as the Lyons' House came into view. She was relieved, as she had feared it would not be there any more, or that she had somehow imagined it.

'Oh no, Beth,' Millie said. 'It's too fancy.'

'I'll not hear another word. Listen! Music, my dears!'

Betty patted her hair and took a deep breath. Elizabeth walked in and the others followed. The ground floor cafeteria was packed, and there was a queue on the stairs. Elizabeth had not been here since the war. The orchestra in formal dress, and the way they had prepared the wartime rations had made it seem like a feast, a banquet in heaven. It all came back to her as she listened to the Viennese waltz. Eventually they were shown a table, where a waitress in a black dress and a lace apron and cap took their order for three salads.

'Do you still cut the tomatoes like they were a rose?' Elizabeth asked her.

'Yes, madam.'

'This is nice, Beth,' said Millie as she relaxed at last and looked around her.

'Yes, it is, isn't it.' They were playing 'The Blue Danube'. My God, she thought. It might as well be '41.

Betty threw back her head and laughed.

'O Liz,' she said. 'You're the one.'

Their salads arrived, and Elizabeth mixed the salad cream through her beetroot. As the taste spread over her tongue, she sighed with pleasure.

She left them happy and laughing at Holborn tube, but as she descended on the great escalator, the wind blowing at her dress so that she had to hold it down, her weariness returned.

Karl was in the yard, carving. She went out to him, but although he greeted her, she didn't respond, but leaned back against the wall, her hands splayed against it. He put his carving away in the shed.

'What is wrong, Elizabeth?' he asked as he emerged.

'Sam let Betty down. He was drunk for days with his so-called mates.'

'*Liebchen* . . .' he said and, his eyes quizzical, he approached her slowly. All she wanted to do was fall into his arms, but she waited until finally he put his arms around her, and she held him as hard as she could.

'Why are men such babies?'

'That . . . I do not know the answer to.'

She looked up at him and he was smiling, and she couldn't help but laugh.

'Karl . . . I need you just to be with me, for now. Is that all right?'

He nodded, still smiling, as if at something he accepted but did not quite believe. They went to bed, but she did not respond to his caresses.

'*Liebling*, your mind is elsewhere.'

She smiled at that and, to give him his due, he saw the irony and smiled too. She touched his face. He closed his eyes in agreement and soon they fell asleep in each other's arms. It was evening when they woke in the dim light of the curtained room.

He must have thought she was still asleep because he slipped carefully out of bed, and again she marvelled how such a big man could be so graceful and light on his feet. She turned and spread her body luxuriously across the bed. She felt so much better. All she had needed was some sleep and a trusted friend beside her. A body needed reassurance once in a while. She knew she ought to get up. Karl would be hungry. She pulled back the bedclothes and looked idly at her body. She felt so lazy, and it was lovely, and having indulged herself for a little while, she stood out of bed. But this lazy feeling was very nice, so she didn't bother dressing, and maybe it would be nice to be with Karl like that, like she used to, in just a dressing gown. She could hear him beating eggs, the devil. That was her job. She licked her lips and lit a cigarette, going to the kitchen as she dragged on it, but slowed to a halt outside the door as she heard Karl's troubled voice.

'. . . I didn't mean to hurt you, Hugh.'

She felt as if she had been hit, and turned on her heel to her room. She dragged on her cigarette again and looked intensely out the window before returning. He was still babbling on.

She felt numb and old. Hugh looked past Karl at her and Karl turned. She stared at Hugh.

'What are you doing here? I thought I threw you out.' She took another deep drag on her cigarette and held it as long as she could. Hugh went to speak, but then continued beating, before looking up again with those cow's eyes.

'I'm sorry,' he said.

'Just look at the state of you.'

She turned and left them, blowing the smoke into the twilight in the hall. Taking clothes from her room, she went to the bathroom and, quenching the cigarette under the tap, she threw off her gown, washed herself at the sink, and dressed. Staring into the mirror, she made grotesque faces, trying to work herself to a pitch of concentration.

This is getting out of hand, she thought. I've got to get it under control. She brushed her hair hard. It badly needed a cut.

Right, she thought. Here goes. She took a deep breath, but she was still very nervous, so she took another, and nodded several times to bolster her resolve, and went downstairs. She swept into the kitchen and ignored both of them.

'I'll make us a decent meal,' she said. She turned on the radio and went to work, but then suddenly it was too much, and her body shook as she wept. Hugh came back after a wash, but nothing was said. How could they just sit there like that?

They ate in silence.

'I will leave tomorrow,' Karl said, as she cleared away the dishes.

'You're not leaving, Karl,' Elizabeth said.

'Then I'll leave,' Hugh said.

'No one is leaving,' she said.

*

At lunch-break the next day, Betty sat with her.

'Thanks for yesterday, Liz,' she said.

'Yesterday?' For a moment, Elizabeth had forgotten about the café. 'Oh yes. We should go there more often, Betty, you and me.'

'And Millie.'

'And Millie.'

'I'm over him, Liz.'

They looked sadly at each other, and burst out laughing, laughing and half crying.

'Oh, what right fools we are,' Elizabeth said when she had finished.

'Oh,' sighed Betty, wiping her eyes with a hanky, 'a girl needs a laugh.'

'You're over him, then?'

They spluttered into laughter again.

Things were strained between them for a few days, but she kept neutral between Hugh and Karl, and gradually the atmosphere in the house relaxed. And as for her sisterly worry over Sam, well, he was a lost cause, so she gave up on him. It was Millie who needed support, and they were getting on well. Betty and Millie had gone to the pictures a few times, all the way to Leicester Square, and it had done Millie a lot of good.

The following Sunday, Millie greeted her with a smile.

'What has you in such good humour, Millie?'

'Sam,' Millie beamed.

'Sam?

Millie leaned in towards her as if to tell her a secret. She was so happy she could hardly bring herself to speak.

'He brought Betty to the pictures last night.'

'What?'

'And he didn't come back!'

'Millie . . .' She hardly dared to smile. 'Millie, do you expect me to think what you're thinking?'

'Wedding bells, Beth,' Millie giggled.

'Are you sure he didn't skip off afterwards with his mates?'

Millie's smile vanished.

'No . . . No, Beth. He's learned his lesson.'

'Did you give him a roasting, then?' Elizabeth asked, only half believing her. Millie hesitated for a moment.

'Not half.'

Elizabeth threw back her head and screamed in laughter, and Millie giggled uncontrollably, falling back onto the sofa, holding her stomach.

Elizabeth couldn't wait to tell Karl. Hugh would be out, he went out on Sunday afternoons. It was Karl she wanted to tell. To her relief he was in the kitchen, listening to the radio.

'Guess what?' she demanded, forgetting herself and holding both his hands.

'What?'

'Sammy and Betty Hindley went to the pictures last night.'

'Is that significant?'

She laughed and danced away from him.

'You can bet your bottom drawers it is! Oh!' She gripped the back of a chair. 'You don't know how I've waited for this, what a lot off my mind it is. At long last. Good old Betty, she'll do the trick.'

'I see.'

'Yes, Karl,' she laughed. 'I can see you see.'

And he bowed. Well blow me down. The gent bowed. The unexpectedness of it touched her, but she recovered quickly.

'Well! Dinner! What do you say?'

'I would say "dinner",' he smiled, and she turned away to prepare the meal, happy as she'd ever been.

The following evening, on her way home from work, she was walking under the railway bridge when she spotted Hugh waiting for her.

'Would you like a sweet?' he asked.

She looked at the bag, amused. Oh dear. Oh dearie me.

'Thank you,' she said. 'I don't know when I last saw a sweet.'

She rolled the sweet around in her mouth, grinning. He had one too, and they walked on home together, easy and happy.

Such a small thing achieved so much. The weather broke, and being cooped up in the house made her nervous, but at least she had made her peace with the two men. Then the weather picked up again, and they sat in the yard like contented pensioners

It became unbearably hot, and as she and Karl had done in previous years, the three of them began to make trips to Southend. Karl seemed to forget himself in the wholesome air, especially after a long swim out to sea. But they stopped going to Southend. The damned place was infested with EastEnders gorging themselves on eels. The eels turned her stomach.

Hugh said he only ever saw her people eat fish and chips, washed back with stout, like himself and Karl – and herself for that matter. She adored the stout now, although it had always been too sour for her before. He teased her. How she managed to look down on her own amused him.

She began to notice that Hugh was looking at her like – what did they say in the pictures? – he was giving her *smoulder-ing* looks. Instead of returning his gaze, she would look nervously at Karl, who seemed oblivious. At night she lay in bed, wondering, shaken that he should be like this, and frightened by what she could no longer control.

She supposed it was inevitable when she found Hugh waiting for her in the hall, and she stopped dead and returned his stare.

'Elizabeth.' There was a knot in his throat. 'I can't stand it any more.' He pulled her blouse out of her skirt and over her breasts and squeezed them, closing his eyes in relief. She was relieved too. Something had happened at last, and he had made it happen, but gently she took his hands away and replaced her blouse, without taking her eyes off him. He faced her, and she smiled.

'Will you come to the pictures with me?' he asked, in a quite dignified way, considering.

Of course she would, but she stopped to consider all the same.

'I'll have to ask Karl if he minds, if that's all right with you.'

'Oh.' He looked away, but rallied. 'Yes.' He rubbed his hand across his face. 'Surely.'

'Thanks,' she said, and touched him lightly on the cheek. He was happy with that, and went upstairs.

In the dusk of the kitchen she cleared her throat, and then again, and then coughed. My God, she thought – the loss of control aside – he had matured a lot in a short time. There was little of the gawkish boy left in him. And for that she could take credit. She drank a glass of water, and looked out the window at Karl.

Why did he make her feel so sad? If she only touched him, his face lit up, and now she wondered if this would set him back again. Well, he was a grown man, and there was no cure for it. Damn it, he'd be fine. What was she worrying about? Funny how he had asked her out only once in a blue moon, in all their time. Of course, they worked so hard, they had always been too tired, anyway. She wasn't tired now, though. She studied his head. He seemed so much at peace, as if he had led a beautiful life.

She went outside, full of affection for him, put her arms around his neck from behind, and kissed the top of his head.

'How are you?' she asked.

'Good. And you?'

She tugged at his hair, pulling it in a circle.

'Hugh has asked me to the pictures. Do you mind?' She knew he wouldn't. She just knew, but she wanted to consider him, or something. Maybe she just wanted him to be part of what was happening. Without turning, he took her hand in his.

'No. I do not mind.'

'Are you sure?' Doubt had ambushed her again. He turned and smiled.

'Yes, I am sure.'

'It doesn't mean anything,' she whispered, relaxing again and trailing her forefinger down his nose.

She turned to go, delighted, but a queer feeling made her look up and, startled, she saw Hugh at his window looking down at them. He waved, slowly, and she didn't know whether to be angry or moved. She went to his room, knocked and opened his door before he could reply.

'Well? What are we going to?'

'*No Sad Songs for Me,*' he said evenly.

'Oh? You don't say.' She smiled. 'I've heard about that. When?'

'Tonight.'

'Well then . . .' she said and, hesitating a moment, she closed the door after her, and felt amazed.

It was a fine evening, but when they came out of the tube on the way back from the cinema, it was raining. They walked across Holloway Road, but then, suddenly it came down in a torrent.

'I don't believe this,' Elizabeth shouted. He took her hand and they ran for the shelter of a plane tree, but it was too late. They were drenched through their light clothing.

'Fuck it,' she said, out of breath. He laughed.

'What are you laughing at?' she demanded, and then she couldn't help herself, she laughed too. 'Well,' she said, 'if you think I'm what's-her-name, and I'm going to ask you not to cry for me when I get fucking pneumonia and kick the bucket, then you've another think coming.'

He roared laughing at that, as she had never imagined he could, and then he startled her by running onto the road, oblivious to the hissing traffic, and kicking at the stream of water flowing into the drains.

'You're mad,' she whispered, and then she shouted it. 'You're mad!'

'What?'

'I said you're *mad.*'

He jumped back onto the pavement and fell on one knee, taking her hand.

'I'm mad with love for you,' he said dramatically. 'Don't die on me, please.'

She tried to laugh.

'That film . . . has gone to your head.'

She pulled him up and, holding hands, they walked at an easy pace through the rain. Under the bridge, she turned to him and held him.

'It was tragic, really,' she mumbled into his breast.

'Yes,' he said. 'I had a lump in my throat the whole time.'

'Get away. You're taking the mickey.' But he wasn't. Sometimes it was hard to know what made a person tick.

Thankfully, Karl was playing his music as she eased in the front door. She ticked off her days in her head, looked at Hugh and then brought him by the hand into her room. She lit the gas fire which hadn't been lit for months, and it spluttered for a time before the elements started to glow.

'You should take off those clothes before you catch your death,' she said, pretending to nurse the fire.

'And what about you?' he asked. She straightened.

'Oh, I'd better do the same.'

They looked at each other as they undressed, as if afraid that the other wouldn't undress completely. As she had more to take off, he waited while she unclipped her stockings. As she bent down to slip them off, she saw that he had a bulge. Poor duck. She unfastened her corset, her heart beating uncomfortably, and turned away as she stepped out of her pants to get a towel from a drawer. When she turned he was standing there with it sticking up.

'Here, sit down on the bed', she said quietly, 'and I'll dry your hair.'

She dried his shoulders and then, vigorously, his hair, her heart skipping away on its own business. She stopped and turned his face towards her, and grinned, but her grin vanished when she saw his eyes were closed, as if his thoughts were in another place. She could see too, that he was soft. She turned his head again and continued until her hands had tired.

'There now,' she said, smoothing down his hair. 'That should do the trick.'

Still looking dreamy, he took the towel from her and, sitting her down in his place, dried her in turn. She gave herself up to her hair being tugged and pushed every way, though it hurt a little and she vaguely feared that he might pull tufts of it out, and she watched her breasts move from side to side, felt herself moist.

Then he finished, and handed her the towel. She hesitated, the towel in her hand, before she hung it on the back of the chair and faced him.

He took her hand.

'I wish it was just you,' she whispered, wondering even as she said it, if that was so.

'Yes,' he said as quiet as you like.

She got into bed without looking at him again and, having hesitated, he followed her.

'Your hair's not really dry,' he said, brushing it away from her face with his hand. 'Maybe you shouldn't fall asleep with it damp.'

She caressed his cheek, ready. Ready to die.

'I don't intend to.'

*

She had never felt so abandoned. On the bus the next morning she thought of the new machine at the factory, the way it vibrated and hummed. Umm ... *something* like that, she thought, looking hard out the window of the top deck in an effort not to smile in a public place at such unmentionable thoughts. But once in the factory, jostling among the women clocking in, she knew it had been madness.

She made him wear a condom after that. He didn't like using them because, she supposed, he was Catholic, and he was embarrassed about buying them at the barber's, but he did all the same, and that was a good sign.

Though Hugh protested, as he liked watching the heavy traffic of ships, their next trip was to Brighton. It was pleasant: the long pier, the large pools of water stranded when the tide went out and the shellfish in these which the children tormented. One pool was so deep that youths, like fish themselves, swam across it, their arms flashing in the water, showing off for all they were worth.

She missed her period and had had to run to the toilets at work to get sick. She couldn't believe it. Her first thought had been to calculate how long she could work.

She looked on Hugh differently once she realized what was happening. He seemed more worthy of respect, seemed older.

It was almost October by now but still warm, so she convinced them to pack a picnic and they scarpered to Brighton. As Karl strolled by the tideline, Elizabeth cleared her throat and told Hugh to keep his eyes off a group of young, skittish women who were playing with a beach ball and to listen to her. She had been to the doctor.

'I'm listening,' he grinned, his eyes lazing on the shapely figures.

'No you're not.'

'I am, honestly.'

'Hugh, turn round, look at me and listen to me.'

'There's no need to be jealous,' he said, turning lazily, then abruptly sobered by her intense seriousness. 'Well? What's wrong, Elizabeth?' He sat up, mollifying her by his sudden, complete attention.

'I'm going to have your son.'

'Be the holy fly . . .' he murmured.

'What did you say?' God, but he could be so irritating sometimes.

'I said . . .' As happiness got the better of his shock, he leaned his face close to hers, but before he could kiss her, out popped two big tears.

'Oh no,' Elizabeth groaned, 'not here, don't make a show of us.'

He caught his breath and controlled himself.

'I love you,' he said.

'That's better,' she smiled. 'I love you too.' She drew her finger down his nose. 'Now I'll have three babies to look after.'

She sighed and rolled away from him onto her stomach and into herself.

She spent most of the journey home on the train feeling like death warmed up, but she pretended she had an upset stomach.

'What you need is a few eels,' he joked, but he didn't try that one again after the look she gave him.

She felt better after a cup of tea when they got home. He had his hand on hers, sitting across the table after Karl had gone upstairs. The lamp was on, but the light was soft and easy, and she could see that he was perplexed. Well, so was she. There was no way around it now, their lives had joined for better or worse, and yet they knew so little about each other. There had to be more to him than just sex, and she couldn't help herself, she wanted to know.

She asked him about his past again. He was uneasy suddenly, but she persisted. His mother was seven years dead and his father thought he was cracked.

He looked cracked, just now, as she had never seen him. She averted her eyes, looking at the table, anywhere so as not to look at his face if it was like that. To see Hugh like that when she thought of her child made her cold all over.

'I see,' she said then.

He asked her about her family. Maybe it was natural to talk about their parents now they were going to be parents themselves, but now she too was upset.

'I'd rather not talk about it, Hugh.'

'All right.'

'My father died of consumption,' she said. 'That fucking basement . . .'

'That was before the war, was it?'

'Yes, before the war . . . I suppose he was lucky. Look, Hugh . . .' She was crying. He took her hand again, and she looked into his face, a few moments ago so hard, now so full of compassion. 'One minute she was waiting for a bus, the next she was blown to bits. There was blood flowing down the street . . .'

He came around the table to her and hauled her into his arms.

'It was terrible,' she whispered. He rocked her in his arms, and she recovered. She blew her nose. 'I'm all right. Here,' she said, getting money out of her purse, 'fetch me cigarettes from Rosenberg's, will you?'

When he was gone, she took down her sewing, but after a few stitches, she looked vacantly out the window. 'I loved you, you stubborn old cow,' she whispered. 'And you too, Dad.' She thought of them in her dream, the night Hugh had come home drunk. She had thought about that dream a lot. They were so young and happy, and the world was in its proper place. It wasn't like her to be like this, letting someone see her cry. But maybe it was different with Hugh. He was the father of her child, after all. She felt better and, blotting out the past, she returned to her sewing.

She looked up as she heard Karl come downstairs, then put her sewing to one side as he came in and smiled, but her smile disappeared fast when she realized he wasn't well.

'Are you all right, Karl?'

'I'm leaving.'

Oh no, she thought. Oh no. She tried to calm things but this time she knew she was out of her depth. He was mumbling nonsense, confused with a gratitude she felt she did not deserve. She tried reason but it was useless. This was what she had dreaded, what she'd denied she dreaded for a long time.

'It's not an idea,' he said, turning to look into her eyes.

Her heart jumped and she felt her strength drain away. His face was like wax, with two blue diamonds for eyes. Only the consciousness of her body and its power to calm him kept her going. She could see he was going into one of those trances and knew she had to act quickly or she would lose him for hours and she would suffer his depression for days. This was the worst she had seen.

'Come on . . .' she whispered, taking his hand.

Karl followed but his eyes were on something or someone in the distance. She closed the door and lay him on the bed and loosened his clothes. It wasn't easy. His body was heavy and stiff. She lay across him, kissing his head, his brow, his face, his lips, but still those blue diamonds did not see her, but stayed fixed on the ceiling.

Sweat had seeped through his pores, sitting like a scum on his deathly skin. Desperate, she abandoned his unresponsive mouth, tore open his shirt and kissed and caressed his body, each fold of flesh, but there was no response and even when she pulled open his trousers his privates withdrew as she lapped at them, sobbing in terror and pity.

'O Karl, come back to me, come back to me.'

On her knees beside him she looked up, her labour useless and defeated, and screamed.

PART TWO

Eight

KARL

October 1950–February 1951

Karl woke in a hospital bed in daylight. A wardsmaid was handing dinner to an old man, but otherwise the ward was empty. A dark-skinned woman prodded him and offered him a plate. He looked at the dish with its aluminium cover. She removed the cover, but he kept staring and she went away.

When he woke again, it was night, and there were many more in the ward, but most were asleep. A male nurse, illuminated by a lamp, sat in his station. Karl drifted into sleep again.

In the morning he was woken by a male nurse, handed a dressing gown and told to get up. He obeyed and was brought to a large bathroom with white tiles. The nurse beckoned towards the toilet, and Karl used it. When he came out he was given a razor, and he shaved in a line with several other men. The razors were collected as each finished, and they showered together under the eye of the nurse, who then led them to the refectory.

Karl was hungry and he ate the bad porridge served to him by the same dark woman who had offered him dinner. One man was groaning, even as he rapidly chewed, but the rest ate in blank silence. When he looked up he saw that the man opposite him was crying. When they had finished, a nurse led them back to the ward.

There was something he could not recall, but he made no effort to remember. He did not care. He registered that a man was shouting, but not his words. The shouting could have been in the ward, or in his head, but again, he did not care. He lay back, wanting nothing except sleep.

A doctor and a retinue of students accompanied by a nurse came to his bed and talked about him.

'Mr Bruckner? Mr Bruckner? Mr Bruckner, I'm Dr Greene.' The doctor leaned forward and examined Karl's eyes, opening an eyelid further with his thumb. 'You've got a bad case of depression, old chap. We're going to bring you down for some electrotherapy,' he said in a loud voice, but there was no response from Karl, who was, at this stimulus, wondering how he had come to be here, and why he kept thinking about a high black wall.

He slept for twelve hours. When he woke, the ward was empty. The wardsmaid he recognized passed through, pushing her mobile oven, and stopped to look at him.

'No dinner for you today, Mr Bruckner.'

He was hungry, but it didn't matter. He was given tablets which made him feel drowsy again. An urge brought him to the toilet. Two nurses were waiting for him when he had finished, one with towels, and this one asked him to shower. He obeyed, they gave him a gown, and asked him to come with them.

Dr Greene and others were waiting beside a table with straps and a console.

'Ah, Mr Bruckner,' said Dr Greene, turning to greet him. 'All set? If you'll just lie down here.'

Karl's interest in machines flickered when he saw the dials and switches, and he looked at them for several seconds before obeying Dr Greene.

'That's fine. Now we're just going to give you an injection to relax you.'

He felt the needle and the drug enter his vein and a pleasant feeling spread through him.

'Mr Bruckner? Can you hear me? We're just going to strap you in to make you secure.' They put something in his mouth, and the straps were the last thing he felt, but he still heard Dr Greene's voice.

'Resistance reading? Right. Voltage and shock duration?

Roger. Safety key. Button guard.' And then all was a white oblivion.

When he woke, his body was trembling and his mind was blindingly bright. He wanted to get up and run. He went to get out of bed, but a male nurse was blocking his way.

'Are you all right, sir?' he asked.

'I've never been more all right in my life.'

'Do you remember who you are?'

'Who I am?'

'Yes.'

Karl was baffled. He did not know who he was.

'Don't be alarmed. You've had electrotherapy and your memory will be affected for a while. Your name is Karl Bruckner, you are a German national and this is a hospital in England. Remember, your name is Karl.'

'Karl . . .'

'Yes. Now don't worry, Mr Bruckner. Your memory will return before too long. If you're feeling a bit shaky, take some deep breaths. All right? That's it. That's it. Would you like to come for a walk in the grounds? Get rid of some of that new energy you have.'

The nurse brought Karl into the grounds. There were banks of flowers, and mature trees, and benches beneath some of the trees. The nurse talked about himself, about Ireland and what it was like at this time of year. Karl listened to the young man with intensity.

'I want to run,' he said, aware of a powerful urge, and cutting across the nurse's description of a dance.

'Ah, I don't think that's such a good idea, Mr Bruckner.'

'Why not?'

'Because I might not be able to keep up with you. Hey!'

Karl broke into a wonderful, liberating run. The tree branches flashed above him, the flower beds passed in a blur. He ran along the high brick wall of the hospital, pushing himself faster and faster, the nurse in pursuit, until his lungs could take no more, and he fell in a heap, gasping and laughing. The nurse caught up with him, and stood, hands on his knees, gasping too.

'Jesus, Bruckner,' he panted, 'you'll cost me my job.'

Karl looked up at him and smiled happily.

'What is your name?'

'Jimmy Fahey,' he said, recovering, 'and my middle name is *stupid* for trusting *you*,' he added. But he was grinning, and Karl was delighted.

They returned to the ward, and Jimmy went to the nurses' station and wrote something. Karl went to the window and looked down on the grounds, recreating his magnificent run, which he knew he would always remember. Karl. His name was Karl.

He woke in the middle of the night to snores and weeping. He had been dreaming about a great fire through which he had walked untouched. A nurse was reading in his station, unmoved by the sorrow at the end of the ward. Then the weeping stopped, leaving only snores of different pitches and tone. Karl followed them, their rise and fall creating a picture of the sea.

The next day he remembered that he was Karl Bruckner, and that his partner in life was Elizabeth Frampton, but it was only after the doctor had gone that he recalled why he had come here. At the thought of Elizabeth's mother's fate, he wept quietly. The doctor had prescribed new medication and once more he took to sleeping for most of the day.

After another electric shock, and a repeat of the consequences, Dr Greene brought him to his office.

'Ah, there you are, Mr Bruckner.'

The nurse who had escorted him closed the door behind her.

'How are you feeling?'

'Tired.'

'Miss Frampton has told me a lot about you.'

'Elizabeth.'

'I beg your pardon.'

'Her name is Elizabeth.'

'Elizabeth. Are you on intimate terms?'

'Yes.'

'I see. Well, she told me that you are very fond of music. Specifically Mahler, I think. Is that so?'

'Yes.'

'I took the liberty of asking ... Elizabeth ... to bring in your records. I hope you don't mind.' When Karl didn't answer,

Dr Greene cleared his throat and opened a record player on a sideboard. Beside it were Karl's Mahler 78s, the maroon titles showing through the buff covers. 'This is my machine – one of those cheap modern thingumajigs, but it can play different records in succession. See? We can stack them up on this thingy here. I believe you are the proud owner of a magnificent horned beast.'

'Elizabeth bought it for me in the market.'

'Wonderful. Wonderful. Let's see. What do we have here. Do you have a favourite?'

'Perhaps the Adagio, Fifth Symphony.'

'Rrright.'

They sat and listened to it, and remained quiet after the arm clicked off.

'It's very beautiful,' Dr Greene said. He hesitated. 'I was in Germany during the war, you know. Medical whatever. Having you in here has brought it all back to me, actually,' he mused, patting his breast pocket and retrieving a piece of wrinkled paper. 'I ah . . .' he faltered, reading it, 'I was friendly with a German nurse and she taught me this poem. Would you like to read it?'

He passed the sheet to Karl.

'It's Goethe.'

'Yes. Good old Wolfgang.'

'You wish me to read it aloud?'

'I'd be jolly grateful if you did.'

' "Wanderers Nachlied II",' Karl read.

'*Über allen Gipfeln*
Is ruh.
In allen Wipfeln
Spürest du
Kann einen Hauch;
Die Vögelein schweigen im Walde.
Warte nur, balde
Ruhest du auch.'

'Lovely. Between you and me, old boy, that poem brings back happy memories.'

'There is another *Nachlied*?'

'So there is. But as I recall, I didn't care for the other one as much, so she wrote this one down for me. Nice handwriting, isn't it?'

'Yes.'

'But I can't understand a word of it now. You'd do me an enormous favour by translating it.'

' "Wanderer's Nightsong",' he began again, simply.

> 'Over the hilltops
> It is quiet.
> In all the treetops
> You hear
> Hardly a breath;
> The birds are asleep in the woods.
> Wait a while; soon
> You too shall rest.'

'Ah,' said Dr Greene appreciatively. 'Not quite as good as the original – no offence to your translation – but wonderful nonetheless. Would you like to copy it?' He offered a pen and paper and Karl copied it.

'Have you had any dreams that you can remember, Mr Bruckner?' he asked while Karl was still writing. Karl finished before answering.

'Yes. Two.'

'Would you . . . care to elaborate?'

'One is of a giant black wall. It is just there. Nothing more. In the other, I am walking through a great fire in a city, but I am not touched by the flames.'

'And is that city Hamburg?'

'I think it is.'

'That's enough for today.' The doctor smiled at him and, as Karl left, he was making notes.

When he returned to the ward, Karl was told he had a visitor. The nurse let him out of the locked ward, and then through another locked door. He walked down the long corridor, aware of the smell of polish, through several double doors, hoping it was Elizabeth, and when he saw her waiting on one of the benches along the wall, he immediately felt strong and happy. As he approached her he saw that she was uncertain, so his smile was hesitant. After all, she had a right to be careful.

'Hello, Karl.'

'Hello, Elizabeth.'

'It's like a prison in here – high walls and locked doors and what have you.'

'That's to keep us lunatics inside.'

'You're no more a lunatic than I am, Karl,' she said, and they both relaxed a little. 'How are you?'

'The doctor played my Mahler records—'

'I hope you didn't mind me—'

'Not at all. It was wonder—'

'Are you sure?'

'Yes, I am sure – and look, he gave me a poem in German.' He showed it to her, then translated.

'That's very nice, Karl.' Her voice was strained and her mind elsewhere. 'Here. I got you some apples. We went especially to Soho. And the Danish pastries you like.'

'Thank you.'

'Hugh wouldn't come. He's frightened of hospitals. But he sent you his best.'

'Good. Come, keep those in your bag for the moment and let us walk in the grounds.'

He took her hand and they walked together down the steps. He told her everything that he could recall, laughing when he told of how he had escaped his nurse.

'Hugh is very upset,' she said, as she was leaving. 'He worries about you. We miss you. You will come home soon, won't you?'

He nodded, but he was drinking in her presence and hardly aware of what she said. He walked back to the ward but the doors were locked so he went into the grounds again and sat on a bench beneath a tree. The branches were bare and he followed the line of each one, absorbed, until a nurse came and brought him back to the ward.

A few weeks later, during a lull in the damp weather, they let him back into the garden again. Jimmy Fahey was never far away, but Karl deliberately ignored this. His emotions had returned with an intensity which sharpened his thought. The ramblings in his head were too simple. It was the same conversation over and over. The same recriminations. The same inability to rise beyond them.

His carvings did not accuse. They stared blindly into nothingness, from nothing. They bore an echoic resemblance to their subjects, it was true, the resemblance he wanted, and which he vaguely knew avoided the reality of his past.

So many weeks here. Or was it months? Months. His family had become so real again that nothing could remove them. He felt he knew them in such a way, they were not just images in his mind but they walked about the room with him, arguing. He even noticed how his father's jaw twitched before he began to speak. He had notched the side of his father's lip with his chisel to emphasize this. He enjoyed these arguments, as for the most part they were about trivial matters like the name of the schoolmistress, their favourite, in Oranienstraße. Jurgen, his brother, argued that she was tall with blonde hair, but Karl contended that she was small, dark and fat. Jurgen was attracted to tall blondes, Karl reminded him, ever since he was a small boy at the circus. There had been a blonde trapeze artist. Karl, with the superior memory of his elder years, he said, remembered her well, and Jurgen's infatuation too. She had not been very tall, it was just that she seemed enormous beside their tiny mother, and so in Jurgen's three-year-old eyes, she was a giantess. He looked up to her as she danced elegantly around the ring after her act, before suddenly stopping in front of Jurgen, gazing, it seemed to him, into his eyes. He was dazzled.

'By her sequins,' Mama rejoined gruffly. 'Immodest whore, corrupting little boys.'

Even Papa guffawed, even Gertrud, but not Mama. She meant it.

'That circus was in Charlottenburg,' Gertrud said. 'We took the tram. I remember it well.'

'I'm the only one who remembers both,' Karl said.

'What do you mean, the only one?' Mama interrupted. 'Upstart.'

'Of the children, I mean, Mama,' he said, head bowed. 'Of course you remember more than I do.'

'Why do people always think that older memories are the sharpest, those that remember most?' Jurgen complained. 'It's just not true – I can remember more than you, Karl, from when I was about eight. How much do you remember from then?'

'Everything!' It was bravado. In reality he remembered very little, which Jurgen knew well. But Jurgen didn't press his advantage. Papa reached for his pipe, but a glance from Mama reminded him of his bad chest. He scratched his bald head. She lapsed into brooding on the old days. There was a faint trace of a smile. Perhaps the memory preceded her marriage. She had married beneath her station, a fatal mistake, but her father had no sons and had faith in his manager's ability. So much for the judgement of men. Her head lolled pleasantly as the family chattered around her. Her beautiful foolish father. Foolish but beautiful. She had not known he was foolish until she was a grown woman with children, but she had always seen his beauty. In fairness to Frederick, how could a woman ever be satisfied with a man, having loved a god? In her girlhood he could do everything, be everyone, be everywhere. Night and day, asleep and awake.

'That circus whore was a torture mistress in a camp,' she said out of the blue.

'What? How can you know that, Mama?' Gertrud was half contemptuous. Jurgen and Karl were dumbfounded.

'Yes, yes, Mama has always maintained that such was so.' Papa sucked his invisible pipe.

'How would you know,' Mama snapped. 'What would you know of such things?'

He shrugged, sucked a cavity in a back tooth. He had sheltered the family of a Jewish friend, whom he could not save. It had not been forgotten.

Papa beaten near to death in an alley by thugs who could have been his grandsons. Gertrud taken by the Gestapo, tortured, raped. They threw her in a canal when they had done with her, left her for dead. Jurgen survived, to die on the Russian front. Mama tried to starve herself. And then they . . .

Only Karl escaped. He had left them to die.

'You should remember,' Mama said, trying to make Gertrud look at her by the force of her stare. 'Don't you remember her?' In a low voice so the men would not hear well, but would hear nonetheless. 'Don't you remember her making you spread your legs, making sure you were clean for her filthy beasts, her monsters?'

'Don't, Mama, don't . . .' Papa said, weeping silently.

'I'm not a whore, Mama.' Gertrud's eyes were closed. 'I fought them, I fought them to my last breath.'

Inside his grief, Papa smiled to himself in gratitude.

'Better you hadn't, daughter. It made them want you all the more. Better you hadn't.' Mama was losing concentration, losing her rage, her contempt.

'She fought,' Papa said. 'She fought like a true woman. She was true to nature. A sin against nature to couple with a monster. She was true to nature.'

Mama recovered.

Jimmy touched him on the arm.

'It's getting dark, Mr Bruckner.'

Karl allowed himself to be led back, but he was staring ahead, and Jimmy had to lead him like a blind man.

'There's some nice spam for tea this evening, Mr Bruckner,' Jimmy laughed. 'That's your favourite, isn't it?'

'That is so,' Karl said.

Karl waited until he was alone before returning to that twilit argument.

'Then we are all beasts,' he mumbled, and he turned away. 'I am a beast, and you, Mama, are a beast.'

'I am a victim!' She shrieked this out. Papa reprimanded him, using such language after all they had suffered. But Gertrud looked at him as if to say, *Du hast Recht, mein Bruder.* You have felt what I have seen. He caught her glance and felt in some way justified, and yet this was too simple.

He tore himself away from them. The only consequence of his ill thought out morality was that he communed with ghosts in a darkened room, ghosts whom he used as a ventriloquist will use a doll.

His conclusions had repeated themselves for months now. If he could overcome his doubt, he would find strength enough to return to the world. Suddenly he realized it depended on a decision. He could decide to doubt or believe.

*

That night he woke again to the sound of weeping and snoring. He sat up and thought of Elizabeth, of her mother and, as he stared into the shadows, he felt himself float out of the ward into a much deeper darkness, where the air was chilled. As this darkness gave way to dawn he found himself looking into the cold eyes of a seagull. When he looked down all he could see was the dull grey of water, its waves rising and falling. There was something unusual on the horizon and he watched it slowly take shape. There were three tall-masted ships, their white sails full, towing a metropolis, and one by one he recognized the buildings and monuments. It was London, being towed across what he now realized was the North Sea, the London of the late 1930s, untouched by war.

On the opposite horizon, as he had half expected, another flotilla of three masted ships was towing a second city towards London. He journeyed ahead and long before he had reached it knew that it was Hamburg, prior to the war. There it was, the roller coaster of the Hamburger Elbbrüke, with its castellated towers; the Rathaus and the Hauptbahnhof, the steam rising from the old engines as if nothing would ever change.

And yes, there they were, the early morning crowd at the Messberg market. He was full of love for them, as they bought and sold their fruits and vegetables, absorbed in the ordinary. And there again, the Jungfernsteig, with the Alster steamer coming into dock, people strolling along the promenade, a flag billowing above the turret of the Alster Pavilion.

The two cities sailed towards each other all day. Karl was hungry and thirsty, but he could do no other than endure. To sustain him, he let the second half of the Eighth Symphony, the final scene from Faust, flow through his head. It grew and grew until it spilled out of his skull and poured into the sky above the North Sea.

It was late afternoon when the German tall ships sailed up the Thames, and the English tall ships sailed up the Elbe until they locked together as one.

Jimmy woke him.

'Mr Bruckner, time to get up. Washey washies. Brekkie brekkies.'

'Eh?'

'Race you?'

'Oh yes,' Karl smiled. His outstretched arms ached badly, and he realized that he had been flying for most of the night.

Elizabeth came again, and he wanted to tell her about his journey above the North Sea, but he was afraid it would upset her. He wasn't mad, of that he was sure, but he had no doubt it had actually happened, not in the material, logical world, but in that realm of existence where reality was ordered and repaired.

'... *balde* ... *Ruhest du auch*,' he repeated to himself. Yes. Soon you too will rest. But there was another journey to be undertaken before he could rest. It would lead him to the spirit of his family. He thought about this on his daily walk. He knew that to be allowed his walk like this was a privilege, as many never left the ward unless in supervised groups.

He did not tell Dr Greene about his journey. The doctor had asked him about dreams, but this was a journey, not a dream. Instead they talked a lot about his childhood, at first in Erxleben and Berlin, and then in Hamburg. Karl remembered it well, but the faces of his family were blank.

And then, quite suddenly, it was Christmas. The nurses decorated the ward, and made them all wear hats, which made them look truly mad. They had special meals all day and some of the nurses smelt of brandy. The Romanian wardsmaid was tipsy and when she thought no one was looking, she kissed him, forcing her tongue into his passive mouth.

'What is your name?' he asked as he burned away, embarrassed.

'Marta,' she said without looking back.

Marta.

As it grew dark, a group of nurses sang carols.

Where had the months gone, and where was Elizabeth?

One afternoon in the New Year, he was sitting under his favourite tree when Hugh came down the steps towards him, looking apprehensive. Of course he was apprehensive. Karl remembered that he was afraid of hospitals, so to relax him, he smiled and offered his hand, which Hugh shook.

'Sit down, Hugh, it's good to see you.'

'How are you at all, Karl?'

'I'm good, Hugh. Things got a little too much for me, that's all.'

'Should we go inside?' Hugh asked, looking up. 'It's going to rain.'

'It won't rain just yet.' Karl looked up too, but into the naked branches of the tree. 'Do you know the legend about this tree?'

'A legend? I don't. What tree is it anyway?'

'It's a white poplar. Hercules won a battle, the story goes, and on the mountain there was a grove of these trees, and he made a garland of its leaves to celebrate his victory. Soon after, for what reason I forget, he descended into the place of tears and gloom, the underworld. When he came back to this world, the top of his garland was darkened by the smoke of hell, but underneath was stained white by his sweat.'

'That's a good story.'

'If it were not autumn, I could make you a garland.'

Hugh laughed.

'Actually it's winter, Karl.'

'Is it? There are many fine trees here. Would you like a tour?'

'Are you sure it's not going to rain?'

'It will not rain. Not until we are ready.'

'Right, so.'

They walked among the trees and shrubs, Karl educating Hugh about them.

'I heard a story once,' said Hugh, 'that long ago in Ireland, the names of the trees were the same as the letters of the alphabet.'

Karl stopped and looked at Hugh in surprise.

'Hugh, you have astonished me again.'

It started to rain lightly and they walked back to the hospital.

'How is Elizabeth?' Karl asked him in the hall.

'She's grand. I suppose she told you I was frightened out of my wits about coming here?'

Karl smiled, shaking his hand.

'When are you going to marry her?'

'Ah now!' Hugh exclaimed, and he shuffled from foot to foot. Then he left.

*

'Will we play some music?' Dr Greene asked him at their next session.

'The Eighth,' Karl said emphatically.

'Is it here? Yes, it's here.'

'The final scene from Faust. They should be all together.'

'The ah . . .' said the doctor, examining the labels, 'the final scene from Faust. Here we are.' He looked at Karl before putting on a batch of records. Midway through, as the choir began to sing, Karl, his eyes closed, began.

'So much destruction . . . the bricks piled high in the street. So high . . .'

'Is this Hamburg?' came a soft voice. 'Hamburg during the war?'

'This *was* . . . Hamburg.'

'Go on. If you can.'

'Did you know that bricks fall intact after a bomb? I've seen it in London, you know. You can take a brick from a bombed building, tap the brick with a trowel to clean it, and then put it straight into a new wall. They fall intact and clean. So many of them, lying in every possible relation to the other. It leaves whole streets like a great river of brick in flood.'

He felt himself go deeper.

'But night is falling, and soon they will be here again.'

'Who will be here?'

'The bombers, of course.'

'You are waiting for them?'

'I have been waiting for them half my life. Night has fallen.

There is silence, and I am lying down, waiting for them. The bricks are uncomfortable, but I am not here for comfort.'

'You are on the street? Why not a bomb shelter?'

'There . . . a dog, and now another, and another, and another, howling. I can hear their howls above the sirens, and above them both I can hear the drone, getting louder . . . and then louder still. At last. At long last . . .'

The drone of the heavy bombers went on, and on.

'They are overhead for hours, and yet . . . I'm still waiting for the bombs to fall.'

He could bear it no longer. He had waited too long, and this time he had been sure it would happen. His tears spilled over. The record stopped, and Dr Greene put on another.

Ah. The soft voice of the tenor, and the slow beat of the music lulled him until the harp struck and the choir soared and in his head he opened his eyes.

Everywhere was on fire. As far as he could see. On the rubble of a collapsed building, three lonely men pumped water onto the mountainous, ravenous flames. Around him, thousands of people were running, their screams sucked away by the tumult of the fires and dwindling air.

A roar gathered until it deafened him and the sky darkened, the fire shining a dark red and dull white through the airborne debris until it was shut out and darkness prevailed. Then a huge fire ignited like a great spit, illuminating a young girl, her mother running after her. Karl watched, powerless from a distance of years. The tar melted beneath her feet, and screaming, she could not drag herself from it, her mother's fingers almost touching her; but as her mother was stuck too, they would never reach each other.

The fire consumed them.

The tar had melted beneath his feet also, and he fought to drag his shoes from it. A terrible wind came through the streets and alleyways, gathering power as it joined and multiplied within itself. It blew him almost onto his back, his shoes still stuck to the tar. But there was no air.

'I can't breathe,' Karl choked, 'I can't breathe.'

The soprano and contralto sang in harmony as he rose within the whirlwind.

Here, there was no more fire, no turmoil as with a multitude of others he rose higher and higher within the spiral until he could see the clear light of the evening star. And then he saw that the bombers had not departed, they had waited for him after all, waiting above the city they had destroyed with their incendiaries. He could feel the wind from the propellers as he moved among them, and he saw the young, tense faces of the crews as the soprano's voice rose into a hushed purity.

He wandered among the suspended planes, thousands of them, and saw that they were Lancasters and Flying Fortresses and Junkers Ju 88s and Messerschmitts, waiting for him, for others, down the years, down the centuries.

At last. At last he knew where he was. He walked among the suffocated and incinerated people of his city, blowing air between their lips to cool their boiling lungs, pouring oil over their charred bones. The young crews of the warplanes stared into infinity, intent on survival, no room in their terrified hearts to know what they had done all over Europe.

'Play "Alles Vergängliche",' he ordered the doctor from 1944, and he waited until the choir sang before turning to greet his family as they made their way out of the massed dead piled between the planes. The soprano's and contralto's and tenor's voices rose into the great chorus as Gertrud called out his name. Like Mama and Papa she was bloodied and in rags, covered in the torment of the storm. Jurgen was frozen in his Wermacht uniform, but he saw past all of that into the life they had shared as he embraced them.

Nine

BRENDAN

July–December 1950

Brendan threw his bag to one side and sat at the table, still in his work clothes. It had been a hard day, and he had driven himself to blot out his bewilderment, as he had done since Hugh left. He sat there, not caring to wash or eat.

Eventually he washed and changed, and went over to Sally's just before she closed. She asked about Hugh, if he was unwell.

'That's kind of you, Sally. The truth is, he's gone back to Ireland, to look after the place at home.'

'I see.'

'Oh, sure it was going to rack and ruin, since his mother died. I'll be joining him, as a matter of fact.'

'That's nice for you, Mr Kinsella, isn't it? But I'll miss both of you, all the same. He's such a quiet, nice mannered chap. A credit to you, in fact.'

'Thank you. I appreciate that. You were always very civil and kind to us.'

So she was. She was a lady. He liked the English, he thought as he made his meal. Oh, true enough, he had come across NO IRISH NEED APPLY signs in his time. He had been spat on, jeered, made little of; but the usual run of an English person was a decent skin. Sure what did they know about what had gone on in Ireland? And what had it gained the English working man or woman, only their sons in a foreign grave?

He turned on the radio, losing himself in the plush English voices.

After his wash and meal, he fell into his routine, putting on his slippers and glasses, and settled in to read the evening paper.

Hugh would come back, he thought, even as he read. All right, he wanted to live on his own. He let the paper drop into his lap and looked around him.

That was natural. Sure wasn't he a healthy young man, wanting to live his own life? He'd be all the better for it. Make a man of him. But he'd come back. He had an inheritance, and no man, no matter how proud, threw that away.

He lay awake in bed that night. Sarah was right. He had allowed him no life. But if he came back, he bargained, all that would change.

Five years. That was all. Sure he'd be beat by that time anyhow. And then they'd go back with enough, put a new roof on the house, tear down them mud outhouses and put up something decent. And Hugh could get a fine local girl, no bother. He wouldn't stand in his way. In fact he'd give the lad a push. Maybe that young one he was soft on was still around, but sure once he had money he could have who he liked.

The thought of children running around his feet on Croghan made Brendan smile. He had seldom been around the place for Hugh, he had missed all that, but he was ready now, or would be in a few years, once he had enough in the Post Office.

Hugh, grandchildren, Máire, Sarah, they were all of a sudden gathered in his head, wanting attention. Even as he hurt at what Máire had done, he pitied her, his old unspoken love still flowing through his veins. He was glad of it, of the good feeling it gave him in spite of all. He shouldn't have left her alone on that mountain, but sure what could he do? She wouldn't live in London, wouldn't leave her bit of the earth, as she called it. Nor would she bring him to the West after their wedding. He had been glad at the time, but, especially since she died, he had wondered why, and he knew now that she had kept many things from him.

He had accepted it as womanly business, but suspected there were some things he should have known, that were his right to know. He recalled their wedding in 1925 in Holy Joe's in Highgate. Her brothers, two big, dark, silent men, who paid for the wedding breakfast and left after it, were her guests. Brendan had had a cousin and a Dublin painter from a big job they were on in the City, who, now that he thought of it, had been his only friend all these years. Poor Liam had been caught in the Blitz. It's a wonder they weren't all blown up that night, bloody fires everywhere. Poor bastard.

Lord, he hadn't thought of him this long time. Poor fella. Bertie and Flynno, they were caught too, later on, or so he had heard. Jesus. How had he survived at all? Pure luck, like everyone else. But what was he thinking of? The wedding.

As soon as her brothers were gone, Máire came to life, laughing like someone free after being in prison. He remembered marvelling, and felt it still, at how beautiful she was when she was laughing and happy.

It turned out a great day altogether, even though they didn't become man and wife that night, nor for a month after. And she never then nor after showed signs of enjoying it. Not like Sarah, who although she said not a word, shook like a frightened calf and held on to him as if her life depended on it.

Begod, that was something, and he thought over it for a while before getting her key out of his Sunday jacket in the wardrobe and, throwing it on the table and considering it, knowing that his acceptance of it had thrown his life in a new, uneasy direction.

He went back to bed and lay awake for some time, the idea of living with Sarah vague and static, and he drifted into sleep. In his dream he floated through derelict passages, dimly lit, water seeping from moss on the walls. He had a terrible drought on him, but when he sucked on the moss and his thirst was slaked, he saw that it was slime that he'd drunk, and his body was burning with fever. He clawed at the walls, which seemed to be closing around him, to find pure water, but as he tore away the rotten bricks, a putrid air rushed through the opening he had made, and he put one hand over his mouth and nose, continuing to claw at the brick with the other. One moment he was in a frenzy, the next he was quiet and in a gloomy room, a thin slit in the wall providing its only light, and the stench of piss and shit was terrible. As his eyes adjusted, he saw that women and girls were lying on dirty straw, and that all of them were thin and ghostly, and some of them were breathing their last.

It was then he saw his grandmother, a girl of seven, feebly clutching her mother who was almost dead. He had gone back to 1852, to the workhouse in Gorey, and his great-grandmother was dying of cholera. The child whimpered as her mother's death rattle stopped. The skeleton she had for a body settled with a shallow sigh, and Brendan reached across the child to close the woman's eyes. He found some pennies in his pocket, and placed one over each eye, the pennies turning black. With a rag he wiped the gunge from her mouth and jaw, straightened her head, and with the same rag pulled up her chin and tied the rag across the top of her head, so that her mouth was closed and she could be buried in dignity.

'Come, child,' he whispered to the girl, 'come out of this place, or I'll never be born.'

The girl turned her head, her eyes sunk into her skull, and slowly recognized him. With great effort, she raised her bony hand and touched his face.

As soon as he brought her into the sunshine of the open yard, the flesh began to fill on her bones, and her hair regained its shine.

I'll bring her home to Croghan, he thought, and I'll bring her up myself, a Christian and a decent human, who'll be a good wife for my grandfather.

But when he called her to come with him and take his hand, she turned and he saw that her eyes had turned to stone. She would never smile again, and neither would her daughter, nor her daughter's daughter, his sister, who had died young.

He could stand it no longer, and sat up in bed as he woke, sweating and shaking. He turned on the light and sat on the edge of the bed, smoking, trying not to think. Unwilling to return to bed, and unwilling to admit that he needed the presence of another breathing body, he lit another cigarette.

'Forgive me, Máire,' he said aloud, 'but I'm going to live with another woman.'

He felt that she was present, and gradually he calmed.

'I'll never love her, Máire, like I love you, but she's a good woman, and I can't live alone any more. I can't.'

He wept silently as he felt that Máire was blessing him, and letting him go. All these years, he had been faithful to her, even in death, and his love for her had supported him, but now she was letting him free, and he hadn't the strength to refuse.

The next evening, he washed and ate, and went downstairs to Mrs Dempsey.

'Good evening, ma'am.'

'Mr Kinsella! Come on in!'

He stepped into the room. Both young Dennis and the baby were asleep, Dennis on the sofa, the baby in the cot. Behind the clock on the low mantel, was a white plastic holy water bottle in the shape of the Virgin, capped by a blue crown.

'Sit down, Mr Kinsella, and I'll put the kettle back on.'

'I won't stay, ma'am. I was just wondering if you could give Mr Silverstein two weeks' rent for me.'

'Are you leaving us?'

'Ah sure, I don't know if you knew already, but the young fella's gone back to Croghan, and the room's too big for me.'

'I thought I missed him. Poor Dennis'll be heartbroken – he never stops asking about him.'

'Right,' Brendan smiled. 'They were good friends, right enough. But he had to go back in a hurry. Family business.'

'That's a shame. And have you somewhere to go?'

'Oh I have. I'm grand, thanks.'

He gave her the money and she insisted that he have some tea.

'I'll waken the childer,' he said, but nevertheless he sat down and accepted tea and a biscuit, and before he was aware of it, she had him freely talking about Wexford and Connemara, Máire's place, where she knew people. It wasn't the first time she had engaged him in conversation. He had always adroitly if politely refused to be drawn, but now it was good to talk about

Máire, about how fine a woman she was, and that she had been his best and only true friend.

He bade Mrs Dempsey goodbye, thanking her for her kindnesses and, despite her protests, left half a crown for Dennis.

As he put his things together, he found a packet wrapped in brown paper and tied with string at the bottom of his suitcase. He had forgotten about it, but it was a packet of photos including those of his wedding, and Hugh's communion and confirmation. He unwrapped them and stared at the image of his dead wife. She was a sight for sore eyes, with her long black hair flowing away from her wedding veil.

He put it aside quickly, and lit a cigarette and dragged on it, filling his lungs. He coughed, saltwater streaming from his eyes. Then he looked over the other photos, of Hugh and Máire and himself. He repackaged the photos and placed them carefully at the bottom of the case.

It was still light when he let himself into Sarah's. The house was warm after a hot day, and he could feel a sheen of sweat tickling his lip. He left the suitcase in the hall, and explored the rooms, testing Sarah's bed. He was more discreet in Deirdre's room, with its dolls and picture books which for him were of another world. In the kitchen he made himself a cup of black tea, and sat looking at the floor where they had done the deed. It seemed so long ago.

She hadn't said where he was to sleep, but there were two flats in the basement and, finding one empty, he set himself up in it. He would pay her the rent. That was best, in case he had presumed too much. Why should anyone love him, or take care of him, anyway? His own son had declared him worthless by leaving him like that. In a rush of anger and heartbreak, he threw the suitcase across the room, its contents scattering, and left, blindly heading for a pub he knew in Camden Town.

He threw open the doors of the pub, pushed his way to the bar and ordered an Irish whiskey. He threw it back and looked around him, glowering at the drunkards he despised before ordering and drinking another, this time more slowly. A man with a West of Ireland accent asked him where he was from. He turned and looked at him darkly before telling him to fuck off.

'Well, fuck off yourself,' the man replied. 'You're not the only...' He pursed his lips and shook his head in bafflement. 'Ah feck you,' he said then, turning away and draining his pint amid the loud laughter and the surge and ebb of talk in a confusion of accents, in Gaelic as well as English.

Brendan had never felt more alone, and relied on the fire of the whiskey to distract and soothe him. He drank steadily until closing time, then bought a naggin and pushed his way through the thinning crowd, and got a taxi home.

'Fuck him,' he muttered to himself in the taxi. The face of the man who had tried to befriend him would not leave him alone. 'Fuck him.' He kept this up all the way home, and like a prayer, it made him forget himself.

He let himself in and drank from the tap in the kitchen, and then on the turn of the basement stairs he stumbled, but his looseness saved him from injury. 'Blast him anyway,' he roared about no one in particular, but partly about Hugh, and certainly about God.

The next morning he woke early and drank back cups of water at the sink. At work he pushed himself hard, harder than ever. Once home again, he made himself something to eat and went to the pub once more, finding himself a corner near the bar where he could be alone. On Saturday evening, on his way to the pub, the door of the flat opposite was opened, and a little girl looked up at him, the whites of her eyes huge in her black face.

'Begod!' he whispered, startled. 'Hello, young one,' he said then, and she disappeared. 'Well, that beats all,' he said to himself. It was only afterwards that he realized she must be the daughter of Sarah's black friend.

He was early, but the pub was packed and loud, and most of the men were drinking hard.

'I've been watching you all week,' a Dublin man challenged him towards closing time. 'Why do you bother your arse coming in here if you haven't the manners to talk to anyone?'

Brendan's fist shot out and hit the Dublin man flush in the face. The Dubliner fell back, and several men cursed as they were knocked back, their drinks sloshing.

On Sunday he slept all day. On Monday evening, he found another, less boisterous bar, away from the Irish. No one paid him attention and, even when drunk, he still had enough care to be quiet and unobtrusive.

The following Sunday evening he was lying down, preoccupied with a hangover which had lasted all day, when he heard Sarah and Deirdre arrive back. It was odd; he knew it was them, but the sound of their footsteps made them seem like strangers, and the uneven weight of Sarah's footfalls made them stranger still. They laughed. That they were happy together was surprising, somehow. He didn't feel he had the strength, but having willed it for some time, he got himself off the bed and went upstairs.

'Oh!' Sarah stared at him, and Deirdre clung to her skirts, keeping one eye on him. 'Don't do that, Brendan,' she said, recovering.

'I moved in downstairs.'

'Oh. Grand. You don't look well.'

'I'm all right. I've been here for more than a week.' He took money from his pocket and put it on the table. 'Is that enough?' She looked at the money but didn't seem pleased.

'Well, say whatever it is.'

'Brendan, can we discuss this tomorrow? We're tired, and I have to get up for work in the morning.'

He was tired too. As tired as Methuselah.

The following evening he was careful to remove any dried mud from his boots before tramping through the hall and downstairs to the flat. He was washing when there was a knock on the door, and he pulled on his trousers and shirt, his body still wet.

'Will you come and join us?' Sarah asked. 'There's plenty.'

'Begod,' he said, avoiding looking at her, 'that's good of you.'

She kissed him lightly on the lips, and he felt his cheeks and neck burn.

'It's as well for you to live down here until Deirdre gets used to you about the house.'

'Right. Right. True enough.'

'Remind me to give you a key for the basement door. It'd be handier for you. And if you keep paying me rent I can feed you every evening. I have to cook for two so I might as well for three,' she added, trying to be light.

'Aye. True enough.'

She bit her lip like a young girl and smiled before returning upstairs. He closed the door, then looked up at the ceiling as she limped across the floor above. He took off his clothes and shaved carefully at the sink. He should have been delighted. Here was a good woman who was fond of him and he could live with her in comfort. But he wasn't delighted. He was depressed and it baffled him.

He stopped short of putting on a tie – that was for Sunday – but he wore his cleanest shirt and trousers, adjusted his good braces and went upstairs.

The smell from the kitchen was wonderful. Deirdre was reading a book, but looked up and greeted him with a smile.

'Hello, child,' he said, easy with her.

'My name is Deirdre, you know.'

'Oh I know that,' he laughed, and sat in beside her. 'What are you reading, or may I ask?'

'*The Water Babies*,' she sighed.

'*The Water Babies*? And what class of a creature are they?'

'I won't be a second, Brendan,' Sarah said, coming in. 'Deirdre, clear away those books now, and bring in the salad.'

O Christ, not salad, he thought as Deirdre obeyed. I'll starve to death.

She set the plates and cutlery carefully as Deirdre brought a large wooden bowl of salad. There was a fresh cloth on the table.

We have our best linen out tonight, he thought. At home in Ireland, this would happen only after a funeral, or a wedding maybe, in a spotless parlour cold from lack of use. She had proper glasses, and a bottle of red wine with ne'er a label on it.

Then she brought out a steaming earthen casserole.

'We got this in France,' she said, smiling almost to herself. 'I thought we might try it out.'

'Good, good,' he said. Begod, I smell meat, he thought,

relieved. When she took off the lid, he thought he spotted some suspicious looking vegetables, foreign stuff surely, but so long as there was meat, he could sort them out and leave them to one side if the worst came to the worst. And potatoes, bedad. He felt on surer ground as she brought in a plate of steaming, floury potatoes. But if I have to eat the salad, he thought, it'll ruin the taste.

'Now, will I serve you?'

'Oh. Right.'

'Just this once,' she said happily.

'Lord that's good,' he said as he ate.

'Oh,' she said, gratified. 'Would you— No, I forgot you don't like wine.'

'Ah sure I'll try some,' he said.

'Really?'

He regretted it as soon as it was out of his mouth, but held out his glass to be filled, and Deirdre leaned across the table to pour it expertly.

They watched him as he drank it back, and exhaled, licking his lips.

'Be the hokey,' he said, 'that'd warm the cockles of your heart.'

Sarah rubbed the back of her hand across her forehead as she laughed.

'Deirdre,' she managed, 'you'd better pour him another.'

She was pleased, he could see, when he asked her about France and, as she talked, he noticed she could throw back the wine herself. Before long, she had another bottle on the table.

'I was going to keep it', she said, 'for a special occasion. But sure this is a special occasion.'

It was great. He had hardly to say a word, she was happy to rattle on, and he could eat heartily. Even the salad, to his surprise, went down like honeydew.

Deirdre left the table, her mother hardly noticing, and lay on the floor with her book, Sarah talking on about France until he could feel the soft evening heat as they drank wine together under the shade of a French tree. He wondered what it would be like to work in such fields, the sun beating down on your head, the sweat blinding you and the wheat as hard as shot. He thought of Croghan, soaked in misty rain every other day. Even the crows perched on the roof were like drenched black flowers, until, maybe, in a break of a week or two, the air danced in the heat and the eye could take in miles in all directions, the ships like islands easing up and down the Irish Sea.

'I'm talking too much,' she said, her eyes on her glass as she twiddled with it.

'Lord, not at all,' he protested. 'Sure wasn't I with you every step of the way!'

She smiled.

'You should have a chance to get a word in edgeways.'

'I'm not travelled in the world like you, Sarah.' When she spoke like that she seemed like a young girl.

'Well . . .' She looked dreamily at Deirdre, who was happily reading on the floor. 'It's time for bed, pet.' Deirdre finished her page, placed her bookmark and rose. 'I'll put her to bed now, Brendan, if you don't mind.'

'Right. Thanks for the meal, Sarah. It was mighty.'

'Mighty!' She laughed. 'It was indeed.'

'And the wine was Trojan.'

'Goodnight,' she said, lightly touching his hand as she passed.

'Goodnight, Brendan,' Deirdre said.

'Goodnight, sweet child.'

Once in his room he felt again the unease of leaving old loyalties behind. He put his head in his hands. This, all of it, was something he hadn't known since Hugh was a small child – to be a guest in the civilized lives of women.

Poor Máire, she had been rough and ready. No wine or fine food in her cupboard, and how could she have? And would he have let her?

He went to bed and imagined making love to Máire, as one last proof of his love and desire for her, and the release calmed him. He was almost asleep when the door opened and she whispered his name. She eased in beside him, in the dark, and kissed him. Her death had been a nightmare, and now in woken life she had come to live with him in London as he had wanted.

He put his arm around her but could not stay awake, and when he woke in the morning she was gone.

*

At break that morning, he cleared his throat and addressed Seán Dubh, the new brickie.

'With a name like that, you wouldn't be from Connemara, by any chance?'

'I am.'

'You speak Irish, so.' Seán Dubh's face brightened.

'*An bhfuil Gaeilge agat?*'

'*Níl.*' No, Brendan hadn't Irish. '*Níl,*' he repeated. 'But my wife's from Connemara. I thought you Irish speakers stuck together,' he added quickly in case Seán would ask whereabouts in Connemara she was from.

'My brothers and neighbours are all in the Midlands— Northhampton and the like. But I prefer London. There's great life down here.'

'You speak English well for a Gaelic speaker . . .'

'Sure I've read any good book there is to read in Irish. So I read in English all the time.'

The whistle sounded and Brendan fell back into his usual silence. Wasn't Máire the right one, all the same, to slip into his bed like that, without a word. It was obvious what had happened. She had decided to come to London, as he had always wanted, and had got herself a little place, and maybe even a job. More likely she was in a women's hostel, and that's why she had to slip away before light.

His happiness made him work feverishly, and Seán Dubh found it hard to keep up with him and the other bricklayer. The rhythm of the work took over, his concentration total, but when there was a lull, his thoughts drifted back to Máire. He tried, half-heartedly, to think of where the women's hostels were. Maybe he'd turn up at the one she was in, surprise her, make her blush in front of the other women as he had done before they were married. Now that she'd decided to live with him, they could get a place – sure there were lots of fine big houses going for half nothing. And Hugh could come home. The damn houses were so big he could have his own flat and marry some young one and make children in it. His thoughts drifted pleasantly into imagining the wedding in Holy Joe's.

That evening he washed and went upstairs for his meal in high good humour. Sarah smiled to herself but went about her business. During the meal, smiling broadly, she asked him about his day, and for the first time he talked about Seán Dubh, the young man who had replaced Hugh.

'You know, I'd say there's more men speaking Irish over here than there is back in Ireland.'

'Do you think so?'

'Aye!' He could see she was only humouring him, but he didn't mind.

'And what might have you in such good humour?' she asked, clearing away the plates.

He was glad to see her in such good fettle herself. She was a fine-looking woman when she was in good form.

'Well, for one thing, Máire's back.'

Sarah put the dishes back on the table. All of a sudden, she looked ill, and he thought she was going to topple over.

'Who?' she whispered.

'Máire. My wife. You didn't let her in the other night, by any chance?'

'No, Brendan. I didn't let anyone in.' She took a deep breath, and looked at him a little strangely. He smiled at her.

'Well, she's in London, anyhow.'

'I see,' she said, gathering up the dishes again. On her way to the kitchen she turned. 'I'll tell you one thing, Brendan. You'll never be dead while your son is alive.'

'O be the hokey,' he laughed. 'That's true enough.' But even as he laughed he could see she was angry. Even Deirdre, who was on the floor with her book as usual, looked up at him with her mouth open. He smiled at her weakly and left.

It wasn't until he reached his room that he felt his resentment. They're jealous, he thought. They're fucking jealous! They had no one. Well, it was too bad. Fuck them. He closed his eyes and ecstatically reached out to embrace Máire, his one true darling.

She didn't come that night, or the next. He began to suspect that Sarah had locked her out, and on the site the thought burned into him as he worked, rolling the cigarette along his lips, his eyes squinting against the smoke. She had kept him from Hugh too, the scheming bitch.

On his way home, he had fish and chips in a café. He didn't trust himself with Sarah, and in any case he couldn't be sure enough, to accuse her. Maybe Máire had been held up. He'd give it till the weekend.

Deirdre knocked on his door.

'You're dinner's ready, Brendan.'

'I'm not hungry.' He sensed she was still at the door, and opened it. She looked up at him with her big eyes. 'Tell Sarah I won't be up this evening,' he said quietly.

'Shall I say why?'

'I'm tired.'

She nodded and skipped away.

He closed the door and went to the barred window. It was raining, and he watched the path of a drop on the pane. He was very tired, because he knew that it hadn't been Máire after all, and that after Hugh was born she had been cold to him. Cold as the grave. It was Sarah who had got in beside him, held him like a human being. He should go upstairs and ask her forgiveness, but he was too tired.

Yet he went upstairs, like someone whose soul had left him, and sat at the table. Deirdre, her fork halfway to her mouth, stared at him, then dropped her fork, the peas spilling around the table, and threw herself out of her chair against her mother's breast. Sarah stroked her head and looked at him in silence, but he was beyond caring, so long as he was not alone.

'Come on, pet, and we'll get Brendan's dinner,' she said very softly. Deirdre looked around at him in terror.

'I'm sorry to frighten you, child,' he said bleakly. 'I frighten myself.'

Deirdre whimpered, clinging more tightly to Sarah.

'Come on, Deirdre.'

Jesus. To frighten a child was the lowest of the low. A sweet innocent child. That was how low he was. He heard the scraping of the saucepan and the pot, and Deirdre's whimpering.

'All right, all right,' Sarah said patiently, before returning alone with the steaming plate.

'I don't know what's wrong with you, Brendan, but you'll have to eat downstairs this evening. You've upset Deirdre.'

The woman was so reasonable.

'I've done you a great wrong, Sarah.'

'What do you mean?'

'As you know ... only too well, my wife ... Máire ... is dead this seven year.'

Somehow he gathered the strength to take the food to his room. He put the plate on the sideboard and lay back on the bed, watching the rain. What frozen demon had taken her over after Hugh was born? He had beaten her once, with an ashplant, God knows, but God also knew that it was wanting her that drove him to it. He slaved all year, wanting her every minute, and all she could talk about was that gom, living on his own with the clouds for company. Living in a hovel, as if he'd been evicted from the poorhouse. And God knows, he had frightened a child before now, when he beat Hugh's mother in front of him. At last, tears flowed at the shame of it. There were plenty other men whose wives didn't want them, not wanting any more childer, and who could blame them, but there were few like himself who didn't give way to the longing for the comfort of a woman's body. He had stayed faithful, like a fool, all those years, those ten thousand years she thought less of him than a dunghill. He shook his head at the stupidity of it. And that gom at the top of Croghan helped carry her coffin at the end. If he hadn't been so numb, he would have killed the bastard rather than let him nearer than a mile of her corpse. The gom was at the wake as well, now that he thought of it, demolishing the soda bread the neighbours had made, and the whiskey, but whatever about hitting a woman you couldn't get away with hitting a God's fool. The worst of it was, she died before they had a chance to grow a little older and maybe wise, when they could at least be friends.

It was all gone now, into eternity. Exhausted, he slept, his food untouched.

He woke moments before the alarm, as usual, and worked his half Saturday. He had been depressed all morning and went to the pub as soon as he was paid, and stood his foreman a drink to get that out of the way. There were several women at the bar, chattering away, God blast them, so he found a corner away from their screeching. After two pints it came to him what was wrong. He had no contact with his flesh and blood. Sarah knew where he was, but the bitch wouldn't tell. As he drank, his anger grew, like the notion that he'd beat it out of her if he had to. The cheek of her, keeping him from his flesh and blood, the one thing he shared with Máire and his last consolation in the world.

He found her in the kitchen, washing up.

'Where is he?'

'You've been drinking.'

'Aye. I've been drinking. I had a few pints after my day's work. Now where's my son?'

'I don't know, Brendan.'

He dragged her into the dining room and held her up straight, gripping her shoulders. She winced.

'Where the fuck's my son? Come on, you whore, you know well.'

'Let me go, Brendan. I swear. I don't know where he is.'

Don't hit her, he kept telling himself, don't hit her. He pushed her away and she fell back against the table, and eased herself onto a chair. As she got her own breath back, her anger grew to match his.

'You've only yourself to blame, you big stupo.'

'What are you on about?' He was breathless with anger, unable to look at her.

'You treated him like a spalpeen.'

'What?' He swung around to face her. 'My own son?'

'Like a squireen's slave, Brendan. All work, no money, no life. I told you before. He's a man. Not very mature, thanks to you, but if you treat a man like a spalpeen ... you can't expect him to take it for ever.'

'Ah woman, what do you know?'

The grief came up, and he bent over.

'What do you know ... My land on this earth is on that mountain. The Kinsellas have been there longer than a thousand years.'

He straightened, though not altogether, and stared blankly, speaking to himself, hardly knowing his tears were falling.

'Our land was robbed on us. We came through poverty, dirt and ignorance. All of that. All of it. We came through famine and cholera. Landlords, by Jesus. We fought the bloodsuckers. And still we were there. Our bit of land, bounded by our cousin's land. And now Ireland, or my part of it, is free, and it's all over.'

He put his hand over his face and rubbed it hard.

'What's to become of me? One day I'll fall over on the street.'

He looked around at her. Her eyes were flooded, and he pitied her, then himself, and everyone who had lost their birthright.

She looked away from him, smiling against the odds, and he turned to see Deirdre, clutching her golliwog, taking it all in. He wondered why she wasn't afraid. He must look a sight, unshaven, in his filthy working clothes, crying like a woman. He hunkered down, cement dust on the callused hand he stretched out to her.

'O lovely child. You have your life ahead of you. Work hard at your lessons, and your French, and don't be an old fool like me. Maybe then, maybe one day, you'll go back to Ireland and help make it a decent place. What do you say?'

She stepped forward and with her free hand she touched his drenched cheeks, her soft fingertips like down.

He was amazed. No one had ever touched him so tenderly, not his own mother, and surely not poor Máire. He looked into her deep, steady eyes.

'Thank you,' he whispered.

She ran into her mother's arms, and Sarah, her eyes closed, hugged her tight.

'Good girl,' she whispered, 'good girl.'

He stood and looked at them, bound to each other. It was a

lonely sight for him, but he knew he was now part of their lives, all the same, for better or worse, and he took his courage and touched Sarah's head softly with the fullness of his hand. Neither woman nor child moved, as if lost in their embrace. He went downstairs, feeling that all his years of loneliness had brought him something unexpected and good. He touched his face lightly, trying to recreate the girl's downy touch. Silently he thanked her again.

Sarah knocked, waking him from a deep sleep, and he let her in.

'Are you all right?'

'I'm grand. Nothing that a wash wouldn't cure.'

'I just wanted to say ... I just wanted to say that in a few years' time, Deirdre will leave me too. It's the way of things.'

'It is.'

'Well, dinner'll be ready in a few minutes. Will I see you then?'

'I'd be a fool to miss it.'

She smiled, and left.

To his relief, while Sarah was quiet, Deirdre was her usual self over dinner and filled in the silence between the adults, humming to herself, quoting characters from her story book in a prim voice.

After dinner, Sarah handed him an evening paper, and as she let him know he was in the way as she cleared the table, he went downstairs to get his glasses, before settling down in the living room to read. She looked in briefly and nodded. The satisfaction of a woman was something he had forgotten. Later, Sarah came back with Deirdre as she was putting her to bed.

'Goodnight, Brendan.' He looked up, the glasses on the end of his nose, and smiled.

'Goodnight, Deirdre.' He felt a surge of happiness as they left, but repressed it and continued reading. He finished the paper in a few minutes, as he lost interest when he couldn't find any mention of the dogs, and looked about the comfortable room. The armchairs had doilies, and a picture of water buffalo hung on the wall. Her books, dozens of them, were stacked neatly on shelves, and he leafed through some of them. Daphne du Maurier, *The Hungry Hill*. By Jesus, he knew one hungry hill. He took another. *The Wandering Scholars*, Helen Waddell. Another woman. He opened a page at random and read down to some verses, which he read aloud, faltering on the unfamiliar words.

> 'At the gates of summer,
>   Love standeth us to greet.
> The earth to do him honour,
>   Burgeons beneath his feet.
>
> The flowers that aye attend him
>   Laugh at the golden prime;
> Should Venus not befriend them,
>   They die before their time.'

Well, he thought, replacing the book, maybe he wasn't going to die before his time, but why an educated woman like her took an interest in him was beyond him. But that was up to herself.

'Don't tell me you're reading books?'

'Ah,' he said turning. 'Sure I've read two already.'

He expected her to laugh, but she didn't.

'I don't want any more sadness in my life, Brendan.'

'O Lord,' he said after a while, 'who does?' He sat beside her. 'No one I know, anyhow.'

She looked at him and her eyes were full of hurt. As if he were taking a newborn into his arms, he held her and, although she didn't resist, he felt how stiff she was, how unresponsive, and he thought of poor Máire. He didn't want sadness any more either, with more than his fair share, and while all his instincts told him to leave her be, that she didn't want a fool like him, he held out, held on to her, and suddenly she relaxed.

'I'm sorry.'

'That's all right,' she whispered.

*

The loss of Hugh never left him alone, but his late affection for Sarah, and Deirdre's childishness, helped him to bear it. By autumn, when Deirdre was back at school, they had settled into a routine that suited them. At weekends, she came to his bed and stayed the night. Sometimes during the week she came for an hour or so, and sometimes she did not. It all depended on Deirdre, who often had nightmares. Then again, there were times she just wanted to talk, and she'd ask him up to the sitting room for a glass of wine. Sometimes they'd get drunk, and she'd cry for no reason, but mostly it just loosened her tongue, and she'd rattle on about France again, and maybe he liked that best of all, especially when, on Sunday afternoons, Deirdre played with her black friend in her room. The black girl gloried in the name of Delilah, but Deirdre called her Delly. And Delly called her Dree, from Deardree. The English couldn't pronounce Deirdre, he had noticed, and how could they? The names tickled him, and the sound of the girls playing their games of pretence was a glory unto God.

He was still in awe of Sarah. She worked as a secretary to a surgeon in the Royal Northern. He wondered how she could talk to a doctor, never mind a great man like a surgeon. Yet she spoke of him as she would of an ordinary man, except she admired the great things he did, saving people's lives, though not always the limbs. He had learned his trade during the war. It was hard to stop her when she talked about the hospital. She yakked about the great thing penicillin was, and the antibiotics which were supposed to be great yokes altogether, and how something called radium would cure cancer and that soon TB would be only a memory, even in Ireland. He caught her wonder about all of this, and began to think he was part of a wider world where it might be good to live.

It sustained him for a month, but as he took his domestic contentment for granted, Hugh's absence troubled him again. He went through the motions with Sarah and, one night in bed together, she confronted him.

'Don't do this to me, Brendan,' she said.

He respected her for that, and was grateful she had made him think about it. Left to his old ways, he would have gone on, head down like a mountain goat, blinded by the futility of it all. She pulled it out of him, picking away, until at last he had the words. It was a queer kind of love, but thick as he was, he knew it was love all right. He opened his eyes at last and touched her face.

'The thing I dread, Sarah, the thing I dread, is for me to die and he not knowing who he is, who his people are, nor where he comes from.'

'Sure we're all the one lost tribe since the Famine, Brendan.'

'No!' he shouted and, to her credit, she didn't blink an eye. 'No,' he said quickly. 'We're not lost. We're still in with a shout. Croghan Kinsella,' he whispered. 'As long as that bloody mountain stands, we're not lost. As long as I can walk about it in my head, and name the fields and the bog, and fifty fields beyond it, and as long as I can count the seed, breed and generation of my cousins and neighbours – sure then how could I be lost? It's only if Hugh reneges on it . . . Do you see what I'm on about? A man, and a woman for that matter, must know the name and history of the field he walks on, or he's nothing. That's why, Sarah, I have to make friends with him.'

*

They settled into winter.

Sarah opened a bottle of wine. Brendan had lit a fire in the sitting room.

'Now, we'll just let that sit for a while,' she said to herself, and sat into the armchair beside the fire opposite Brendan. Deirdre was in bed.

'Are you tired?'

'Ah, I'm all right,' she said. 'We were busier than usual, for some reason.' She yawned.

'Winter,' he said. 'More people get sick in winter.'

They had grown easy and content with each other, and Brendan had thought of asking her to marry him. The only thing was, she made him use those yokes now when they were having the how's-your-father. The only place he had seen them before was in a barber's, so she must have got them in the hospital. More often than not, though, he couldn't keep things going, having to deal with an awkward yoke like that; but she wouldn't budge unless he had one on. He could see her point. She had her child and, of course, so had he. That didn't stop him cursing their invention.

Besides, he was still enough of a Catholic, even though he had given up Mass after Máire died. And there were other things in the back of his mind that gave him pause. He wasn't comfortable with Sarah's friendship with the black woman downstairs, for example. Or worse, Deirdre's friendship with Delly. It was all very well, now that they were innocent children, but what would happen in a few years' time? And his thoughts hardened against what Delly might lead her into.

She handed him his glass of wine. He had always thought that wine was for priests on the altar, and for bigshots, but he had grown used to the idea, and sure Sarah was almost a bigshot herself. She had taught him that wine should be sipped.

'I've been thinking,' he said. 'A spalpeen was a different class of person in our part of the world. He was a travelling trades-man. I was just thinking about it the other day. They had a spalpeen fair outside Gorey. My mother told me about it when I was a young fella.'

'The Considines have been in Clare a good while, too.'

'Right.' He thought about it for a while. 'That makes us all square, so.'

'All square,' she said, looking into her glass.

'Hugh always thought you were a Protestant. Did I ever tell you that?'

She laughed.

'Maybe I am.'

He never said anything about Deirdre and Delly's friendship, but whenever he got the chance, he told Deirdre about growing up in Wexford, how people went to each other's houses at night and played cards and told stories and danced and sang. To his delight, she loved this and sat herself up on his knee while he told her about the *bean sí* wailing across the bog when someone with an old Irish name died; or about the evil Hunter Gowan in 1798, who lived beyond Hollyfort in the Mount, Mount Nebo; or about the gold that could be found on Croghan, which one day would make them all rich. It was a much better way of keeping her Irish, he decided, than interfering in an innocent friendship. Maybe he was getting sense at last.

Two weeks before Christmas, the frost hit in earnest, and the ground was harder than stone. The foreman handed him his cards. He didn't need to be told that there'd be nothing doing till February, if he was lucky. This was when he had packed up and gone home to Ireland for a few months to be with Máire and Hugh. As he shopped for Santy with Sarah, he decided the place could look after itself just this once. He'd send his cousin Johnny a few pounds for Christmas, and ask him to light a fire in it to keep the place aired. He could still go in time for Máire's anniversary, but for now he was too comfortable to make the winter journey, and looked forward to a civilized Christmas with a good woman and a child he now almost thought of as his own, the daughter he never had. Besides, he realized he would spend his idle time tramping the streets in hopes of catching sight of his flesh and blood.

Ten

HUGH

October 1950–February 1951

Hugh switched off the radio as Elizabeth returned. She came into the kitchen and laid her bags, full of fruit and biscuits she had bought for Karl, on the table, before slumping onto a chair.

'Well? How is he?'

'He's still away with the birds. There was no point in bringing all this, I can tell you that much.'

He sat down. She tore a piece from the wrapping from the biscuits and twisted it, then absently ate a biscuit.

'So what did the doctor say?'

'He said he'd probably recover.' She put her head in her hands. 'He asked me questions till I thought ... Questions, questions. Nothing but questions. He knows as much now about Karl as I do, that's for certain. He said there was no point in going to visit, for a week at least. I'm to bring his records, the next time.' She munched on another biscuit.

'His records?'

'Yes. He thinks music can help certain kinds of people.'

'What's he like?'

'The doctor? He needs a haircut.'

'But is he kind?'

'Kind? Yes, I think so. Hugh, I need a drink.'

'Do you want to go out?'

'O my God yes. I need to get out. Where shall we go?'

'The Nag's Head?'

'Do you know, I've never been.'

'Well, now's your chance.'

'Am I all right like this?'

'Some lipstick and you'll be grand.'

She took lipstick and a mirror from her bag, and he watched as she rouged her lips in slow, deliberate movements, her mouth open, before she carefully pursed the lips and examined herself from every angle.

'How's that?' she asked confidently.

'It's mighty,' he said with conviction, and she checked one more time in the mirror.

'Am *I* all right?' he asked as an afterthought, half in earnest.

'You're *moighty*,' she said, punching him lightly in the ribs.

As they walked up Holloway Road, he said, 'You'll never get the accent.'

'Never mind, love,' she said. 'If I had no fault, you'd be bored.'

'True enough,' he said.

*

'Lord, there's Seán Butler,' he said as they entered the pub.

'Who?'

'The barman. I used to work with him. He used to come to the reading classes. You know, that Sarah I told you about. Her classes.' She settled gratefully onto the side bench. 'What are you having?'

'Well now, let me see. I'll have a port, kind sir.'

'I'm fierce kind,' he grinned over his shoulder. He hailed Seán at the bar.

'Ah! If it isn't the bold Hugh Kinsella! Good man, Hugh,' he said, shaking his hand. 'What has you in these parts?'

'Sure I live around here now,' Hugh said, scratching the back of his head. 'How're you doing, anyway?'

'Powerful. Gave up the buildings as you can see. It's a great city, this, Hugh,' he said leaning forward. 'A great bloody city.'

'Less of your jaw, Butler, and get us a drink,' an Irishman called down the bar.

'I'm serving a gentleman,' Seán called back. 'What can I get you, Hugh?'

'A port and a bitter.'

'Are you with a lady friend?'

'I am.'

'Well, sure I'll bring it down to you.'

'Is there going to be a row?' Elizabeth asked as he sat beside her.'

'At the bar? Lord no. They're only slagging.'

'Slagging.'

'You know.' He ducked and weaved, grinning foolishly.

'I see.'

'There you are now,' Seán said. 'Is the port for you, miss?'

'That's right.'

'Seán, this is Elizabeth Frampton.'

'How do you do.'

'Pleased to meet you, miss. Are you all right there now? Just give us the nod if you want another round.'

'Good man, Seán.'

'He called me "miss". Fancy that.' Her mood swung upwards. 'I didn't know you had such nice friends.'

'Well, if he's a friend, apart from yourself and Karl, he's the only one I have.'

'Stick with him, chuck, is my advice. He looks like a good man to have around if you're in a fix.'

'Sarah used to be a friend, as a matter of fact.'

'So what happened?'

'She was friendly with my father too. So once I . . . well, you know.'

'Is your father that bad?'

'No.' He was surprised by a rush of affection for his father, a deep sympathy for the way he was. 'No, he's a good man. He's just . . . just caught by an idea.'

'Which is?'

'Well . . .' He had to think hard. 'Well, his whole life is lived in the future. Always. Always thinking, day and night, about going back to Ireland.'

'What's wrong with that?'

'He forgets everything else.'

'Including you.'

He didn't answer that, but it was good to talk about it.

'Land is everything in Ireland.'

'Yes? Go on.'

'You know. The few acres of farm. If you have a few acres, you're somebody. You can look down on someone who hasn't. It might earn nothing, but you won't starve altogether. And if it's been in the family, then it's where you come from. It's in your blood. It's like something sacred, that you can pass on.'

'But he wanted something better.'

'Yes.'

'To pass on to you.'

It was true. Hugh realized he had always known that, that his father had spent his life working for him, and he felt the regret of not being able to live up to his father's dream.

'Make peace with your father, Hugh, or when it's too late, you'll regret it for the rest of your life. Go see him on Sunday. Tell him he has a grandson to look out for.'

'No. I can't.'

'Oh!' She drank back half her port. 'You can't see Karl, and now you can't see your own father. What will your son say to that when he asks about his granddad?'

'You keep saying *son*. What makes you so sure?'

'Oh, women know these things,' she said airily.

He supposed they did.

'I just wish I had my parents to tell. They wouldn't be half proud. Their Liz.' She smiled to herself, lost in a lost world he would never know. She turned to him. 'They had a lousy life. I swore I'd never put up with what my mother did. No sir. They never had a chance. I can tell you, my duck, we live in a better world, for all its faults. A pity my fool brothers had to die for it.'

She looked annoyed at that and took a quick drink.

'I'd like to meet your father. I know what it's like to work my arse off for a decent life in my own place. I bet he swore he'd never put up with what *his* parents did. We'd get on. I know we would.'

'Yes. I have a feeling you would.'

'Well, go and see him, then.'

'I'll think about it.'

'Do, my darling.' She finished her port. 'It's time to call your Seán, I think.'

They made it a regular date in the Nag's Head after that, just for a few hours on a Saturday evening. She liked the place and he could see it was good for her, and Seán would sit and talk with them if he wasn't busy. He could see that she liked Seán a lot, but then most women did. Once, when he was very tired, he got upset by it, fearing the worst, but then he saw that she could like Seán without wanting him.

He was tidying up in the yard, while there was still light, when he heard her return from the hospital. He went inside immediately and found Elizabeth leaning against the door jamb. That was a sure sign she was depressed.

'They gave him electric shocks. They wouldn't let me see him.'

He had enough wit to say nothing, to dam his consternation and love, to just be there for her, quiet and calm, and she came to him and he held her and kissed her neck.

'I miss him. Don't you?' she asked.

'Very much.' She stood back to look at him.

'Really?'

He bowed his head and nodded. She lifted his head by the chin and kissed him. They hadn't made love in weeks, she had been too sick, and his longing for her overwhelmed him. As they made love in her room, their passion was brutal, their pleasure building towards a pain which obliterated all other pain. It left them haggard, still unsatisfied.

'I hope we didn't hurt the child,' he said.

'Good training for him,' she said. She went to the kitchen, not bothering to cover herself despite the chill, and returned with a lighted cigarette. 'Do you want one of these?'

'No.'

She lay back and blew a plume of smoke towards the ceiling. 'Are you hungry? I'm starved. I'll make us something in a mo.'

'I could eat a landlord's arse through a hedge.' He had heard that one in the old schoolyard.

She laughed and slapped him on the chest.

'Here, none of that bad language.'

*

Very quickly the days got shorter. He was tidying the yard on a Saturday afternoon while there was just enough light to do so when there was a pounding on the front door. A strange, Cockney voice rose in the kitchen, and Elizabeth pleaded with it. Hugh put his brush against the wall, not quite taking in what was happening, and moseyed into the argument. Elizabeth turned, disbelief written all over her.

The stranger sized up Hugh.

'Who the fuck are you?'

'Hugh Kinsella.'

Elizabeth almost laughed.

'That's very interesting. Now what the fuck are you doing here?'

'He's my lodger,' Elizabeth answered nervously. Hugh caught his breath at the description.

'A fucking lodger fucking my fucking sister,' the stranger shouted, taking a punch at Hugh in a wide arc that connected against the odds. Hugh staggered but didn't try to defend himself.

'A fucking Irish lodger, to cap it all!'

He caught him again, and again Hugh was passive. He glanced at Elizabeth who didn't believe this was happening. He was tougher looking, but Hugh knew he was by far the stronger.

'Hit him! Hit hit!' Elizabeth screamed.

The stranger stopped dead, scowled, then punched her in the face. She fell backwards, crashing against the table. Hugh straightened and, as the stranger turned to strike again, hit him with all his strength and weight on the chin. He fell where he stood, unconscious.

Elizabeth, hand to her face, stared at the heap on the floor, and a curious interval passed before Hugh asked if she was all right. She mumbled something, her voice breaking, and turned into his arms, asking him the same question. Both their faces were beginning to swell.

'You've a bruise coming up already,' she said, delicately touching his face.

'Your beauty's going to be spoiled for a day or so too,' he said. He found it difficult to smile.

'Is he dead?'

'Not my brother,' she said. 'He wouldn't do me the favour.'

'Your brother?'

'Will you check him, Hugh. I'm scared.'

'Your bloody brother,' he said, settling on his hunkers and patting Sam's face. 'Are you all right, there?' He patted him harder and Sam opened his eyes. 'Do you want some brandy, or something?'

'Brandy? Yeh,' Sam said weakly. He was very pale. Elizabeth found some, a mouthful in a forgotten bottle, and knelt to give it to him while Hugh cradled his head.

'You sodding nuisance, Sam,' she said as he sipped. 'Why don't you mind your own bloody business.'

He recovered and they helped him to his feet.

He looked comic, his Brylcreemed hair askew, his jacket crooked, but Hugh was too tired and sore to laugh. Sam looked at Hugh and whistled.

'Blimey, Paddy, I never saw it coming.'

'His name is Hugh,' Elizabeth said. 'Hugh Kinsella. Hugh, this is my wretched brother, Sam Frampton.'

'Wotcha, Hugh,' Sam said, extending his hand. 'I respect a man with a good punch. Don't mind at all,' he continued as Hugh accepted his hand, 'don't mind at all you being the father of my neph.'

'How did you know that?' Elizabeth shot at him. He scratched his head.

'Millie! I'm your flesh and blood, Beth. Your flesh and blood, remember. Didn't know he was Irish, though.'

'Well then.' She said it as a challenge.

'You're a good bloke, Hugh. I can see that. Well,' he said, looking at Elizabeth, 'how about a celebration?'

'Celebration?'

'Yes, I think we should celebrate,' Hugh said.

'Time enough when the bastard is born,' Elizabeth said, annoyed.

'Bastard? Bastard?' He looked from Elizabeth to Hugh and back again, a fleeting anger turning to puzzlement. 'Ain't you two getting hitched, then?'

'No,' Elizabeth said. 'He's going to be a bastard.' The word rang strange in Hugh's ears. But Elizabeth seemed to enjoy the notion.

'Oh,' Sam said, scratching the back of his neck. He looked up at Hugh. 'So you ain't going to be my brother-in-law after all.'

'Looks like it,' Hugh said.

Without warning, Sam punched him in the face and he fell back, dazed. Sam laughed heartily.

'Gotcha, mate.'

Elizabeth stood back and kicked him as hard as she could in the arse.

'Hey!' he shouted in pain and surprise, holding his arse.

'Get out of here, you bleeding jailbird. Get out!'

'Aw, sis, I was only malarking.'

Hugh was laughing silently, holding his face with one hand and his aching stomach with the other.

'See that? See that?' Sam was triumphant.

'O Christ, Hugh, don't encourage him.'

'He's a real man, sis. We're going to get on. It's going to be just great. That right, Hugh mate?' he added, turning to Hugh.

'Out.'

'Kicks like a mule, she does,' he laughed to Hugh, holding his arse again. 'Cheery-bye,' he said, backing out. 'Here, look at him,' he said, still bright and smiling, to Elizabeth. 'Laughing his head off.' He disappeared into the hall. 'He's a good bloke,' he called back as he closed the door behind him.

Elizabeth laughed then too, gingerly holding her face.

'Oh no.' Trying to hold back the laughter, she steadied herself against a chair. 'We'll be two swollen pumpkins in the morning.' This made them worse. She couldn't help herself, and soon both of them were laughing hard, the pain temporarily forgotten.

He hadn't noticed the leaves falling, but there they were, all of a sudden it seemed, bronze and huddled together, before they corrupted into the earth. Even if they were in the gutters, he thought, they were going to the earth. He mused about this for weeks, the notion coming back to console him when he let his thoughts drift, dreaming of Elizabeth's swelling belly and their little bastard. The word had shocked him at first, but now it amused him.

At first she went through the mill, standing over a conveyor belt all day, but as her belly swelled, Elizabeth also became softer and happier. How she could eat beetroot and chocolate at the same time was beyond him, but apart from her demands that he keep her supplied with these, she also became more indulgent, and more at ease about Karl. This made life simpler and happier for Hugh, too.

He loved the naked, true trees of November and, for the first time in his life, he didn't resent winter and its hardship. You could see how strong those trees were, how they were only waiting for spring.

To ease Elizabeth's burden, he had taken to shopping on Saturday afternoons while she went to the hospital. He had never really understood the ration coupons, but he liked shopping in the markets as darkness fell and the lights came on in the stalls.

One evening he was returning in the rain along Hornsey Road, a full shopping bag in each hand, when he spotted her walking under the railway bridge. God, she's lovely, he thought. How in Christ's name did I have the luck to find her? By the time he turned into Citizen Road, she was home, and he marvelled at how fast she walked, though she was pregnant.

She was waiting for him, sitting at the table, when he got in. Parts of her hair were stringy where the rain had seeped through her scarf. He put the bags on the table, and almost immediately small puddles of water formed around them.

'They let me see him,' she said. Then she started crying, silently. 'He's in prison, you know. And I put him there.'

'Sure he has to be there', he said, sitting down in front of her, 'for his own good.'

He glanced at her bag, lying empty and crumpled on the table.

'At least you didn't have to bring the apples and biscuits home again.'

Her smile was gone almost as soon as it started.

'The doctor gave him a poem in German. He was very excited about that. Maybe the doctor's mad too. He is mad, you know, Hugh. I mean, he's not violent or anything and what he says makes sense, but he grins all the time, and his eyes – ugh' – she shivered – 'they're so ... they're so ... starey, and bright, as if they were hiding something. And worst of the lot, he doesn't seem to mind being in that place. He trotted off happy as you like when I said goodbye.'

She kept going to see him, and all he could do was admire her courage and feel bad about the lack of his own. Each time she prepared to go, she asked him to go with her, and he knew what the solitary journey cost her, but he couldn't, even when, with just over a week to Christmas, he was laid off. It was very cold now, and yet she said they went into the gardens when she visited, sitting under a favourite tree. He began to see trees differently. When he looked up at them, black in the winter light, he shuddered.

To make himself feel useful, he started to cook. She laughed at him at first, but exhausted by work and her visits to Karl, she was pleased, even if what he made was almost inedible. So she taught him the basics, and each night made a menu from her ration cookery book for him. There was still a lot lacking in comparison to her easy touch, but she didn't seem to mind.

'I could get used to this,' she laughed. She said that almost every night.

The Saturday before Christmas they were in the Nag's Head. It was crowded and they had to raise their voices to be heard.

'Millie and Sam want me to spend Christmas with them.'

'Oh. Right.'

'Why don't you invite Seán to stay with you? I can make you a chicken and a plum pud! Of sorts.'

'That'd be grand.'

'Go on now, ask him in case he makes other plans.'

He made his way through the crowd. Seán was working flat out but spotted him.

'Same again, Hugh?'

He nodded.

'What are you doing for Christmas, Seán?' he asked as he paid him.

'Christmas Eve and I'll be on the vomit bucket home to Thomastown.' Seán cackled and was away to another customer.

'Well?' Elizabeth asked as he returned.

'Oh, sure he's delighted,' Hugh said.

'That's settled then. I'll make you a feast before I go.' She was relieved.

'What about Karl? Won't they let him out for Christmas at least?'

'No.' She shook her head. 'No, he's not well enough.'

'God, it's awful,' he said, putting an arm around her.

'Hugh . . . not here,' she said, freeing herself.

*

The shopping crowds brought home to him the reality of Christmas. He knew he ought to buy her a present but he was at a loss as to what she might like. Now that he had time to himself, he was thinking back a lot over the past months, marvelling at how his life had changed. It brought him back on the underground, reliving their first kiss, their happy time browsing in the market. He wandered amongst the stalls, so different in winter to that showery summer's day. He remembered she liked the portrait of a boy, and he was excited about this, as if everything was falling into place, but there was no portrait of a boy to be found.

'Like some jewellery for your lady, sir?' He turned to see an African grinning at him.

'What have you got?'

'Earrings, bracelets, necklaces, chains. I think you'll find what she'll love you for here.'

Hugh looked up from his browsing and grinned back at him.

'D'you think so?'

'Nothing more certain.'

He liked the tall, thin African, grinning in his ill-fitting brown suit and loose overcoat.

'Is this gold?' he asked about a ring.

'That's African gold, my good fellow. The best in the world.'

Hugh tried to fit it, but as he hoped, it wouldn't. He remembered how he had thought about her fingers as he had travelled home alone on the tube, and yes, this ring would fit her ring finger.

On Christmas Eve she was up early to cook the chicken. The pudding was already on the sideboard from the night before, decorated with a sprig of holly. He could smell the chicken while he was still in bed. The cold on the stairs woke him fully, but there was a blast of heat as he came into the kitchen.

'Morning, love,' she said. She fussed over him as she made him breakfast. She was in high good humour because the foreman had said she could work as long as she felt up to it. One of the women had twigged she was pregnant and had spilled the beans. He wanted to sack her on the spot, but relented when she told him that her husband was out of work till the spring. It was funny how people couldn't resist looking sideways at your ring finger as soon as you mentioned a husband, but she didn't care as long as she could keep the shillings coming in, tough and all as it was.

'Husband?' Hugh had asked, cocking one eye at her. 'Well, you know . . .' she'd grinned.

'That's right,' he'd said, 'be sure to treat your husband well, like a good little wife.'

She had hit him over the back of the head with a dishcloth.

Now she sat with him, having a cup of tea as he finished his breakfast. He stretched back, trying to be casual, then pulled a red velvet bag from his pocket and gave it to her.

'Your Christmas box,' he said. She was taken aback, but untied the ribbon and peered inside, then took out the ring and put it on her palm.

'What's this, then?' she asked quietly.

'What does it look like?'

'Does this mean we're getting married?'

'If you like.' Now that she had put it so plainly, the idea alarmed him, but it was obvious, really.

'I don't know. I'll have to think about it.' She slipped the ring back into the bag, and deliberately tied it. 'It's nice,' she said.

'It's African gold,' he said.

'African gold. Fancy that.' She couldn't look at him, and seemed lost in herself, soft but distant. He had never seen her look like that. 'Well, I should get ready.' She took the pouch and without looking at him, went to her room.

'What about the chicken?' he called after her.

'Oh. I'll see to that before I go.'

He laid his head in his hands.

'O Christ,' he whispered. 'O Christ.'

He sat there until he heard her door close, then he grabbed her menu book and pretended to read it. She came in, placed her hat on the table, and with a dishcloth to protect her, she prodded the chicken before taking it from the oven.

'Isn't your mouth just watering,' she said, without looking at him.

'It is, begor.' Her make-up made her look like a film star. She was dressed in her blue suit. Her stockings had a black seam up the back.

'What time is Seán coming?'

'Oh, in his own time, I suppose.'

'Well, wish him Happy Christmas, then. I'm leaving this in the pantry box with the pud. Just pop it in the oven to heat it.'

'How long are you going for?'

'I'll stay for Boxing Day, I think. Well then, I'm off.' At last she smiled at him, lifting his heart. He rose.

'Happy Christmas.' He went to kiss her and she offered her cheek.

'Can't ruin my make-up, darling. Don't know why I dressed up, but there you are. Happy Christmas.' She touched his face with her left hand, and he saw that she was wearing the ring. Then she twirled around.

'How do I look?'

'You're like a film star.'

'Oooew, you are nice!' she laughed. 'Tooraloo. And don't you boys get up to mischief.'

And then she was gone. His heart was pounding. He ran out and called after her.

'Tell Sam and what's her name I wish them Happy Christmas!'

'I will,' she called back. She was wearing her blue coat, carrying a small case, and those new Seeba shoes made her rear end stick out nicely.

Beside himself, he watched her walk up the road until she was out of sight. Once inside, he pinched a morsel from the chicken. It was delicious.

He was at a loss what to do. He made his bed. As he looked in the mirror in his room, he thought of Karl, and wondered if he could make it to the hospital. It didn't seem right, to have him in there Christmas Eve, with a crowd of madmen. But he knew he wouldn't go, even if it had been practical. Thinking of Karl drew him to his room. Elizabeth dusted it down every few weeks, but apart from that, no one had been in there and, as he opened the door, he knew he was breaching a trust. Everywhere there were books, and in a corner were records, the mauve labels visible through the buff covers, some tattered at the edges. By contrast, the table was neat, with just one or two books, and a metal box. He opened the box. A compass, some pencils, geometrical drawing tools. He closed it. One of the books was actually a sketchbook, half full of careful geometrical drawings. He picked up the other. *Stars in their Courses*. So Karl was an astronomer, too.

He flicked through the pages, pausing at the black and white photos. That night in the bomb-site, the night he had seen the reflection of a star in a pool of water, came back to him. It all seemed so long ago, part of a time which had fallen asunder after Karl went into hospital.

He shook his head. There was no point getting upset about it all over again, and he waited till the Nag's Head opened. With Seán on the vomit bucket, he had no point of reference, and fell in with some Irish and, as he had intended, got drunk. The men left him, said they were going to Dublin on the last boat out of Holyhead. He wished them luck, and he was alone for a few moments.

'Young fella, would you buy a melodeon?'

'I don't play.'

'Feck it, can't you learn!'

'There must be something wrong with it if you're selling it.'

'Wrong with it?' The man opened the wrinkled leather straps and played a lively reel, beaming at Hugh. 'Now,' he said, 'what's wrong with that? Not a ha'porth. Not a ha'porth, boy.'

'Then why are you selling it?'

'Were you born suspicious ... or has life made you that way, young fella?' He leaned back against the wall, weary. 'I promised my mother I'd see her for Christmas. But I've pissed the fare into the Thames. I haven't seen that poor woman for ten years.' His eyes lifted, without bitterness, towards Hugh. 'Now are you happy?'

They struck a deal and the man bought him a drink for luck. 'I'll just make it,' he beamed, and he drank back a pint without pausing for breath.

'Give your mother my regards,' Hugh said as the man exhaled loudly.

'I will. By God I will. And may God bless you,' he said, before leaving.

'And you too,' Hugh said to himself. He left the drink and went home, tempted on his way to invite some Irish who had gathered outside the pub. He had visions of a party, with whiskey and music and chicken and pudding, with him playing the melodeon as if he had played all his life, but they started fighting over two women in the company and he slipped away through the fog. It was so bad he could hardly breathe, and when he got inside and blew his nose, it left black smudges on his hanky. The fire had almost died, so he shuttled in some coal and, sitting as near to the range as he could, he opened the straps on the melodeon and tried it.

He would have given that poor sod twice what he asked. He wanted it as soon as he saw it. His father had had one like it, and he recalled how he would play some tunes when the neighbours called. Or sometimes, for no reason, he would take it down in the weak light of the tilley lamp, and play it before the fire, the flames breaking the shadows across him. Hugh loved it most of all because his mother loved it, and often she would harmonize with her mouth music. Brendan had taught him one slow air, 'Eiblín a rún'. He practised it over and over until it was fluent, and then played it through, at one with his perfect memories.

On Christmas morning he slept till late. He made himself a cup of tea and toast, piling on the marmalade. Despite a hangover, he was hungry and then remembered the day it was and her chicken and plum pudding, but when he opened the pantry box he found a bottle of Irish whiskey in front of them. Neatly arranged either side of the food were two crackers.

'Happy Christmas, darling,' he whispered. He kissed the bottle. 'Happy Christmas.' He put them all on the table and got himself a glass. 'Here we go again,' he thought as he put a glass of whiskey to lips, but he didn't drink it. It wasn't right keeping all this to himself on Christmas Day. And besides, he'd have to eat and drink twice as much as he wanted or else Elizabeth would be offended that Seán didn't like her cooking. So he gathered it all in a bag and as darkness fell, he went to a bomb-site where he knew there were people sleeping out.

They were easily spotted by the light of the fires, and he chose one, a small group of three men and a woman.

'Happy Christmas to you, people.'

'Ah! The Salvation Army! What kept you?' shouted an Irishman.

'That's no Salvation Army,' said the woman, who had a Cockney accent, 'that's a Paddy.'

'I've a small bit of grub and a bottle of Irish whiskey,' Hugh said by way of introduction.

The one who had hailed him fell to his knees.

'A bottle . . . a whole bottle . . . of Irish whiskey?' He clasped Hugh to him by the legs. 'The blessings of the prehistoric Irish gods on you . . .'

'Enough of your guff, O'Flaherty. What has the decent man brought us?' said another Irishman. O'Flaherty stood, and grandly introduced himself and the company.

'My name is Cathal,' he said.

'Of the Blood Red Eyes,' guffawed the other.

'Never mind that Protestant,' said Cathal. 'This is Annie of the East.'

'How do,' said Annie.

'The finest flower of East London. And this is Stefan, from the wilds of Europe. He says very little and we know him, because of his big belly, as the Lance Corporeal.' The Lance Corporeal said nothing but took the whiskey from Hugh and drank back several mouthfuls, nervously watched by the others. 'And this', said Cathal, relaxing only when the bottle was handed to Annie, 'is George, the only Protestant Irishman in the grand bombed palaces of London.'

'You're just a spalpeen, O'Flaherty,' said George, drinking back his share.

'He still thinks he's on horseback,' Cathal said, pulling the bottle from him and drinking deep. Hugh patiently waited his turn, but Cathal handed the bottle back to Annie, who purred with pleasure. Then Cathal took a deep breath.

> 'Go deo, deo, arís, ní raghad go Caiseal
> Ag díol ná ag reic mo shláinte
> Ná ar mhargadh na saoire im' shuí cois balla
> Im' scaoinse ar leataobh sráide.
> Bodairí na tíre ag tíocht ar a gcapaill,
> A fhiafraí an bhfuilim híreáilte.
> O téanam chun siúil tá an cúrsa fada,
> Seo siúl an Spailpín Fánach.'

'What does that bleeding mean?' Annie asked. 'He's always rambling in Irish,' Annie cackled to Hugh.

'What does it matter a fuck what it means,' Cathal said,

suddenly bitter. 'Give us that,' and he grabbed the bottle of whiskey.

'It means,' George said dryly,

'Never, ever again will I go to Cashel
To sell my health to the highest bidder.
Or to the market place, sitting against the wall
On the side of the street like an eejit,
The big bucks of the country arriving on horseback
Asking if I'm hired.
Come on, let's go, the road is long.
This is the way of the Spalpeen Fanach.'

'Blimey, I'm as wise,' Annie said.

'Nothing much has changed,' George said, taking the bottle back from Cathal, who had sat down.

'Fuck you,' Cathal said. 'Fuck you, George . . .'

'I've a little bit of food,' Hugh said. 'Maybe we can share it.'

Annie scrambled over to him and took the food, taking her share and dividing the rest among the others. Dumbfounded, Hugh watched as they devoured it. The Lance Corporeal threw the empty bottle away.

Apart from the pinch of chicken the night before, he had had not one scrap or drop of the Christmas dinner Elizabeth had so lovingly prepared. Now that he had no more to give, they ignored him, and talked and cursed among themselves. He took the crackers out of the bag and threw them on the flames. They exploded, but still the party ignored him. He went back to the empty house, and whiled away the time until Elizabeth returned the next day.

She came back laden with biscuits and cake and some duck.

'Sam nicked them,' she said grimly. 'The blighter'll have us all nabbed for fencing.'

'Are you serious?'

'I better tell you, darling. That brother of mine spent five years in Holloway. Stay on the right side of him. He's got a big heart, but don't get involved in any of his crazy schemes. By the way, like all jailbirds, he's very moral and he wants us to get married. He got drunk on the spot when he saw my ring.' She raised her hand to admire the ring and grinned.

' "This I have to celebrate, sis," he said. Not that he needed an excuse.'

'Are we getting married, then?'

'Millie says she's looking forward to a day out in the registry office.'

'The registry office?'

'You're the one who wants to get married. Sam and Millie think you're very upright.'

She went to her room in high spirits. He looked around him in bewilderment. He was getting married. A registry office!

That Friday he went to the Nag's Head. Seán was back, and he got straight to the point.

'Seán, when you see Elizabeth, you're to thank her for a wonderful dinner on Christmas day, all right?' Seán's mouth dropped. 'The chicken was delicious, and you haven't had a plum pudding like it in years, do you hear me? And the whiskey – sure you were legless with your man – that's me – filling up your glass before it was properly empty. Have you got all that?'

'Oh, a mighty chicken altogether,' Seán said. 'And as for the plum pudding, well, words fail me. And your man here,' he said to the absent Elizabeth, 'he never stopped pouring. I was so drunk that I fell asleep at the table, and we had to finish the bottle on Stephen's Day.'

'And the crackers,' Hugh said, remembering.

'God, was I *that* drunk?' Seán asked, surprised. 'I don't remember the crackers.'

'It's like this, Seán. Get it right, and you'll be my best man. Get it wrong, and I'll be a bachelor for the rest of my life.'

'God, you're a hard man, Hugh, there's no doubt. My Mary does a lovely "Ave Maria", if you're looking for a singer for the wedding.'

*

Elizabeth's good humour lasted. Nothing seemed to bother her any more, not even Karl's incarceration. It made life easier for Hugh, but he knew that his life was moving in a certain direction and he had no control over it. After mulling on this for some time, he realized why. There were certain things he would not face, and so he lost control. Seeing Karl was one of them, and meeting his father again was another. He took the easiest solution first, and in early January he surprised Elizabeth by announcing that he was going to the hospital.

'My,' she said, 'what brought this on?'

'There's certain things I want settled before the chap is born. What are we going to call it, anyway?'

'Not *the chap*, that's for certain. How about Charles?'

'You're going to call my son after the Prince?'

'Well, it's the English for Karl . . .' she ventured.

'Oh. That puts a different slant on it. That's a good idea, in fact. Fair dues to you. Can I call him Charlie?'

'That's what I'd call him.'

'That's settled then. What was your father's name?'

'Jack. John.'

'Charles John Brendan – Brendan after my father. What do you say?'

'Done.'

'Done.'

On his way to see Karl he thought about Charlie, who seemed to take on a reality now that he had a name. She had said, *I'm going to have your son*, and now he wondered why. Not child, but son, with a certainty which left no room for doubt. So much so that he hadn't questioned it till now. Reflection, that was the word he was looking for. She wanted to see him reflected as a child, and now he did too. Perhaps it would explain many things.

Charlie, that would be his name. After Karl. They were excited about that. Karl, who had no family, would be commemorated in naming a new life. Hugh wished he could tell him today, but as she hadn't told him about the child, Elizabeth had advised him to say nothing. *Wait till he's better*, she had said.

Charlie would grow up in the city, with an English accent, with no conception of the mountain. Excited, he realized that he could bring him to Ireland, to the mountain, when he was old enough, maybe in three years or so.

In the tube, the rattle and hum of the train lulled him. He wasn't thinking, although as always Elizabeth was with him, so maybe he was thinking about her.

Karl was in the garden. A nurse pointed him out under a tree. Someone, maybe Elizabeth, had given him a hat. He was well wrapped against the cold in a brown overcoat and scarf. Hugh had taken off his cap when he entered the hospital. He supposed it reminded him of a church, and it stayed in his pocket. Hugh went down the steps towards him, very nervous. Karl smiled and offered his hand, which Hugh shook.

'Sit down, Hugh, it's good to see you.'

'How are you at all, Karl?'

Hugh was surprised that he looked so ordinary. Other-worldly, sure, but not in any frightening way. He could have been a monk. Maybe he looked a bit scary when he talked about the myth of the tree they were sitting under, but it didn't take a genius to see that the story was about some hard suffering. Suffering was always scary but it wasn't mad.

They walked among the trees and shrubs, Karl jawing on about trees, and just for something to say, Hugh told him how the old Irish alphabet was based on trees. That impressed him mightily.

It started to rain lightly and they walked back to the hospital.

'How is Elizabeth?' Karl asked him in the hall.

'She's grand.'

Karl smiled, and shook his hand.

'When are you going to marry her?'

'Ah now!'

Jesus! He might or might not be mad but he was no fool. Hugh was on the point of telling him but in the end he couldn't. Christ! He couldn't make out why he was so upset. It was as if he had opened his big mouth and betrayed a secret. And yet he hadn't. He had stayed true to Elizabeth's wish, so why did he hate himself, want to be a thousand miles away? By the time he reached home he was drained. She opened the door to greet him, and he walked past her into the kitchen without a word.

'Well?' she asked, quietly.

'He wanted to know when I was marrying you.'

'I thought we agreed not to tell him yet.'

'I didn't tell him. He just knew.'

'Oh. We'll have to tell him the next time we go out.'

'I can't go out again. I can't face him.' She didn't insist. 'It was grand for a while but . . . he looks into your soul, Elizabeth.'

'It's all right, love. It's all right.'

But it wasn't, and Hugh, with time on his hands, remained troubled at what Karl might see when he looked into his eyes.

The weeks passed and the onus fell on Elizabeth to visit Karl, until in February she signed the papers for his discharge. Hugh met them, Elizabeth linking Karl's arm, outside the walls of the hospital. They took a trolleybus, sharing the lower deck with an old woman with false fruits on her hat and a young woman with two squabbling infants. They changed to the underground that took them to Holloway Road.

Hugh walked ahead with Karl's bags, grateful to be of use.

'There now, it's good to be back home,' Elizabeth said as they entered Citizen Road. He could hear the emotion in her voice. They had hardly exchanged a word more than necessary on the journey. It wasn't going to be easy, in the months ahead. Karl had said that he wished to live alone, but Elizabeth wouldn't hear of it. 'It's not right,' she said more than once.

'Now, we've kept your room spick and span,' she said, leading him up the stairs, and he did not protest. Hugh followed with the bags. 'There,' she said proudly, 'clean as a new pin.'

'Thank you,' Karl said.

'It'll be as if you'd never been away,' she said as she stood on her toes to kiss him on the cheek. 'You'll see.'

'It's great to have you back,' Hugh said.

'Thank you,' Karl said again. Hugh thought he looked calm and removed. He had got thin and a bit grey, his clothes hanging loosely.

'Come on, Hugh. Let Karl settle in. It must be a little strange after all this time,' she said, turning back to him, but he only bowed slightly by way of an answer.

In the kitchen she sat at the table and gnawed at her knuckles, distracted.

'Is there a cigarette anywhere?'

'You gave them up.'

'I thought I hid one somewhere for an emergency.'

'Oh.'

'I shouldn't, I suppose.' She looked up. 'I don't know what to say to him, Hugh. Help me. You're not as nervous now that he's out of the hospital. It's me that's nervous now.'

'It'll be all right. Really.'

'I can't get it out of my head that he's going to kill me.'

'Ah, no. Ah, no. Why would you think that?'

'Because of Charlie,' she said, placing her hands on her belly. 'It was obvious so I had to tell him. Because we're going to get married. Because . . . because', she whispered, 'he's mad.'

Over dinner he was polite and sane. He complimented her cooking, saying that it tasted of freedom. The colours of his room were beautiful. He had forgotten the beauty of colour since autumn had passed in the hospital grounds. The eyes became dead without colour. Hugh relaxed and he could see that Elizabeth realized her fears had been unfounded. She was chatting to him, so Hugh cleared the table and washed up.

'But I realize that only two books matter to me,' he said. 'Goethe's poems, and the life story of Beethoven. I will leave the rest to you when I find somewhere to live.'

'What do you mean?' Elizabeth paled.

'You are to be man and wife. That is clear. Besides, I cannot bear the squawking of children.'

'Please stay here, Karl. I need you. Hugh needs you.'

Despite Elizabeth's protests, he was determined and, by the following weekend he had packed a few essentials and the few things that Elizabeth had given him, like the gramophone, and was gone, refusing to give them his address.

*

Two Irish boys and a Pole were killed at work. After a week of heavy rain, an underground river had undermined a gable wall and toppled it. Hugh had been lucky. When the bodies had been taken away, he found his billycan, crushed like a jack in its box. He went home to Elizabeth. She gave him brandy in tea, which he managed to get down, and then put her arms around him which was what he really needed.

'I often heard of those rivers,' she said. 'I hear tell there's hundreds of rivers under London. If you saw the basement at home when I was a kid, you'd believe it.'

She covered his face in light kisses and stroked the back of his neck, like she might have a little boy woken from a nightmare, but her gesture was sensual, not maternal and he was grateful and calmed.

She had been moody when Karl left. It was guilt, she said. Guilt that she was happy to see him go, for the sake of the baby. And yet she missed him terribly, and she was grateful that Hugh missed him too. It was something else they could share. She gave up her job, and was upset over that, but then her mind was taken up with the baby and forthcoming wedding, which they still had to plan. She decided it was time for him to meet her family and her friend, Betty.

'You've never asked me about them, really, have you?' she asked.

'I was waiting for you to tell me.'

She laughed.

'Do you know, that's one of the things I like about you, my darling. You let me have a life of my own. It's why I'm going to marry you by the way, so I hope you've no grand ideas about poking into everything I do once you're legal.'

She laughed, but he knew she meant it.

She needed a sense of being separate, he had known it from the first. She was a strange fish that way. There was always a part of her which drew back, refusing to be available. Now she was opening that secret life slowly. He told himself to remember what that might cost her.

She got up in the middle of the night to go to the toilet, and he woke as he always did. He had been dreaming about Karl and was glad to be out of the dream, although he couldn't remember it. Her original belief that he was going to kill her had never stopped bothering him, much as he had tried to put it at the back of his mind.

'Sorry, love,' she whispered as she came back. 'I know I should use the pot but I can't stand the smell. It reminds me of when I was a child.' She climbed back in. 'What are you thinking about?' she asked.

'I was just wondering what would have happened if Karl had attacked you. I know he wouldn't have. But just suppose. He's a big man. Would I have been strong enough to protect you?'

'Why, you're the strongest man I ever came across. Look at those arms. When did you last look in the mirror? Go on, flex those muscles!'

He roused himself from her, looked at his naked right arm and, after some hesitation, flexed his biceps.

'Cor, look at that,' she grinned.

'Ah, you're just making fun of me.'

'But I made you smile, didn't I? Which is nice for me.' She gathered him in her arms again. 'Because usually it's you who makes me smile, with that wicked brogue of yours.'

'I don't have a brogue! Wexford men don't have brogues! And as far as I can make out, the only one I ever heard speaking with a brogue was a certain Englishwoman of my close acquaintance.'

'Hey!' She gave him a wallop on the arm. 'I wouldn't mind if I had your accent,' she said then, snuggling in to him. 'It's a terrible pity I can't get the hang of it, I'd much prefer your accent.'

'Well, you'll just have to listen to me very carefully in future, won't you.'

'True. I can't sleep. Can you?'

'No.' There was no point in trying to sleep if she couldn't.

'Tell me about your father. What was he like when you were a child?'

'There's nothing to tell.' He yawned. 'He was in England for most of the year – oh, for as long as I can remember. He'd come home around Christmas and stay for a few months, but there was hardly ever a word out of him. He was a stranger, I suppose. The only other man I remember early on was an oul' fella who lived further up the mountain on his own. He reminded me of a bird. He was huge, and yet he looked so light that you'd expect him to fly away if he stepped off the side of the mountain. He used to help my mother in the winter to get firing and keep the well clean. That fed a stream which flowed into a river in the valley. I never saw my father drink except when the police sergeant came to the house to see why I was missing so much school. They were great friends, the father and the sergeant. Of course they call them "guards" over there.

'"Young Kinsella", he always called me. They always talked about London. My father loved that, especially after a few drinks. He loved talking about the Blitz and the sergeant would always have a question that puzzled him from the last talk. As if he went away every time, going over what my father had said and there was always something that didn't quite fit. I suppose it occupied his policeman's mind, made him feel like a detective.'

'Did they love each other?'

'My father and mother? They never showed any signs of it when they were together. Not in my presence anyway, although maybe that doesn't mean much in a country like Ireland. Huh! I've just remembered ... Once, when he was home, I followed him when he went fishing below in the valley. Oh, he went as far as the moor. There was a sandy patch there – Lord, now that I think of it, it was a small beach – in the bend of the river, and there was a pool there where he was fishing for brown trout. He never saw me following him all that way. And then I couldn't bear to keep hiding anymore, and I walked out onto the beach, sure he'd give out like hell. But he didn't. He just smiled and went on fishing, and when I went up beside him he handed me the rod, and the next thing I knew I'd caught a big trout. He was delighted. "Good man! Good man!" He was shouting this. "Good man!" Huh! I'd forgotten about that till now.'

'There you are. And what happens to the farm when your father dies?'

'I'll own it, I suppose, though God knows I wouldn't know what to do with it.'

'And what's this place called, then?'

'Croghan. Croghan Kinsella,' he added proudly.

'No less. Are you one of those Irish descended from kings, then?'

'High kings,' he joked.

She smiled at that and lay back.

'Tell me about this sweet factory.'

'Oh that. Nothing to tell.'

'There must be something.'

'Well . . .' Then she brightened. 'Did you know that there are different stages to boiling sugar?'

'I did not.'

'Well then, let me see. There's . . . *small thread*, *large thread*; then there's . . . *little pearl*, *large pearl*; and then there's *the blow*; and then . . . what's after that? Oh yes: *the feather*; *ball*; *crack*; and . . . *caramel*!'

'That's it?'

'That's it.'

'Do you know something? That's poetry.'

'Ho!' she said, lying back on the pillow, grinning. 'I suppose it is, in a way. Yes. For the first four stages you have syrup. And then with *the blow* and *the feather*, you have crystallization. And then when you get past *the feather*, you have candy . . .'

Within a few moments she was asleep, and he reached across her to turn out the bed lamp.

*

'Will you come and meet Millie on Saturday?' she asked the next morning before they got up. 'You know Sam.'

'The jailbird? I feel I know him.'

'You watch it, luvvy. Don't cross him. Will you come?'

'Of course. I like Sam.'

Before they went on Saturday she went to the local shops to get a few things. To fill in time, he put a pillow under his shirt to see for himself what it might be like. Immediately he felt unwieldy, the pillow pressing on his belly which in turn pressed upwards against his lungs. Thinking of her increasing difficulty with her shoes, he tried to bend down to tie his own, but he couldn't reach within a hand's length of his feet. Then he remembered that when she lay down, she usually lay on her back, and so she had woken him several times with her loud snoring. He lay on the bed with some effort as the pillow seemed to have changed his centre of gravity and, when he tried to lie on his side, the bulk of the pillow pushed him back again.

'Jesus Christ,' he whispered, breathless, the giant tumour on his belly obscuring his feet. And to think that she put up with all of this, and the Lord knows what else, with good temper. Most of the time, at least. In fact, lately, she seemed to wear a permanent smile, as if she had her mind on higher matters. He got his breath back, pulled out the pillow and smoothed it out.

They went to the East End, and Elizabeth was in high good humour – amused, even.

'So this is my street,' she said. 'Do you like it?'

He looked about him, taking in the grimy yellow brick terraces. A sleek black car cruised past. A pub, the Jolly Buccaneer, came to a point at the junction of two streets, forming a V.

'That's Harry's pub. A friend of the family since before the war, our Harry boy. Maybe we'll have a drink in there later.'

Something in her voice made Hugh look at her closely. Her accent had changed, but it was more than that. She put the key in the door, and there was something defiant about her.

'Millie? Millie, where are you?'

'Hang about,' Millie called. 'Ooh,' she said, as she came into the sitting room. Her eyes dropped. 'You must be Hugh.'

'Hello, Millie,' he said, as warmly as he could. She still looked away as he shook her limp hand, which annoyed him.

'Sam's gone to fetch Betty. Said he'd meet us in the pub later. I have some sandwiches ready.'

'I'll help you, Millie,' Elizabeth said, already on her way to the kitchen.

'No,' Millie said quietly but firmly. 'You sit there with your fiancé. I'll get them.'

Elizabeth stopped dead as Millie passed, and turned, raising her eyebrows.

'Fiancé, if you please.'

Maybe it suited him, but the two women ignored him and talked gossip, mainly about the factory, and Sam and Betty.

'He's giving Betty the old one-two, isn't he?' Elizabeth asked.

'That's none of my business, Beth. More tea, Hughie?'

'Hugh,' Elizabeth said. 'His name is Hugh. Hugh Kinsella, and he's descended from the high bleeding kings of Ireland.'

'That's all right,' Hugh said, embarrassed.

'No it's not all right.'

'Hugh,' Millie said, joining her hands and squeezing them until they were white.

'Is that damn pub open yet?' Elizabeth demanded. Millie looked at the clock, but said nothing. 'I'm going to water the lilies,' Elizabeth said, getting up from the sofa with difficulty.

'I thought for a moment she said "millies",' Millie said, barely smiling. 'I'd have swung for her if she had. Would you like more tea, Mr Kinsella?'

'Please call me Hugh.'

She poured him a cup of weak tea.

'Don't take any notice of me, Hugh. I'm just not a social person.'

'That's all right, Millie.'

She looked him in the eye, as if sizing him up, before clearing away the tea things, and he was on his own until Elizabeth came back. He made up his mind to be kind to Millie, although he knew that if he had to live with her he would probably wring her neck.

To get out of the house, they went for a walk. Elizabeth asked Millie if she wanted to come, but to her relief, Millie insisted that they go alone. When they got back, Sam still hadn't arrived, and Millie said she'd stay to let him know where they were, so they went to the Jolly Buccaneer. They sat down and she called over to Harry, introducing Hugh.

'I've heard all about you from Sammy,' Harry said, concentrating on pulling a pint for a customer. 'He says you pack a wallop. Knocked him on his arse.' He put the pint on the drain to settle, and looked at Hugh. 'But then all you Paddies are great fighters, ain't that so?'

'I wouldn't be a match for Sam,' Hugh said.

'No?'

'I want no cockfighting, Harry. That's the truth,' Elizabeth called over to them.

'Would you like a drink instead?'

'I'd like a nice hot port, if you please.'

'Won't it harm the baby?' Hugh asked over his shoulder.

She hooted. 'It'll put him to sleep, hopefully.'

'And the gentleman?'

'I'll have a stout and mild, thanks.' He returned to Elizabeth. 'Is he kicking you?' he asked quietly.

'Here, have a feel.'

'In front of everyone? Ah no, no, it's all right.'

'Come on, silly, never mind these geezers. Don't be afraid. Press.'

He wasn't sure. It was very faint and could have been a pulse. Then he thought he felt a kick.

'Jesus Christ.'

'There you are,' she laughed happily. 'Your son. A footballer.'

For a moment he thought of football in the Croghan valley and Bridie Kavanagh watching him score a goal. He smiled weakly, the life in his lover's belly making him dizzy. 'It's a miracle,' he whispered.

'Go on, you old softie. Get me that port off Harry before he pisses in it.'

Harry didn't look at him as he accepted the money. Well, they didn't know him. He was a foreigner, so what could he expect?

To cover his nerves, he drank back half the pint in one go.

'Mmm,' Elizabeth moaned in appreciation as she sipped her port. He drank back the other half of the pint and went up and got another. He was being a drunken Paddy, true to form, but to hell with it.

'I've been thinking.'

'What, my love?' she said, perfectly content.

'Elizabeth, I'm not on for this registry office lark at all. I want us to get married in a Catholic church.'

'Hugh! You're always springing things on me. Will you never learn to work up to something gradual?'

'Well, I am a Catholic.'

'But you haven't been to church since ... well, since I've known you at least.'

'Mass. Only Protestants say church. Catholics don't say *I'm going to church*, they say *I'm going to Mass*.'

'Oh you are an old bigot.'

'Ah now, Elizabeth, that's not fair. That's an awful thing to say. Orangemen are bigots, but not the likes of me.'

'Oh, shut up, Hugh. I suppose you want me to marry you in a long white gown.'

'No, Elizabeth, you can't wear white – sure you're not a virgin.'

'But I want to wear white!'

'We've left it a bit late. The priest'll see you're ... ah ...'

'Up the spout.'

'Yes, and he won't allow white.'

'Oh bollocks, Hugh. What difference is it to him what colour I wear. No white, no wedding and the child will be a bastard and that's that. It doesn't make any difference anyway. He won't turn blue because his mother and father aren't married in a Catholic church.'

'Please, Elizabeth. I want to do it in memory of my mother.'

'Oh.' She brooded for a while. 'Oh, all right. How about cream? I like cream.'

'Cream sounds grand,' he said gratefully.

'And a nice big church, Hugh. If it's going to be a Catholic church, then I want it to be a big one.'

'I know just the one – St Ignatius's above in High Road.'

'High Road, and all. Their eyes won't half pop back here.'

'I'll see the priest tomorrow after Mass. Will you come?'

'To church? No, I don't like preachers.'

'They're not preachers, Elizabeth. Only Protestants have preachers. They're priests.'

'Priests. I'm beginning to know a bit about you.'

'He'll want the child brought up a Catholic . . .'

She looked at him in disbelief.

'He? The priest . . .' Hugh nodded. 'But what do I know about . . . I suppose he'll make me sign on the dotted line.'

'That's what they do in Ireland anyway, or so I'm told.'

'Blimey . . . Hugh, you're not keeping anything from me, are you? I don't have to become Catholic or anything like that?'

'I was hoping you wouldn't ask me that one.'

'Oh no, I can't stand this.'

'Till I see the priest, I mean. I'm not sure.' He saw she was beginning to get cold feet and decided to compromise. 'All right, love, you've promised enough. If you have to become a Catholic, we'll call the whole thing off.'

'I haven't promised anything,' she said, throwing him for a moment, but then he saw she was mollified.

'You're really very good – you're great. This means a lot to me. I'll make it up to you.'

'Good job my mother don't know about this – she'd turn in her grave, she would. She went to church regular, you know. She thought the Pope was the Antichrist.'

She grinned.

'God, that's what the Orangemen say.'

'Who the hell are the Orangemen?'

'Why don't I get you another port and we'll forget religion and weddings for tonight.'

She sighed in relief.

'That's the first sensible thing I've heard you say all day.'

'I want to meet your father,' she said as he got the drink. 'Soon. He's Charlie's only grandfather, you know.'

'All right,' he said quietly. 'I'll go up to Wedmore Street after I see the priest.'

'That's my boy. Oh, here's Sam and Betty, the charge of the late brigade.'

'I heard that,' Betty said.

'Hello, Betty,' Hugh said, as he stood to greet her.

'Look at you, you're as handsome as anything!' and he laughed in surprise and pleasure.

'Elizabeth told me you were special,' he said. 'And now I see why.'

'Isn't he nice?' she laughed to Elizabeth. Sam had his arm around her and they both looked relaxed and happy.

'He's a good bloke,' Sam agreed.

'Can I get you two fine people a drink?' Hugh asked.

'Told you he was a good bloke,' Sam said, and they laughed.

'Where's Millie?' Elizabeth demanded.

'What's the toff word?' Sam narrowed his eyes in concentration. 'She's . . . indisposed.'

'She'll be decomposed if she keeps carrying on like that.' Betty laughed.

'Poor Millie,' she said then, 'she's had a hard time, losing her little sparrow like that.'

'We've all had a hard time, Betty.'

It turned into a happy evening, and they ended up singing above the noise of others singing in the bar. Even Hugh sang, as if he knew the words, but they didn't care. They were together and they were happy.

*

He had a hangover, but Elizabeth made him get up, and after breakfast he got the bus on Seven Sisters Road. The journey was longer than he had imagined and, when he got to St Ignatius's, people were filing up to communion. The church was a fine big one, and he knew that Elizabeth would be very proud to be married here, but as he watched the mainly Irish faces as they came back from the altar rails, that old feeling of being an outsider returned. There was no going against it. He didn't belong.

As the Mass ended, he went out into the grounds, along with the few men who couldn't wait to light up. He listened to their accents: Mayo, Donegal, Cork. He had hoped for a Wexford accent, and maybe if he held on he would hear one. He looked up at the fine, brick building and swallowed the lump in his throat. It was all over. He would never go back and, just as the main congregation streamed out, he turned and left.

He got off the bus where he guessed Seven Sisters would be

parallel to Tollington Park, and walked north through a maze of streets. He wondered why he was so upset. The church was beautiful, that was why. He thought of his mother, praying in Irish by the fire at night, praying, no doubt, that his father would be safe and would earn enough to come home and look after her. The neighbours and family looked after her, saw that Brendan's wife was all right, but she always knew she was an outsider, and that was how she died. And now he too was an outsider, and that was how he would die. He thought of Betty and Sam, how grateful he was to them for making him welcome. Betty, in her own way, was almost as beautiful as Elizabeth. He remembered her sympathy for Millie. He found it impressive.

There were several children playing in Sarah's front garden, despite the cold. He looked up at the sky and wondered if it held snow.

> 'Ring a ring a rosy
> Pocket full of posy
> At-choo At-choo
> We all fall down!'

One of the older children, a girl, sprawled over a male friend, abruptly stopped laughing and rose to face Hugh.

'Hugh? Hugh! Hugh...' Then she recovered her composure.

'Deirdre...' Her face lit up.

'Have you sweets for me?'

She didn't say *sweeties* any more.

'I've no sweets,' he said as brightly as he could, 'but I have a sixpence.'

'That's just as good.'

'Oh.' He produced the sixpenny bit.

'Thanks. This will buy lots.'

'Where's your mother, Deirdre?'

'Inside. Brendan lives here now.'

He groaned.

'Pardon?'

'Eh?'

'Are you going to see Sarah now, then?'

'Yes. Of course.'

He looked up at the house. Perhaps his father was watching him at this moment, and that he couldn't bear. He angled for a way out.

'Does your mother come to the park any more, Deirdre?'

'She said there was no point when you didn't come. She sleeps on Sundays now. She sleeps with Brendan. I'll tell her you're here, shall I?'

'No! Don't tell her . . .' He shifted uncomfortably. 'I want to see her,' he added hastily, 'but not my daddy. He doesn't like me.'

'He was horrid for a while, but he was lonely. Now he's nice.'

'Is he good to you, Deirdre?'

She nodded.

'Sometimes Sarah and Brendan drink, and then Sarah's horrid and calls me names.' There were no tears or self-pity. She seemed to accept it as a regrettable part of growing up.

He smiled and touched her face.

'You go back to your friends,' he said. 'I'll see you in a little while.'

'All right,' she said. 'Thank you for the sixpence.'

He smiled again, and went up the steps, hardly believing what was happening. He wanted to run, but there was no turning back now. Sarah opened the door in her dressing gown, her eyes bleary and her hair askew.

'O God,' she said. 'I thought you were Deirdre.' She hesitated, and then stood back. 'I suppose you'd better come in.'

'Thank you, Sarah.'

'I'm afraid I'm hungover.'

'So am I.'

She looked at him and tried to laugh, but obviously her head hurt too much, and she led him into the kitchen.

'I've just made a pot of tea. Do you want a cup?' She cleared her throat.

'That'd be great.'

'I suppose Deirdre told you that Brendan is living with me now.'

'Yes. She did.'

'And how do you feel about that?'

'I think it's great.'

'Do you? Good. Thank God you're back, Hugh. He has me driven demented talking about how he has to see you and make amends.'

'Really? He said that?'

'Here.' She handed him his tea. 'You're his son, Hugh. No matter what arguments you've had in the past, you're his son. He loves you.'

He suddenly felt overwhelmed.

'I never thought I'd hear that,' he stammered.

'Hush,' she said quietly, touching his hand. 'He's in the basement. Why don't you go down and hear it from himself?'

'He's downstairs?' he asked superfluously. It seemed an outlandish thought.

'Drink up your tea and go on down. It's the door on the right.'

He drank back the tea and made his way down the dark stairs. He had never felt so strange, and again he had the urge to run, but having stood looking at his father's door for some time, he finally knocked. There was no answer, and he wondered if it was the right door. He waited and was about to knock on the door again when it opened, and there was his father, his braces hanging from his waist. They looked at each other in silence and for the first time in his life, Hugh saw him not as his father, but as a man.

'Well, come in,' Brendan said softly, and stood back to let him in. 'Sit down, sit down.' He drew up the single chair, before sitting on the bed.

'Well, well,' he said.

'How are you?' Hugh asked. Brendan had a heavy grey stubble, and his eyes were bloodshot, but lively.

'Ah sure, just dandy. Great altogether,' he said, his voice still very soft. 'I suppose Sarah told you we're . . .'

'Yes. It's great.'

'Do you think so?'

'I do. You were alone long enough.'

'That's true enough, by God. And you? Have you a little girl?'

Hugh smiled at the thought of Elizabeth as a little girl.

'That's what I came to tell you, as a matter of fact. You're going to be a grandfather.'

Brendan's mouth dropped open, and he stared at Hugh. Eventually, he recovered.

'Be the hokey,' he said.

Eleven

ELIZABETH

February 1951–June 1954

'Oh, get out,' she demanded of Hugh, as they lay in bed. It was a Sunday morning and she knew it was unreasonable, but she had been awake for hours, uncomfortable as hell, and she wanted to spread herself across the bed. 'Get some air in your lungs. Do something. But if you hang around another ten minutes I'll swing for you.'

'Give us a chance to get up, will you? Sure amn't I going to see the priest about the wedding?'

'Oh. That.'

She kissed him and tossed his already tossed hair. He was still half asleep, and now she wanted him to stay with her until he woke, but he kissed her back, smiled that lazy smile he had recently perfected, and left her be. Without thinking, she got up and made him breakfast, and saw him off. But as soon as he was gone, she missed him, and looked about her, bored.

As well as the business about Karl, she was on edge worrying about money. In reality she had nothing to worry about. She had counted up her loss of income between work and Karl's rent, but her savings would last for several months, and Hugh had some put by to tide them over. It was funny, that, how they were so naturally supporting each other now. But still, still!

Once she settled, it was great to have him out of the house. She lay down, hardly able to breathe, but once she spread herself out, it was bliss. She thought back over Christmas, how nice it was to be with her family, although a few days was more than enough, thank you very much. And knowing that Hugh had Seán to keep him company had helped her to relax. They must have had terrible heads on Boxing Day! She laughed. At last, life felt like it should. Of course, Millie had got maudlin, as usual, after a couple of ports. Elizabeth knew she was jealous of the baby, but somehow that didn't annoy her any more, and she thought tenderly of her sister.

Thoughts of Karl drifted back. All those times she had visited him in hospital. Of course, he noticed she was pregnant, but she hadn't the courage to put words on it, and they kept the conversation as light and meaningless as possible. She remembered, horrified at herself, how she had wished they'd keep him in for ever, she so much dreaded having to cope with him. It had all worked out, but at a price. Every damn thing had a price.

She woke as Hugh put the key in the door. It had been a deep sleep, and she badly wanted to pass water. She sat on the bowl in exquisite relief, then looked up as she thought she heard him in his room. It would be Charlie's, in a short while. She threw water on her face, and dried herself, refreshed and happy. She looked at herself in the mirror. There was something older about her, but that wasn't frightening. In fact it comforted her. Things were fitting into place.

She knocked and looked into his room.

'Hello, there.'

'Hello.'

'And what has you so quiet?'

'I met my father.'

'No!' She sat down quickly on the bed and beckoned him to sit beside her, agog.

'Well?'

'It was grand.'

'It was *ghrand*. That doesn't tell me anything!'

'I told him about you.'

'And what did he say?'

'He was delighted.'

'Really?'

'He wants to meet you.'

'Oh! At last. I know we're going to get on, Hugh. I just know. How about next Sunday? We can invite him to dinner. What do you think? Hugh? Hugh, what's wrong?'

'Nothing. It's just – it just takes a bit of getting used to, that's all.' She waited for him to continue. 'He was so quiet,' he said, very quiet himself. 'You'd think he had never raised his voice. And he was happy to see me!'

'Of course.'

'I'm glad you're so sure. I still can't believe it. By the way, I've decided not to marry in a Catholic church. It's going to have to be the registry office.'

'What?' She stared at him, not knowing whether to be pleased or annoyed. 'I don't believe it. After all you said, Hugh. I was looking forward to getting married in a church, and now you want to do it in a godforsaken registry office!'

'I couldn't do it to you, Elizabeth. The priest'd want too much. Especially of you. As long as someone sings "Ave Maria" I won't mind. I'd like "Ave Maria". Seán Butler says his girlfriend does a mighty job on it. We'll invite her on condition she sings it.'

She shook her head.

'Sorry, love,' he said. 'He won't turn blue, you know, just because we're not getting married in a church.'

'What am I marrying?' she asked the ceiling.

Knowing he'd leave it on the long finger, she sent Hugh the following evening to invite Brendan. He invited Sarah too, and said he had wanted to invite her daughter, but Sarah insisted that her friend would mind her. Elizabeth would have preferred if it had been just Brendan, but what was done, was done.

She was taken aback when she opened the door to them. She hadn't expected such a tall man, and at first she said nothing, only smiled at his big, weathered face, before looking at Sarah, whose neat good looks surprised her too.

'This is Brendan, my father...' Hugh was at her shoulder.

'I'm so pleased to meet you, Mr Kinsella.'

'... And this is Sarah. Sarah Considine.'

'You're very welcome, Sarah.'

'Thank you, Miss Frampton.'

'Please come in,' she said, stepping aside. She could feel Brendan's eyes on her.

'To your right, there,' Hugh directed from behind. He squeezed her hand as they followed them into the kitchen. That helped.

'Now,' she said brightly. 'Do sit down.' As they sat, she noticed that Brendan was giving the room a once over.

'Would you like a sherry?' The sherry and glasses had come from Harry's pub. She was very happy.

'Oh! I'd love a sherry.'

'Good!' She poured and Hugh gave Sarah her glass. 'And you, Mr Kinsella?'

'Well now,' he smiled, 'it's far from sherry I was reared, but if Sarah here has a taste for it, then it must be good.'

'Does that mean yes?' she grinned.

'It does,' he smiled back. 'And I'd be obliged if you'd call me Brendan.'

'I think it would be nice if we were all on first name terms,' Sarah said, and although she was smiling, something in her voice warned Elizabeth to observe the boundaries.

'Here's your sherry, so . . . Brendan,' Hugh said. Unable to look at Hugh, he accepted the drink in silence, and tasted it immediately. Hugh was waiting for Brendan to acknowledge him, but instead he looked up at Elizabeth and smiled weakly.

'You've got a grand snug little place here, Elizabeth.'

'Why thank you, Brendan.'

'The young fella's landed on his feet, I'd say.'

'Hugh,' Hugh insisted quietly.

'Hugh,' Brendan concurred, looking into his glass. 'I say he's landed on his feet. Well, here's to happiness.' He raised his glass and they leaned towards him.

'To happiness,' they said in unison, but stiffly.

It was embarrassment, that was all, Elizabeth decided. It would pass in a minute or two, and then she was sure it would be a happy afternoon. She really believed that and, to her surprise, she even believed in happiness itself.

'I've heard a lot about you, you know,' she said to Brendan as they started the dinner, 'but I'd like to hear it from yourself.'

'This is great grub,' he said, eating his pie. He swallowed. 'Don't mind me, Elizabeth. I'm just an ignorant brickie. What this woman here sees in me, I don't know. I don't know if Hugh told you, but she's an intellectual.'

'Tst. Stop that, Brendan. He thinks,' Sarah said, looking directly into Elizabeth's eyes, 'that if a someone reads a book now and then, that they're intellectual. I'm a humble secretary.'

'To a surgeon,' he rejoined, as if it settled the argument. He filled his mouth with food.

'Really? Where?'

'The Royal Northern.'

'On Holloway Road? You don't say! That must be interesting.'

'Yes, it's interesting.' The strength of her eyes unnerved Elizabeth.

'You never told me,' she ticked off Hugh, to break away from it.

'Sarah's a woman of many parts.'

He was still down. Could the old boy not call his son by the name he gave him?

She managed to smile at Sarah.

'And you?' Brendan asked.

'Hugh's made me into a woman of leisure,' she laughed, clearing the plates.

'No better man,' Brendan said, which she thought was a peculiar remark.

'She used to work in a sweet factory.'

'Hugh! That's not of any interest.'

'Yes it is. Tell them about the different boiling points of sugar.'

'Oh that . . .' she said as she laid the dessert. The blighter. She had told him that in their bed, all snuggled up. What else would he blab? 'Well . . .' She sat down and went through it all. Her bit of poetry. Hugh was as proud as anything.

'Oh, that's *very* interesting,' Sarah enthused, taking Elizabeth by surprise. She hadn't expected that.

'There you are now,' Hugh said. 'What did I tell you?'

'I never heard the like of that,' Brendan said.

It was ridiculous, but they made her feel important, and it was a nice feeling.

'You'll have another sherry to finish off?'

'Indeed, and I might have two,' Brendan laughed.

'Oh dear, I hope there's enough,' but Brendan had one eyebrow raised ever so slightly, and she relaxed. She realized she was the slightest bit tipsy. Or was that giddy?

'The perfect end to a perfect meal,' Sarah said, reaching out her glass for a refill. She looked so content it was almost comical.

'How nice of you,' Elizabeth managed, and she grinned back at Brendan.

'I've something to show you,' Hugh said to Brendan as he refilled his glass.

'Oh? And what's that?'

'I'll bring it down.'

As they waited, they looked upward, placing his steps, then followed the footsteps back down.

'A melodeon . . .' Brendan whispered, as Hugh stood at the door, holding out the instrument by the strap in one hand. 'Where did you get that beauty?'

'In a pub.' Hugh gave it to him and, without looking at him, Brendan accepted it reverently, stroking its contours, making it wheeze, before settling it in his lap and testing the buttons.

'Can you play?' Sarah asked, surprised.

'Play something, please.' Elizabeth was delighted.

'What'll I play?' he asked Hugh, looking at him directly for the first time since he came.

'I don't know,' Hugh said quietly, but his emotion was obvious. 'How about "The Mason's Apron"?'

'Oh that!' He wiped his lips with the back of his hand. 'I don't know if my old brickie's fingers are up to it.'

Oh but they are, Elizabeth thought happily. And he knew it.

He closed his eyes and fluently played a tune she supposed was an Irish jig. She thought that perhaps he played a couple of different ones, though she couldn't have sworn to it. No matter. Her foot tapped to the rhythm, and she felt an urge to dance, and would have, if Hugh had asked her and showed her the steps. And then all too soon, as she longed for Hugh to ask her, Brendan stopped.

'Talk about hiding your light under a bushel!' Sarah declared.

'Ah sure,' he said, trying to cover his pleasure. 'Here.' He handed it to Hugh, who took it reluctantly.

'You expect me to play after listening to that?'

'Sure play a slow air, can't you? You used to play "Eibhlín a rún", remember?'

'That's the one you tried to teach me, more like,' Hugh said, but nevertheless, he ran his fingers over the buttons until he had a feel for it, and played "Eibhlín a rún". Halfway through, he looked up at Brendan, who was smiling proudly, and he smiled back. Elizabeth was moved. The two men were lost in each other, their old arguments forgotten in the music.

'That's so sad,' Elizabeth said as he finished, and wiped her misted eyes with her hanky. 'What's it called?'

'Eibhlín a rún,' Brendan said. 'It means "Eileen my dear".'

'Well now,' Sarah said, 'a family of musicians. And here was me thinking that sort of thing only happened in Clare.'

'Oh we can play in the Model County too,' Brendan said. He looked so happy. 'Well now, missus,' he said to Sarah, 'don't you think it's time we got going before dark?'

'Do you think so?' she groaned. 'I'm so comfortable here. And besides, I wanted to ask Elizabeth about the wedding. Which church it is, and all that,' she smiled at Elizabeth.

'There's no church, I'm afraid.'

'No church?'

'No.'

'It's going to be in a registry office,' Hugh said, nervously.

They said nothing for what seemed minutes on end before Brendan recovered.

'It's all the fashion now, I hear,' he said, turning to Sarah.

'Oh yes, of course.'

'Loads of young fellas on the site, now. They tell me they couldn't be bothered with a church wedding.'

'Thank you, Brendan,' Elizabeth said, and she kissed him on the cheek. 'And you too, Sarah,' and she kissed her too. 'Well!' she said.

Hugh was scratching the back of his neck.

'We'd better be going, Elizabeth. Deirdre'll be wondering if I'm lost.'

'Aye,' Brendan said. He shook hands with Hugh. 'All I can say is, you've found yourself a great woman. Good luck to both of you.'

'Thanks. She's a great woman, right enough,' Hugh said, turning to Elizabeth. 'A powerful woman, in fact.'

'Get away!' she said, drinking in the compliments.

They stood at the door in the winter dusk until Brendan and Sarah were out of sight.

'That went all right, didn't it?' She shivered as they went inside.

'Yeah,' he said quietly. 'Yeah it was fine.'

She ran her fingers along his cheekbone. She loved the way his cheek ran into a hollow, and she kissed him there.

'It's all right between you and your father, isn't it?'

'Mmm, it is. I still can't get over it. I always thought he was hard. And he is.'

'He wants to tell you how he feels. He just doesn't know how.'

'Yes. As long as I know that, it's not so bad.'

They went to bed early that night. They had got out of the habit of making love, and he seemed to accept it as part of childbearing. She had her back to him in the darkness and he was lying on his side towards her. She put her hand behind her and brought his to her breast.

'It's all right, love,' she whispered when he hesitated. 'We can touch each other, can't we?'

He cupped her breast, then stroked the nipple with the pad of his thumb, and she closed her eyes, realizing how much she had missed his hands. She lay in towards him, on her back, and they kissed, lightly, his stubble brushing against her skin as he kissed his way towards her breasts.

Little Charlie would have them soon. The brat! She loved the idea of it, had dreamt about it for so long, and now it would happen soon, and as Hugh put his mouth over her tit, she knew it must be like this. She caught her breath as he tugged with his teeth and a current of pleasure surprised her. His erection prodded her. She grasped it, and he delved between her legs. 'Higher, love,' she whispered, more and more agitated. 'Higher. There. There.' She waited until he had a rhythm, then gave in to it, groaning.

'It's gone,' he said, baffled.

'No, no, keep going!'

He picked up the rhythm again until she was beside herself.

'Harder. Harder!' she shouted, and he rubbed her in a frenzy until she arched and pushed him away.

When she woke, he was gone. She looked at the clock. Eleven. She had never slept that late in her life. She got up and pulled aside the curtain. It was drizzling. The house was cold so she put on an overcoat over her dressing gown, and got the fire going and made herself a cup of tea. Thinking back, she realized that she had fallen asleep almost immediately, without as much as a thank you, sir. She put her hand to her mouth to stifle a laugh. Oh dear! He must have thought she was a selfish old cow. Poor boy, stranded like that, with a pregnant whale of a woman, snoring her head off, without a doubt. She wondered if he had relieved himself, and for a moment the thought detained her. But no, she decided, he was far too polite to do it in her presence. She'd make it up to him, and he would love her for ever, a slave to her skills and blind to her stretch marks. Pooh!

Sam was hardly ever there now on Sunday afternoons, and she was beginning to resent going all the way to the East End just to see Millie. Why couldn't Millie come to see her, for Christ's sake? Hadn't she enough sight left to see that she had to carry an extra weight with her wherever she went? She worked herself up on the trolleybus, determined to show Millie how selfish she was. But when she saw Millie's face, her anger turned to concern.

'What's wrong, Millie?'

Millie didn't answer but went into the living room ahead of Elizabeth and sat down, her hands joined on her lap, tears in her eyes.

'Well?'

'I've lost my job.'

'Millie, what happened?'

'The doctor says it's depression.'

'You can get over that, can't you? We all get depressed.'

'I don't want their old job anyway. I always hated it.'

'So how will you live?'

'I just want a few weeks to myself, Beth. I'll get another job then. A nice one. I could almost live off my war pension, you know.'

'I know all that. But what to do all day, Millie?'

'Don't you fear.'

When Elizabeth got home, Hugh was still out, at Brendan and Sarah's, she supposed. Damn him. She couldn't rest until he came in an hour later.

'Guess what?' she said before he could greet her. 'No sooner have I fished Sam out of the fire, than Millie jumps in, head first. Why do we have families, I ask you? They're nothing but trouble.'

They got the licence. She went with him, as he was too nervous to go alone, poor boy, though he tried to hide it and be manly. She supposed that she would have been just as nervous if he had brought her to a Catholic priest, so she resisted the temptation to tease him. She went to see Harry about the reception, and looked him in the eye. What else could he do but say yes? Life was going her way. She knew it. She could do anything she turned her mind to.

'Harry was very pleased I asked him.'

Hugh wasn't impressed. He didn't like the idea of Harry at all.

'Hugh! Darling! He's warmed to you now he knows you're going to be my husband. I'd have boxed his ears for him if he didn't behave himself.' She shadow-boxed his ears. 'It'll save us a lot of money,' she coaxed him, reaching out and curling his hair around her finger. 'And the bride should be in her home place, shouldn't she? That's the way it is in Ireland too, isn't it? Go on! Smile.'

He smiled.

'That's it.' She laughed. 'Whoops! Here, feel it! He's jumping for joy . . .'

But he ignored the baby and put his arms around her lightly, kissing her neck.

Seán Butler agreed to be the best man, and when she asked Millie to be her bridesmaid, she accepted with a faint smile, as if it was her due, all her practical questions prepared.

She had forgotten about the damn dresses, the flowers, the bouquet.

*

All she could think of at the wedding was the smell of Brylcreem. Hugh's face shone he had shaved so closely. He had cut himself on the upper lip, too. Her nerves were in tatters after a night with Millie. Sewing this, ironing that. In the end, she had to get Millie ready, she was held together with hairpins, although Betty had arrived to save the day. It was one thing being late for a church, but it didn't seem right in a registry office. Hugh was afraid that Sarah and his father wouldn't turn up, but there they were, with little Deirdre, the picture. You could cut war bread with the crease on Brendan's trousers. Sarah had enough fruit and flowers on her hat to start a shop.

'And now you may kiss the bride.'

She looked at Hugh directly for the first time since they had arrived. He looked stunned, and then, slowly, very slowly, he leaned towards her and kissed her. Everyone clapped, and she felt herself smiling, and they both turned around, smiling, as if they had practised it.

Mary Flynn, Seán's girlfriend, had been nervous about singing a hymn at a non-Catholic wedding, but Seán had persuaded her. It was obvious she would do anything for Seán. It was what Hugh had wanted, that 'Ave Maria'. Their give and take. She sang it so beautifully, even Sam stopped shuffling and listened. And they all clapped again when she was finished.

'You ought to be in Covent Garden,' Betty told her.

After the tension of the ceremony her mind was empty. Millie affected a false gaiety.

'Is Millie all right?' Hugh whispered.

'She's thinking of her own wedding,' she whispered back. 'She'll be all right after a few drinks.'

Taxis took them to the Jolly Buccaneer, and outside, Sam took photos with his Kodak.

'It's nicked,' Elizabeth whispered to Hugh.

'Jesus,' he said, and then he whispered back, 'They'll never come out.'

A special table had been set aside, the food and drink laid on as a wedding present. Sam stood and called for attention, and welcomed Hugh into the family.

'He's got breeding. How do I know that? 'Cause he landed me on my arse with a sucker punch, that's why.' That got a big laugh. 'And they'll be very happy together. How do I know that? 'Cause she kicks like a Covent Garden nag, that's why!'

'So watch it,' Elizabeth said.

Sam bowed to Elizabeth and sat down to laughter and applause. Brendan rose awkwardly and cleared his throat.

'Well now, I don't have Sam's gift of the gab, but I'd like to welcome Elizabeth into the Kinsella clan. I knew from the first moment Hugh introduced me to her that she was a fine woman who would do our family proud. And thank you all for your hospitality. That's all I have to say.'

Drink quickly made them boisterous. Harry played his ornate accordion. The old Cockney lady and her friend in their long black coats raised their glasses of stout, raised their skirts and sang and danced to 'Knees Up Mother Brown', egged on by Sam. Elizabeth sang 'We'll Meet Again'. The old reliables.

'That's my girl,' Harry said.

Oh dear, there he was, at it again. What the heck. He'd never change, that was for sure, and he had put on a good spread. And Sam said it was the nearest thing to Vera Lynn he had ever heard, so she was mollified.

Warned by Elizabeth, Hugh had got the words of an Irish song and had practised for a fortnight. The booze didn't help the nerves one bit, and he sweated as he sang 'She Moved Through the Fair'.

For some reason it reminded her of Karl and, for the first

time that day, he came flooding back with all his power. She had felt something was missing, and now she knew what it was. He ought to have been here. It wasn't right, him out there on his own, with no one. He should be here, taking his place, singing one of those sad German songs of his. If it was all right for an Irishman to marry her, well then, it was all right for a German to be her dearest friend. The anger rose in her, but then Hugh put his arm lightly around her and whispered in her ear.

'A pity Karl couldn't be here, isn't it?'

She looked at him in amazement and gratitude.

'He would have loved it.' She knew that wasn't true, but she wanted it to be true.

'Aye,' Hugh said. 'He could have sung one of those songs of his.'

Elizabeth knew that he too wanted to believe the impossible, and somehow that made it all right, and she squeezed his hand and smiled.

Sam insisted that Millie sing.

'She's got a voice like an angel, she has,' he said, looking around him as if challenging anyone to contradict him. So he was pleased when she stood and cleared her throat. '"Apple Blossom Time", Harry?' Harry nodded and they tried the key.

'Now Hugh and Elizabeth, you can dance to this one.'

There was a roar of approval.

Oh no, Elizabeth thought. But she took a deep breath as Hugh took her hand and there was a space made for them. Harry started, they danced, and Millie sang.

> 'I'll be with you in apple blossom time.
> I'll be with you to change your name to mine.
> One day in May, I'll come and say
> Happy the bride
> That the sun shines on today . . .'

O Millie . . . She must have been practising for weeks. How sweet! She was a bit flat, but she was getting by. And Hugh could dance so well! He looked so happy, poor boy, and so proud, and she realized that she was proud and happy, too. Harry changed the key and Millie followed. It really was a pretty tune, one that she had often hummed but never learned. And then it was over, the rituals had been seen to and now the party could begin.

'That's a grand music box,' Brendan said to Harry. Harry looked down at the accordion and beamed.

'Not half bad, is it?' he said, caressing it.

Give it to the man, Elizabeth shouted in her head. Give it to him!

'How about an Irish tune, Mr Kinsella?'

How about that! Elizabeth thought.

'Well . . .' Brendan hesitated.

'Go on, Brendan. He plays beautifully, you know,' she said to no one in particular.

'Sure maybe a little waltz,' Brendan said.

'Perfect,' Harry said.

She smiled gratefully at Harry, and he smiled back. She had worried about Harry, how he might take all of this, but he was all right. He'd come up smelling of roses.

Hugh took her out to dance again, and Sam and Betty and some other couples, old regulars, joined them. For the first time, she realized she was married. It was all right. She didn't feel trapped, as she had feared. There was a kind of peace about it as her fine, gentle husband guided her around the floor. She felt safe, and knew that with the seal of marriage, everyone had accepted her loving a foreigner. He wasn't the first foreigner round these parts, that was for sure.

What was it? Respect, that's what it was. And then Harry tapped Hugh on the shoulder, and Hugh gave way.

She smiled at him, remembering as she had no doubt he was remembering their one night of passion under the stairs in her mother's house when the second all-clear of the war had sounded. The first siren, she remembered, had sent them pushing and running under the stairs, but when nothing happened – no bombs, no invasion – their disbelief in the war could last for another while. Yet when the siren went off the second time, she had held her breath, frightened, crushed among the other frightened tenants, and when a man took her hand it was damp.

She remembered it all so vividly as she danced with him. When the all-clear sounded, the relieved tenants, and many of them would be killed in the Blitz, shook themselves down and trailed away, chatting amongst themselves. But Harry, Big Harry, who had been visiting, stayed behind, and they made urgent love as if desperately holding on to something which was falling away, for ever.

*

Hugh surprised her with tickets for Joseph Locke at the Finsbury Empire. He said it was time she got out, and it was true. It was like being in Ireland, Hugh said, he heard so many different Irish accents. Seán and his girlfriend were there, and it turned out that Seán had got the tickets for Hugh. Locke's pure voice carried her out of herself, but twice in the show, Charlie startled her with a kick.

As the weather grew warm, it seemed like it was going on for ever, and that he'd never pop. She went two weeks over her time, and the contractions came and went, and each time she thought this was it, but Millie told her not to fret, and then, just before Millie arrived and she was having a peaceful cup of tea, her waters burst.

'O Millie, this is definitely it,' she said when Millie arrived.

'There's nothing to fret about.'

'Are you sure?'

'You have lots of time, and I'll look after everything.'

At first there was such a time between the contractions, she had time to recover, but as the day went on they became closer and more intense, lasting much longer, and still Millie wouldn't let her go to the hospital. No sense in it, she said, hanging round. She leaned on the table, to give her relief.

Nothing to fret about. Suddenly Elizabeth remembered the stories she had heard of women who had died in childbirth. There had been times when she wished she was dead, but not now. Not now.

At last, when she had barely time to catch her breath between them, Millie relented, and calmly put on her coat and fixed her hat in the mirror.

Elizabeth glanced at her. She had never seen her so confident, and she felt something like awe for her sister.

'How can you be so calm?'

'Well, I've been through this lark before, ain't I?'

O Christ. Poor Millie.

'So ... For crying out loud, Millie, you're not supposed to look so happy!'

Millie smiled, and the sadness was there, nothing surer.

'It's nice to be needed, that's all.'

Yes. Yes it was always nice to be needed. Good for her.

'Where are you going?' she asked, panicking as Millie left.

'To get a taxi, of course.'

'Oh yes.' Elizabeth tried to laugh, but she was too scared.

And then, without realizing it, she was calm. She took her bag, prepared for weeks now, left it in the hall, and put on her light coat and that dressy light scarf she had got in the market. She waited in the kitchen a while, but when Millie still hadn't come, she went back into her bedroom and stood in front of the mirror and looked at herself as she would never be again, if she had anything to do with it.

'This is women's work,' she said aloud, as Hugh floated to the edge of her thoughts. It was as if he didn't matter any more. He might never have existed. Funnily enough, Karl was more real. What might have been.

Still, she left a note for Hugh. Millie would tell him when it was all over, as arranged. He wasn't to worry. And she wrote it down: *This is wimmin's work.* That made her feel good. And then, to ease his worry, she wrote: *I love you.*

Another one came, and she staggered against the wall, gasping. Hurry, Millie. Hurry.

The taxi arrived, and she met Millie, who took her bag, at the door.

'Nice and calm for the cabbie,' she whispered. 'Don't want to put the wind up him, do we?'

She took a deep breath, and pulled the door behind her.

'The Mothers' Hospital, Hackney,' Millie instructed as they settled.

Blimey, Elizabeth thought. We could be on our way to

Downing Street. Millie as Minister at the Foreign Office. They were that calm.

But her fear returned when she was settled in the ward. She was for it. It wasn't death she feared, it was the bleeding pain. This was it. You didn't get any more real than this.

The friendliness of the nurses made her more nervous. Her only reality arrived every five minutes with the contractions. They were all very calm about it, sticking their fingers up her. To see was she dilating, they said. Then a nurse put a funnel on her belly and listened, checking her watch. The heartbeat. You could hear the heart beat? Nothing to worry about. It was her first baby, they told her, as if she didn't know.

It had been going on nearly twelve hours and she was so tired she didn't know how she was going to push the little blighter out.

The light in the birthing room was so strong and white, it occurred to her that maybe she had died after all, without anyone noticing. And then she got a terrible urge to push, but they wouldn't let her. *Don't push, don't push*, they shouted. The pain was terrible.

'It's on its way now, Mrs Kinsella,' a male voice said. 'Keep it up. Push. That's it.'

She screamed in her final effort and felt him leave her.

And then it was all over and she heard his tiny bawling, and she saw him, all wet and slimy, and all her pain was forgotten.

'A boy, Mrs Kinsella. A fine healthy boy.'

She couldn't believe it. His eyes were open, and she laughed with joy.

'Are you sure he's all right?'

'He's perfect. It's six minutes to four, Mrs Kinsella,' a nurse said.

He came to her out of somewhere where time didn't exist, a beautiful little interloper. He lay on her belly, his face to one side, his arms sprawled, as if he too was worn out. He had had a long day too, a long day and a long night, and the little creature was worn out like herself, and she held him by the bum to support him lying there. She had never been so happy in her life.

And then they gave her her nightgown and dressing gown, and brought her back to the ward in a wheelchair. She held her little bundle, looking down on him, wondering what she had done by bringing him into the world.

When she had settled in bed, they took Charlie away, so she could get some rest, they said, and a ripple of anxiety spilled up from the depths of her exhaustion. There was no light in the ward, apart from a shaded lamp at the nurse's station, and no sound except snoring women. Then they let Millie in for a moment, just a moment, they said.

'You never heard me,' she whispered, 'when you were wheeled up the corridor. You never heard a word I said. Fancy.'

'I'm so tired,' Elizabeth said, not bothering to whisper.

'It's only natural,' Millie whispered. 'He's beautiful, he is. What weight?'

'Eight pounds eleven ounces.'

'A whopper! A real whopper. Right then. I'm off to tell the proud father. You sure it's all right I stay the night there?'

But Elizabeth was falling into a black sleep.

She woke, dazed, to bustling nurses calling out names. She sat up, blinking in the May light, as a nurse gave her a tray.

'Nurse, where's my baby?'

'Don't you worry your head, now. He's snoring his head off in the nursery. We'll bring him in after breakfast.'

'Oh.'

She nibbled at her toast and sipped the grey tea, vaguely aware that she was crying, and that she was empty. Her breasts were sore and, when she looked down, she saw that her milk had seeped through her nightdress. When she had finished breakfast, they pulled the screens around and gave her a basin. No such thing as time to relax here. She was itchy and it was a relief to wash, and while it took all her strength she felt better after it

When they took away the screen, the babies were being returned to their mothers, and the doctors were on the rounds. For a moment, she was gripped by panic, thinking they had forgotten Charlie, or that they had given him to someone else, but then a nurse handed him to her. He was bawling for all he was worth.

'He's a beauty, Mrs Kinsella. This is your first, isn't it?'

'Yes. Yes it is.' She was hardly aware of anything but this beautiful stranger in her arms.

'With a name like that,' the nurse asked, tidying the bed-clothes, 'you're not Irish, by any chance?'

'My husband,' she mumbled, pulling aside her gown to give him her breast. Tired as she was, satisfaction flowed through her as he sucked. And then, like a revelation, she realized again that she was a mother and that her life had fundamentally changed.

She had to feed the little blighter every few hours, and it passed the time, but she wondered if she could keep this up for years. Imagine having child after child. Feeding, changing nappy after nappy, washing them. It had all seemed easy before, as if she had been fooled somehow, but now it was as plain as day that it wasn't easy at all. As if reading her mind, a woman called over to her as Charlie sucked peacefully.

'Cow and Gate, love, that's what I say. Cow and bloody Gate. God's gift.'

Elizabeth looked around to her, but said nothing. Cow and Gate. The powdered milk stuff. Millie had talked about that too.

Several times, she wondered why Hugh hadn't come. Other fathers came in the afternoon, but it was evening before he came, smelling of drink as he kissed her.

'Where were you?' she asked evenly. His face dropped.

'Millie said I should let you rest.'

'Oh. Thank you very much, Millie. Did you go to work?'

'I thought I might as well, if you had to rest. Are you all right?'

She was angry with him and didn't answer, but sat on the edge of the bed and took Charlie from his cot.

She held the baby so he could see him and Hugh stared at him, his mouth open.

'He looks a bit scrawny,' he whispered.

'Don't you think he's beautiful?'

'He looks a bit like a *bonnamh*, to tell you the truth.'

'What's a bonnav when it's at home?' she demanded, hurt again by his lack of enthusiasm.

'A young pig.'

'Hugh! Your own son!'

'That's an awful thing to say,' Mrs Dried Milk interjected, but they ignored her.

'Well, they have the same wrinkled skin.'

'You bastard,' she said, holding Charlie close, pouring attention on him and freezing out his loutish father. She knew she had wounded Hugh, but then he deserved it. Or did he? Did he? What was wrong with her? This was supposed to be the happiest day of her life, and she was miserable. Whatever the rights and wrongs of it, she should make an effort, so she looked up at Hugh, mutely pleading forgiveness. He smiled weakly in response, and for a wild moment she thought that maybe he understood what was happening to her.

'Come here to Mama,' she drooled, trying to make it light and harmless. 'After all I went through for you, my little coojy-coo, he calls you a piglet.' She forced herself to smile at Hugh. 'Don't look so glum. He'll fill out and you'll like him then. Here, do you want to hold him?' She held him out, but he hesitated.

'I'm afraid I might let him fall.'

She laughed. Men all over. The boy woke, and she could feel Hugh's fascination as she uncovered her breast and this strange creature, who was their flesh and blood, sucked. She felt content again, and Hugh's undivided attention made her more so.

'You're smiling,' she said, looking up.

'What?'

'That's the first time you've looked happy since you saw him – you didn't even know you were smiling, did you? Admit it.'

'It's a sight for sore eyes . . .'

Yes, it was all that. She felt a wave of pity, and wanted to cry for all three of them, but she just whispered, 'I love you, Hugh,' and she stretched out her free arm and made them a trinity.

'Everything will be all right,' she whispered. 'We're going to be very happy.'

Millie and Hugh came to bring her home, but then Millie insisted that she would look after her.

'Never you mind, Hugh. You've got to work. I'll look after her, don't you worry your head.'

That stunned Elizabeth. She wanted her husband to bring her home, but she said nothing. Went along with it just like he did.

'I've a surprise for you,' Millie said as the taxi pulled into Citizen Road.

'Another one?'

That stopped her in her tracks.

'You'll be in the dumps for a few days. It's only natural.' She paid the driver and opened the door ahead of Elizabeth, who never took her eyes off the child, closed the door behind them, and led her into the kitchen.

'Now,' she said, 'what did I tell you?'

'Brendan!'

'Hello, Elizabeth,' Brendan said. He was standing, at his full height, and smiling.

'I thought you were at work?'

'Well, I took the day off to see you, and my grandson.'

'O Brendan!' She tried to hold back waves of emotion but gave in and hugged him.

'Here. Here he is.' She held Charlie around for him to see.

'Lord, he's a handsome young fella, there's no doubt,' he said, tenderly pulling away the cover which hid his face. 'He has his mother's good looks, I'd say.'

'He's a Kinsella, Brendan.'

He went all dewy-eyed. She knew how much this meant to him.

'May God bless you, and reward you.' The years seemed to fall away from him as he said that.

'Sarah can't wait to see him, but she said you needed some rest for a while. She said I had special permission,' he laughed.

'Tell Sarah thanks from me for giving you permission.'

'I will!'

'And she can come as soon as she likes. Deirdre too.'

'Well now, I can tell you that Deirdre's dancing up and down with the excitement.' Delicately, he took Charlie's hand and pressed a new half-crown into it, closing over the tiny fist. 'For good luck,' he said to Charlie, as if they were cronies.

'Millie, will you make some tea for Brendan?'

'No, I'll leave you now,' he said. 'Sarah warned me you'll need your rest.'

Millie insisted on staying with her when Hugh was at work, and Elizabeth was too apathetic to argue. She let her change and bathe the baby, and Millie glowed. Elizabeth knew it was her role, but she didn't want it. All she was interested in, all that gave her pleasure, was suckling him. And looking into his eyes. She could stare at him all day, baffled that she had brought him into the world. Millie left as soon as Hugh came home, and Elizabeth felt better, even if she had to change the nappy herself. Millie insisted that she wash the soiled nappies, and Elizabeth left them in a bag for her. If Millie had the energy, well then, that was fine by her. Charlie cried a lot at night, so much that Hugh had to sleep in a separate room, and slept a lot during the day, so Millie got the best of him.

Hugh stared at him just like she did, and she recognized the same bafflement. When they talked in bed, any reference to Charlie made his eyes go wide with anxiety. She identified with that, too. Everything had changed; their freedom which they hadn't known they possessed was only a memory, and maybe Hugh especially was too young for that. But every so often, especially when she was nursing Charlie, that queer smile would cross his face, and she knew that the child had changed him, made him deeper.

She was jealous of him for that, shaking her head in disbelief that she was jealous, that unlike him, she could find no happiness in the child. Beyond the pleasure of nursing him, there was just emptiness. It will go away, she told herself. It will go away.

As time passed and he filled out, he developed a personality, a way of looking at her that seemed as old as the hills. This intrigued her and distracted her from that void in her belly.

'See, I told you he'd fill out,' she said when Hugh remarked on it.

'He's like an oul' fella,' Hugh laughed.

Hugh had bought the most expensive pram in North London for his son, but it remained idle, taking up space in her bedroom which was the only place they could fit it. Millie never stopped telling Elizabeth to go for a walk, especially when the weather was so warm.

'Let me take him then. If you don't want to get some air in your lungs, then. Charlie deserves some.'

'No.'

'This is getting a bit much, Beth.'

'You don't have to stay.'

'Oh. I see. So that's the thanks I get. He'll get pneumonia, you know. Then you'll know all about it, let me tell you.'

'I'm going to bed.'

'But you're only just up!'

Elizabeth took Charlie from Millie and brought him to bed with her.

Millie opened the door, in tears.

'I see I'm not wanted here.'

'Millie, you've been ever so good. Really.'

'It's no trouble, Beth. No trouble at all.'

'I don't know what I'd have done without you. Honest. But you have a life of your own and maybe it's time you saw to it again.'

'I've no life.'

'Yes you have. Thirty-six is not as old as it used to be, you know. Don't lie down and give up.'

'There's no one left for me, Beth. The war saw to that.'

Millie closed the door behind her and a few minutes later, she left.

O God. All Elizabeth could think of was Karl. Millie needed someone to look after, that was obvious. That was the way she was and life meant nothing to her otherwise. For the first time since Charlie was born, Elizabeth felt she had a purpose, and got out of bed, thinking what a good match it would be. It would ease her conscience about Karl, too. And keep him in the family. He was part of her family, of that she had no doubt, and it made her realize how important her family was to her.

I'll see you right, Millie! But even as she thought this with surprising passion, she hoped that Millie wasn't coming back. The only problem was, she didn't know where Karl was. She dressed for the street, put Charlie in his gleaming pram, and set off to she didn't know where, dazzled by the summer light.

Hugh was pleased when he heard she had been out.

'I'm worn out,' she said. She resented his easy solution.

'Maybe you should take it easy for a while.'

'I don't think Millie's coming back.'

'Is that so?'

'I see you're pleased. So am I.'

'Well, you said she was getting on your wick.' He put an arm around her, and she stiffened at first.

'Leave the washing up,' she said. 'Let's have an early night, before his nibs starts up. I tell you, he's worse than the Blitz when he gets going. Oh yes, you can laugh. You're not up half the night.'

They talked in bed until Charlie started crying, and then Hugh went upstairs. As she fed the baby, she thought again about how she might find Karl. But he was a clever dick. She would never see him again, that's the way he planned it and wanted it. And yet . . . and yet. Why was life so complicated?

Charlie settled down, and she lay back in bed, longing for a smoke, or some excitement, like a burglar, or for the roof to fall in, to shift her out of not caring about anything at all.

Her life settled into a routine dominated by Charlie. She felt obliged to bring him to the East End, and mend fences with Millie, who just needed a little coaxing and flattery to get her out of her huff, and so it was worth the long trudge with a baby in the growing heat.

As summer continued, her spirits rose. It wasn't that she was enthusiastic, but at least she didn't feel so tired and hopeless. She found herself going to the park, taking the pram although it meant walking all the way, and that having a baby gave people, especially women, a licence to talk to her. So she heard a lot of life stories and a lot of hard cases, which made her seem fortunate by comparison.

She was delighted when Hugh began to bring her to see Brendan and Sarah on Saturday afternoons, and Deirdre fussed around Charlie, entertaining him, delighted when Charlie gurgled at her efforts. It soon became a ritual, and she looked forward to those outings very much. The only thing was, she could never get Brendan on his own, and he was less himself in company, preferring to let others do the talking. She missed that conspiratorial grin, that special consideration for her, though when she thought about it his discretion made her smile, and she was content just to be in his company. He made her feel secure, in a way that her poor husband, for all his love, could never do. Maybe it was experience, simply.

As soon as she was on holidays, Deirdre dragged Sarah along to see Charlie as often as she could get away with it.

'You should be getting ready to go to France,' Hugh teased her.

Deirdre smiled, but still could not take her eyes off Charlie, brushing his barely existent hair.

'We're not going to France this year, are we, pet?'

'No? I thought you went every year,' Hugh said casually as he smiled at Charlie.

'We decided to give it a miss.'

Something in her voice made Elizabeth wonder if Deirdre's fascination with Charlie was the real reason they weren't going to France.

She asked Hugh about it later but the only reason he could think of was lack of money.

'I wonder if she had a fancy-man there?' Elizabeth asked, intrigued.

'Sarah?' Hugh laughed. 'Nah. Not Sarah.'

But Elizabeth wasn't so sure.

By mid-August it was so hot that it was a choice between the park and the sea, and Elizabeth was adamant she wasn't going to bring a baby all the way to Southend or Brighton. So on Sundays, with thousands of others, they went to Finsbury

Park, leaving the hood of the pram up to protect Charlie from the sun. Karl had been on her mind again. They used to come here together too, and the place was full of wistful memories. But maybe it was time to respect his wishes and cut off the past.

'Don't you think we should rent Karl's room?'

Hugh looked at her sharply.

'No,' she said, fussing over Charlie's bonnet. 'No. Forget I ever mentioned it.' She looked Hugh over. 'You should cover up. You're getting burned.'

'Do as you think fit,' he said. 'It's your house to do as you want.'

'No, Hugh. It's our house. It's our family's house.'

But her innocent question had spoiled the afternoon, and she had to put up with his dark, wordless mood, taking refuge in Charlie. A year ago she would have told him where to get off. But not any more, as if being married to him changed all that, and moods were what she should expect and accept. Funny old world, and no mistake.

As long as he wasn't bundled up, Charlie seemed to like the warm weather and slept more and more, giving her some ease. The more he slept, the more her spirits lifted and gave her room to feel she loved the child, and she took a deep pleasure in the way he suddenly looked around at her and smiled. Then his gums bothered him, and her nerves started to fray again.

One afternoon in September, she visited Millie. As usual, Millie fussed about Charlie. She had bought him a new cap, for the winter, she said, although winter seemed far away to Elizabeth. They had almost finished tea before she noticed that Millie was embarrassed.

'Out with it, Millie. What are you keeping from me? Come on, you can't keep a secret from your little sister.'

'It's nothing . . .'

'Millllie . . .'

'I'm seeing Fred,' she blurted.

'But he can't see you,' Elizabeth laughed, and immediately regretted it. Millie was mortified, even if she seemed to expect wisecracks like that. But there was something hysterical about Millie seeing Betty's old brother-in-law, blinded in the war.

'I'm sorry. That wasn't funny, Millie. Is it serious?'

'Why not?'

'Millie, you've said it. Why not?'

'Well, if you can marry a boy half your age . . .'

Elizabeth took a deep breath and let it pass.

'Is there going to be a wedding?'

'Maybe. He hasn't asked me yet.'

'Well, it's good to have someone to look after.'

'Oh, he looks after me, Beth.'

Her eyes shone when she said that, and Elizabeth felt a surge of affection for her.

'Good for you, my girl. Good for you.'

*

Hugh had by now taken to fatherhood. It seemed to make him more solid and self-assured, as if he felt he had done what was required of him. With knobs on, actually, she thought with satisfaction. Elizabeth spent most of her time absorbed in Charlie, as she changed him, washed him, fed him, brushed his hair.

The general election almost passed her by. She voted Labour as always, but Churchill got in, and she didn't mind so long as it was him. 'The Rt Hon Winston Spencer Churchill' they called him in the papers. The old boy had guts, and he was going to leave welfare alone. Hugh said he voted Labour too, he didn't care much for Churchill and he got a right old shock when Labour lost. He couldn't get over how Labour had more votes than the Conservatives, but less seats. It was funny, she hadn't realized that Hugh was able to vote in England. But of course he was Irish, not German.

And then, it got on his wick that Guy Fawkes Night seemed like a celebration for the Tories. She didn't care, though. Guy Fawkes was Guy Fawkes, and that was it.

Suddenly, it was Christmas. It was their first Christmas as a family, and that made it very special, especially when Hugh brought them to see the crib up in Holy Joe's, as he called it, in Highgate. She hadn't thought of Christmas like that before, and it made her feel – oh, part of something universal. Or something. Around the middle of January, Hugh was depressed. It turned out that his mother had died on the 15th, so they went back to Holy Joe's to light a candle in her memory. Charlie started bawling in the church, but it didn't seem to matter. They were the only ones there, anyway. It was a nice custom, lighting a flame to remember someone. And it seemed to do Hugh a lot of good.

He had not been prepared for the expense a child would entail, and was convinced that Elizabeth had no sense of it. No sooner had he shelled out money for clothes, and then shoes, than she had her hand out again. He worried about what would happen if Charlie got ill, or if she got ill, or if he suddenly lost his job. Such questions ate away at him, and they had rows over money. He wanted to save; she needed money for immediate needs. She understood how he felt. After all he was a young man with no experience of these things. But it couldn't be helped.

The months passed like that, so quickly.

In February the King died, and the Princess had to come home from Kenya to be at her father's funeral and to be made Queen. The Coronation wouldn't be for ages, but at least it was something to look forward to. Charlie was going to grow up in a new era, and she tried to imagine what it would be like. The new Queen was so young! It made Elizabeth feel old, in a way.

They sat around the radio for Churchill's speech, and Elizabeth cried silently. She had loved that man without even knowing it. He hadn't been well for a long time, but he had kept going with a thrilling dignity. She had been sure he would live for years.

'Shh.'

'I never said a word,' Hugh whispered.

'*The King was greatly loved by all his peoples,*' Churchill intoned. '*He was respected as a man, and as a prince, far beyond the many realms over which he reigned.*'

She loved that bit.

When it was over Hugh said, 'He was a fine man, by all accounts.'

'A real gent.'

'Well, the Lord be good to him.'

It went on like that, one day like the next, her time taken up by Charlie. Her greatest excitement was when Hugh got a fridge after Easter. Everyone was getting one, he said.

'There now,' she said to herself, admiring the fridge when it was installed. 'There now.'

It was a luxury, a lifetime away from the want of the war years, and yes, it gave her a certain pleasure. So why did she feel let down?

On his first birthday Sam took photos of Charlie in the white suit Millie bought him, and he ignored their pleas to hide the tip of his tongue as he stared into the camera. Elizabeth cried in bed that night.

'We're just caretakers, Hugh.'

'Hush, love. We're more than that and you know it.'

Charlie was crawling, then it seemed no time at all before he was standing, with the support of Elizabeth or Hugh. They laughed, delighted, at each new achievement and the wonder of it. You'd think he were the first child in the world to take a step on his own and fall on his face, screeching.

He was toddling around, giving them lots of laughs, but the novelty wore off as a new eye tooth tormented him, and their nerves wore thin from his screams and their lack of sleep; but with one smile, Charlie was forgiven everything.

Everything revolved around him. All her waking hours were spent with him, watching him as he grew, sometimes taking his progress for granted, and then, as a whole, understandable sentence escaped him, she would shake her head in amazement that she was his mother.

Christmas 1952, his first real Christmas stole up on them, and they had strange emotions about it, realizing that it wouldn't mean anything without him. Time was passing fast, but events took on a new significance with Charlie around. It was as if they were seeing things for the first time through his eyes, and as he grew she became panicky suddenly if she left him alone, even while he slept, having to tell herself to calm down, he'd be fine.

*

She felt easier going to the East End now that Millie had a man. She was still the same old Millie, always would be, but at least she had someone else to think of now. Fred was a good bloke, and if he was blind he could see right through Millie, but they accepted each other, as if they had come to an unspoken understanding. That was nice. Real nice, and Elizabeth looked forward to her visits nearly as much as she looked forward to seeing Brendan.

She was returning home from Millie's on a Sunday evening the following May when she spotted Karl. Her heart was racing, but she didn't even stop to think, and got off the bus at the next stop. Thankfully Charlie slept through it all as she ran after Karl, pushing the pushchair before her. He had turned a corner and she dreaded losing him after all this time. She wanted to call after him, but his name stuck in her throat. Out of breath, she slowed as she saw him go into a new block of red-bricked flats, built away from the road with bushes and flowers growing in the front.

Something made her look up to see Karl at a first floor window, pulling back the curtains, and she felt like running away. He hadn't noticed her, and so she stayed. The front door was open, and she parked the pushchair in the hall, taking Charlie upstairs in her arms. At least she could say that she wanted him to see his namesake. Her excuse didn't stop her nerves as she wavered outside his door.

Why am I so nervous? she thought. I love this man.

And it was true, she loved him. Not in the way she loved Hugh, but she loved him all the same. Not daring to think any further, she knocked.

'So this is where you've been hiding on me?' she said brightly when he opened the door. She had meant it to be light, but immediately it sounded like a mistake. Not that he seemed to notice, standing there, so gentle he looked empty.

'Elizabeth,' he said simply, as if he saw her every day. He glanced at Charlie, and without him even smiling she knew he loved him.

'Come in,' he said, and then he smiled, just about, making

way for her. 'Sit down. I was just making tea. Would you like a cup?'

'Please.' She was never more in need of one, but his eyes, his eyes were warm and full. Yes. That calmed her down a bit. It was all right. And Charlie was still asleep. Instead of sitting, she looked around her. As far as she could make out, there was only one bedroom.

The flat was modern and comfortable, but bare of pictures or books. He had the gramophone, sure enough, and there beside it, his German records. But no books. She sat on the sofa with Charlie on her lap.

He brought the tea, and she remembered how domesticated he had always been, making her sandwiches for work in the morning, cleaning up after himself, even cooking for himself when she wasn't there.

'Karl, I can't imagine you without your books. Aren't you going to collect them?'

'No. I don't read any more,' he said, pouring. 'Except Goethe.' He looked up, handing her her tea. 'I read him in bed before I sleep. So this is your little boy.'

'Charles.' She felt right proud. 'He's two now, almost. No bother at all, he is. We call him Charlie.'

'After the Prince.'

'No, Karl. After you.'

'After me.' He considered this for some time, but showed no emotion.

'Will you come to his birthday party?'

He smiled, ever so slightly, in reply. Another time and she would have been mad with him, but all she could think of was his dignity. He was like a king, sitting there, calm and above it all. It made her forget herself for a while, forget everything around her, except Karl. There he was, she fancied, floating above the clouds with only her as witness.

'All right then,' she said at last. 'You know you're welcome, and as long as you know that, my mind's at rest.'

Charlie woke and he started to cry.

'You don't mind, do you?' she asked as she opened her

blouse. He shook his head, and looked on as she suckled the child, as if it were something he saw every day.

'My library is his,' he said.

'You what?'

'Everything I left in the room now belongs to Charles.'

'Karl . . .' She met his gaze, and then looked down at Charlie, and smiled. She felt very happy and at ease. Everything seemed so natural and in its proper place. Her nipples had gone so big from the sucking. Hugh wouldn't kiss them any more, said they smelt of milk and made him feel all queasy. But he had another think coming if he thought she was going to give it up. Not yet. Not until she had to. She remembered an old woman saying it was the best way to stop getting pregnant again. Her mind drifted over all of this, and her years with Karl, who loved to suck her nipples. For a moment she let herself fantasize that Karl was Charlie's father. The legacy of books allowed it, in a way. And yet she couldn't bring herself to change how Charlie looked, to allow for a different father. Before he was born she'd done that. More like before he was conceived. But it could have been. If Hugh had been in that caff ten minutes later than he was, Charlie would be very different. High cheekbones, for instance. It was all right to think all these things in front of Karl. Everything was all right.

When Charlie was finished she looked up at Karl again. Neither his position nor expression had changed. How did he do that?

'You're a gent, Karl.' He had lulled her into forgetting the question she most wanted to ask him, but now she remembered. 'Is there someone in your life – you don't mind if I ask?'

For the first time, his gaze dropped.

'Yes. She's not beautiful, or intelligent. In fact, her only quality is that there is nothing exciting about her at all.'

She didn't know what to say to that. He looked at her directly again.

'You are probably thinking there must be something about her that is attractive. Well, yes, there is one thing: like me, her family is dead.'

'I see. She'll look after you, though, Karl. Won't she? I mean, she's capable and all.'

'Oh yes. She doesn't cook like you, but her skills are adequate.'

That made her smile. He still had his humour, that was for sure.

'You'll bring her to meet us? No? All right, then.'

He rose, hesitated, and then sat down on his hunkers to look at Charlie. Charlie looked around at him and smiled. Karl offered his little finger and Charlie grasped it.

'Charles,' Karl said, ever so quietly.

'There,' Elizabeth said. 'Mates for life. His birthday is on the 31st of May, in case you have the inclination.'

'The 31st.'

'That's right . . . Does she live here?'

'No. Not until after we are married.'

That took her breath away. For some reason she hadn't considered he would marry. But why not? She took it for granted that the premarital chastity was the woman's wish, but then she wasn't so sure. He had changed from the old Karl, much as he looked and sounded like him. And she decided she liked the change.

'But she comes to visit you.'

'She will be here shortly.'

'Oh.' She coughed. 'Well, I'm off, then.' She laughed quickly. 'Don't want to play gooseberry, do we.'

'We have dinner. She cooks. I listen to Beethoven.'

'Nothing much has changed, then,' she said, turning to him at the door.

'Old patterns are too reassuring to change.'

That tricky humour again.

On a shelf beside the door, she spotted an envelope with his name and address.

'Can I have your address – in case I need to contact you?'

He removed the bill and gave her the envelope.

She secured Charlie on her hip and touched Karl's face. To her surprise, he returned the gesture, sending a warm current through her, and they stayed like that, looking at each other, not saying anything at all.

She left, not sure whether she was happy or heartbroken, inclined to tears but determined not to let them come in case she met that woman on the street. She couldn't help it, she looked closely at the women she met who walked alone, suspecting and rejecting each one as his bride-to-be.

He never came for Charlie's birthday. Somehow she had hoped he would, but she put it from her mind and told herself to leave him be. He had a life to live. But in quiet moments, when Charlie was asleep, or amusing himself, she thought wistfully about that half hour with Karl. It didn't seem like a year, as they tried to get Charlie to blow out his birthday candle. Her wrinkles were getting more numerous, time was slipping away, and her life was set on a course which had very little meaning except for Charlie.

It had been over a year since she had been to a show, and then, just as she was about to complain, Hugh suggested they go to the pictures. Millie jumped at the chance to mind Charlie, and brought old Fred with her, and as the lights went down in the cinema, she felt an overwhelming relief.

Yet twice, when she was most caught up in the film, Charlie startled her by his absence.

One afternoon she couldn't find the little blighter, until she looked up to the top of the stairs and her heart stopped to see him disappearing on his hands and knees along the landing.

In June they joined the crowds to greet the new Sovereign. Charlie was just two, so it was possible he would remember something like this. They were too far back to see anything, but she got Hugh to raise Charlie over the crowd so he would see the young crowned Queen, a great moment in history, and maybe remember. She bought him a Coronation cup, all for himself.

He was like a little tank, crashing into everything around him, and a real chatterbox; and they were surviving, getting used to the pressure, getting used to their hearts in their mouths when he jumped off a chair or the table. They began to talk to each other in bed again, mostly about Charlie – what he had done on the day, about his future; rarely about themselves, but it drew them closer together.

*

He had had a friend at his second birthday. There was a hole in the dividing backyard wall, just enough to see each other's eye, and Charlie and Nancy, the little girl next door, discovered it. After the birthday, Charlie spent a lot of time in Nancy's house. Elizabeth spent her unaccustomed leisure reading fashion magazines, or old articles on the ideal homes that she had always meant to read, but the novelty soon wore thin – although it was something neutral to chat about with Nancy's mother – and she became restless until she realized that she should just relax until Charlie came back. It was never more than an hour or two, anyway.

As the summer passed, they went to Brighton, and Charlie pottered around in the sand, comical in his white cotton hat. It could have been a mistake to go. She saw a balding man swimming out to sea, and almost said, *Look, Hugh, there's Karl*, as the memories flooded back. But that was all past, now, and you couldn't stay away from a place because of memories. Southend would have been worse.

After the first trip to Brighton, the bitter-sweet memories made her desperately want to see Karl again, but his probable marriage stopped her from making a fool of herself. She was living in a daydream, with no one to talk to but a child all day. All that saved her was when Deirdre and Brendan visited while Sarah was out shopping for the weekend. They did that every other weekend, but what she liked most of all was when Brendan came alone, in the evenings, which helped to break up her time with Hugh.

'How's my little fella?' Brendan always said, bouncing Charlie on his knee, and Charlie always squealed in delight. It was a great solace that Charlie had a grandfather. He had no grandmother, which would have made things complete, but a child needed a grandparent, she thought – to make it a real family.

She managed to give up thinking about Karl.

On a Saturday in July, they visited as usual. Hugh didn't notice a thing, and sat talking about horses and going through the racing pages with Brendan, but Elizabeth saw that Sarah was pale and Deirdre was not her lively self. She waited until she and Sarah went inside to make the tea.

'Is there something wrong, Sarah?'

Sarah stopped what she was doing and bowed her head, before composing herself.

'Deirdre and I have had some bad news.'

'Oh, I am sorry, Sarah.'

'Thank you. Elizabeth . . . of course I told Brendan we had sad news and he was very good about it.' She looked directly at Elizabeth in that unnerving way of hers. 'I have to tell someone . . . Can you promise not to tell Brendan – or even Hugh?'

Elizabeth sat at the table and Sarah sat with her.

'Deirdre's grandmother died last week.'

Elizabeth leaned over to touch Sarah's hand.

'I didn't go to the funeral.'

'Why, Sarah?'

'I hated her.' Sarah struggled to compose herself. 'I mean I loved her but I hated her for . . . O God I hated her for so many things, but most of all because she wouldn't accept Deirdre.'

'Yes. Yes.'

'I kept hoping . . . I kept hoping that she'd write and say that this had gone on long enough, that we were welcome home.'

'But she never did.'

'No. Johnny wrote begging me to come home, because it took her a few weeks to die.'

'Johnny?'

'My brother. But she never did. And now it's too late.'

'I won't tell anyone. You can be sure of that. Is Deirdre all right?'

'She's a little sad that she doesn't have a granny any more. But she had no connection with her, really.'

'Good.'

'Thank you. I feel better now.' She washed her eyes at the sink. 'Well,' she said, rallying, 'we'd better get these men their tea.'

'You'll be fine,' Elizabeth said, rinsing the pot.

They went to Brighton again as the weather became hot. This time Charlie was able to waddle about on the sand in his altogether except for his white cotton hat, wildly swinging his bucket and spade. Hugh helped him to make sandcastles, and they brought him to the shore to get his feet wet and be thrilled by the splashing waves. It was all so like when she was a child here with her family, and the dream about her mother and father walking the promenade came back to her. As she lay on her towel, letting father and son build yet more sandcastles, she wondered if she would live to see herself a grandmother, coming here with Charlie and his children.

The next Guy Fawkes Night, Hugh got some rockets and put them in milk bottles in the backyard for Charlie to light.

'He'll burn himself,' she fretted. 'Don't be an idiot.'

'Ah it's all right,' Hugh insisted. 'Don't be worrying yourself, I'm not a gom altogether. I've put a taper on the end of a brush handle for him. Here you are, Charlie son, grab a hold of this,' and Hugh gave Charlie the brush handle, the other end of which immediately fell to the ground.

'Like this, Daddy?'

'Now hold on, and I'll light it first, and then I'll give you a hand.'

'No, Daddy, I want to do it myself!' Charlie insisted.

'Let Daddy give you a hand...' Elizabeth suggested, but they both ignored her. Hugh lit the taper, and then helped Charlie hold it up, and guide the flame to the rocket.

Whooossshh.

Charlie jumped back, letting go of the handle.

'Look, Charlie, look!' Elizabeth and Hugh said together, pointing up.

Charlie looked up in time to see the rocket explode and cascade across the sky. He was lost in wonder, and she took a deep breath.

'Another one!' Charlie shouted, breaking the spell. 'Another one, Daddy!'

'Oho, you're going to be a rocket scientist, aren't you?'

'Yes,' Charlie said, taking his end of the handle again, and concentrating hard.

They lit six before they went to see the bonfire.

*

Christmas came, and they brought him to see Santa Claus in the West End. Charlie was terrified. On Christmas morning, Charlie woke to find that Santa had brought him a rocking horse. Elizabeth and Hugh had had an argument about that, the rooms were too small, but she had given in to Hugh's enthusiasm. Charlie was two and a half already, and seeing his eyes light up when he saw the tree that Hugh put up made her forget her sadness that he would never be a baby again. Hugh spent hours playing with him now that they could talk to each other in their childish language, and there were times she felt left out. Maybe that's how Hugh felt when he was born, but it didn't make it any easier. She knew it wasn't fair to resent Hugh, but that didn't stop her stalling him in bed, and they would go for weeks without sex, until she couldn't bear it any more.

Charlie was all that mattered when all was said and done.

She got depressed all the same, and a week after Christmas he got it out of her.

'Well, isn't it depressing? All there is is Christmas, going to Brighton in the summer, Guy Fawkes, and then Christmas again. I never saw it before, but since Charlie was born, it's as plain as day.'

'Well sure, we'll go on a world cruise this summer, what do you say?'

'Oh that's right, make a joke of everything.'

'Will we get a television? I hear they're great yokes altogether.'

'We're still paying for the fridge.'

'Oh. Right.'

It played on her nerves. She couldn't get over how each day seemed to drag, but before you knew it another year was gone. That puzzled her, just as Charlie seemed to grow behind her back. The short, bleak, winter days didn't help, and you couldn't bring a child out in the filthy air in case he'd get some awful

280

lung disease. Sometimes the air was almost yellow, there were so many coal fires burning through the London winter.

They had a break at Easter when Brendan arranged that they all go to the zoo. At first she considered it something she should put up with, for Charlie's sake, but it turned out to be a wonderful day as they strolled around the zoo, mocking the monkeys, enjoying the fine day. When they came to the pool with the walruses, Sarah took Charlie from the buggy and held him on her hip.

'Look down there, Charlie,' she said. 'See that big fella?'

Charlie pointed, without a word.

'That's a walrus,' Sarah said.

'A walrus,' Charlie repeated. Sarah looked so young and happy, holding Charlie like that, and Elizabeth wished she had a camera. Sarah described the other animals splashing about, and Elizabeth remembered that she was a teacher back in Ireland.

Deirdre took over pushing Charlie's buggy, and they chatted, entertaining themselves, and in the end it was as good as a holiday. Brendan and Sarah were holding hands, and Hugh nodded at them, grinning, and then took hers. Ah well.

He could have thought of it first, though.

They made love that night, slow, relaxed, loving. It had become something of a duty for her, something to be got over, but this reminded her that they were still lovers once they got the chance. That cheered her a lot, made a lot of things seem not too bad. And when Brendan suggested that they go to the Derby together, all her old energy returned.

Brendan, Sarah and Deirdre came to Citizen Road, and Sarah and Elizabeth packed a lunch.

'Well,' Hugh said to Charlie as he bounced him on his knee, 'you're going to the races, old son, and you can ride a big horse on the roundabout, all on your own.'

'The gee-gees!' Charlie shouted.

'On his own?' Elizabeth protested. 'Not on your life.'

'I'll go with him, if you like,' Deirdre said eagerly.

'Deardree will come with me, Mammy!'

'All right, then,' Elizabeth relented. 'As long as you hold on to him tight.' She smiled and pinched Deirdre's cheek.

They took the tube to Victoria station and then a Green Line bus to Epsom.

'Well, I presume you have a tip for the big race,' Hugh asked Brendan, laughing.

'Indeed and I have,' Brendan said. 'You can put your shirt on Pinza.'

'Pinza? What a name for a poor horse,' Sarah huffed.

They had to shout over the noise of the engine.

'How much?' Elizabeth asked Brendan, whose eyes were shining.

'He'll probably end up at five to one.'

'Will you put a bob on for me, then?'

'I will, surely.' He turned to Hugh. 'As for you, you gom, you cost me a pretty penny that time you ran off with your present wife.'

It was difficult to hear, but Elizabeth fixed her attention on Brendan.

'What are you on about?' Hugh asked uncomfortably.

'I was all set to put a pound – a sterling pound, I'll have you know – on Galcador at a hundred to nine. But your disappearing act distracted me. And needless to say it won by a mile.'

'So how much do I owe you?' Hugh asked, trying to make light of it.

Brendan glanced at him sideways, and grinned.

'Begob, it's great to get out of the city,' he said, stretching.

They settled into the journey, but Hugh had gone quiet, and Elizabeth knew why, especially when he took Charlie from her and entertained him. He always did that when he had something on his mind.

At the racecourse, they found a spot to settle and had their lunch. The tea from the flask was foul, reminding her of the canteen tea at the sweet factory, but no one complained. You put up with a lot because of the novelty of a picnic. Charlie couldn't wait to ride the gee-gees, so they went to the roundabout after they'd eaten.

'Look, Mammy, look, Daddy, look at me!' Charlie shouted each time he came around, Deirdre holding him tight.

The men went off to place their bets on Pinza, but on the

way back, Brendan took Hugh aside, and they went off to the beer tent.

'What are those two up to?' Elizabeth protested.

'My bet is that Brendan is telling Hugh that he's sorry,' Sarah said quietly.

'Sorry?'

'Ah, he treated Hugh like a slave, you know, and it's been on his conscience. You have a different way of looking at things when you have a bit of happiness and security, as we all know too well, I'm sure.'

'Yes . . .'

'So I've been at him to have it out with Hugh, and this is his opportunity. I'm only guessing, mind you, but it looks to me like this is his chance.'

'I see. Then we'd better let them at it.'

They came back looking relaxed.

'You two been boozing, then, behind our backs?' Elizabeth asked wryly.

'Sure aren't we having a day out?' Brendan said, grinning.

'Nothing to the day out we'll have if Pinza comes in,' Hugh said.

It did, at five to one.

A few weeks later, Hugh came home with Charlie from the park, looking confused.

'What's bothering you?' she asked, unstrapping Charlie from the pushchair and taking him in her arms.

'I met Karl.'

'Oh?'

Blimey, she thought, what's coming now?

'Why didn't you tell me you'd been to see him?'

'I saw him once, Hugh,' she said turning into the kitchen and taking off Charlie's coat. 'I spotted him, just by chance, when I was coming home from Millie's. Anyway, it was ages ago. Near as makes no difference to a year ago, in fact.'

'He said you were in his flat. That you have his address.'

She let Charlie free, and he toddled into the backyard to look for Nancy. She looked out the window at him for a while before answering. It was obvious that Hugh was upset over this.

No doubt he thought she had been unfaithful, or more likely, didn't know what to think, the silly git.

'I followed him to the flat. Wouldn't you have? I was curious. But he didn't want to know, Hugh. I invited him back, even invited him to Charlie's birthday party, but he wouldn't have any of it. I think he was relieved to see me go. So I just had my cup of tea and left.'

'Just like that.'

'Just like that. I didn't tell you because ... oh I don't know. I'm sorry if you're upset. There didn't seem to be any point, when we weren't going to see him again. I suppose I thought you'd be hurt that he didn't want to know us.'

'He was friendly today.'

'Is he married?'

'Well, he had a woman with him. Marta's her name.'

'Marta ... What's she like?'

'Dark. Quiet.'

'Come on, Hugh. You can do better than that!'

'Ah ... black hair, neat, very thin, that's for sure. She didn't say anything. Karl did all the talking.'

'A foreigner.'

'I suppose so. He's back working as a bricklayer.'

'He must have married her, then.'

She brooded about it for several days. One afternoon, when Charlie was having a nap, she held her head in her hands. Why couldn't he stay out of her life?

There was tension between them and while Karl was never mentioned, he was behind it all. She picked a row with Hugh when he was five minutes late home from work, and she burned the stew. He fought back, the frustration spilling out, and they shouted at each other in a most shocking but relieving way. They stopped abruptly, fuming. Then Hugh said, quietly but with conviction: 'It's Karl you love. The real one. Isn't that so?'

Startled, she hesitated, looking away to consider the possibility. Then, slowly, a smile brightened her face and she said, 'No, dash isn't sho.'

'You still haven't got the accent. After all this time listening to me. Jesus.'

She threw back her head and laughed, allowing herself, in a feeling of wonderful freedom, to be carried away by her laughter.

They made love which wasn't hurried, which they hadn't done since Easter, delighting in each other, knowing their old love was still there. It was too easy to forget that, sometimes.

'We should be like this all the time,' he said at breakfast. The glow of being close was still with them. 'And yet it happens so seldom.'

'Things get in the way, Hugh. It's not just us. Everybody's like that. Something annoys a body and she closes off. The best about you is that you make me laugh. A good laugh washes off a lot of the pong.'

'Well maybe I should do my best to keep you amused.'

'You do that. Make sure you do,' and she tugged at his quiff.

For a time after that, as soon as Charlie was in bed, Elizabeth and Hugh made passionate love, sometimes even spontaneously and in the kitchen, something they had never done before. The idyll lasted a month but suddenly it faded. There was something missing, and they both knew it was Karl.

'We should invite Karl and Marta to eat.'

She stared at him.

'Her too?'

'Her too.'

'Why?'

'Why? Because', he protested, 'she's part of him now, whether we like it or not. Just like you are part of me, Elizabeth.'

'I'm not part of anyone. I am myself. Completely.'

'You know what I mean.'

'No. No I don't know what you mean.'

'What I mean is . . . that whether we like it or not, we now have to consider Marta when we consider Karl.'

'Maybe you're right,' she conceded.

'I know I'm right,' he said hopefully.

She didn't answer, but put the cups and plates into the sink, rinsed them, dried her hands on the tea cloth and went to bed. When he joined her, she turned her back to him without a word.

Elizabeth remained in her dark mood and Hugh in his limbo for four days. Then, having brooded her way through it, she said in the middle of dinner, 'Do you think Sunday afternoon would be a good time?'

He swallowed his tea, licked his lips and looked at her.

'For what?'

'To have Karl . . . and Martha, for something to eat, silly.'

'Marta. That sounds like a good enough time to me,' he said off-hand, and continued eating.

'That's settled then.'

'Right. If it suits them.'

She couldn't help herself, she had to strike out.

'You've forgotten, haven't you?' she said, looking up.

'Forgotten what?'

'You're so anxious to please this Marta woman, you've forgotten your son's birthday is on Saturday.'

'Jesus . . . But don't blame Marta. Please, Elizabeth.'

'He's three on Saturday. Poor child!'

'Already. What do you mean, *poor child*?'

'Soon he'll know what a rotten world this is.'

'Elizabeth! Elizabeth . . .'

The tears just flowed, helplessly, without fuss. He put his arms around her and she pressed her head fiercely against his chest.

'I thought we went through this before,' he said. 'Of course he'll see the bad things, but he'll see the good things too. He has a right to see both, that's what will make him know who and what he is.'

She stared at him. Then she pulled away.

'Make sure you're here Saturday afternoon.'

'Elizabeth, you know I always am. Religiously.'

'It's a teddy, remember?' She was businesslike now. 'He just loves that Rupert the Bear.'

'Aye. The bold Rupert.'

'Will you get some candles from Beecham's – no, no I'll get them myself. We'll invite little Nancy.'

'A proper romance.'

'Yes.' She paused and smiled. 'Maybe being a child is not so bad after all.'

He was late again the next evening, but in high good humour, and winked, and she couldn't help but smile. It must have been a fine teddy. To Charlie's delight he lifted him up at arm's length, face to face.

'Who's a good fella, then?'

'I am, Daddy.'

Hugh and Elizabeth laughed in one of those moments of happiness which seem airborne.

Nancy had arrived with her mother when Hugh arrived home with a large parcel. Already the children had slipped into their private world and Elizabeth was having a hard time making small talk, so she was relieved to see him.

'Will you be all right, Nance?' her mother called, but Nancy pretended not to notice. 'I'll call for her at five, if that's all right,' but as she turned to go, Nancy ran to her for a reassuring hug. Hugh shoved the package under the stairs and exchanged a nod with the woman as she left. Elizabeth closed the door in relief.

'You got it then?' He nodded, grinning. 'After tea, ask him to tell you *Little Red Riding Hood*.'

'Can he remember all that?'

'We've been rehearsing for days,' Elizabeth said dryly. 'Here, you're going over it, aren't you? Just in case your darling boy misses a beat!'

'Where's the book?'

'You old softie, you,' she laughed, pulling at his shirt.

When tea was finished and they were stuffed with buns and had burst two balloons, it was time for the story.

'Once upon a time ...' Elizabeth prompted.

'... There was a little girl and her name was Little Red Riding Hood,' Charlie continued. He entered a world of his own and she watched and listened, but mostly watched, entranced. He left out parts of the tale but invented adventures to fill the gaps, making it his own. He hesitated, taking several breaths, searching his memory or maybe his imagination.

Elizabeth prompted and he began again, the tale becoming richer. Later, near the end of the story, he stopped once more, his nose screwed up in concentration, and this time, Hugh, obviously caught up in the world of the forest and wolf, prompted him.

'No no, Daddy, that's not it,' Charlie protested and continued his own version, his father laughing and blushing, caught out, tender. Elizabeth loved Hugh very much, just then.

When Charlie said happy ever after with a flourish, they clapped and Nancy shouted hooray, and looked around her for approval, and Elizabeth clapped Nancy too. Then Elizabeth produced a big box of sweets with a picture-book of *Little Red Riding Hood* and the children stared in amazement for a moment.

'Look, Nancy,' Charlie screamed then, 'sweeties!', and Elizabeth had to restrain them, rationing them out one at a time, and the book was examined as a pretext for keeping an eye on the chocolate toffees. Hugh brought in the package, helping Charlie to unwrap it. The child looked in awe at the giant toy, then hugged it crying, 'Rupee! Rupee!' as if it were a long-lost friend.

That evening, Hugh put Charlie to bed, and told him the story of Oisín in *Tír na nÓg*, The Land of the Young.

Elizabeth stood at the door, marvelling at how alike they were, father and son. She could see that Hugh filled in the gaps in his memory with his own invention and at times had to pause to gather the threads of the story, or to soften the scary parts. But by the time he came to where Oisín becomes mortal again after three hundred years, having left his magic white horse, and falls down dead with the weight of age, Charlie was asleep.

He lit the night candle for him and took a last look at Charlie, who was worn out by the day's excitement, and kissed him on the forehead.

'Goodnight, my boy,' he whispered.

'It's been a big day for us all, hasn't it,' Elizabeth said quietly, beside him. He smiled and reached out an arm to hold her but she leaned forward and kissed Charlie lightly, lingering over his face.

The next morning, Hugh brought Charlie to Finsbury Park,

with some bread for the ducks. Elizabeth wanted them out of the way to prepare the dinner. She was on edge, dreading the afternoon, and regretted inviting them. Had it been Karl on his own, that would have been a different matter. She knew so many ways to connect with Karl, one way or another, but the presence of this woman would block all of that, leave them like strangers, really. It was her love of cooking that got her through the next few hours.

When they returned Charlie was asleep in his father's arms.

'Well done,' she said, and took Charlie from him and put him to bed. Through the house, there was a heavy smell of meat roasting.

She washed and tidied herself up then. She even put on powder and lipstick.

'Do I look all right?' she asked Hugh nervously.

'All right? You look a million dollars.'

But she wasn't assured, and kept looking for dust, tidying up the artefacts on the mantel, making sure the cutlery was perfectly in line. Even the chairs had to be perfectly arranged.

'Elizabeth, relax. You're making me nervous.'

But she ignored him, until they knocked.

'Do I look all right?' she asked again.

'Lovely,' he said, but she could see he had just said it. Why couldn't he be nice to her, just this once?

'You let them in.' She checked herself in the mirror one last time, and took a deep breath, her mask falling into place.

Her first surprise was that she didn't hate her. She must have been pretty as a girl, as she still had good bones, but her teeth were bad, preventing her from smiling. Her skin was grey and wrinkled, and she had no curves that she could see, being almost as thin as those poor Jewish mites she had seen in newsreels after the war. She could see nothing about her that a man might find attractive and, while the small talk of introductions went on, all she could think of was what Karl had said about her having no one.

She never said a word until there was a lull during the meal, and even then she looked nervously at Karl before saying anything.

'It tastes well. It is good to have meat again. After the rations.'

'Good. Eat up then,' Elizabeth said.

'It tastes very well,' Hugh said.

She could see everyone was savouring it and it made her happy. It really was very good.

She caught Hugh's glance. He was proud she had made a special effort. He was happy too, enjoying the moment, but then, suddenly, she realized that it was only her and Hugh who were happy and relaxed, and that Hugh was blissfully unaware of any tension. He looked at Marta, obviously thinking of a way to include her in the conversation, and if she could have she would have reached out to stop him.

'Where are you from, Marta?' That big broad smile of his.

'Romania,' Karl cut in.

Her face brightened as she was asked the question but now she was downcast again. That was Elizabeth's second surprise. Not only was Karl dominating the conversation, he was determined that Marta wouldn't speak. Elizabeth was appalled until she remembered he had been like that a bit when she had introduced him to Hugh.

Hugh caught the tension at last and silence followed, broken by a rattle of knives and forks on emptying plates. Karl was the first to finish, and sat back, his eyes on the table. Marta had been eating slowly, but when she saw that Karl had cleared his plate, she stuffed down her food nervously and finished too, ahead of Elizabeth and Hugh.

'Let me help,' she said as Elizabeth moved to clear the dishes. Elizabeth hesitated, then nodded. As the women fussed around the table, Hugh cleared his throat and turned to Karl.

'How's work?' he asked.

'Good,' Karl boomed. 'Good. You should come and work with me, Hugh. I miss you. Men don't seem to work as hard as we did.'

'I'm happy where I am, Karl. I'm plastering now, so I don't work as hard either.'

'Tell me about Romania,' Elizabeth asked quietly at the sink. 'What was it like to grow up there?' She smiled in encouragement as the men talked on. Marta brightened again, glancing at Karl and, reassured that he was preoccupied with Hugh, she opened up.

'It was hard ... but real, you know?' she whispered. 'You understand? It was home.'

Elizabeth stopped what she was doing, and considered this. Then she nodded.

They served the dessert and sat in again. Elizabeth knew Marta had suffered a great deal – no, not a great deal – more than Elizabeth thought she could ever imagine. But then, they had all suffered one way or another.

The talk continued, man to man, woman to woman. Karl had relented, but Elizabeth could see he was still nervous. Thankfully he had always liked Hugh, and they rattled on. Marta and herself served the tea.

'England is a good place,' Marta said. 'My grandmother, very happy if she has cooker like this. We bring the wood long way, for big fire,' she said, opening her arms wide.

'We had to do that too, for a big open fire,' Hugh said. 'Big pots of spuds for the pigs,' he said.

'Yes, yes!' Marta smiled happily.

Karl excused himself and went upstairs.

'Now we can talk,' Elizabeth said. 'I see you have a ring. When was the big day?'

'The wedding?' Marta blushed, and the colour made her look young and rather lovely, Elizabeth thought.

'If you two are going to talk women's talk,' Hugh said, 'then I suppose you don't mind if I turn on the news.'

'Good,' Elizabeth said. 'The louder the better,' and she waited to hear as much as Marta would tell her before Karl returned. It was hard work to quiz Marta, but she persisted. They had been married a few months, after a long engagement. Then, as Marta was talking, Elizabeth instinctively looked up as she heard Charlie's feet on the landing. The little blighter was awake already. She turned her attention back to Marta, and the pips for the hour sounded on the radio. In the pause, there was a distinct thump on the stairs.

'What was that?' She looked around as the announcer's voice

returned. They all looked towards the stairs, but there was no sound in the house except from the radio.

'It's nothing,' Hugh said.

'Elizabeth!' Karl shouted. 'Elizabeth – Hugh! Come quickly!'

Elizabeth led the charge from the kitchen and stopped in front of Charlie, who was lying at the foot of the stairs, unconscious. She took him in her arms, covering his face in kisses as if they would suck back his life.

'Hugh,' she screamed as if Hugh were a distance away.

Hugh hovered around her, staring in fear.

'Hugh – get a taxi.'

He hesitated, reluctant to take his eyes off Charlie, then reacted. By the time she reached the street, he was halfway to Hornsey Road. Elizabeth ran too, though half afraid to run, cradling Charlie's head with her free hand. As she turned into the junction, her breath rasping, she stopped as the sun, coming low over the rooftops, caught Charlie's head in a pale wash of light, and she stared at him as if her eyes had forgotten how to close. As the taxi stopped beside her, she hardly cared, knowing well that her life was over.

Twelve

KARL

June–December 1954

Karl eased into the steaming water until his lips were submerged. He could hear Marta at the living room window, coaxing the birds to eat her stale breadcrumbs.

'Coo coo,' she called. 'Coo coo.' He imagined her, squinting in the sunlight, enjoying her few moments of peace with the undiscriminating creatures.

It had been a grave mistake to marry her. She was ugly and her spirit was crushed. He slipped under the water in an effort not to think, but even there he reproached himself. In his own eyes, his one saving grace was empathy, and yet, and yet . . .

He surfaced, unable to deny his cruelty. She was dutiful and looked after him without complaint, and still this made him look down on her with greater disdain. By his neglect, her own husband, who had sworn to cherish her, crushed the last small light in her soul.

He still craved Elizabeth's body, its unawareness of itself. He thought of her all the time now, if only to blot out Marta, whose body seemed to reproach him and which always seemed to be desperate for somewhere to hide. Those Sunday evenings in summer, when Elizabeth returned from her sister's, her underclothes stuck to her gleaming skin, they were what haunted him most.

He would see her today, know again the agony of not being able to touch her. It was baffling. How had it been so natural before, whereas now it was impossible? And he would look on Hugh, his supplanter. And he would gaze at their son, who so obviously should have been his son that he even bore his name. How had all of it come to be?

Marta closed the window and he set to soaping himself. She needed to bathe too. He did not hate her. It was only that he could not bear to touch or look at her. He got out and let the water drain away. Once dressed he washed away the tidemarks, put the coin in the meter and filled the bath again.

'Your bath is ready,' he called as he passed through the living room, combing back his scant wet hair.

'Thank you.'

In the bedroom he looked at the wall beyond which she was undressing. He could not bring himself to imagine her skeletal body, and he turned away to find a clean shirt and tie. Dressed, he went to the sunny living room to wait for her. The birds were still pecking at her breadcrumbs and he passed the time watching their ceaseless activity and diligence.

When Marta emerged in her summer dress, she had made up her face, but had not blended the powder at the join of her neck and body. He cringed.

'You look nice.'

'Thank you.'

'Your lipstick suits you,' he added, relieved that for once this was not a lie.

She nodded, turning her eyes away, and he knew he had wounded her again.

They left, and he did his best to find small considerations like opening doors for her, guiding her onto the escalator. But once on the tube, all that was left was to put his arm around her and that was far too intimate for him to bear, so he cast about for something to say.

'You haven't met Elizabeth?' he asked before realizing he had asked her that at least twice before.

'No.'

'You'll like her,' he said yet again. What else? What else! His toes curled. 'It's funny, I lived in their house for years.'

'Did you like it?'

'Oh yes. I loved it.'

'Then why did you leave?'

'Why?' He could not tell her the truth, that he left because he could not bear to be in the same house as Elizabeth when he was not her lover.

'To marry you.'

She reached tentatively for his hand and he grasped hers, as he could scarcely do otherwise. It was a compromise which brought them to Holloway Road.

Once in the blinding sunlight, he took her hand again as they crossed the road, but without looking at her. He knew he would regret it, but he had to get through the next few hours. He was always on guard in her presence, and once he was out of her sight he was too relieved to keep her in mind.

Hugh opened the door and Karl forgot his jealousy. In the kitchen, Elizabeth turned nervously from the cooker, but then she smiled and everything was well. She kissed him on the cheek but her proximity meant nothing. Then she turned to Marta and surprised him by the warmth of her approval as they swapped kisses on both cheeks.

'Well,' Elizabeth said brightly, 'dinner's almost ready.'

'You timed it well,' Hugh said, pulling back a chair for Marta. She nodded and sat. Was she going to shame him by not saying a word? But Elizabeth smiled to encourage her.

Marta remained silent through most of the meal, and even then she looked nervously at Karl before saying anything.

'It tastes well,' she said. 'It is so good to have meat again. After the rations.'

'Good. Eat up then,' Elizabeth said.

Hugh complimented her cooking too, and she glanced at him, pleased. Lucky Hugh. Why was it that the young, who had not suffered, took all? While those who had earned some peace continued in torment and deprivation?

'Where are you from, Marta?' Hugh smiled warmly at her.

'Romania,' Karl cut in. He hated himself for this, but he could not help it. Elizabeth stared at him, unable to believe he was like this. A tyrant. He could not believe it either. He could not bear to see Marta brighten, or be accepted by them. How could they love one such as her, and if they could, did their love of him mean anything?

Hugh caught the tension at last and silence followed, broken by a rattle of knives and forks on emptying plates. Karl finished and sat back, pretending to stare at the table but really watching Marta stuff down her food to catch up with him.

'Let me help,' she said as Elizabeth moved to clear the dishes. Elizabeth hesitated, then nodded. As the women worked around the table, Hugh cleared his throat and turned to Karl.

'How's work?' he asked.

'Good,' Karl boomed. 'Good. You should come and work with me, Hugh. I miss you. Men don't seem to work as hard as we did.'

'I'm happy where I am, Karl. I'm plastering now, so I don't work as hard either.'

'Are you making as much?'

'Oh, more. No, Karl, I'm happy enough.'

'I was thinking of buying a house. You can get a good house cheap, I hear. One of the old ones. Lots of rooms.' He had overheard men on the site talking about it. The Irish, they talked about it all the time, how you could rent out rooms to the navvies and the house would pay for itself in a few years. He was half listening to the women talking at the sink. So be it. He felt better now that he could talk directly to Hugh, about male things which were of no real importance. Yes, so be it. He would think it all out later, how yet again the interaction between people inevitably changed his perceptions.

'That sounds great. We're happy enough, though. And we've to think of Charlie.'

'Of course.' Yes, a child had to be thought of. The constant expense and worry. But as Marta handed out the plates to Elizabeth from the pantry and Elizabeth served the dessert, he thought that perhaps he should think more of buying a house. It would be a distraction if nothing else.

'England is a good place,' Marta said to Elizabeth. 'My grandmother, very happy if she has cooker like this. We bring the wood long way, for big fire,' she said, opening her arms wide.

'We had to do that too, for a big open fire,' Hugh said. 'Big pots of spuds for the pigs,' he said.

'Yes, yes!' Marta smiled happily.

Karl stared at her teeth. His family had servants when he was a child. So he had descended to this.

'Excuse me,' he said.

He closed the door behind him and paused, sighing in relief. So much had changed and could never be the same again. Marriage and a child had changed Elizabeth and Hugh. His years of darkness, and now Marta, had changed him. There was a chasm between them, they who had been closer than brothers and sister. He moved his hulk through the narrow corridor and slowly up the stairs to the toilet and relieved his half-full bladder, his excuse to be alone. As the toilet flushed, he peered into the mirror. Was that Karl Bruckner? Had his jowls wasted so much, had the furrows on his face and forehead become so deep and the whites of his eyes so grey and yellow? He curled his lips under the hook of his nose. He was growing old. All that was left to him was to be a rock on which Marta would founder. He smiled bleakly. What a strange pair they made . . . There was no mutual or even one-sided physical or emotional attraction. One day, he told himself, he would sit down and sort it all out, put a name on those needs, and a measure on how they were being fulfilled. He noted with resignation that his once strong teeth were decaying.

He flinched. Why this love affair with decay, with everything that is rotting? He had a job, he had money, he would repair both their *teeth*!

He stopped dead, realizing he had almost shouted this. He had to be careful. If he shouted, he might not be able to stop, he had discovered such a hatred of decay, of Marta as she now was, a reflection of everything he had a sick lust for. And if he could not stop, they would put him away and he would descend into the underworld again. He wanted light! He wanted cloudless skies and sun. He wanted to work, to put brick upon brick, watching the building rise and to relish its completion. No more decay. No more bombs or rubble, he would clear it all. Clean strong buildings rising from destruction. He would build it with holy sweat and profane muscle. Everything must be swept away, their rubble, their pasts and their *teeth*!

He swung around, full of destroying fervour, but stopped abruptly at the bathroom door. No one must know. No one must know of his hatred for rottenness. He had to be careful or they would put him away, and there would never be any hope again. He would build, but secretly, something strong and lasting, a home where there would be peace. Life. Peace. There had to be peace somewhere in the universe.

He seized up as Charlie stumbled from his room, rubbing his eyes, his bare feet flapping on the brown linoleum. He turned at the top of the stairs, almost tumbling down but by instinct clutching the banister, to look up at Karl. At that instant, music came from the kitchen.

'What's your name?' Charlie demanded.

'Karl.'

He marvelled at the boy's clarity of mind. There were no memories, nor horrors, to clutter it. It saw clean and true. He approached him and sat on his hunkers, yet still towered over him.

'And you are Charlie.'

'How do you know?'

'I know everything.' Or at least, he thought, I know too much.

'Are you fierce?' Charlie asked, as if he were asking him if he was tired.

'Yes,' Karl said, trying to be playful, but in reality he was seized by a fear that the child had seen through him.

'Are you a wolf?'

A wolf? Karl trembled, tension building in his forearms and reaching down to his hands and into his fingers. His mouth began to open in an effort to smile and his eyes bulged. Charlie watched in fascinated delight.

'You're turning into a wolf! You are a wolf!' Charlie squealed. He turned, thrilled, to descend the stairs, to tell his mother and father. 'Mammy! Daddy! Karl is turning into a wolf!'

Charlie's body seemed to be suspended in mid-air for a

moment, and then bounded off one, two, three stairs, like ill-struck notes, before glancing off the last and rolling onto the floor, and then was motionless. He had not screamed, or whimpered, Karl marvelled, as if he had accepted his fate. There were five pips on the radio. It was five o'clock.

*

As he stood with Marta on the pavement, watching Elizabeth run up Citizen Road with the child in her arms, some of the neighbours came to their doorsteps, roused by the commotion, but then Elizabeth disappeared at the end of the street and they went inside again. Marta put her hand in his and he looked around to see that she was weeping. For all her wretchedness, she could feel the reality of the disaster and he could not.

'What should we do?' he whispered.

'We must wait now.'

They went inside and Marta finished the washing up. He poured a cup of water from the tap and drank.

'Do you want some?'

She nodded, so he poured another cup and handed it to her. Then he spotted Hugh's keys on the mantel.

'They left these behind,' he said, showing them to Marta.

'You go to them. I will wait,' she said.

He walked up Holloway Road to the casualty department of the Royal Northern. A nurse was able to tell him that they were waiting outside the operating theatre. His heart jumped with hope. Perhaps the child had only sustained some broken bones, but when he saw Elizabeth and Hugh, seated on a bench and holding hands, their faces shocked a marble white, he knew there was no hope.

'I brought you your keys,' he whispered as he sat beside Hugh. Hugh turned, dazed. 'How is he?'

'They shaved his head. They're operating on his head.'

'Karl . . .' Elizabeth peered around Hugh. He nodded. 'My baby's going to die.'

Knowing she was right, he reached over and took her hand. Then he withdrew it and stayed with them in silence. It struck him that they were huddled together in a pocket of comfort, so long as no one moved, or thought, or said anything. A nurse passed and then a young doctor. Down the corridor there was a shaft of light from the tall window. A nurse came through the door leading to the theatre and Elizabeth rose, her mouth open to ask, but the nurse walked down the corridor briskly, as if Elizabeth wasn't there.

She sat, almost collapsing onto the bench again. Hugh put his arms around her, and Karl felt his sense of exclusion again, knowing it to be unreasonable. Hugh turned to him.

'Where's Marta?'

'She stayed behind to mind the house.'

'That was good of her. But . . .' Hugh struggled to think out something. 'Maybe you shouldn't leave her on her own.'

'You're right. We'll wait for you till the last tube, then.'

'Oh, I'd say . . .' Hugh faltered. 'I'd say we're going to be here all night.'

A nurse came to them and they all looked at her with total concentration.

'Can I get you a cup of tea?' Her accent was Irish.

'Then I'll call tomorrow evening,' Karl said.

They nodded their goodbyes and Karl strode away, but once on the street his knees started to shake uncontrollably and he had to lean against a wall to steady himself.

He was grateful to see Marta when she opened the door, and almost embraced her in relief.

The next evening he went straight from work to Citizen Road. Charlie was dead. His first thought was that he was neither shocked nor sad. Perhaps it was because they were not wailing in grief. He sat with them for a time, without a word spoken.

'I should leave you in peace,' he said then.

Elizabeth remained seated, staring at the stained glass cock on the back door.

'Thank you,' Hugh said at the doorstep. 'We'll see you at the funeral, then.'

'Of course.' He tried to allow for Hugh's shock, but he was hurt at being spoken to like an outsider.

'Oh no,' Marta gasped when he told her. She turned away

from him and wept, her shoulders shaking, and once again it seemed she was weeping and feeling for both of them. Was he a human being at all? He shook himself, trying to waken some – any – emotion, and without thinking he reached out and touched her. She turned and he took her hand and stared at its skeletal fingers, the nails bitten down, and forced himself to kiss it. When he looked into her face, her mouth was open in confusion. Please believe me, he thought, and even as he thought it he wondered what it was she was supposed to believe and, although he longed to say something, he remained silent.

*

They took Wednesday off and went to Highgate on the tube. They were early, and walked through the cemetery.

'It is very big,' Marta said. 'We will lose them.'

'Yes, perhaps,' but in the distance he saw a lone gravedigger at work. They walked over to him and with a glance at the small cavity he knew they were in the right place.

'Is this for a child?'

'That's right, guv.'

'We'll wait here,' he said to Marta.

When the funeral cortège arrived, they stood away from the grave. Hugh, once he got his bearings, looked around and came over to them, embracing them each in turn for which Karl felt grateful, then brought them over to the small group, introducing them to his father, and Sarah, and Sarah's daughter, and then more briefly to Elizabeth's family. There was another family there, with small children, and Hugh talked to them also, and a young couple who seemed to be Irish arrived, giving Karl a chance to approach Elizabeth, and with a simplicity which surprised him, he put an arm around her shoulders.

'What am I going to do, Karl? What am I going to do?'

He squeezed her to his side, and made way for Hugh as the undertakers were about to lower the coffin into the earth. Karl expected wailing, but there was none, only a grunt from Elizabeth. They threw some earth on the coffin, and a blind man sang a hymn and then, with frightening rapidity, the child was buried.

As they turned away from the grave, he overheard Elizabeth say to her sister, 'It's my turn now, Millie.' He stared at her, chilled. He looked wildly about him, at the other mourners. *They* would never have such a turn, such loss. Why had it to befall his beloved Elizabeth? Why were he and Elizabeth the ones who were fingered by the Furies? Marta took his hand, and he looked at her quickly, his anger draining away. Forgive me, he thought, calming as they walked from the cemetery, contemplating her dark head, we must all bear the lot we are given.

They accepted an invitation to Sarah's house, and Hugh's father fussed over them. There was an unreal atmosphere. Everyone was acting as if nothing had happened. Even Elizabeth concentrated on being hospitable. He had never seen anything like it, but then, he had never been to a funeral before.

Having nothing to say, they left when they could eat and drink no more. Apart from anything else, he wanted time to himself to sort out the thoughts which had piled on each other, but one awful realization recurred through the overwhelming torrent: he had not lived. He had experienced everything from a distance – the death of his family, all that suffering he had lacerated himself with, even, most horribly of all, his love of Elizabeth. He had not lived until now, when he had witnessed her son tumbling to his death, and saw his coffin enter the ground. The noise of the clay on the white box rattled through his head.

'Shall I make tea?' Marta asked once they were safely back in the flat.

'No. No more tea. I can't eat or drink any more.'

'Then I think I'll sleep.'

'Yes. A sleep is an excellent idea.'

They went to bed and as she turned on her side, he put his arm over her waist.

He woke knowing that he should go to Elizabeth and Hugh and explain exactly what happened to their son. He knew, more than anyone, that to leave the past behind, you had to know where everything lay, in its proper, unchangeable station, no matter how terrible. The manner of Charlie's death needed its resting place, no less than his body did. He shook Marta awake and told her.

'Yes,' she nodded, and the simplicity of the moment amazed him.

Hugh welcomed them with feeling, and Karl thought, with relief. Elizabeth was still in her dressing gown, although it was four in the afternoon, and although she tried to smile in welcome, it was as though her lips were too heavy to move. Nevertheless she made tea and, after they had settled at the table, Karl cleared his throat to speak.

'Marta and I . . .' he said, looking to Marta, 'Marta and I were talking and we thought you should know exactly how it happened.'

Elizabeth and Hugh came to life and leaned towards him.

'Yes, what happened to my darling?' she moaned softly.

'I was coming out of the bathroom, just as he came out of your old room – I suppose that was his bedroom,' he said to Hugh.

'Yes, that's right.'

'He was half asleep, rubbing his eyes, but he wasn't startled when he saw me.' Karl had thought that perhaps he could not bear to tell the exact truth, that he would tell them that the boy got a fright and lost his footing. Now he was confronted with their eager faces, he knew he had no choice but to tell them as it was.

'He asked me my name, very simply, so I told him, and then I said, "And you are Charlie."'

'God, Karl, you remember it all,' Hugh said, but Elizabeth stayed him, intent on Karl's account.

'*How do you know?*' Yes, he remembered clearly, every detail. '*I know everything,*' Karl said, lost in the memory. "*Are you fierce? Yes.*'

'I was trying to enter his world. I was trying,' Karl said as if to himself, 'I was trying to remember myself as a child. So I got down on my hunkers to be close to him. And then he asked me if I was a wolf.'

'*Little Red Riding Hood . . .*' Elizabeth whispered, gripping Hugh's arm, as if she understood at last.

'I smiled at that, of course.' Even now he felt the child was probably right, how somewhere in his head he was a starving wolf, powerful and dangerous. O God, O God, he thought, that is nonsense, the imaginings of a child! 'But it seems my ability to smile is not practised, and perhaps I did look fierce, because he was delighted. *You're turning into a wolf!* He was jumping up and down in excitement.'

'*Little Red Riding Hood,*' Elizabeth repeated, gripping Hugh's forearm again.

'*You are a wolf!* And then he missed his step and fell.'

They stared at him, lost in Charlie's fall.

'Did he bounce off many steps?' Elizabeth asked then.

'Two, I think. It all happened so quickly.' He paused to reflect. 'He didn't cry. I think he was unconscious immediately. So he felt no pain. Or fear.'

'Thank you,' Hugh said.

Elizabeth was lost in her thoughts, even when Marta reached across the table and took her hand. Then she came to.

'Yes, thank you, Karl. It means a lot.'

'Do you think so?'

'Really,' Hugh assured him.

*

As they left, he noticed how Hugh's arm lay across her shoulder, and how, though her face was haunted, she leaned into him, as if taking shelter there.

'You did a good thing,' Marta said on their way to the tube. 'I was proud of you.'

Proud? His jaw dropped in surprise as they kept walking, she oblivious to his astonishment. He shook his head, struggling to associate the word with his notion of himself. No one that he knew of had felt, much less expressed pride in him. Yet this poor casualty of indifference could find it in her abused soul. Touched, he took her hand and held it till they were home. For a wild moment he had the urge to take her in his arms and make love to her, that part of her he could not see, the part which took pride in him. But one look at her reminded him that he could not. Instead, over the next few days he expressed his gratitude in small gestures. He gently corrected her English, smiling encouragement, and he was surprised at how quickly she learned, complaining that the English and Irish wardsmaids in the hospital had never corrected her. He smiled at that, remembering the grammar and dialects they used themselves. He touched her lightly at every opportunity, trying to show her that at last, he was learning to be proud of her qualities too. At last he could see she was kind, intelligent, and most of all, she could feel. He valued that in her most of all. It was the quality that complemented him best, and that was what marriage was, he told himself. Your partner complemented you, brought qualities you did not have. Male complemented female, and vice versa. That was it, wasn't it?

But after his initial flush of gratitude, he could not deny that he found her physically repulsive. Even the taste and smell of her skin, he remembered from their wedding night, reminded him of ash. He could only believe that she knew of his disgust and accepted it as her lot. But he railed against that too, and more and more he became ashamed of contrasting her with Elizabeth, siding with Marta almost, and in this way his tenderness for the woman behind the body grew, offering him a hope he could as yet only dimly feel.

His optimism abruptly ended when he brought Marta to Citizen Road again and discovered that Elizabeth had attempted suicide. Although Marta pointed out that Elizabeth did not want to see anyone, he only heard that she did not want to see him and, racked by remorse, he blamed Marta for encouraging him to tell them about Charlie's fall.

'It would never have happened if I had kept my mouth shut. It brought it all back, and she blames me. You should never have encouraged me.'

'My darling,' she said, fighting back her indignation. 'She do not see anyone. She do not talk to Hugh. He said this more than once.'

'I am not your darling,' he said coldly. 'I never was and I never will be. Elizabeth is the only one I have ever loved, and she tried to kill herself because of me.'

'Not because of you,' she said with an edge of anger. 'She tried to kill herself because of her son.'

He stared at her, then turned and slammed the door behind him.

He walked fast, instinctively heading for the nearest bomb-site, but it was not enough. There were too many intact and rebuilt buildings, and he jumped on a bus until he found a wide expanse of ruin, and did not rest until all he could see was destruction.

This is where I belong, he thought, and he sat on a cushion of weeds and wild flowers which covered the rubble. This is where I belong.

For hours he enjoyed the relief of idle thought, sweating in the sun. Then, as evening fell, he explored the ruins, studying the vegetation, finding small domestic objects like combs and false teeth. He imagined their owners brushing their hair, taking out their false teeth at night, before the madness of nations overtook them. In the distance he could see a band of children, running wild in their perfect playground.

Night came, and he settled in a cavity just big enough to fit him. He had found a cellar and almost decided on that but feared the rats, several of which he had seen during the day. His niche was perfect, as he could see the stars and, despite the glare of the city's lights, they were beautifully clear. He thought of his astronomy book, which he had left behind in Citizen Road, and for a moment he wished he had it now, but it didn't matter really, he could remember most of it. Venus was easy enough. There she was in all her splendour. But what intrigued him most was Neptune, the planet star which could not be seen without a telescope. It was there, as sure as Venus was. There and not there, like his soul. Like his past. Like his present. The King of the Sea. It reminded him that Elizabeth had spoken of the underground rivers of London. Dozens of them, she said. Perhaps there was one beneath where he crouched, there but unseen, like Neptune. Like Elizabeth, locked away in her pain that no one could see or touch, beyond the reach of any telescope. He wept, finally, as much because of his helplessness to ease her pain as for her pain itself.

That's why he had come here. To weep. To be far away from anyone so he could feel without shame. And what had he done to his poor wife? He turned away, and crouched into himself, surrendering to the realization of what he was.

When he woke it was mid-morning and the sky was cloudless. He struggled to emerge from sleep, feeling as if he had been drugged, and breathed deeply to clear his head. Then he panicked as he realized he was late for work, and glanced his head off some masonry.

Scheiße!

Gingerly he felt his pate and it was bleeding slightly. He crawled into the sunlight and standing, examined it again. The odd thing was, he hadn't felt better in a long time.

O God, he thought, as he stared at the blood on his hand and thought of Marta's anguished face, I should apologize to her. She would be at work, but no matter, it would give him time to patch himself up, think things out, and get her some flowers, maybe.

When he walked into their living room she was sitting, waiting for him. She turned her head away. He had not expected this, and knew by her eyes that she had sat up all night waiting for his return. I don't deserve her, he thought. I don't deserve her. Faltering, he fell on his knees before her.

'O Marta,' he whispered, 'forgive me. Please forgive me.'

She put her hand lightly on his head.

'What happened you?'

'What?'

'What happened to your head?'

'Oh. It's nothing.'

'Wait here. It needs to be clean.'

'Eh?' He sat back on his hunkers, bewildered. How could she be so calm, while he was in turmoil? Answer me, for God's sake!

She returned with a basin of water, cotton wool, and iodine.

'Where did you get that?' he demanded, meaning the iodine.

'The hospital.'

'You stole it. Why?'

'For accident,' she replied evenly as she washed his pate. He closed his eyes as she dabbed it dry with cotton wool, and winced as she applied the iodine. He looked at her again.

'Do you forgive me?'

She looked away from him, frowning. She was right. Words meant nothing and were too easily betrayed. Maybe at last he was learning, in his fortieth year, that something like forgiveness had to be earned to be meaningful. Gently, he pulled her face back towards him.

'You are right, Marta, not to forgive me. Not yet. I am a very foolish, blind man. What am I saying – a blind man sees much more than I do. I don't know,' he said, shaking his head. 'Somehow I think you are my teacher, sent into my life to show me my stupidity. We are very different, Marta, from each other as well as from everyone else, but perhaps that is why we need each other.'

'Please, Karl, get up.'

He stood, head bowed, and without a word she went to the bedroom and closed the door behind her. There was silence in the flat apart from the distant hum of traffic, and then her sobs broke into it.

He turned towards the room and stared, appalled. The sobbing stopped, replaced by a whimpering which did nothing to calm him. What could he do? He was desperate, knowing that he could not trespass on her now. Then it came to him.

Food.

The woman needed nourishment. He found the shopping bag and went to Soho. He spent an hour buying the best meat and vegetables and bread he could find. Thank God the rationing was over. He supposed she must have been on rations since her teens and hadn't adjusted. She had been starving for years.

Cautiously cheered, he returned with his laden bag. She came out of the kitchen just as he crossed the sitting room. Her eyes were bloodshot but he could see she had tidied herself.

'What's that?' she asked.

'Food. Good food, Marta.' They looked steadily at each other, and that gave him courage. 'We must build up your strength, Marta,' but what he had intended to sound firm, dropped from his lips as a plea.

'But I eat in the hospital.'

'But what do you eat? Spam? Bangers and mash? You need good food, Marta,' he said, lightly touching her arm.

'Am I too thin for you?' she asked earnestly.

'Not for me,' he said, unnerved again. 'For you. I want you to be healthy, to . . .' He was about to say, *to be full of life*, but feared that would hurt her again. From now on, he realized, he would have to measure everything he said, to nurture her, give her the confidence to rebuild her joy in life. 'To be happy.'

She regarded him in a way he could not fathom until he broke the spell by kissing her tentatively on the cheek. There was no response.

'Marta,' he whispered. 'I want to make peace with you.' He waited for a moment, but still there was no response, so he turned and unpacked the groceries.

'The best English steak, potatoes, and cabbage. Fresh as dew,' he said brightly, with his back to her, but as he turned she left the kitchen and opened the living room window. Deflated, he unwrapped the steak and stared blankly as a fly alighted on it.

'Excuse me,' she said, suddenly beside him again, and he stood aside as she drew off some water for the birds.

'Shall I make the meal now?'

'If you like.'

Well, that was something. As he prepared it, his spirits rose. At last he was doing something positive. Already he had realized that it would not be easy. That was established, but at least he had a plan, and as he worked he plotted it out. First he would build her up and put flesh on her. That, and his attentions, would give her confidence. He wondered how he would broach the delicate subject of her teeth, but then he remembered he needed dentistry himself. They could both go at the same time. And then, then he would ask her to choose a house. She would see her life improve beyond measure. Women got confidence in their men once they saw their lives improve. He supposed.

She sat at the table as he fried the steak and he allowed himself a faint smile.

'I cannot eat so much!' she protested as he laid a heaped plate in front of her.

'No? Then . . . then eat what you can. It is very good.'

She cut a small portion of the medium rare steak.

'A lot of iron in steak!' he said cheerfully. He counted that she chewed the morsel twenty-three times. But that was good. It was an event when she swallowed, and they both laughed.

'All my family were fat before the war,' she said. 'Even me.'

He smiled, but he didn't want her fat; he wanted good, supple flesh. A woman didn't need surplus fat in this climate.

'Even you. And your grandmother too, I suppose?'

'Yes, my grandmother too.'

'Eat up,' he said, not wishing to dwell on her grandmother. 'Eat up.'

She slowly ate more than was comfortable for her, but she couldn't finish it.

'Don't worry,' he said, 'you can build up to it. I'll finish what's left.'

'Then you will be fat instead of me!' she laughed.

He laughed in response, delighted to see her happy. In truth he was enjoying the food. He hadn't enjoyed food so much since . . . he had lived with Elizabeth. Marta gathered the plates to wash up and he smiled at her quickly.

Why was he doing this? If he was true to himself he would think of no one but Elizabeth. It was against all his inclinations to consider Marta, so why was he doing this?

Again they exchanged passing smiles as she came out of the kitchen and turned on the radio. She shared a love of radio with Elizabeth and Hugh. *Mrs Dale's Diary* was her favourite, it seemed. What a Romanian refugee could possibly have in common with the sheltered values of Mrs Dale, he could not imagine.

Attempting to read a book, he brooded on Elizabeth all evening. In thinking about her suffering he couldn't help but think of her physical presence beside him through those years, when in truth he had taken it for granted that he would always have its comfort. Dreadful as it was to recall his loss, it was deliciously tempered by the memory of her breath on his lips.

He looked up to see Marta watching him curiously.

That night he lay beside her as she snored, resisting the temptation to waken her for sex. He had been too long celibate and his body craved to uncoil. In hospital he had acquired the discipline of leaving relief to come in dreams, but fantasies about Elizabeth had tortured him for hours now, and they would not leave him be. Marta would never know, he reasoned, and might well be glad, and he could ease his conscience another time by being considerate. But in the end he realized he could not do this to her, and it was more than a victory of conscience. He wondered what this new feeling was, and in his wonder his frustration ebbed. It was something akin to respect, though nothing so plain as that. Whatever it was, it made him happy and he fell asleep.

*

Marta gradually put on weight, and as they went to the park on Sundays if it was warm, she gained a dark colour which suited her. It made her look healthy, in fact, like she must have looked as a girl, before the war. On their way, on Marta's insistence, they always called by to see Hugh, but Elizabeth remained in her wheelchair, refusing to talk to anyone but Millie. Karl tried not to think of it, and more and more turned his attentions to Marta. One Sunday, lying on the grass, she yawned, and he remembered his vow to get her teeth fixed, surprised that in his preoccupation and even contentment, he had forgotten.

That evening during tea, he suddenly clutched his jaw.

'What's wrong?' Marta asked him, alarmed.

'My tooth,' he groaned. 'Oh! It's dreadful. I must have an abscess.'

'Here, let me see.'

He had no choice but to let her see, but she could find no abscess.

'Then it must be a nerve. It's dreadful.'

He eyed her suspiciously as she went purposefully into the kitchen, returning with a few cloves.

'Did you steal those from the hospital too?' he moaned.

'Here, put these close to your tooth.'

After some minutes he could not keep up the pretence, and was grateful for the excuse.

'That seems to be working,' he said. She beamed.

'My grandmother told me about that. It works for me, very well.'

So she suffered from toothache, but had hidden it from him. The next day he made an appointment for them both for the following Saturday afternoon, with Marta before him on the list, and secretly rehearsed for Friday night.

He waited until they were in bed, then built up from a mild pain to writhing agony.

'You'll have to go to the dentist tomorrow,' she said, appalled.

'But I'm terrified of dentists,' he lied.

'But you have to. I can't see you suffer like that.'

He gripped her wrist.

'Then will you come with me?'

'No.' She shook her head in panic.

'Please, Marta. I'm too afraid to go alone.'

'No.' She shook her head again.

His pain grew worse.

'Please, Marta.'

'Yes,' she nodded fervently. 'I'll go with you.'

'Get me some cloves, will you?'

She leapt from the bed to get the cloves, and he sighed in relief.

The next day when the dentist's receptionist read back their names to him, Marta looked at him first in disbelief, then in terror. He ushered her into the waiting room. She was shaking.

'It will be all right,' he said quietly.

'Why did you do this to me?'

'We might as well get both of us done at the same time. We can support each other.'

She looked at him, shaking her head, but when her name was called, he gave her a nudge and she went meekly.

She came back, stunned, her mouth bloody and swollen. He put his arms around her, and when his name was called, spoke softly to her.

'You'll be all right here. I won't be long.'

'Now, what's the problem?' the dentist asked as he lay back in the chair.

Karl put his finger against a back tooth.

'This one,' he said. 'It has to come out.'

The dentist examined it, looking doubtful.

'It looks perfect to me, Mr Bruckner.'

'I cannot endure it a moment longer,' Karl insisted. 'It has to come out.'

'Very well,' the dentist said, frowning. 'Your front teeth need cleaning. I'll do those first.'

On his way back to the waiting room, Karl stopped in front of a mirror, and made sure there was a streak of blood across his lips.

'Are you all right, Marta?' It was very difficult to speak.

She looked through him, but nodded.

'We'll get a taxi home, I think.' She nodded again. 'No steak for us tonight, I'd say,' but this time there was no response. She had had her top and bottom front teeth and four back teeth removed, and she didn't open her mouth in front of him until she got her dentures a few weeks later.

'Let me see how beautiful you are.'

She laughed with her mouth closed.

'Go on,' he teased. And then, suddenly, she smiled happily, and tears of pride sprang to his eyes.

'They're lovely,' he said.

'Do you think so?'

'I do,' he said. Her smile widened, and her eyelids dropped, and he was so absorbed in the change in her that it took him several moments to realize she was waiting to be kissed. He put his fingers under her chin and raised her mouth to his. She glanced at him quickly, then closed her eyes again as he kissed her. He drew back and caressed her face, hardly believing the fortune which had brought him this far.

'We must celebrate,' he whispered. She smiled, and he drew in his breath.

They had a bottle of wine with dinner that night, and she grew giddy after one glass. Laughing, she confessed that she had

had several lovers in Romania. Then she noticed that he was put out and said, 'I was young. They were boys. It was nothing.'

She went quiet after that, and he regretted his jealousy. He smiled and said, 'Forgive me. I had several loves too.'

'Yes?' she laughed again, like a girl, and he was delighted.

That night as they made love he was surprised by her response. Afterwards, as he lay sweaty and exhausted, he whispered, 'We must buy a house. I'll buy a house for you, fit for a queen.'

She snuggled in to him, and he felt his old need to retreat. Everything had moved so fast from awfulness to happiness, and that was not right. It had to go slower, he had to feel his way towards it, become accustomed to every earned stage, as he might build a house on a good foundation, and then brick over brick.

'It is nice you are a dreamer,' she said.

'What do you mean?'

'Karl,' she laughed, 'people like us do not have money for a house.'

'I do,' he said.

She raised herself on her elbow and stared at him.

'I have earned good money for several years. Out of that, I have paid only rent and subsistence.' As he spoke the memory of his journeys to Southend and Brighton came back to him. 'And some modest travel.'

'Then it is true,' she said after a while.

'Yes.'

The next evening and over the next two weeks they looked through the papers together. It was part of their new intimacy. Yes. Yes, he was learning, and that was good. Eventually they looked at three, and decided on the second, a large house in Putney. It still had its air-raid shelter at the bottom of the garden. Karl would have bought it for the fine garden, where the soil was black and deep, and he dreamed of growing vegetables. He would have a surplus in a soil like that, which he could bring to Elizabeth and Hugh.

He was surprised at how reticent Marta had been when they looked over it, even though she was insistent that this was more than she had ever dreamed of. It wasn't until they had moved in, and he had paid the removal man, that she walked about the house with nervous excitement, handling the curtains which had been left, and opening musty-smelling cupboards.

'You can decorate it as you wish, of course,' he said. She looked at him quickly and smiled, looking so tense it seemed she was holding back, not believing she was mistress of this castle of ten rooms, if you counted the basement flats. He followed her around as she checked everything, which she had left to him when they had viewed it. In one cupboard were old letters and writing materials. She looked through the letters one by one before showing the bundle to him.

'1942,' he said looking through them, '1944; 1944; 1945; '45; '46; 1946. They're all from the war. What do you think we should do with them?'

'Keep them. In case the owner comes back. It's like Sarah's house,' she said looking around her.

'It's bigger. An extra floor. A bigger garden.' That gave him a deep satisfaction.

She continued her discovery of the house, totally absorbed, so he let her be, and wandered down to the front hall where he found the phone. He picked it up and listened to the tone, realizing it was almost useless as he knew no one with a phone. Unless he could ask Hugh to phone him. That would make it real. Remembering the writing materials, he went upstairs and found them. The fountain pen was dry, but although it had almost evaporated there was just enough ink in a jar. It made his handwriting look spidery and jagged, but it was still legible and he wrote to Hugh with his address and number and an invitation to visit. Licking the envelope, he looked around him, wondering where Marta was. He searched a few rooms, and then through a back window saw her in the garden, touching the leaves of an apple tree. The apples were rotting into the soil, but Karl felt very happy, and at once, all the reasons why he should be unhappy flooded back. But now, for some blessed reason he had the strength to refuse them and enjoy his wife, lost in her innocent joy.

They settled in, gradually buying furniture and making the

house their own. The leaves had fallen and as he watched them turn golden in the garden, he knew he should dig the garden before winter took hold, and the following Saturday afternoon after work he set about it until darkness fell.

It was weeks before they had their first phone call, and Marta and Karl looked at each other in surprise.

'You answer it,' she said, and he could see she was too nervous, so he hurried downstairs, swallowing hard before he picked up the receiver.

'Yes?' he demanded in a strained, exaggerated voice.

Thirteen

BRENDAN

June–December 1954

Brendan was bone tired as he walked home from work in the sunshine. He wasn't a young man any more, and yet he had to keep up with young men, brick for brick. Maybe it was time to check the savings and go back to Ireland. There was young Charlie, of course, and Sarah and young Deirdre, and he allowed himself a daydream where they would all return with him to Croghan, taking life easier with a few bob in his pocket. He looked up and recognized the black woman and her daughter ahead of him. They continued on past the house. He scratched his head and yawned as he let himself into the basement. A wash and a good feed were all he needed. Tomorrow was another day.

When he went up for the bit of grub, Sarah was crying and Deirdre was hugging her, crying too.

'Maybe you should sit down,' Sarah said.

He sat. He always knew that himself or Hugh would be hurt on the buildings, and now he waited for the worst.

'Charlie had an accident yesterday. He died this afternoon.'

Deirdre sobbed into her mother's breast. What was the woman talking about? Yet his flesh was going cold and the blood was draining from his head, so if his mind refused to believe it, his body knew it was true. He couldn't speak or think.

'They were up all night,' Sarah continued after a while. 'I

met them . . .' Her voice broke. 'I met them in the corridor in the hospital. They weren't crying, or anything.' She stroked Deirdre's hair. 'Too shocked, I suppose.'

Sarah and Deirdre, the room around him, blurred. He was going to faint. Then Sarah handed him a glass of brandy, and he sipped, the liquid burning him into awareness again.

'You too, Deirdre. We all need one,' she said.

'We'll have to go and see them,' he said. His voice seemed far away to him.

'Yes.'

Deirdre spluttered as she drank the brandy.

'I think maybe we should go right away.'

'Yes,' she said. 'I think you're right. Dry your eyes now, Deirdre. We're going to have to be strong and brave for Hugh and Elizabeth.'

'I don't want to go,' Deirdre said.

'Drink that up and you'll be all right.'

'I don't want to go!' Deirdre shouted.

'Hush, pet,' Sarah said, holding her to her. 'Hush. Hush.'

In the end, Deirdre came. She was tipsy, so they decided to walk, each holding her by the hand. That gave Brendan a grip on things as they walked through the streets. They had decided to walk, to brace them. Brendan knew he had to be strong, to be a good father for his poor son, and poor darling Elizabeth. God love them. O God love them! He tried not to think of Charlie too much. Not the laughing boy who climbed onto his granda's knee. To think that the little creature was gone from the earth was too much to bear. What had Elizabeth said to him when he was born? He had felt like a man redeemed that day, when she said that. But he couldn't think of all that now. He'd think of it later, but not now. Now he had to think of his son and his son's good wife. He thought of Máire. He had been through this before. He knew what it was all about.

Before they turned into Citizen Road, Sarah checked Deirdre again, and took out a hanky, dampened it with her spit and rubbed Deirdre's eyes, as she had done before they left the house, though they were perfectly clean as far as Brendan could see.

'Now we're all going to be strong, for Elizabeth and Hugh's sake, aren't we?'

Deirdre nodded.

His heart was sore, like they talked about in songs, but it was really sore, and he had to keep taking breaths in case it would leave him in a heap on the ground.

Elizabeth's sister opened the door when he knocked.

'O Mr Kinsella! And Miss Considine. I'm so glad you came.'

Why wouldn't he come, to see his own family in their hour of need? But the poor woman had to say something. She smiled weakly at Deirdre.

When he went into the kitchen, Elizabeth and Hugh were sitting at the table, pale as fleece, holding each other's hands tightly. Elizabeth's brother sat against the sink behind them, and nodded to them.

'Hello, Dad,' Hugh said. Elizabeth looked up, stared at him, and then jumped to her feet and into his arms. She said not a word, but held him tight.

'What happened, in the name of God?' Brendan asked no one in particular.

'He fell down the stairs,' Hugh said.

'He fell down the stairs, Brendan,' Elizabeth repeated into his heart. 'He fell down the stairs.'

'It was a clot on the brain in the end,' Millie said.

'Millie, get Brendan and Sarah a whiskey, will you?' Elizabeth turned to Sarah who held out her arms and they embraced. 'Thank you, Sarah. Thank you for coming.' Sarah looked into her eyes, and stroked back her hair. He knew Elizabeth was grateful for the motherly gesture. Elizabeth turned from her to Deirdre.

'And what will you have to drink, Deirdre?'

'Nothing.'

'Nothing?'

Deirdre jumped into her arms, and the two of them swung out of each other, their faces knotted with pain.

'O Deirdre, what are we going to do?'

'Take the weight off your legs, Sarah,' Hugh said, rising and pulling back a chair.

She staggered towards him and put her arms around him.

'Hugh, Hugh . . .' she whispered.

'I know,' he said. 'I know.'

Sam shuffled, embarrassed.

'Right, I'm off,' he said softly to Millie.

'Good luck,' Brendan said, and Sam let go his breath and nodded, before slipping away.

Brendan had expected there would be wailing, but there was none.

They stayed for two hours. Before they left, Brendan spoke to Hugh in the hall.

'Do you want me to arrange the funeral?'

'Sam's doing it. He knows someone, who knows someone. Highgate on Wednesday morning.'

'Oh. What about a priest?'

'Sure he wasn't baptized.'

'Right. I forgot. So no priest.' Somehow that hurt terribly, worse than not being asked to help with the funeral, and his first impulse was to blame Elizabeth. But he shied away from putting blame on that girl, so he blamed himself for at least not asking that the child be baptized. He should have done that, at the very least. Then he saw that it was all beyond blame now.

'Can you come?' Hugh asked.

Brendan looked at him with pity. He must have been stunned, the way you stun a beast before you kill it, to have asked a question like that.

'Isn't he my own flesh and blood?' he asked quietly.

Hugh nodded.

The others gathered in the hall, and they left. It was dark, and Deirdre was falling asleep, so they took a taxi, and didn't speak. He carried Deirdre in his arms from the taxi, and laid her on the bed for her mother to undress her. Sarah turned to him as he was leaving.

'Will you stay with me tonight?' she asked.

When they had settled in together, holding each other, all she said was, 'It'll be a long, hard road for them now.' There was nothing he could add to that, so he said nothing, but stayed awake long after Sarah turned onto her back and snored.

They slept it in, and didn't wake until Deirdre came and got in beside Sarah, holding her tight. She didn't seem to pass any heed that Brendan was there. He got up, and stared out the front window onto the road. Sarah and Deirdre got up then, and they had a cup of tea.

'I must tell Mrs Dempsey,' he said. 'She'd want to know.'

'I should ring the hospital,' Sarah said.

He walked to Wedmore Street, glad to be out in the fresh air, to not have to think. Mrs Dempsey wasn't in, but he remembered where she worked. She was pregnant again, he noticed.

'O my God,' she said, going pale, though she had never met Charlie, to the best of his knowledge. He was telling her for his own sake, and for Hugh's sake. She asked about the funeral and said she would be there. They shook hands, and she said she was sorry for his trouble. He was surprised at how grateful he was about that, the way she said it in that particular Irish way, and the way it was a matter of course that a neighbour would go to a neighbour's funeral. That, he realized, was what was missing in his life in London. He had no neighbour. He had never belonged. After all these years, he was still a stranger. You needed a neighbour in a time of need.

Sarah sewed black diamonds into their sleeves, and they went to the morgue on Wednesday morning. Deirdre stalled as they were leaving, getting cold feet again.

'Be a brave girl,' Brendan said. 'For Hugh's and Elizabeth's sake. We'll all have to be brave.'

She thought about that, and they left together, walking in silence. Hugh and Elizabeth were already there, with Millie and her boyfriend, and Sam and Betty. The lid of the white coffin was open, Charlie's face, his shaven head, impossibly pale against all that white. They exchanged muted greetings.

'Do you want to kiss Charlie goodbye?' Hugh asked Deirdre quietly.

She leaned over the coffin, completely taken up with him, and then she kissed him quickly on the forehead. Sarah kissed him then, whispering a few words to him that Brendan couldn't hear, and then he took his turn. Goodbye, Charlie, precious boy. Keep a place warm for me, he thought, lingering over the child, his heart breaking.

'Elizabeth would like you to say a few words,' Hugh said, as he turned away.

'Just give him his blessing for the next world,' she said.

He didn't know what to say, sure he wasn't a priest, and yet he could not refuse. He walked around the coffin and faced them. He still didn't know what to say.

'Charlie, dearest son . . .' he faltered, 'dearest grandson, nephew, and friend . . .'

He took a deep breath.

'We want to thank you for all the happiness you brought us on your short stay. As for myself, well, I had great notions for you, and it's as sure as daylight that your mammy and daddy had too. We could see you as a fine big man, doing great wonders and making us prouder and prouder. We were even looking forward to you having children of your own, and coming from a fella like you, they would have been some children, that's for sure. So we have to leave all those dreams behind us now. And that's hard, Charlie, that's very hard.

'No doubt you've better things to be doing where you are, but think of us, poor banished children of Eve, in our sorrow at your leaving.'

He licked his thumb and made the sign of the cross on Charlie's forehead.

'Dear precious Charlie, we're wishing you well for your journey, and I'm sorry my spit is the nearest thing to holy water I could find at short notice. This is to send you on your way, to guide and protect you.'

Looking up at Elizabeth, he continued, 'In the name of the Methodist God, as well as the Catholic God.'

He turned back to Charlie.

'Because God has many mansions, Charlie, and may he welcome you in them all.'

Sam nodded to Brendan in acknowledgement, and Brendan nodded back as he came from behind the coffin.

'Thank you, Brendan,' Elizabeth said, her eyes red as the setting sun, and she drew in her breath.

'Thanks, Dad,' Hugh said quietly. Hugh squeezed his arm before turning to Charlie with Elizabeth. With his arm around her, Hugh and Elizabeth leaned over Charlie, whispering to him, caressing him, kissing him.

Then it was time to let him go, but Elizabeth wanted more time, and then she wanted more time still. She would have stayed there till doomsday, but gently, Hugh took her away and, supported by Millie and Betty, she stared into the distance, as if she were looking at Charlie as he faded into eternity. Deirdre clung to Sarah, whose face was as dark as he had ever seen it. The undertakers put the lid on the coffin and screwed it down, and Hugh carried it to the hearse.

To his surprise, Mrs Dempsey's husband and children were there with her at the graveside. He went straight to them, and thanked them. Mr Dempsey shook his hand and said he was sorry for his trouble. Young Dennis looked up at him, obviously knowing that something strange was going on.

'Hello, Dennis,' Brendan said. 'Lord, you're growing up at a mighty rate.'

There were two foreign-looking people at the graveside too, and Hugh and Elizabeth embraced them. Hugh introduced them as his friends, Karl and Marta. Then Seán Butler and his girlfriend, the one with the lovely voice who sang at the wedding, arrived, rushing in case they were late.

As the coffin lay at the graveside, Millie's boyfriend, who was blind, was brought to the front by Millie, and sang 'Nearer My God to Thee'. His voice seemed to fill the cemetery.

Then the undertaker lowered the coffin into the grave and, following Hugh's example, they threw in some earth on top of it before the gravedigger filled it in. Elizabeth grunted as she stared at the earth rising above her son, blocking off his breath for ever. Brendan tried to repress the thought that she sounded like Sarah sometimes did when he was pushing inside her.

As Hugh and Elizabeth turned from the grave, Millie was in front of them. The two sisters looked at each other, and then Elizabeth said, 'It's my turn now, Millie.'

Sarah had arranged for Delly's mother to prepare some tea and sandwiches for them, and Brendan invited the Dempseys and Karl and his wife. Thankfully they came and stayed an hour, so they were able to make small talk and look after people, and pay attention to the children. Deirdre disappeared with Delly.

When Elizabeth and Hugh, the last to leave, were going, she said to him, 'Brendan, I hope you won't take it bad if we stay to ourselves for a while.'

'No, Elizabeth,' he said, 'I won't,' and he remembered his emptiness when Máire died. 'I know what that's about.'

'Thank you,' she said, and kissed him on the cheek. Her paleness was breaking his heart.

He understood it well, and respected her wish, but as the weeks passed and Hugh stayed away too, he began to see it as a rejection. He needed to see them, to talk to them about Charlie, if nothing else.

*

When Hugh had gone his own way, putting aside a few bob every week to secure Charlie's future had given a lift to Brendan's step. He had looked forward to giving the lad a good sum when he was twenty-one. He nearly said it at his funeral, nearly shouted it. He had kept it to himself, since the child was born. Twenty-one years. It had seemed like a long time but hadn't three years passed in the blink of an eye? Now there was nothing, no future to work for, and it felt like a crushing weight. He had to tell someone and, having decided, he hurried home early from work to tell Sarah. She wasn't home yet and he had to wait impatiently for her return. She was in a bad mood, and tired, they had both slept badly since the funeral, but she asked him what was wrong, so he let it spill out.

'You should give it to Hugh,' she said, and there was no mistaking the hard edge in her voice. 'He's your son.'

'It doesn't mean the same if it isn't for a child. Hugh's future is set.'

'Well, suit yourself.'

It would be a hard battle not to drink it. Sarah knew it. He could see it in her face.

It consoled him to think of drinking, and yet he didn't go

near a pub. It was Sarah, caught in one of her silent depressions, who started.

Deirdre always took any chance she got to see her black friend in the basement, and as soon as she was gone that Saturday, Sarah took out a bottle of brandy and sat in the armchair in the front room, drinking. There was no talking to her when she was in a mood like that, so he went to his room and tried to think out what was happening. It wasn't the usual huff. Maybe she was reacting to Charlie's death, a delayed shock, maybe. Whatever it was, no one was talking, not even young Deirdre. They were like rabbits in headlights, helpless unless one of them could break out of it. He hadn't the words, but something had to be done. *Break a window, or some crockery, or something.* Break the fucking silence somehow.

Yet he endured the emptiness where his grandson should have been. It had brought back the time when Máire died. It had made him go over the time Hugh had left. It all seemed to be in a line, starting out all those years ago when he had married Máire, and it was still going on its way, and the Lord only knew its destination. He endured it all, going to work, and looking after Deirdre when Sarah took to the bottle, letting her show him how to make a salad. He could see it in her tense young body that she was trying to avoid the thought that her mother was drunk and beyond her reach.

The only consolation was that something clicked in Sarah on Sunday evenings, when she would lay the bottle to one side, and this way she managed to work, holding on till Friday night.

The weather had gone humid again, and he was lying on the bed, sweating and thinking how lucky he was to have Sarah at a time like this, when it came to him. She was suffering like this because of Hugh. She loved Hugh. That explained a lot. He had seen it a hundred times and thought nothing of it, but now he remembered the evening Charlie died, the way she looked at him, how she had looked crucified with love. It was a maternal love, of course. She loved him as a son, and he knew how powerful that could be. It dawned on him that he had always wanted to be of first importance in someone's life, and never had been. To be put first. And now there were two ways of looking at this. Either she loved Hugh because he was his father's son, in which case he had got his wish, or she put up with him because she loved Hugh. Maybe it was as well to consider the possibilities before he stepped out into eternity himself. You had to know these things, and face the consequences, because they told you who you were.

Ah, shite, he thought. I'm doing my head in for the sake of a stray thought, for nothing at all.

He drove himself at work until he physically hurt and he fell into bed as soon as he had eaten. But he didn't sleep for weeks until one Saturday night when he went to bed at nine and slept for twelve hours. He felt changed when he woke. His exhaustion was gone and it seemed as if he could see everything clearly at last. He sat on the bed, thinking over the last dreadful time, and felt strong. He looked at the clock and decided he would go to Mass. It was a beautiful morning, but as he walked to Everleigh Street, clean as a razor in his blue serge suit, the sadness returned to him. He longed for Charlie to be walking beside him to Mass, and for a moment Tollington Park was a country road to Ballyfad or Coolgreany. It was a relief to sit in the church and let the Latin flow over him. He hadn't been to Mass for years. It gave him solace, although exactly why he could not say. Maybe it was because it was all about eternity, and he had been acquainted with that recently, but for now he didn't care why.

Buy the Irish Press! Keep the boys at home.

He surprised himself by buying a copy. When he returned, the women were still in bed. He made himself some breakfast, and Deirdre came from her room, rubbing her eyes. She said nothing, passing him as if he wasn't there, and made herself tea and toast, holding the bread over the gas jet with a fork.

'It's a grand day, Deirdre,' he said as she ate in silence. 'Would you fancy a walk in the park?'

'I'm going downstairs,' she said.

'Oh. With your friend.'

She drank back her tea, cleared away her cup and plate, and left without a word. That was young ones for you, nowadays. The sun was flooding the back garden, so he took a chair and sat there on a bench, reading his paper. The girls came out, chattering and laughing, not paying him a whit of attention. When he went back in to make himself a cup of tea in the afternoon, Sarah was up and having a sup herself.

'That was a mighty sleep you had,' he said.

'I need more,' she yawned. She poured herself some tea and went back to bed.

Begod, the women were fierce sociable today, and no mistake. He poured a cup. It was lukewarm, but it would do, and he went back into the garden to sun himself. After about an hour, he was drowsy, and went to his room for a nap.

It must have been nearly seven when he answered a knock on the main door. There was no stir upstairs so he went up to answer it.

'Would you say there's a God?' Hugh asked.

'Well now, that's a big question. Maybe we should go down to my room. Sarah's asleep.'

He hadn't seen him since the funeral, and he had gone into an old man. They went down without a word, and Brendan pulled out the chair for him, and sat on the bed. Hugh sat, staring at the ground, pushing against the lino with the side of his shoe.

'Elizabeth was hit by a car this morning. They say she threw herself under it.'

'O my Jesus.'

'Yeah.' He looked out the window. 'Yeah.'

'Hugh, for Christ's sake tell me she's not dead.'

'Dead? No. She's not dead.' He considered this for a moment. 'As a matter of fact, she got away lightly.'

'Are you sure?'

'Aye, I'm sure. A few bruises, that's all.'

'Thank God!' Brendan let his head roll back in relief, and his thanks to God were heartfelt. He rubbed the back of his neck and took deep breaths to calm himself.

'Yeah.' Hugh nodded. 'Thank God.'

'She tried to . . .'

'There's nothing serious.' Hugh got up and looked out the

window. 'A few bruises.' He half turned. 'The thing is, she won't say a word to me. Pretends she's asleep, or unconscious. She's not, though.'

'Sure she's ashamed.'

'Ah no. No, it's more than that. She talks to Millie and Sam. A bit, maybe. But it's more than that.' He sat on the chair again, hunched up.

'Like what?'

'Sure she's hardly said a word to me since Charlie died.'

'The woman's in mourning, Hugh. You've got to expect things like that.'

Hugh was struggling, and then it came out.

'She blames me.'

'You? But sure you weren't near the child when it happened!'

'No, but I invited the man who was. They came to see us last weekend.'

'Who's "they"?'

'Karl and Marta. I introduced you to them at the funeral.'

'The foreigners.'

'Karl told us exactly what happened. It was good to know, and that's the truth. Elizabeth said as much herself. Said it made her feel better to know. Karl said it was a weight off his mind to tell us. It was the best feeling we had since Charlie was alive. Sure Karl is the best friend we have. But we must have doubted him till he told us what happened. You could feel the relief in the room. And I thought to myself, well, maybe now we can begin to talk to each other at least.'

He rubbed his face, slow and hard.

'Ahhh! . . . Well, we didn't talk too much, not about Charlie, that's for sure. But it was better, for a day or so. And then it got in on her. She couldn't stop thinking about it. Anyhow,' he said wearily, 'I thought you should know.'

There was nothing Brendan could think of to say. This was outside of anything he knew, so neither of them spoke for a while. Finally he asked him if he would like a drink.

'I'm too tired for drink. I was never as tired in my life. I'm off home to bed.'

'Will I go and see her tomorrow?'

'If you like.'

'She's in the Northern?'

'Aye. That's where she is.'

When Hugh was gone, Brendan sat, staring into space, on the side of the bed. Then, he reached out for the pillow and deliberately placed it upright between his knees. First he ripped the seam of the case, then slowly tore the cotton into strips, dropping each one onto the floor. When he had finished with the case, he ripped the seam of the pillow and pulled out the feathers in fistfuls, dropping them over his head. When it was empty he tore the lining as he had torn the case, coughing as the smaller feathers were sucked in by his heavy breath.

He considered the destruction around him, then lay back in the middle of it. He lay there until a howl worked its way up, and he turned on his side, aware of nothing but his convulsive grief. It wore him down, until he was quiet.

Another feather was trapped in his nostril, and he removed it. He sat up again, weary, realizing that he should tell Sarah. Shaking off the feathers, he went upstairs and woke her. She looked at him sullenly.

'She's all right, but Elizabeth threw herself under a car this afternoon.'

That woke her all right. Her face came together of a sudden, completely alive.

'O no.' She put her face in her hands. 'What next?'

She glanced up at him, then stared.

'What are you doing with feathers in your hair?'

'What?'

'Feathers!' she pointed.

He looked up, as if the feathers were on the ceiling, then back at her.

'She won't talk to him, Sarah. To Hugh.'

She considered this, absently tugging the strands of hair away from her eyes.

'We should go and see him, this minute.'

'No. He's worn out. He went home to bed.'

'Then we must see her.'

He was surprised by how suddenly she was calm and practical. But then, it was no wonder she was fresh, having slept all day. Within minutes, she was neatly dressed.

It was after visiting hours when they arrived at the hospital, but she knew the night porter, who rang the night sister, and they walked along the quiet halls which smelt of polish. The nurse was expecting them, and showed them to Elizabeth's bed, but she was asleep.

'Elizabeth?' he called her softly. There was no response, and he looked to Sarah for guidance. She beckoned him to the door and whispered that she would leave them alone and wait for him in the hall.

'She looks up to you,' she said quietly. 'You get along, maybe she'll talk to you.'

'Right,' he said, and cleared his throat. 'I won't be long.'

'Be as long as it takes.'

*

'Elizabeth? It's Brendan. I'm on my own.'

Her eyes opened cautiously.

'Are you sure?'

'Yes. Sarah's in the hall.'

She lifted her hand to him and he took it with both of his, appalled that she looked so ill.

A drip was bandaged into her right arm.

'What happened you, girl?'

'Here I am,' she said. 'Here I am, not a hundred yards from where Charlie died.' She looked away from him then, towards the window where the light was failing. 'I stink of iodine,' she said after a while.

He could find nothing to say. He looked down at her hand, still in his, all bones and indifference, and felt helpless. She turned to him again.

'I want to die, Brendan. I messed it up.'

'Lord, Elizabeth, don't say things like that.' He stroked her hand, and she gave a little laugh.

'When they asked me my name . . .' She looked away again.

'Kinsella,' she whispered. 'How strange that sounds, attached to me. But not part of me. You know?'

She took her hand from him and examined her wedding ring, the dull gold which gave her this foreign name. 'Hugh said it's an ancient name, belonged to kings of Ireland, it did – or was it chieftains? Is that right?'

'So they say. The kings of Leinster.'

'Fancy that. Made me proud, it did. Once. *And your address, Mrs Kinsella?*' she mimicked the doctor. 'Mrs Kinsella . . . How strange. My life hanging on Hugh's name, like washing on a line. Hmm. *A telegram for you, Mr Kinsella.* Fancy.' Her eyes filled with tears, but she took a deep breath through her nostrils and held them back.

'Do you know what's driving me mad? As soon as he got my name and address out of me, the doctor said, "Now you rest, Mrs Kinsella." Like that. As if it was the easiest thing in the world. But do you know something? There's no rest. Everything, always, pushes you along. Hmm. Oh, it's life to others, it is. Action. This must be done. That must be done. Relations have to be told. Everything you do affects someone or other, did you ever notice that? You live, it affects. You die, it affects. A doctor, a husband, a nurse, a sister, a driver on the Holloway Road, a mortuary porter. Someone, it affects someone.'

'Shush. Don't be upsetting yourself.'

Her eyes flooded again, and she looked at him, her hand reaching out for his again.

'I feel like screaming, Brendan. I feel like shouting at them, tell them that I want to be alone. I don't want to affect anyone. I don't want anything I do . . . to have any consequence, any importance for anyone. But I can't rest. They won't let me. No, no, no.'

He rubbed her hand, as he could think of nothing to say. She fought back the tears again.

'I had to be responsible, hadn't I? That's right, my role. Hmm. 'Cause a doctor and nurse were waiting to tell my husband what he'd be happier not knowing for the rest of the day. He had to have his great news, because the world doesn't take account of such things, Brendan. It's not designed for it. It was a lovely day. He could have enjoyed it. He probably would have thought I was at Millie's.'

'Shh.' He squirmed in distress.

'It was good of you to come,' she sniffed.

She looked out the window again, and her eyes began to close. It was obvious that she was very tired, and he knew he should leave her be, but he couldn't go without asking one more question.

'Elizabeth, Hugh says you won't talk to him.'

'I can't, Brendan. I want to, but I can't.'

'He thinks you blame him.'

'It's not fair, is it? No, it's not fair, but I can't help it.'

'You'll have to talk to him sooner or later.'

'I know.' She yawned. 'I know.'

'So you will? That's all I want to know.'

'Just give me a few days. I need a few days to myself. Please.'

'All right, Elizabeth. I'm sorry. And thank you.'

She smiled at him, drowsy, and he leaned across and kissed her on the cheek.

'Rest now,' he whispered. 'Rest well. I'll see you tomorrow.'

He had almost forgotten that Sarah was waiting for him in the hall. She rose to meet him.

'How is she?'

'She'll be all right,' he said. 'Have you a pen and paper?'

She didn't but asked the porter in the hall. Brendan sat while they chatted. She handed him the pen and paper, and he wrote to Hugh, telling him that everything would be all right, she just needed a little time.

When he put the note through the letter box, he waited a while, hoping that Hugh would open the door and they could talk, even for a minute or so, but the house remained silent and he walked away.

After work the next day, he washed and shaved and put on his Sunday suit before going upstairs to eat.

'I looked in on her today,' Sarah said. 'She had a nurse taking her pulse, so I didn't speak to her.'

'Oh. How is she?'

'Not as pale, thank God. I see you're going to see her.'

'Aren't you coming?'

'No. I think maybe it's best if you get to see her yourself. I'll look in on her again tomorrow.'

'It's powerful that you're in the hospital, Sarah.' He was grateful that she looked better too.

When he got there, a bunch of flowers in his fist, Sam and Millie were there. Millie and Elizabeth were talking quietly to each other and Sam was pleased to see another man. The women hadn't noticed Brendan's arrival, and Sam stood away from them to talk to Brendan.

'You all right, mate?'

'Not so bad, and yourself?'

'Hospitals give me the creeps,' Sam said, looking around him and at the ceiling, as if he suspected a vampire might be waiting to jump on him, or something.

'Any sign of Hugh?'

'Left about ten minutes ago.'

'She won't talk to him.'

'You know that, then.'

'Brendan?' Elizabeth had spotted him.

'Do you know something?' he said, grinning as he bent over to kiss her on the cheek. 'You're looking a power better than you did yesterday.'

'Go 'way, you old charmer.' But she didn't smile.

'Here,' he said, handing her the flowers, which he had kept behind his back, embarrassed at being seen with them.

'O Brendan . . .' she said, taking them from him and smelling them.

'I see they're not the first you got.'

'Hugh brought some earlier,' she said, concentrating on the flowers. 'Millie, could you get a nurse to bring a vase? Sam and Millie brought me grapes. I haven't had grapes since before the war. Everyone's so good.'

Yes, she was brighter than she had been, but she was putting on a show of liveliness, and it was a strain.

The nurse came with a vase and arranged the flowers, chatting away, relieving them from each other for a moment.

'She's Irish, of course,' said Elizabeth when the nurse was gone.

They settled into a pattern all through the week. Sarah dropped by to see her every day, but she was either asleep or there was a nurse by her bed.

When he went in on Friday evening, Millie was looking worried. Elizabeth spotted Brendan and her face changed.

'Sarah's looking in on you, by the way. But you always seem to have nurses around you.'

'Sarah?' She beamed. 'Tell her ta from me, then, will you?'

'Our Beth's going to be just fine, she is,' Millie blathered, smiling for all she was worth.

'No I'm not,' Elizabeth retorted.

'Oh, poor Beth,' Millie whispered.

'Don't call me that,' Elizabeth shot back. 'You know I hate being called that.'

The tears dropped onto Millie's cheeks.

'You all right, sis?' Sam moved from foot to foot, trying his best not to look at Millie.

'I'd be all right if I were left alone,' Elizabeth grumbled into her bedcover.

It was the first time Brendan had heard her speak in a plain Cockney accent.

'Sure you're worn out,' he said gently to her. 'We should go and let you sleep.'

'I'll be all right,' she said in a stronger, conciliatory voice. She smiled quickly at Brendan, but she was away with the birds.

'Run along now – I'll be fine.'

Sam was relieved, Millie anxious. They turned to leave, but she called Millie back.

'That husband of mine, Millie – where's he been? You'd think he'd have come to see me by now.'

Millie was startled, but then smiled happily, the two men assembling behind her. Brendan felt weightless.

'He'll be in, Beth, just like he's been here every day since your accident. Never fear.'

'That's right, sis. Every day he's been in, he has,' Sam added, relieved he had something neutral to say.

They left slowly, looking over their shoulders, as if caught between decorum, love, and the desire to leave. Elizabeth was smiling.

Brendan was elected to tell Hugh, but when he got to Citizen Road, he wasn't there. He searched in his pocket for a cigarette, but the packet was empty. To hell with it. He was in such a hurry to tell Sarah that he got a taxi and, when he got home, Hugh was having tea with Sarah and Deirdre.

'Well,' he said, heartily slapping Hugh on the shoulder, 'what are you doing here when your wife's dying to see you? Eh? Well, don't gawk at me as if I was the Angel Gabriel. Get up off your arse and get down to her.'

Without a word, Hugh got up to leave. At the door, he turned and frowned at Brendan.

When he was gone, Brendan helped himself to a cup of tea.

'Is it true?' Sarah asked.

'We've turned the corner now,' Brendan said.

'Is Elizabeth going to be all right?' Deirdre asked.

'She is, my pet,' he said. 'She is.'

She smiled up at him, like she used to, her eyes shining. Jesus, what a selfish fucker he had been! It had never occurred to him that the child might have had her world turned upside down, no less than his own.

'She's going to be grand,' he managed to say. 'Everything's going to be grand,' and she ran to her mother.

The excitement got to him, so he gave in and had a snooze. When he woke, he felt as fresh as a daisy, and went up to Sarah in high spirits. She was having a drink, so he joined her. It was nice to have something to celebrate for a change, and he thought that Sarah hadn't looked as good in a long time, even if she was in a bit of a strange humour. He hadn't been in the mood since Charlie died, but he was now.

But although she brought him to bed and he was all set, her heart wasn't in it and she turned on her side and went off to sleep, as calm as you like, leaving him high and dry. He resigned himself to it after a while, but he couldn't stay in the same bed, wanting to touch her like that. It was too much, so he slipped away downstairs.

Ah, these things happened, he thought. He was still frustrated, all the same. He drank a glass of water at the sink, and his thoughts drifted back to Elizabeth and Hugh.

They'll be grand, he thought. They'll have another child and they'll be grand.

*

She had been discharged over the weekend, Sarah was able to tell him on the Monday evening.

'Will we go on down to see them?' he asked her, unable to hide a smile.

'Maybe we should give them a few days. She went home in a wheelchair, you know.'

'Oh. Right.' But she would need that for a while. No use staying in a hospital when you can be among your own in a wheelchair. 'So is Hugh taking time off work?'

'I suppose he must be.'

But he couldn't wait, and the next evening, he went straight to Citizen Road in his work clothes, his face covered in grime. Hugh answered the door.

'Oh. Dad,' he said. 'Come in.'

'Well, where is she?' he demanded when Hugh brought him into the empty kitchen.

'She's asleep.'

'Oh. Right. She needs the rest,' he rallied. 'There's not a ha'porth wrong with her that a good long rest won't cure.'

'Well, there's nothing seriously wrong with her . . .'

'But?' Brendan heard the alarm in his voice.

'But she refuses to walk.'

'What . . .?'

'She says I have an invalid for a wife, for the rest of my days.'

'What? But sure that's ridiculous.'

'That's what she says.'

'She needs a good kick up the arse, that's what she needs,' Brendan said, his anger taking him by surprise. He glared at Hugh, who just looked at the table, then regretted his outburst. 'Ah . . .' he said. 'Ah, don't mind me. What would I know. I'm only an old fool.'

'Oh, you're no fool,' Hugh said, rubbing his finger along the table. 'You're no fool.'

'Well, that's as may be. I'll drop by tomorrow.'

'She doesn't want to see anyone.'

Brendan stared at him.

'She's arranging for Millie to come and look after her while I'm at work. I'll mind her in the evenings when I come home. That's it. No one else.'

Brendan was stunned and hurt. He had fooled himself into thinking that she preferred his company to anyone's.

'That's it?'

'That's it.'

'Well . . .' He dragged himself to his feet and left without a word.

*

The barman had asked him for the price of the whiskey, and Brendan looked around him, dazed. What was he doing here? How had he got here? He remembered that he had left Hugh, but had no recollection of what had happened in between. He fumbled in his pocket and the barman took the money from the palm of his hand. Then Brendan counted out enough for four more whiskeys. Here's to nothing, he thought, and drank back his first before calling for another. He dragged on a cigarette, idly noting that his fingers were stained brown by the tobacco. It didn't take him long to finish the four, and he walked home in the evening heat, just letting the tears go any way they wanted, trying not to think of the truth of what Hugh had said.

'What happened you?' Sarah asked. 'Deirdre was wondering where you were.'

'Deirdre?' He slumped down at the table. 'Lord, Sarah. She's threatened never to walk again.'

'I see.'

He stared at her. You see? What do you see?

She took his dinner from the oven and gave it to him. He looked at it, and ate, but his heart was tired. Somehow he finished it.

'Have you any of that brandy left?' he asked her.

'Drink isn't going to solve anything, Brendan.'

'God, you're the one to talk.'

'All right. I'll join you, so.'

They drank steadily. Sarah sat on the edge of the armchair, one hand massaging the back of his neck, drinking with the other. O Lord. O Lord. O Lord.

When Deirdre let herself in she curled up her nose when she saw them.

'Where were you till this hour?' Sarah demanded. It was almost dark.

'Pooh!' Deirdre said, holding her nose. 'This place stinks of drink. Again.' She glared at Brendan. 'Are all you Irish drunks?' Then she turned and went to bed.

'Sure she's Irish herself,' Brendan protested.

'Little bitch,' Sarah muttered.

*

He began to stay mostly in his room. Sarah humoured him and when she had looked after Deirdre, joined him, bringing him his dinner, having a cup of tea while he ate. It was kind of strange having her there.

'Will you have a drop?' he'd ask her of an evening, as if it was some class of a ritual they had.

'Hmm,' she'd say, off in her own private world. At first he found it a bit queer in her, and he'd stop and wonder what was going on, but after a while he paid her no heed.

It went on like that for weeks, and more than once when she went back upstairs he could hear Deirdre shouting and screaming at her. Then she decided she wouldn't come down any more, and made him go upstairs for his dinner, and she stayed off the drink. For Deirdre's sake, she said, and Jesus yes, they had to think of the child or else they were worse than useless. He could stop drinking if he wanted to, he was sure of that, and remembered how he had gone through this after Máire died. So when Sarah asked him to stop, it took him a week or so, but then he made the decision and did it.

Giving up drink was one thing, and getting back to normal was another. There were nights when he could hear mother and daughter going at it, hammer and tongs, so it wasn't all plain sailing between the two of them. And Sarah would let it all out on him and, still not over the hurt he had been through, no more than any of them was, he lashed back. They argued over nothing, cursing and abusing each other, conscious all the time of where the laceration was coming from, and somewhere he dimly knew that it was a kind of love. The worst of it was, the child could hear it all and, naturally enough, she kept being troublesome, and so the hell's roundabout continued.

Sarah matched him, but once she had gone beyond a certain point, she'd lose interest and stare out the window, even if it was dark. He'd continue, but in a low voice, to himself. He had to keep going, keep talking, calling her all the names he could think of.

If it was really bad, young Deirdre would slip away and stay out till nearly dark. Once or twice, in the calm after the storm, as he sat across the room from Sarah, he'd hear Deirdre cautiously closing the door behind her, slip along the hall and away up to bed.

'Sarah,' he'd whisper, 'she's gone away up to bed.'

'Hmm? Oh. Yes. Thank you.' And bone weary, she'd drag herself up to say goodnight to her daughter.

She looked awful, and her hair was going grey at a fierce rate. What had once been a spotless home was getting like a dosshouse, with dust everywhere. Sometimes in a quiet moment he would sit, smoking, watching the dust float through the sunbeams in the evening.

He was no oil painting any more either, with lines under his eyes, and his stubble, which he grew for days on end, was grey, pitted with clots of blood where he had cut himself shaving after a dream about Máire which troubled him for several nights. In the dream it was always that quiet time of the morning before the city wakes. But he would wake, only to see Máire, a baby on her hip, mocking him.

So, he thought in his dream, she's not hiding it any more. I'll get the bitch. 'I'll get you,' he shouted, 'I'll get you, by Christ.' He got the poker from beside the fire and lunged at her, but she stepped out of the way, and he fell on his face. Her laughing went through him like a knife. By Jesus, he muttered to himself, catching his breath, by Jesus ... He got up again and chased her around the armchair where Sarah was snoring, lunging at her, but she was as supple as a dancer, far more so than he ever remembered, and he wondered if she was a banshee, or what. Maybe that's what she was, and sure enough when she turned to laugh at him again, her face had turned to rotting flesh, and now it was fear, before anger or revenge, that made him want to want to kill her. But then she ran up the wall, out of reach, before turning to laugh at him again, the rotting child on her hip. Then she disappeared.

That was it. He could remember every detail, and had a job convincing himself that it was a nightmare. It was enough to make any man cut himself shaving.

The morning after one of their rows, he went upstairs before going to work for some breakfast, only to find Sarah crying at the table.

'What's the matter?' he asked, tenderly, leaning over her, putting his arm around her. 'What's the matter?'

She didn't answer, just went on whimpering like a child. He sat across from her and poured himself a cup of tea.

'This has got to stop,' she whispered.

'Yes,' he admitted. He took a couple of slurps of tea. Yes, she was right. It would have to stop. He coughed hard, his chest hurting, and he lit a cigarette to calm his alarm. 'I've been a right bastard.' His heart was going like a steam hammer as he realized what he might lose. He dragged deeply on his cigarette. 'You're some woman to be putting up with me at all.'

She sniffled, but stopped crying.

'Do you want some porridge?'

'Ah no, I'm not hungry.' He was hungry all right, but he needed some means of being considerate. 'A few cups of tea'll do me grand.'

With their truce, Sarah rallied back to her old self, keeping a sharper eye on Deirdre, but although she shouted at her if she came home late, she didn't beat her any more. That made him feel easier, as he knew his behaviour had been the straw that broke the camel's back.

It had taken quite a while, but at last Deirdre settled into school. She was a bright child, and good at learning and, with a bit of calm in the house, Sarah kept her at her lessons. But as Sarah said, you couldn't be up to them, and only the Lord knew what'd happen when two young ones got together like that. Sarah said that they were going off to the bomb-sites, and he could see she was worried. Now that she had pulled him up, jerked him out of his destructiveness, he could see a muckle more. He never had to deal with any of this stuff with Hugh, Máire had done all that. It was women's work, the difficult, tricky things in life. All men had to do was slave their guts out.

Deirdre wouldn't admit to whether they were with other children, but although she said nothing about it, he knew Sarah's worry was that they were prey to older boys. Worse still was the thought of what desperate, crazy man was lurking in those places.

Work got tougher at the site as winter drew in. He hadn't had a drink for weeks, and some of the boys were slagging him about it, so it was a relief to give in and go for a few pints on the Friday evening. Apart from anything else, they lubricated his weary bones. It meant that Sarah would be wondering where he was, his dinner going dry in the oven, or so he expected, but when he arrived home there was no sign of either herself or the young one, though the lights were all on. Sure enough, the dinner was in the oven and dry as old cowdung, but he was never more grateful to have a meal ready for him as he sat in to the table, Methuselah weary.

He sat back, his belly full, and opened the paper. His mind wandered to where it always wandered these days, wondering how Hugh and Elizabeth were faring. Then the front door and basement door slammed, one after the other, and Sarah threw Deirdre into the living room. They were both covered in grime and mud. Sarah just stood there, looking absently at the floor. Deirdre dared to peek up from where she lay.

'Get into the bath, you, and don't let me see you again tonight, or I'll swing for you,' Sarah whispered without looking at Deirdre. Deirdre scrambled from the floor and disappeared. He folded his paper and put away his glasses. He was so taken aback that he forgot to ask what happened.

'My hip is killing me.' She sat at the table and pushed the hair out of her eyes. 'She's not to be let out of the house from the moment she comes from school, Brendan, do you hear? Alice is under strict instructions until one of us is here. Make me a cup of tea, will you?'

Despite his weariness, he didn't hesitate, relieved to be doing something useful when he had nothing useful to say.

The next day, he wasted no time in coming home. Sarah was late, so he had a hot stew ready for Deirdre when she came up from the basement looking for her dinner, and had Sarah's meal waiting for her in the oven.

'I can't let you out of my sight, Deirdre, you know that,' he said as she ate.

'I know,' she shrugged.

'What were you up to, anyhow?'

She shrugged again.

'Was it fun?' he grinned.

She looked at him in surprise, then slowly grinned herself. 'Yes!'

'Aren't you the quare one, all the same.'

She giggled, and he laughed with her, because it warmed his heart to hear her laugh like that in front of him, he who no more deserved such a gift than the lowest thief.

She went off with herself then, to her room, happy as Larry. God, it took so little to bless a man with peace, once he had the sight to see what lay in front of his nose. He cleared the dirty plates, whistling softly. He hadn't to wait long for Sarah, who came in all damp and weary, laden with shopping. He took the bags from her and left them in the kitchen. She was still giving him queer looks when he handed her the steaming stew.

'Deirdre's in her room,' he said. 'All is well.'

The Saturday after that, they finished the job, and he was handed his cards. It was too late to start another job before Christmas, the foreman said, so with the weather getting worse, there'd be no work until March, maybe. Christ, he hadn't expected that. Normally he'd expect to be laid off a week or two before Christmas, but this was nearly a month early. Confused, he hadn't the wit to have one or two and leave it at that. It was like a wake, and one drink followed another, and after that, nothing mattered except the next drink.

It was late when he got home, muttering to himself, indulging in maudlin fantasies, his self-pity at all that had happened to him returned with all its destructive force. His tears mingling with the driving rain, the November wind whipped at his face. He sheltered his cigarette in the cup of his hand, and miraculously it stayed lit, glowing in the wind as he sucked on it. The house was in darkness, and it took him a long time to manoeuvre the key into the lock, but eventually he got in. A fit of coughing hit him and he hacked for a long time. There was something he meant to ask Sarah, about whether she really knew where Hugh was that time he skipped it, so he went upstairs, forgetting the convenience of light, but when he stepped into the darkness of the kitchen, the question was gone. The darkness calmed him, and he listened hard, convinced it would tell him something. He coughed some more, and his chest hurt. Then weariness came over him, and he lay on the floor and was instantly asleep.

When he woke it was daylight, and Deirdre was kneeling beside him, timidly shaking him. Their eyes met for a moment, and then he noticed Sarah's legs moving about below the tablecloth. She was preparing breakfast, and the smell of rashers wafted to him.

'Why do you and Sarah drink?' Deirdre asked.

'Hah? Sure Sarah doesn't drink any more . . .'

'Why do you drink, then?'

'Why do I drink?'

She swallowed nervously, but kept looking him in the eye. Begod, she had guts, so she did. He felt so awful he almost told her to leave him alone, but looking into her earnest eyes, he knew that that was what he had always done with Hugh, and here and now was a child giving him another chance.

'I drink . . .' He sat up, his head hammering, but he steadied himself, because this was important. 'Well . . .' It was hard to say this but he fought to say it. 'I suppose I drink because there's a lot of pain in this life.'

'Pain? What kind of pain?'

'What kind of pain? Lordy Lord. That's a tough one.' The

girl was right, there were all sorts of pain, and he could give her a list as long as his arm, but did any one of them drive him to drink? He squeezed his eyes shut in an effort to give a truthful answer.

'You don't have to tell me if you don't want to.'

He stared at her, astounded by her consideration. He rearranged himself, and knelt before her.

'O child of grace, I do. I do. And this minute I'll tell you what it is. It's the pain of not knowing.'

Was that it? It had tumbled out as if it had been waiting to fall from his lips.

'Will you know soon?'

'I hope so,' he said fervently, taking her hands in his. Then he whispered, 'As long as you're my friend, I think I'll know soon.'

She smiled at that, and he felt that she was the old, wise one, and he was the witless child.

'You're awake,' Sarah said, as she laid the table. 'Do you want some breakfast?'

'I'm starving,' he said, still looking into Deirdre's eyes. Her smile had gone, but she looked at him steadily.

'We better have some breakfast,' he whispered to her.

'I'm starving too,' she said primly, coming back to life, and for a second she looked and sounded much younger – about five or six. As he stood, he coughed until his eyes watered.

'What are you looking at me like that for?' he said to Sarah as he sat in.

*

November was a hopeless time to look for work, but he got out his bag and went out in the rain. He trudged the remaining sites, brooding about Hugh and Elizabeth. It was ridiculous that he couldn't see his own family, but there it was, the baffling way of the world. He was tempted to go on a batter, but he couldn't face Deirdre like that again. He got a bad cold, and that kept him off the streets for a week.

He kept trying the pubs on pay day, when the men were in good humour and might be generous, but he didn't have any luck. Yet he had no alternative but to try. It meant buying drink, and drinking himself, the accents of Ireland singing off each other around him, but as long as he kept to brown ale he was all right. By the middle of December he was in despair, and with it the temptation of the easy option grew. He sat at the bar in the Nag's Head, a glass of whiskey in front of him, but he kept seeing Deirdre's eyes, which considered him as he had never been considered, and he left it untouched, and walked out.

Wondering what to do next, he hesitated outside the pub, hands in pockets, looking up and down Holloway Road as if it might give him inspiration. Across the road, Mrs Dempsey was pushing a baby pushchair, with Dennis and young Joseph by her side. He watched her as it sank in who she was. Of course, she had had her baby by now. Cheered, he decided to cross and talk to her. She was on her way to register the baby, it turned out, another boy, so he decided to be sociable and walk with her some of the way. A crowd was gathered outside the prison, and as they passed, Mrs Dempsey remarked that a notice was being posted. A gasp ran around the crowd.

'Someone's been topped,' Brendan said.

'Come on, Dennis,' Mrs Dempsey said, 'we can't wait around.'

Talking to Mrs Dempsey cheered him, and it was good to see Dennis and young Joe again. Walking back alone, he was tempted to continue to Citizen Road. He could tell Hugh he had been speaking to them, and Hugh would be delighted. But he didn't. He went home.

The next morning he was up early and looked through the paper until he found the short paragraph.

'Lord God above, they've hanged Christ and it only ten days to Christmas.'

'What are you talking about?'

'Ah, the poor fucker they hanged yesterday.'

'Oh. I heard about her. She murdered her daughter-in-law.'

'A woman?' He looked back at the news item.

'Greek Cypriot, I think.'

'Be the hokey,' he said in disbelief, adjusting his glasses as he read over the report. 'They hung a woman.'

'No wind of anything?' she asked before she left for work.

'No. Don't suppose there will be now, till March.'

'Keep trying.'

He tried every day, the weather and therefore prospects worsening. Sunday came as a relief, though he didn't lie on. Instead he went to Mass in Everleigh Street and prayed.

O Jesus, forgive me for all my sins. Forgive me for being a coward. Help my family, Jesus, and give me a job. I don't know what I can offer you in return. I'll do my level best. That's all I can do.

He even went to Communion, though he hadn't been to confession for years. To hell with what the priests said. Jesus would understand that he wanted the comfort of Communion.

Trudging around the streets all week had left him very tired, and he slept for a while in the afternoon. It was almost dark in the basement when there was a knock on the door. Coughing, he pulled on his trousers and a shirt.

'Hugh . . . Come in, come in!' he said, looking away to hide his emotion. He switched on the lamp and turned to Hugh. 'Hold on there now till I get my shoes on. Sit down. Sit down!'

Fourteen

SARAH

June 1954–July 1955

Sarah looked across her cup of weak tea to the other side of the canteen where the wardsmaids and porters were having their morning break. It had never occurred to her before, but if Brendan were working in the hospital, that's where he would be, segregated from her because of her education, limited as it was. She was very tired, but glad to be back at work after the trauma of the funeral. What the shock of it would do to Deirdre, she didn't know. She had become very quiet, but maybe it would pass.

She opened the letter Johnny had written to her before her mother died. Why she had taken it to work this morning, she couldn't say, unless it was to cancel out one pain with another.

Come home, for God's sake come home. I have to tell you that she is stubborn to the end, and won't give in with regards to yourself and Deirdre. The Lord knows I've asked her, but each time she turns her head against me. For reasons best known to herself, she has to believe that Deirdre doesn't exist. I know it's asking both you and your daughter a lot, but I feel sure she will forget everything as soon as she sees that lovely child, and die in peace. What I'm trying to say is that it's the abstraction she won't acknowledge – the flesh and blood girl would be a different matter altogether.

She closed the letter, wondering if she was any better than her mother, any the less stubborn. She should write to Johnny, and ask for his understanding if not his forgiveness. Poor Johnny, always caught in the middle. The other secretaries rose to go back to work. She had told them there had been a death in the family, and mercifully they'd left her in peace. She finished her tea and went back to work. Dr Hubbard passed her on the corridor and winked. Usually his youthful cheek made her smile, at least inwardly, but not today. Back in the office, as she went through Mr Baird's correspondence, she wondered if someone as young as Dr Hubbard could imagine the consequences of his vigour, or if he even cared.

Somehow, she got through the day. Her hip ached badly, to the point of pain, and she felt her leg dragging as she walked home. On top of everything else she had to support Brendan's grief. Like Deirdre, he had become silent, but now as she opened the door he was waiting for her, agitated.

'What's wrong with you?' she asked as she slumped onto the sofa and kicked off her shoes and moaned in relief. 'You've a face on you as long as a wet week.'

'Sarah . . . I've got to tell you something.'

'Well then, tell me.'

'It's like this. I've been saving money for Charlie, you know – a few bob every week . . . well, since I gave up on Hugh coming back home with me to the farm.'

'So?'

'So now I've no one to save for.'

She swallowed hard, the blood draining from her head as she realized the implications of what he was saying.

'You should give it to Hugh,' she said coldly, turning away from him. 'He's your son.'

'It doesn't mean the same if it isn't for a child. Hugh's future is set.'

'Well, suit yourself.' Clenching her teeth, she made Deirdre something to eat. By the time it was ready, Brendan had gone off with himself to worry about his bloody farm or money or whatever he was worried about next. Deirdre was playing with

Delly on the pavement and Sarah called to her so sharply that she jumped and came running.

Just how innocent could a woman get? She had thought she had put bitterness behind her, but now it came flooding back.

As Deirdre ate, she stared at her.

'Don't rush your food,' she commanded. Deirdre stopped, then chewed slowly.

Christ, she thought, don't let it out on the child. Hasn't she been wronged enough for one day? She steadied herself and asked as gently as she could how she had got on at school. Deirdre perked up.

'Jimmy Flynn stole sixpence to buy a holy water bottle of the Blessed Virgin and he was caught!'

Sarah smiled in spite of herself and Deirdre laughed.

'Yeh!'

'You mean *yes*.'

'I mean yes and the nuns brought his mother into the class! His mother thought he had stolen the Virgin and brought her back!'

'Brought who back?'

'The Blessed Virgin. You should have seen his face!'

'And what happened then?'

'Sister Mary and his mother brought him out of the class and we all started laughing!'

'All right. Finish your tea and you can play with Delly but don't go too far from the house.'

Deirdre stuffed the rest of her food into her mouth and skipped away to find Delly. It was the first time she had shown any liveliness since the funeral.

Instead of clearing the table, Sarah sat where she was and stared into space, the evening sun on her back. She had given that man a home, and comfort, not to mention herself, and his only thought had been for his grandson. The worst of it was, it was right for him to think like that. Charlie had been his flesh and blood, his descendant. He wasn't her husband, and he wasn't Deirdre's father, and what was most bitter was that she had codded herself into thinking he was both. No, she had no husband and Deirdre's father might as well be in Timbuktu, scrimping to save five pounds a year for a daughter he had never seen.

It wasn't the money. She told herself she would provide for her daughter, come what may. What mattered was that she lived without dignity, carrying on as her mother had predicted.

Tears dropped onto her cheeks as she remembered what her mother had said when she told her she was pregnant. '*You little whore*,' Sarah whispered. '*You little whore.* You were right, Mam. As always you were right. I have no dignity, and a woman without dignity is nothing.'

She endured it until Deirdre was in bed, then she took down her last bottle of wine and drank it, brooding about Clare, the water gushing through ditches after heavy rain, the drops of water clinging to the stillness of fuchsia. She let herself roam over the hills which brushed against the Atlantic and, in the distance, to the south, if she and her brother walked far enough on a fine Sunday, they could see the Shannon as it enters the sea. She adored her brother in those innocent times. He, of all of them, had stood rock-steady in her disgrace, in his quiet way, but even he couldn't stand against her mother's fear of shame, between Sarah and her banishment into the mouth of war, with ten shillings in her pocket and an overcoat on her back. It dawned on her that that was why Tom was obsessed with Deirdre having a winter overcoat. The last time they kissed, he had unbuttoned her heavy coat to touch her breast. She put her hand over it and imagined him doing that once more. He might have made her a whore in her mother's eyes, but at least he had the guts to give her a child, even if he hadn't the guts to claim her in front of everyone. There was a dignity beyond public shame or morals, and it was called Deirdre.

For years she had put them all out of her mind, had become hardened to Tom, to her soft-hearted brother, and most of all towards her mother. She had become realistic, efficient, had made something of her life and best of all, had given back something too. But it had all become undone since Brendan had come to live with her. All of it. She didn't even bother to teach any more, and teaching had been something which had given her pride and purpose, and secretly connected her to her past. More and more often, she thought of her people with their music and stone walls and their reverence for the Church and de Valera.

It hadn't always been like that. What was that song Tommy Fox used to sing? 'I'll Marry You Without Priest or Witness'. She hummed a few bars of it, trying to get it right. The old songs taught you a lot if you listened to them, things the priests were so cocksure the people had forgotten, they never saw their significance.

'Huh huh,' she laughed. She couldn't bring herself to damn the clergy but it made her feel good to know they hadn't always been so powerful. There you are now, Tom, she thought as she drained the bottle. You could have married me without priest or witness. The song says so, and I agree – so you haven't a leg to stand on.

Tom could sing a song, hundreds of them. Sure wasn't that what made her fall for him before anything?

*

She continued drinking like that for a few weeks, managing to go to work, though she drank every night. She realized that she was becoming more and more lonely. She had hardly spoken to Brendan for weeks, and he had not slept with her since Charlie died.

One Saturday she went to the West End and bought a bottle of Irish whiskey and a bottle of rum. She hid the whiskey and brought the rum to the basement. When Alice opened the door, she held up the rum.

'Do you feel like a drink?'

Alice laughed.

'Woman, I have never felt more like a drink.'

'Me neither. And drinking alone is hell.'

They settled in. Alice's husband was at sea. She was frank about her frustration to Sarah, and told her she was reduced to looking at white men out of the corner of her eye. As they drank, her remarks became more ribald, and Sarah gave in to wave after wave of convulsive laughter.

Delly and Deirdre came in and stared at them, baffled at this strange behaviour.

'You see, Deirdre?' Sarah said triumphantly. 'Delly's mother likes a drink too.'

'Yes, young madam,' Alice addressed Deirdre, 'I like a drink,' and they collapsed into more laughter.

The girls looked at each other.

'They're crazy,' Delly said.

'Girls,' Sarah said, holding her stomach, 'go on upstairs and get Brendan to get the pair of you something to eat.'

'All right,' Deirdre said, turning, 'come on, Delly.'

'And we're not crazy – we're just having a bit of crack, for once.'

'They're crazy,' Deirdre said to Delly before they left.

Their hilarity lasted until they finished the bottle, but then Sarah had to hold Alice's head over the toilet bowl while she got sick, clean her up and put her to bed. As soon as she lay back, Alice passed out. Delly came back and Sarah hushed her to bed.

Sarah thought she was fine. It wasn't until she went upstairs that her world started to spin. It was almost dark. In the back of her head she knew Deirdre was in bed. She made it into bed before she too passed out. She woke in bright sunshine, her bladder insistent, so she went to the toilet, barely conscious.

She went down to the kitchen and made herself a pot of tea.

'That was a mighty sleep you had,' Brendan said. He was in his shirtsleeves, and looked warm from the sun. It was actually a beautiful day.

'I need more,' she yawned. She poured herself another cup and went back to bed.

Someone poked at her for a long time before she woke, and when she opened her eyes, it was Brendan's father. She glared at him, furious that this old man had disturbed her, and then as she focused she realized it was Brendan himself.

'She's all right, but Elizabeth threw herself under a car this afternoon.'

'Oh no.' She put her face in her hands. 'What next?'

He sighed, and closed his eyes.

Then she remembered that he'd said she was all right, so maybe things weren't as bad as they sounded, but instead of clarifying this she was distracted.

'What are you doing with feathers in your hair?'

'What?'

'Feathers!' she pointed. The man looked like a village idiot. Was he cracked, or what?

He looked up, as if the feathers were on the ceiling, then back at her.

'She won't talk to him, Sarah. To Hugh.'

She considered this, shifting the hair from her eyes, but it kept falling back.

'We should go and see him, this minute.'

'No. He's worn out. He went home to bed.'

'Then we must see her.'

When they got to the hospital, Elizabeth was asleep, or pretending to be, so she left Brendan with her. Elizabeth looked up to him, she told him. Maybe she would talk to him.

She went into the hall and sat on a bench. She had been fine, but now that nothing was expected of her, for a while at least, she felt nauseated and very tired. It seemed to come in waves, almost with every breath. If she could stop breathing, maybe. At least it kept her mind off Brendan sweet-talking that young one. Great, isn't it? The centre of the world. You demand attention and everyone comes running. Try to keep the best side out, and a woman's ignored. She'd be all right. Her type always were. It was the stoics who went under, slowly, bitterly, hating themselves for allowing the world to ignore them. Oh, she'd be fine.

Hugh, the little fool, adored her.

Her rage at Hugh's adoration of Elizabeth brought an unwelcome surge of blood to her head, and at once her jealousy faded into insignificance. She tried to stay perfectly still, not to think, but as soon as Brendan appeared, buoyed up, she stood, somehow leaving her hangover to one side for the moment.

'How is she?'

'She'll be all right,' he said. 'Have you a pen and paper?'

She didn't but asked the porter in the hall. She handed

Brendan the pen and paper, and he wrote to Hugh. She wanted to ask him to send her love, but she let it go, unable to open her mouth.

'You go on home,' he said to Sarah. 'I'm just going to put this through Hugh's door.'

Off he went down the front steps without her. Now, Sarah, she thought, heed what your daddy says and go on home, like a good little girl, while he goes about looking after his real family, like a man should. She went home, and called in to Alice for Deirdre. Alice was ill too. Sarah could hear the girls in Delly's bedroom.

'O Sarah,' Alice said weakly, 'come in.' Alice took a large, weary breath. 'Would you like some tea?'

'No, Alice. I think it would poison me.'

Alice tried to laugh.

'Why does pain always follow pleasure, Sarah?'

'Oh, the more pleasure, the more pain, Alice.'

Unable to laugh, they both grinned, painfully.

'I'm sorry I left her with you so late, Alice. We had a bit of an emergency.'

She managed to stay off drink that night and felt reasonably human the following day. When she got home, Brendan was washed and shaved and in his Sunday suit. His ordinary clothes were obviously good enough for herself and Deirdre, but not for Madam Kinsella.

'I looked in on her today,' Sarah said. 'She had a nurse taking her pulse, so I didn't speak to her.'

'Oh. How is she?'

'Not as pale, thank God. I see you're going to see her.'

'Aren't you coming?'

'No. I think maybe it's best if you get to see her yourself. I'll look in on her again tomorrow.'

'It's powerful that you're in the hospital, Sarah.'

'Yes. Well . . .'

Long after he had gone, she was still tapping the handle of the fork against the table, in a regular, slow pattern that she needed to maintain.

She looked in on Elizabeth during her break every day that week, relieved that she either had the attention of a nurse or was asleep, so she didn't have to force herself to be nice.

In the evenings, she busied herself with Brendan and Deirdre, but once they were in bed she took a bottle of brandy from under the kitchen sink and sat up till after midnight. She longed for some good French wine, but her stock was long gone.

During those evenings, her jealousy of Elizabeth turned to a hatred of Hugh. Far from being upset, she found that she delighted in her fantasies. It was the nearest thing to the sensuous she had felt in some time. She didn't want to see him injured, no, not that. Not physically. What she wanted was that Elizabeth should torture him emotionally, and she knew that Elizabeth was just the woman. It had taken Sarah three nights to arrive at a refinement of what might happen to him.

At last, she told herself, she wasn't drinking to blot out hurt; she was drinking to celebrate something. She could see it going on for years, Hugh becoming grey and old before his time, never giving up his infatuation and paying the price, day after day. Because that was all it was, infatuation. Thinking it all out like this was exquisite, the justice of it. By her third glass, she found it hilarious, and began to laugh, at first to herself, but then she found it so outrageously funny that she couldn't help herself and laughed out loud until the tears rolled down her cheeks.

As she recovered, she realized that Deirdre was standing, in that accusing way she had mastered, at the door.

'What's wrong with you?' Sarah demanded.

'You're drunk.'

'How could I be drunk? I've only had one glass.'

Deirdre looked pointedly at the bottle.

'No you haven't. You're drunk.'

'Well, what about it, you little bitch. Go on back to bed and mind your own business.'

'You're a rotter!'

'A rotter?' Sarah repeated ironically. 'I see. The grand little English lady thinks I'm a rotter.'

'I'm not English!' Deirdre protested.

'No? With an accent like that? You could have fooled me.' Sarah laughed.

'Stop that drinking and go to bed!' Deirdre countered.

'Ah go and fuck yourself, madam.'

'I mean it!'

'So do I.' Sarah leapt from the table and dragged her screaming daughter to her room and threw her on the bed. 'Now understand this, missy,' she said in a low voice which broke with rage. 'You're the child around here, and I'm the adult. So while you have no right to decide what I do, I have every right to expect obedience and respect from you.'

'How can I respect a drunk?' Deirdre managed to say through her tears.

The remark stung Sarah, but she recovered.

'None of your cheek. Now shut up and go to sleep.'

Shaking, she went back to the kitchen and poured herself another glass, Deirdre's words sloshing through her brain, and drank it back before pouring another. Yes, she was a drunk. Just for a while. She needed it just for a while, until she got the energy to be human again.

She managed to get through the week. She still drank in the evenings, but fear of Deirdre's reproach made her more careful, and she stopped short of getting helplessly drunk, brooding about Deirdre as well as Hugh. She had failed both of them. Her children, she thought, getting sentimental and tearful. She had failed them like her mother had failed her, even if it had been in a different way. She resolved, no matter how difficult it might be, to give up the drink for their sake.

Hugh came on the Friday evening and, despite his dejection, it never occurred to her that she had cursed him to a lifetime of misery. She fussed over him, making him tea, telling him that he shouldn't worry, that Elizabeth would be fine and back with him before he knew it, all with an energy and happiness she had not known in ages. Deirdre was happy to see him too. Sarah realized that Deirdre was now old enough to sense Hugh's pain, and to sympathize with him. That moved her, and made her proud. They could both love Hugh, nurse him back to strength, be needed.

But then Brendan, as usual, ruined everything. He came bursting in, full of energy and all the joys of life, and then stopped dead, before bounding over to Hugh and almost knocking him off the chair with a slap on the shoulder.

'Well,' he demanded, 'what are you doing here when your wife's dying to see you? Eh? Well, don't gawk at me as if I was the Angel Gabriel. Get up off your arse and get down to her.'

When he was gone, Brendan helped himself to a cup of tea.

'Is it true?' Sarah asked, staring at Brendan.

'We've turned the corner now,' Brendan said.

'Is Elizabeth going to be all right?' Deirdre asked.

'She is, my pet,' he said. 'She is.'

She smiled up at him, God bless her, all excited.

'She's going to be grand,' he said. 'Everything's going to be grand,' and then Deirdre ran to her, as well she might, and she held her precious daughter close.

The prize bitch. Could she not have left it for another hour? There you are, sitting up in your hospital bed like the Queen of Sheba, ruling other people's lives. O yes, snap your fingers and they come running, don't they? Could you not have waited another hour?

Deirdre was humming, happy that things would turn out all right. The Lord love her, she was too young to know that life wasn't that simple. And look at him, the cat that got the cream!

She tried to look pleased as she gave Brendan his tea, but the effort was too much, and as soon as she could, she went to her room and closed the door behind her in relief. It was then, remembering how Hugh had jumped to the command, without even so much as glancing at her, much less a word of thanks, that she felt her hatred of him again. How could he be like that? Did he not know that his bloody wife was turning him into a servant?

Well, let her. He deserves it all. He wasn't man enough to turn to her and say *Thank you, Sarah, I'll be right back. Your kindness means a lot to me.* No. Not a word. Not as much as a word, to acknowledge her existence . . .

She threw herself on the bed, weeping. Was that too much to ask? A kind word, after all the kindness she had given him? And Brendan, the old fool, under her spell too, just like Hugh. O God, it was too much to bear. Too much.

She cried herself to a point where she didn't care any more. She shivered, then sat on the edge of the bed, feeling vacant. Eventually she shook herself, washed her face in the bathroom, and somehow put on a cheerful face for Deirdre. Brendan had gone down to the basement and Deirdre was downstairs with Delly. She could just about hear them laughing. She was tempted to have a drink, but resisted it, mostly because of Deirdre, but partly because she felt so tired. Empty, that's how she felt. If she could only stay that way.

She pottered around, cleaning up, until it was time to call Deirdre. She came happily enough, content in her own world.

'What about a French story, love?' she asked.

Deirdre stopped and looked at her in surprise.

'No thanks,' she said airily.

'Oh. I suppose you and Delly tell each other all the stories you want.'

Deirdre just stood there, trying to hide a smile, unable to look her mother in the face.

'Hmm. Off to bed with you, won't you?'

Still grinning, Deirdre did as she was told.

'Have you done your homework?' Sarah called after her.

'I'll finish it tomorrow,' Deirdre called back.

Of course. It was Friday night. Well then, one little one perhaps.

On her second glass, Brendan came in, smiling.

'I'll join you,' he said.

'Help yourself.'

He found a glass in the kitchen and poured, reaching over to refill hers.

'Here's to the full recovery,' he said, tinkling her glass.

'Yes,' she said without enthusiasm, and then he leaned over and kissed her. He hadn't touched her since before Charlie died.

'You're a powerful woman,' he whispered, his forehead against hers.

It was all she could do not to burst into tears when he said that. It was his way of paying her a compliment, but the irony was too much.

'I was thinking I might stay up here tonight,' he whispered.

'Well, come on, then. I'm too tired for words.'

In bed she switched off the lamp and turned her back to him.

'Goodnight, Brendan,' she said.

He didn't reply. Obviously he had expected more, and the Lord knows she wanted to be touched more than anything, but she couldn't let him near her when his good humour was all down to that woman. Maybe in his own slow but sure way he would realize after a while that he had to consider these things, and give her her due. It was odd to think of it like that.

He was gone when she woke, and she wondered if he had stayed the night. She was refreshed but subdued. Elizabeth crossed her mind. Oddly, she didn't hate her any more – why should she hate her? Wasn't she the only one she could confide in when her mother died? A pity Brendan wasn't still in bed with her. She would have liked to have kissed him quickly before getting up, touch his cheek and smile, just to show some affection.

She made an effort to be pleasant that weekend, and gradually they relaxed with each other, going about the ordinary business of accumulated housework, doing ordinary things. She caught Brendan looking at her once or twice, intrigued, or so she hoped. They even had a few laughs, and once, when she was giving him his tea, she touched the back of his head lightly, quickly, and the pleasure of it made them both smile. Maybe things would turn out all right after all.

She had a few glasses of wine on Saturday evening, but they were with Brendan, and they talked quietly about several things. He seemed more thoughtful about Elizabeth and Hugh, after the euphoria about her recovery. It wasn't going to be easy, he said. They still had to go through the loss of Charlie, and that would be terrible for them. But, for the first time, he asked her about the difficulties of rearing Deirdre, and she was surprised by his observance of her approaching puberty, and the signs of her rebellious streak.

They kissed before going to their separate beds that night. She was too superstitious to call it happiness; she preferred to think that she had been comforted.

It was good to be back at work with a clear head and a calm heart, and she enjoyed the morning, absorbed in her work. After lunch she went to see Elizabeth, but she had been discharged – in a wheelchair, the nurse added pointedly, and Sarah stared at her as she strode away, wondering why the nurse had been so curt about it. She was relieved, though, that she hadn't to speak to Elizabeth, and realized that there was still a barrier between them.

Deirdre was very perky when she told her, and got excited when she heard Brendan's footsteps coming up from the basement.

'Well,' said Brendan when he saw her, 'what has you so bright and airy?' He winked at Sarah and once again she felt that comfort.

'Sarah has good news!'

'Oh?' He looked at Sarah, as if the good news might possibly be bad.

'They let her out today.'

'Will we go on down to see them?' There he was, full of beans again.

'Maybe we should give them a few days. She went home in a wheelchair, you know.'

'Oh. Right.' He considered this. 'So is Hugh taking time off work?'

'I suppose he must be.'

The following evening, Brendan did not return from work at the usual time. Deirdre missed him too, but she reasoned that he would have gone to see Hugh and Elizabeth. As his dinner turned solid in the oven and the hours passed, she began to wonder if he had had an accident at work. When he returned, he was drunk and confused.

'What happened you?' Sarah asked. 'Deirdre was wondering where you were.'

'Deirdre?' He slumped down at the table. 'Lord, Sarah. She's threatened never to walk again.'

Her heart went cold.

'I see.'

He stared at her, as if she had insulted him.

She took his dinner from the oven and gave it to him, sitting at the table with him in silence while he ate without much interest. So her fantasy was coming true and, stunned by guilt, she wondered if she had cursed Hugh by indulging it with such pleasure.

'Have you any of that brandy left?' he asked her then.

'Drink isn't going to solve anything, Brendan.'

'God, you're the one to talk.'

'All right. I'll join you, so.'

Brandy. There had to be some somewhere. Then she remembered the emergency stash in her bedroom.

She poured them two glasses, and he clutched his absently before he drank back a mouthful. As she drank, she ran her free hand through his hair, letting it run down his neck to caress the hollow. He let his head fall back as he stared into space, her hand supporting him, and she continued like that for a while, drinking with one hand to catch up, holding him with the other, all the while remembering her curse had come true. She was going to have to live with that. Jesus Christ and His Holy Mother, but how would she live with it? She tried to reassure herself that it was coincidence. The days of witchcraft were long gone, even in Clare. Biddy Early, Lord rest her, was the last of her breed. But the more she tried to be rational, the more she believed she had brought this about with her stupid jealousy. Please, she thought, let her get over this nonsense now. The trouble was, it wasn't nonsense. The woman had lost her child and was out of her mind.

When Deirdre let herself in she curled up her nose when she saw them.

'Where were you till this hour?' Sarah demanded. It was almost dark, and she sat upright, horrified that she had forgotten about her.

'Pooh!' Deirdre said, holding her nose. 'This place stinks of drink. Again.' She glared at Brendan. 'Are all you Irish drunks?' Then she turned and went to bed.

'Sure she's Irish herself,' Brendan protested.

'Little bitch,' Sarah muttered. It was all she could say. She had no right to go in after her and beat her to a pulp, which was what she felt like doing. She had forgotten about her. How could it have happened? It was true she had forgotten about her before, but not at this time of night, when it was obvious even to her clouded brain that the child had been roaming the streets.

The bottle was finished, so Brendan went to bed. She sat where she was, trying not to think of the possible horrors which might have befallen Deirdre, all because of her. What must Alice think? She knew she should go down and check if she had been with her, but she was too ashamed. And then she remembered a detail. Deirdre had a book with her. She took a deep breath in relief. She must have been reading it with Delly.

She was soul-weary, and was about to leave everything as it was, but then realized she did not want Deirdre to confront the smell of alcohol, so she opened the windows and cleared everything away. As she washed the dishes and glasses, she recalled Deirdre's jibe about the Irish. She hadn't thought that one up herself. The Lord knows what dirt she heard on the street from other children, and here she was, coming home to see it was true.

Sarah cried as she worked, but then as she finished, she wiped the tears away with the back of her hand and clearing her throat, steadied herself. The light was still on in Deirdre's room, so she knocked on the door.

'Go away!'

Deirdre had been reading but when Sarah opened the door she hastened under the bedclothes.

'Deirdre,' Sarah said quietly. 'Deirdre, you should let me know if you're staying late with Delly.'

'As if you care,' came the muffled reply.

'Yes, well ... We got some bad news about Elizabeth this evening.'

Slowly, Deirdre emerged from the bedclothes and sat up to

face her, her face dark with concern. Sarah realized with a pang that her little girl was fast leaving childhood behind.

'What bad news?'

'She's not able to walk, and probably won't be for a long time. Brendan was upset,' she added, suddenly anxious to justify herself, 'so we had a drink. I'm sorry.'

Deirdre looked away, taking it in. Quietly, Sarah left her be and shut the door behind her.

The following evening Brendan neglected to come home. She presumed he was in a pub, though she could have sworn she heard the basement door bang, the way he always shut it, but she put him out of her mind to look after Deirdre, who was still subdued.

'I'm sorry 'bout what I said yesterday,' she mumbled as she finished her meal.

It stopped Sarah in her tracks. She left down the plate she had just picked up. Deirdre was unable to look her in the face, but Sarah felt a surge of love for her.

'That's all right. We all say things we don't mean to, from time to time.'

Their eyes met then, and Deirdre bit her lip, but without a word, she went down to Delly.

'You'll let me know if you're staying late, won't you?'

Deirdre stopped in mid-stride, and half turned.

'Yes,' she said, before leaving, closing the door carefully after her.

Sarah took a deep breath, got her bearings and cleared the table.

She waited a while before going downstairs, bringing him some food. She stopped outside Brendan's door, distracted by the laughter coming from Alice's, and crossed the hall to listen. Alice was mock-haranguing the girls and they were laughing. It was almost strange to hear Deirdre laugh. How rarely she laughed now in front of her own mother. Well, she thought, trying to be philosophical, that was the fate of mothers.

She went back to Brendan's door and knocked.

'Brendan?' There was no reply, so she opened the door,

stopping her nose against the stale air, and stepped into the gloom. Then she saw him and almost shrieked. He was seated by the sink, a cup in his hand, a cigarette butt glowing in the other, staring vacantly past her. A whiskey bottle was on the floor beside him. She recovered and limped over to the sink, rinsing out a stained cup. 'I see you intended keeping that bottle to yourself,' she said as she poured. He coughed.

'Help yourself,' he muttered, still coughing, and he lit another cigarette.

She made it back upstairs that evening, just before Deirdre came in.

'Hello, Deirdre,' she smiled, but even as she said it she knew she was swaying, and Deirdre stopped dead, her mouth open in disappointment.

'You rotter!' she shouted, turning on her heel to her bedroom.

'Don't speak to me like that,' Sarah protested feebly. 'I'm your mother.'

'You rotter!' Deirdre shouted from her room.

She managed to work, look after Deirdre when she came home, and be at home when Deirdre came up from the basement, but every evening, as soon as Deirdre went downstairs, she went to Brendan's. As if arranged, he was seated near the sink, a cup of whiskey in one hand and a cigarette in the other.

Mindful of Deirdre, she'd have a cup of tea with Brendan, but then he'd ask her if she'd like a drop, and before she knew it she was through a glass of whiskey and feeling like another.

It all depended on Alice. So long as she behaved in her discreet, predictable way, it all worked.

They were both managing, she reflected, as she brought Deirdre shopping. They never missed a day's work and, against the odds, she was holding back from letting her life go altogether. Deirdre was troublesome, and fought with her, but that was better than silence.

She needed to go through this with Brendan, drinking in silence. It was like going to a holy well, and drinking until you had found grace. That they might never find grace was, she knew, an essential part of it all.

As the summer ended, and she was back at school, Deirdre got more difficult, shouting and screaming at her and staying downstairs later and later. It was getting too much and Sarah knew she would have to stop, as she was near exhaustion.

One night Brendan followed her upstairs.

'Make me a cup of tea, will you?'

As she had noticed before, once they were out of the basement everything changed, became more domestic and everyday. She gave him his tea and he put his arm around her haunches.

'We'll be all right,' he said. She put her arm around his neck.

'I know,' she said. 'I know.'

'We'll just get through this.'

'Yes.'

She had some tea with him, then looked at the clock. Deirdre would be back soon, and Sarah hoped she would see them drinking tea instead of alcohol. After a while she looked at the clock again, vaguely anxious, and she started when there was a knock at the door.

'Is Delly here?'

'Alice . . . I thought Deirdre was with her.'

They turned as the basement door closed and the girls giggled in the hall below. Deirdre came clattering up the stairs and appeared behind Alice.

'Is Delly back?' Alice asked her, her voice rising.

'Yeh!' Deirdre said, cool as you like.

Alice turned and ran down the stairs. As Deirdre walked past her, Sarah caught her by the hair and slammed the door in one movement.

'Where were *you*, madam?'

'The sites, that's all,' Deirdre winced as she tried to release her hair.

She squealed and fought, but Sarah dragged her into her room, old dirty necklaces and bits of coloured cloth spilling from the pocket of her dress.

'And what's this, you little cow? What dirt are you dragging home now?'

''S none of your business!' Deirdre managed to say as she tried to ward off the blows buffeting her.

'I'll teach you . . .' Sarah gasped, hitting her blindly as hard as she could, 'I'll teach you what's my business . . . and what's not.'

Sarah staggered out of her daughter's room, appalled by what she had done. Her own mother had beaten her several times, and she had sworn she would never subject her daughter to the humiliation. But now she had done it. Brendan was nowhere to be seen, had skipped it just when she needed him. Breathless, she leaned against a chair in the kitchen, then poured herself a glass of water, before going downstairs to knock on Alice's door.

'Alice, I'm sorry,' she said when Alice answered.

'Lord, that girl's ass is sore, I swear to you, Sarah. Come in.'

Alice's anger was some small comfort.

'No, Alice, I can't . . .'

'Curfew for her. As soon as she's in from school. I swear. Curfew.'

'For both of them.'

'Right. I won't let them out of my sight, I swear to you, Sarah.'

Sarah realized, to her horror, that Alice was blaming herself.

'Alice, it's my fault. I've been neglecting her. We . . .' She had been about to give an excuse, but there was no excuse. 'But it won't happen again, I promise you. Truly. I promise you.'

The first thing was to stop drinking. She didn't want to but there was no other way, and to give him his due, Brendan saw the necessity as well. You couldn't go on like that with a child in the house, holy well or no holy well. The trouble was, it had been their haven and now that they were thrown back on themselves, it got too much. They rowed at the slightest excuse. They weren't ordinary domestic rows. Oh no. A good row to clear the air, that would have been constructive, or so she imagined. These were something else altogether, more like mortal combat. And yet, and yet . . . Somewhere in the back of her head she knew it was a kind of love-making. It tired her to the bone, shouting like that, letting everything that had ever hurt her fly at this man, and he gave as good as he got. But after a while, her mind would close down and, when she wasn't fighting back, he'd whisper his abuse, like a voice from the past. She didn't know how, or why, but it made her stronger, or maybe immune. Yes, that was it. Like those injections for smallpox. The thing about it was that he didn't leave her. He stayed, and she knew he needed her as much as she did him. She needed a lot of proof, but with every day that passed, it was there. And he'd tell her when Deirdre sneaked in, though she heard her herself, and he'd tell her so softly, full of care and regard.

She followed Deirdre upstairs to wish her goodnight. She was lying on her belly on the bed, reading, ignoring her. Her white ankle-socks needed washing.

'Would you like a drink of milk?'

'No thanks.'

A blind man could see how sad her little girl was, how bewildered, and it hurt her to the bone.

'Did you have a nice time with Delly?'

'Mmhmm.'

She wanted to explain, but didn't know how. How could she, when she had no idea what was going on herself?

'Goodnight, darling,' was all she could manage.

'Goodnight.'

She went to bed and after a while, Brendan slipped in beside her, quiet as sunlight, and just lay there, his arm over her belly, saying nothing. He reminded her of a big woolly dog who knew that its owner was troubled. She fell into a black sleep.

She got up early the next morning, and sat at the breakfast table with a cup of tea. She had no right to be working out her own troubles when her daughter was still growing. Why else bring a child into the world unless you were willing to put her first? She would be gone soon enough, and she shook with remorse. What if she never forgave her? What if she was wounded beyond forgiveness? Oh you forget the bad times in your childhood, or think you do. But what if Deirdre held her a grudge, like she did against her own mother, a festering secret? What then? There would be nothing left. Nothing.

The tears rolled down her cheeks and she wept, mostly silently but every so often a weak sob escaped her. Brendan came to her and put his arm around her.

'What's the matter?' he asked softly. 'What's the matter?'

She couldn't answer him and just went on crying to herself. He sat and poured himself a cup of brewed tea.

'This has got to stop,' she whispered.

'Yes,' he admitted. He took a couple of slurps of tea. He coughed hard, spilling the tea, and the idiot lit a cigarette. 'I've been a right bastard.' He dragged on his cigarette. 'You're some woman to be putting up with me at all.'

Deirdre had to come first. She wasn't quite sure if she could cope without Brendan now, but she'd cross that bridge if she had to.

'Do you want some porridge?'

'Ah no, I'm not hungry. A few cups of tea'll do me grand.'

*

The leaves were falling and Deirdre tried on her tweed coat, delighted she had grown into it. Red suited her, actually. Sarah realized that time was passing all too fast, and she would soon be old. But at least they were holding things together now, and there would be a space to pause and relish that, or so she hoped. Brendan was a changed man, and on good terms with Deirdre again. He still got depressed about Hugh and Elizabeth, but that was no wonder. He wasn't made of stone and she felt it herself. If it wasn't one thing it was another, but she rallied Brendan by convincing him that it was a mourning time that had to be got through, and they would be all right, and in the end she believed it herself. What else was there to do?

Apart from that, things were back to an up and down normality until one Friday evening in late October. It was after dark when Alice came to the door looking for Delly and immediately both women knew. She grabbed her coat and a torch and they set out for the nearest large site still uncleared, down near the railway.

'The little bitches!' Sarah muttered for the tenth time as they arrived. 'Alice, we're going to break our necks in here.' A light rain had begun to fall, but as it happened the darkness helped them as they saw a bonfire in the distance.

'It could be old drunks,' Alice said doubtfully, but they had no choice but to stumble over the rubble towards it. Sarah gritted her teeth as her hip played up, and they made good headway across the site.

'Thank God I remembered the torch, Alice.'

'Shh! Do you hear what I hear?'

Sarah stopped to listen and yes, it was the raucous laughter of young boys, voices on the verge of breaking.

'That's where they are,' Sarah said grimly, and then it was confirmed as the girls' giddy laughter floated over to them.

They were in a hollow around a large bonfire, only the top of which Sarah and Alice had originally seen. Deirdre and Delly were with six boys, and the women could immediately see what the game was. Each boy was allowed to crawl between the girl's legs and look up her skirt. But the pay off was that he had to carry the girl on his shoulders three times around the bonfire. Sarah looked on as her daughter rode the shoulders of a boy, clutching his hair with one hand, her free hand wildly punching the air.

Without a word both women moved simultaneously, Alice grabbing Delly and Sarah hauling Deirdre from the shoulders of the startled boy. The boys disappeared as if they had never been there, and a weird silence replaced the laughter, the girls too surprised to respond as their mothers marched them home. Alice kept up a continuous tirade against Delly so that Sarah felt sorry for her, and held her peace with Deirdre until she got her inside, dumping her on the floor. Brendan looked up from his paper and stared at them over his glasses. Maybe it was delayed shock, but she couldn't think of anything to say. Deirdre looked up at her from the floor, and she was genuinely afraid, but would accept whatever happened as her due. Sarah turned away, unable to face her.

'Get into the bath, you, and don't let me see you again tonight, or I'll swing for you.' Deirdre scrambled from the floor and disappeared. Brendan folded his paper and put away his glasses, his mouth still open in surprise.

'My hip is killing me,' she groaned. She sat at the table and pushed the hair out of her eyes. The rain had been light but she was drenched nonetheless, and covered in mud and dirt, much the same as Deirdre, no doubt. 'She's not to be let out of the house from the moment she comes from school, Brendan, do you hear? Alice is under strict instructions until one of us is here. Make me a cup of tea, will you?'

When she came in from work the next day, she was taken aback to see the table set and the smell of good food from the kitchen. Brendan looked out and waved to her to sit down. Too surprised to do otherwise, she sat in to the table and he handed her her dinner, a perfect stew.

'Deirdre's in her room,' he said. 'All is well.'

She ate her dinner without a word.

He kept this up for a while, but then he didn't come home from work one Saturday afternoon. He didn't come that night either, his dinner drying to a cinder in the oven, and she lay awake in the dark, listening to the rain against the window, not knowing what to think. It was very late when she thought she heard the front door opening, and then a while later, a thump, but she lay there, her ears aching with anticipation.

The next morning it didn't take a genius to see what had happened. This was too much.

'Why bother?' she said out loud, stepping over him. She put on some rashers and eggs, enough for the three of them, and if he didn't want any she'd eat them herself, or share them with Deirdre, or whatever. Why bother? she kept asking herself. She set the table while the food was frying, then went back to watch over the pan as the kettle boiled.

'Why do you and Sarah drink?'

Sarah froze. Deirdre was up, and confronting Brendan in a soft, but determined voice. It was enough to put the heart crossways in a person.

She put the rashers and eggs on the plates and brought them to the table like a maid discreetly fascinated by the behaviour of her employers.

It was obvious that Deirdre was scared of Brendan just now, but still she persisted in asking him why he drank.

He sat up, his mouth open in an effort to concentrate. With his bloodshot eyes and stubble and tossed hair, there was nothing to distinguish him from a tramp, and it chilled her to think that a short time ago, she must have looked the same. And Deirdre had endured it all.

There was a lot of pain in this life, he told her softly. What kind of pain? she asked him. Sarah was taken aback by the gentleness in her voice. She seemed to feel for Brendan in a way you would never expect from a child, much less Deirdre. And Brendan was astonished too. He gathered himself and knelt before her on both knees. 'Child of grace' he called her. It was a long time since she had heard that phrase.

'And this minute I'll tell you what it is. It's the pain of not knowing.'

'Will you know soon?' she asked with all the power of her innocence.

My God. How could you answer that? But he did. He did.

'You're awake,' Sarah said, breaking the spell as she laid the table. 'Do you want some breakfast?'

'I'm starving,' he said to Deirdre, and then he whispered something to her.

'I'm starving too,' she said, like the little madam she used to be. As he stood, he coughed until his eyes watered.

He has TB, she thought. There's nothing surer. The drink has worn him down and he has TB.

'What are you looking at me like that for?' he asked her as he sat in.

*

Ever since the night she had dragged her home from the bonfire, Deirdre seemed to have become quieter, and reflective. And to think she wasn't yet twelve years old. Sarah had even discovered that Deirdre was reading French stories. She had intended tidying her room, which was in a mess, when she found the book under her pillow. Careful to leave it back exactly the way she found it, she eased out of the room like an intruder, which from now on was exactly what she would be. Where had the years gone? But along with sadness, she felt proud of her, this wise young girl who was her flesh and blood.

A blessed peace settled in the house. Brendan got a cold, looking for work in the rain, and she nursed him. The weather was miserable and it was unlikely he would get a building job so close to Christmas, but it wasn't the most important thing in the world. Most building workers would be laid off around Christmas anyway, until the weather improved in the spring. What was important was to have peace. As long as she had her job and they weren't drinking, they would survive. They had become a family and she discovered that she loved that, without ever being consciously in love with Brendan. A closer bond than before Charlie's death had sprung up between himself and Deirdre, and they talked in an easy way that she could never do with her daughter. He was the father she never had, and Sarah found herself standing back sometimes, just for the beauty of seeing them together, and also because she knew Deirdre needed this. And how pretty she was turning out to be!

Her own good looks, if she had ever had them, had passed, she thought a little too wistfully, and passed unnoticed. She shook herself out of all that nonsense. It was the way of the world, and she had a lot to be thankful for. Brendan was sleeping regularly with her now. It had quickly become obvious that he was impotent – after all the emotional disasters, she supposed – but she didn't mind. It was better, really, to have him with her like this for now at least, and she didn't want to risk another child at her age. He was upset at first, but she put his mind at ease so that he too enjoyed just being with her, kissing her, stroking her breasts and between her legs, making her enjoy sex like she had never done. She looked after him too, though each time he went into a fit of coughing even as he climaxed. This upset her greatly, but never stopped her doing it, and as soon as his coughing stopped, she forgot about it, determined to clutch at the comfort of being at ease with him like that.

And then, before Christmas, Hugh turned up, full of the

joys of life. She went cold with embarrassment when she opened the door and saw him there, but he leaned forward, his hands on her shoulders, and kissed her heartily on the cheek.

'Hugh,' she said, barely able to raise her voice above a whisper, 'come in.'

'*Hugh!*' Deirdre jumped up from the table when she brought him in and leapt into his arms.

'Oho, Deirdre!' he shouted. 'It's good to see you again. Let me look at you,' he said, holding her at arm's length. 'Begod, as soon as I turn my back, you grow another foot.'

'I do *not*,' she protested. 'Sarah, tell him he's dreaming.'

'I'm not sure,' Hugh said, winking at Sarah, 'I'm not sure now whether you'd turn up your nose to some sweets, but I brought a few anyhow.'

'I hardly ever have sweets,' she said, bashful all of a sudden.

'She has to mind her figure now, of course,' Sarah teased.

'I do *not*.' Deirdre blushed and took the bag from Hugh, offering him one, before offering one to Sarah. '*You* don't deserve *any*,' she said.

'I know,' she said, taking one, enjoying the chocolate centre.

'I suppose you've guessed by now why I'm here,' Hugh said.

'Is Elizabeth well again?' Deirdre asked.

'She is, love.' Hugh looked so content as he said that, she was sure he was going to fall asleep on the spot. It was hypnotic to watch. 'I mean, she's not walking, but she's come around.'

'That's great news,' Sarah said, turning to him. He would never know just how relieved she was.

Deirdre started another sweet, never taking her eyes off Hugh.

'Here, what am I thinking of – a cup of tea!'

'Ah no, I'm grand. Is the oul' fella out at the pub, or what?'

'He's off the drink, Hugh.'

'Oh?'

'We both are,' she said, looking at Deirdre, who was twisting a sweet paper. 'For good. He's looking for work. Actually, I dare say he's out at the sites this minute.'

'I heard him come in a few minutes ago,' Deirdre said.

'Well, I better go down to him so. With my news, like,' he

said, grinning again. 'And maybe I can get him a job, you never know.' He kissed Deirdre on the cheek, and she blushed a deep crimson, before he kissed Sarah. He held her shoulders and looked into her eyes. 'This is going to be a happy Christmas, Sarah.' Turning to Deirdre, who seemed rapt and distant at the same time, he asked her if she would visit them soon. She nodded, and smiled beatifically.

They stood in silence as he left. This was a Hugh she had never seen, a generosity in him she had never expected. Yes, she was relieved.

She looked at Deirdre, who was now, she realized, almost as tall as herself.

'Stop biting your lip,' she teased, gleefully poking her arm, 'or you won't have any lip left for you know what.'

'Stop that,' Deirdre said, blushing again and pushing against her, and Sarah laughed.

'You're a rotter,' Deirdre said, and left to take refuge with Delly.

Oh yes, Sarah thought when she was alone, it's all happening by the day.

*

Brendan and Hugh came back upstairs, Brendan unable to hide his grin, demanding a pen. Amused, Sarah handed him one, and he in turn handed it to Hugh, who scribbled an address.

Hugh left then, in a shower of good wishes. He didn't want to leave Elizabeth too long alone.

'Well,' Brendan repeated when he had gone, this time looking from Sarah to Deirdre, 'what do you think of that for a turn of events?'

'It's wonderful,' Sarah said. 'Really wonderful.'

'Isn't it now?' he demanded, grinning, and patted Deirdre on the shoulder. 'Isn't it now?'

'How long will it take for her to be really better?' Deirdre wanted to know.

'Oh, the Lord knows,' Brendan said. 'But sure what does it matter, as long as she gets better?'

'What's the job?' Sarah asked lightly.

'Eh? Oh.' He peered at the already crumpled paper. 'Night watchman.'

'Night watchman? Don't take it, Brendan.'

'No?'

'Deirdre, are you going down to Delly?' Deirdre didn't need prompting a second time, and left. 'No,' Sarah continued. 'Out all night. Think what it would do to your chest. It's bad enough as it is.'

'But what am I going to do, Sarah? I can't kick my heels around the house all day.'

'Why not? What did you do every other year when the building stopped?'

'Ah you just want me as your gigolo, that's what you're after.'

'Maybe I do,' she laughed. 'Maybe that's what I'm after.' She touched his face, ran her finger along his lips. 'You've been through so much, Brendan. Why not rest now, and be fresh for work in the spring?'

He kissed her fingers as they passed over his lips.

'I'm a very lucky man,' he whispered, and held her tight in his arms.

When they went to bed that evening, she was not surprised that he was potent again. She wanted him to be and was ready for him.

'O my gigolo!' she groaned as he slid into her, and they both laughed, the dark seriousness of passion breaking down into something slower, more widespread, delightful.

*

She was relieved when he agreed to rest, but just as she had known at the back of her mind that she would not conceive when they made love, she checked her post office account to make sure she could tide them over. It would be close, but better to be in debt than to have him dead, and she knew he had some put away too, so she didn't bother him with such a question.

He turned out to be the housekeeper she had always wanted. Every evening now, as she came out of the smog and darkness, she was greeted by a fire and a hot meal. He swept and cleaned the house and his own flat every day. He even polished her meagre collection of silver. She noted that he had no eye for the smaller details of cleaning, but it was easy to rectify this when he was absent. He looked much younger and she felt much younger. Even her hip didn't bother her so often, despite the winter damp and cold. And Deirdre was happy too. That was no small thing.

With a fine mix of trepidation and excitement they went to visit Elizabeth and Hugh, laden with flowers from Brendan and Turkish delight from Deirdre and bottles of port from herself.

'Be the hokey,' Hugh exclaimed when he saw them. 'Santy isn't in it,' he joked to Deirdre.

'There's no such thing,' she replied sniffily.

'Oh, will you listen to her,' Hugh laughed.

Hugh closed the door behind them and they waited nervously for him to lead them in.

'Look what I have here!'

Elizabeth gasped and threw her hands over her face when she saw them come laden with gifts like that. When she looked over her fingers her eyes were flooded and she kept shaking her head. It was then that Sarah noticed that while seated at the table, she was still in a wheelchair. She was pale and had lost weight, with grey smudges under her eyes, but when she took her hands away to allow Brendan to kiss her cheek, it was obvious that her strong life-force had returned.

'Deirdre!' She held out her arms, sniffling, and Deirdre rushed to her.

'I brought you this,' Deirdre said shyly after they had embraced.

'My favourite!'

'Really?' Deirdre was delighted.

'And I brought you something stronger,' Sarah laughed, putting the two bottles firmly on the table.

'Sarah, you shouldn't have – but I like it!'

'Oh,' Brendan muttered, remembering the flowers, and lifting them with a flourish. 'I brought you something delicate.'

'Brendan . . .'

'Lord, it's an awful pity we don't have a camera,' Hugh said. 'It's at a time like this that I really miss Sam.'

Sarah and Brendan glanced at each other as Hugh opened a bottle of port and poured four glasses, but they took them and drank, Sarah giving Deirdre a few sips from hers. Deirdre protested at first, whispering to her that she hated smelly old drink, but when Sarah whispered back that they were celebrating with Elizabeth, she relented, and seemed to enjoy it and it helped her to relax in adult company.

There was a lot of laughter that afternoon as they finished a bottle, but when it was obvious that Elizabeth was tiring they left early.

'Doesn't she look great?' Brendan enthused as they walked home in the dark. Because of the smog, it was difficult to see where they were going, despite the street lighting which looked like the sun trying to break through cloud on a misty day. Sarah agreed. Elizabeth's colour had certainly improved after the first glass. They passed a pub, which was eerily quiet. 'Lord,' Brendan declared, coughing after a drag on his cigarette, 'it's a shame to stop celebrating just as we were getting going.'

Sarah glared up at him.

'Oh,' he muttered, crestfallen. 'Right.'

Brendan was disappointed that Hugh and Elizabeth were to spend Christmas with Millie, but Sarah was secretly delighted. She wanted an intimate Christmas, and Brendan soon rallied and they went shopping together just like a normal family, to Deirdre's obvious satisfaction. They even brought her to Piccadilly to see the lights, and for a while she was a child again, enchanted by everything.

Sarah got a nice joint to roast, but on Christmas Eve Brendan arrived home and heaved a large, unplucked bird onto the table. Sarah's mouth dropped open.

'What's that?'

'What do you think it is – it's a turkey!'

'Brendan . . .'

'All right, all right, I'll look after it, don't worry.'

She sat at the table and put her head in her hands. He touched her lightly.

'Sure, Sarah,' he said softly, 'won't we need it if you're going to invite Delly . . . and her mother – sorry I can't think of her name.'

'Alice,' she said, looking up. 'Do you know something, in all the years she's been here, I never thought of that.'

'Sure it's only right, isn't it, for Christmas?'

'Huh,' she laughed, 'you chancer. You only thought of that to get you out of a hobble.'

He tried to hide a grin.

'All right, go on, pluck your duck.'

'It's not a duck, it's a . . .'

That night, before she went to bed, she turned out the light and watched the fairy lights blink on and off. She had worried as to why she hadn't asked Alice to Christmas dinner before, but when she went down to ask her, the answer was obvious. Alice's husband was home for the holiday, and Delly was on high doh. So they would have to tackle the duck, as she insisted on thinking of it, themselves. It was a small problem at what was a peaceful end to a tormented year, and it was hard to believe that the torment had passed. It was a time to be very grateful, and she would sacrifice a lot for it to continue like this, though she knew in her heart that it was borrowed time. She shook herself. It was sinful to think like that, after all they'd been through. Borrowed time! It was their time. They were happy now, and the rest was in the hands of God.

She found her presents for Deirdre, a skirt and the colourful socks she had talked about, and for Brendan, a shirt and silk tie, and placed them under the tree. When she slipped into bed, Brendan seemed to be asleep, but when she reached out to turn off the lamp, she felt his arm lie across her waist.

Brendan was up when she woke late on Christmas morning, and so, she discovered, was Deirdre.

'Happy Christmas, Mammy!'

'Mammy?' she laughed as she hugged her. 'Mammy,' she laughed as she hugged her. 'You're a bit old to be calling me "Mammy", aren't you? Happy Christmas, Brendan,' she said, turning to him, and for the first time in front of Deirdre she kissed him on the lips. She blushed as she glanced back at

Deirdre who was grinning at this. 'Go on, you, open your presents. You too, Brendan,' she said, as Deirdre leaped to the bottom of the tree.

'And how about yourself, now?' he asked, squeezing her to him. 'Are you going to leave yours unopened?'

'Me?'

Deirdre danced about with delight as she discovered the clothes. Subdued, Sarah opened her parcels. Deirdre had given her a box of chocolates, and Brendan a book, *The Stories of Sean O'Faolain*.

'Brendan . . .' She flicked open a page. He had inscribed it, in a spidery scrawl,

To Sarah
Christmas 1954
Love Brendan

'Well, well, I'll look a right gent in this,' he said, holding up the shirt and tie against his chest.

Sarah laughed.

'Look, Sarah, look!' Deirdre said, hardly able to contain her excitement.

'Let me see.'

'*Irish Fairy Tales* by . . . James Stevens.'

'Look, Deirdre, it's illustrated . . . And Brendan has inscribed it.'

'You like it, so,' Brendan said.

Deirdre closed her eyes and drew Sarah and Brendan to her. Sarah looked up at Brendan as they both held Deirdre in response, and his eyes, like hers, were misty.

'Well,' she said, trying to be businesslike, 'we'd better get this duck in the oven. I hope you've plucked and cleaned it, Mr Kinsella.'

'Lord, but she's a hard woman,' he said over his shoulder to Deirdre, but Deirdre was already engrossed in her book.

The day passed happily. She ate too much, in a way she had not done since coming to London and, after dinner, when Deirdre had gone downstairs to Delly, they fell asleep in front of the fire.

Deirdre stayed up late, but as soon as she was gone to bed, Brendan suggested a glass of wine. She hesitated, but relented when he said he had got a bottle of French recommended to him in a shop in Soho. He went downstairs to get it. She realized he must have gone to a lot of trouble and paid a good bit for it, and she was touched by this thoughtfulness at not producing it in front of Deirdre. It had been a perfect day for her – for all of them.

He came back with the bottle and brandished it at her.

'May you live to be a hundred,' he said as he handed her a glass and poured.

'I don't think I want to do that, actually,' she said, sniffing and then sipping the wine. 'Oh, that's very good, Brendan.'

'Good, good.'

'What made you think of it at all? Oh, it's lovely to enjoy a glass of good wine again, to enjoy it, instead of . . .' She glanced at him.

He nodded.

'Ah . . .' He cleared his throat. 'I'm not very good at this,' he said, taking a small black box from his pocket and giving it to her.

She put aside the drink and opened it. The ring's five small gems were for all the world like a star. She could not take her eyes off it, could not speak, her mind blank.

'I thought,' Brendan faltered, 'seeing as how we've been through so much together and all . . . that we'd probably make it the whole course.'

'Here, you put it on,' was all she could say, and she handed it back to him.

'It was made for that finger,' he said as he slipped it on.

She sat back and looked into the fire, glancing at the ring every so often.

'What do you think?' he asked at last.

'It's lovely,' she said, glancing at it again, then reached to retrieve her drink.

'Will I fix a date, so?'

'Whenever you like.'

'Right then, I'll . . . drop around to see the priest in Everleigh Street. After Mass . . .'

'Grand.' She sipped her wine. It was delicious.

Deirdre slept late the next morning, and it was almost one o'clock when Sarah knocked on her door.

'Deirdre?' she called softly. She went in and pulled the curtains. Deirdre blinked, and moaning, shielded her eyes. Sarah sat on the bed and held out her left hand.

'Well, what do you think?'

'What?' Deirdre took a while to focus, but when she did she immediately sat up.

'Oh,' she breathed, taking Sarah's hand and examining the ring closely. 'It's beautiful.' She looked up. 'Did Brendan give you this?'

'Of course, silly.'

' 'Bout time,' Deirdre said, obviously pleased. She got out of bed and dressed rapidly, leaving Sarah stranded on her own.

As she heard Deirdre slam the bathroom door, Sarah looked blankly out the window. Deirdre's approval had made it more real, but still she wasn't quite sure this was happening, and for some reason hadn't expected her daughter to be so enthusiastic. Maybe she had hoped she'd be upset, to give her an excuse. She held out her hand at arm's length, and examined the ring yet again. This should have happened to her twenty years before, and she wondered if really it was all too late.

At work she found that she was blushing like she hadn't done since she was a young girl in Clare, which reinforced her notion that it was all too late, that it should have happened long ago. Some of them even thought they could joke her about her Romeo.

'He's my gigolo, actually,' and the looks she got made her regret she had revealed the intimacy.

It was only when they went to see Hugh and Elizabeth in the New Year, crunching through a light snow, that it came home to her what was happening. Even when Brendan had come home from the priest, the date set, it had not seemed real, but seeing Elizabeth, who was now walking unsteadily, being supported so tenderly by Hugh – that brought it home somehow.

And then it had time to settle in her mind when Brendan, buoyed up by the news that Elizabeth was improving, went to Ireland for two weeks in the middle of January to look after some business. Lying awake one night as the wind and rain beat against the window, and as she imagined Brendan alone in the pitch darkness of the mountainside, a fear of losing him took hold in her. His cough was getting worse all the time, and although a hot water bottle warmed her hip through her night-clothes, she went cold as her fear brought back memories of the funerals out of the cottages and small farmhouses of Clare. She remembered the wasted young faces she had grown up with. They had all been so gorgeous, like film stars, some of them. Some came back from the sanatorium with one arm hanging weirdly because ribs had been removed. Others were never seen alive again. So young, many of them barely more than children.

She turned, agitated. Oh, she knew what it was like to be imprisoned like that. She knew what it was like to be desperate for colour, for decent food, for clean air, for something as modest as peace and quiet. She did not want him in one of those places, in a dispiriting ward for months on end. There was a cure for TB now, of course, but still the fear of it ran deep.

She rocked herself as she thought of ways to protect him. He intended going back to work when the building picked up again in the spring, and he was sure to be wet through more days than not until summer. She promised herself he would have a hot bath every evening, on wet days at least. Funnily enough, he had never used her bathroom. Well, she'd see to that as soon as he came back, and she'd get him out of that basement altogether once they were married. The lack of light reminded her of the poorest cottages at home and she was superstitious about that. Of course, he would have to stay there, for Deirdre's sake as well as decorum, until the wedding.

Wedding.

When she thought of that word, it still made her feel inadequate, as if she had grown up on the wrong side of a wall, the other side of which was a mysterious process called life.

A week before the big day, Brendan showed her the will he had just made. Hugh would inherit the farm in Wexford. She would get the money left over after his funeral, which he had arranged.

'Does that sound all right to you?'

'What's all this about a funeral, and we only getting married next week?'

'Ah, it's a long way off, please God. But you have to provide for these things, and, well, I just wanted to put your mind at ease. You're entitled to a few shillings, and I don't want you footing a bill to cart me back to Croghan.'

There was sense in what he said, but she had wanted to feel starry-eyed about marrying him, wanted to feel like a young girl starting out in life. Maybe it was as well to have a little sense. Then came the jubilant news that Elizabeth was pregnant . . .

They had to go to confession, something she hadn't done in years, and indeed it was educational to give such an account of herself. She did what was asked of her without fuss. You could accommodate all those things so long as you were happy in yourself.

She married Brendan Kinsella on a blustery day in March, Wednesday the 17th. A lot of Catholic Irish got married on St Patrick's Day, as it was the only day in Lent when it was allowed. Anyway, it meant that she could have a spray of shamrock mixed through the flowers of her bouquet. Alice was her matron of honour and Deirdre her flower girl. She had not written home to tell them the news, although she supposed the parish priest would have told them, as he had to be contacted to give her the freedom to marry. Imagine!

She laughed to herself at the thought of her family being here, watching her at the altar with her twelve-year-old daughter, and a robust black woman as her matron of honour.

But she put all that out of her mind as she entered the church, with Alice and Deirdre and Elizabeth. They had walked from home, with Hugh and Brendan going ahead. Sam had come too, to take the photos, but Millie was working again and couldn't take the day off. Elizabeth and Alice boosted her by saying she looked beautiful in her blue silk outfit she had bought on her last trip to France, but in truth it was too light for the weather, and the strap of her bag kept sliding along the silk.

Brendan looked magnificent as he turned at the top of the aisle to meet her, all dickied out in his blue suit and the shirt and silk tie she had given him for Christmas. But he'd got thin, she saw that clearly in the light of the church, and she saw that he struggled hard not to cough through the ceremony. And then she was mesmerized when Hugh, who shone like a new penny, produced the ring, and Brendan slipped it on, as easily as he had done her engagement ring, and they kissed.

Coming down the aisle on his arm, she felt happy, very happy, but as if she had experienced everything since the beginning of time. No illusions. That kind of way. And maybe, after all, it was the best way.

As soon as they were outside, Brendan lit up another cigarette, even as he was coughing his lungs out, but she stifled her fear, determined to enjoy the day. The photos were taken with the priest. Brendan had asked him to the dinner but he declined, citing another wedding, and they went in taxis to the Lyons' House on Tottenham Court Road, which Elizabeth had recommended.

In bed that night, he had another fit of coughing.

'Brendan, you'll have to give up those cigarettes,' she whispered when it had eased. 'They're going to kill you if you don't stop.'

'I know,' he whispered back. 'I know.'

But he didn't, protesting that he could not. Hugh found him work on the same site as himself near St Paul's and, while it was difficult for the first few weeks, when he came home stunned with fatigue, as the weather grew better he improved as she watched anxiously for every sign.

Then in early May, just before she left work the heavens opened. She waited for it to ease, but it didn't, so she opened her umbrella and set out for home. As she walked up Holloway Road, she knew with sudden clarity that Brendan was out in it, taking its full brunt.

'O Holy Mother,' she prayed. 'O Holy Mother.' In spite of the season she lit a fire and made sure there were coins for the gas meter and lots of towels. Then she sat and waited. Sure enough he came in like a drenched cat, and she dragged him straight to the bathroom and stripped him while the water was running.

'Do you want to catch your death and die on me?' she muttered as she steered him into the bath.

'Don't fuss, Sarah,' he spluttered, but she poured hot water over his head to burn out the dampness and cold, and he squeezed his eyes shut.

'Jesus,' he exclaimed, shaking his head, the water flying off his head like off a dog.

Despite her efforts he got bad bronchitis, and worse, he refused to go to the doctor and kept on smoking.

'How can you smoke when you're in such a state?' she implored him, unable to understand how he could do it, but he just looked helpless and took another drag.

The cough got worse, and she lay awake at night, appalled by the content of his lungs.

Fortunately Deirdre was outside with Delly, after tea, revelling in the stretch in the evenings and fine weather, when he got his most frightening attack. It got so bad his lips turned blue, and she stared at him, frozen in terror as he wheezed, struggling for breath. Her fist pushed against her mouth as she waited for the blood to bubble up, but it did not. He just lay across the table, supported by his elbows, and wheezed as he fought to get air into his lungs.

'Right,' she said at last, 'that's it. When I go into work tomorrow the first thing I'm going to do is get you an appointment with a specialist.'

When he looked up at her she knew that as long as she lived she would never forget the fear in his eyes.

Fifteen

HUGH

August 1954–August 1956

He sat in darkness, staring at the silhouette of the stained glass on the back door. He rubbed his face and turned away, realizing he felt better. There was something he could do after all – visit Sarah. He checked his keys, impelled by his new purpose, but when he reached the end of Citizen Road he turned left along Hornsey Road, and then up Holloway Road and walked until he came to the hospital. He worked out which window looked into the ward where Charlie died and then he wept as the cars passed in front of him, life going on as normal although one life, more precious to him than any, would never breathe or laugh or play again. A couple passed him and he knew they were staring at him. He hated their health, their hope, their life, and he wept fiercely for Charlie.

As he calmed and turned for home, he was glad he had come. Everything needs its own time, he thought as he retraced his steps. I needed time to be able to come here like this, just as Elizabeth needs time.

He was weary, and yet some life had stirred in him, and it was great to feel again, even if it was only pain he could feel. And he would still see Sarah. There was still that. Elizabeth and himself would pull through. He was sure of that now. Everything needed its own time.

When he reached home, Elizabeth was awake with her bed lamp on. She looked at him as if she knew something had happened, but said nothing.

'Are you all right, love?' he asked her, but she didn't answer. She rolled over onto her side, dragging her leg heavily away from him as he got into bed. It will pass, he thought. He kept thinking that, though he had no reason to believe it. He was jaded, shagged, because there was nothing in life he could rely on and he wondered how, if everyone was like them as Elizabeth had often said, how could human beings adapt to happiness at all. He pictured the ebb and flow of the tides, and felt it must be something like that. A hesitation between happiness and unhappiness seemed like the way to go about it. That way maybe there wasn't too far to fall.

If he caught hold of a moment, it was in spite of himself, as if an outside force had planted him at the correct time – at a hole in time, say – just to taunt him with how good life could be. Look at how he'd met Elizabeth for Christ's sake. But more often than not, there was an invisible wall and there was no passing through it. And life ticked on, second by second, most of it spent yearning for that hole in time to come around the face of the clock again. Thinking of clocks and time and the sea, he drifted into sleep.

The next morning he woke fresh, and at work the idea of the previous night – that Elizabeth's mourning needed time – gave him hope. And Croghan, the mountain he had forgotten during the happy times, returned like a friend to give him comfort.

Croghan was home, at the end of the day, and had given him his part of the earth to be born in and so truly belonged to him beyond any legal document. He was the heir to the small house and land – only a few acres perhaps, but land. That in itself didn't matter.

His new morale made him kinder and more patient. His love was no greater, but he had more resources the better to love her with. And so he persevered, determined when she did not respond. If anything she dug in deeper, as if it was a battle between love and the refusal of love. Perversely, his hope became faith.

Gradually she came out of her numb state, only to be conscious of her misery. She began to drink, glass after glass of port. Millie proved her usefulness by replenishing supplies, and purchasing a bedpan. Elizabeth could not bear his even temper, and one afternoon threw a bottle at him in exasperation.

'Are you a man or what are you?' she screamed.

He smiled, more patient than before.

'Oh, I see, you're practising being a bleeding saint. You're driving me fucking crazy.'

He beamed. She had spoken to him, had shown a great spark of life, after all. The sap was rising in her. It would be difficult, it would perhaps take a long time, but it had begun.

'Why do I always fall for men who go soft in the brain? Get out of my sight, you crazy Irish monk. I hate you. Don't you realize that – I hate the sight of you. No, no, I hate the thought of you!'

She was so furious she forgot herself and rose out of the wheelchair for a moment. Delighted, he withdrew to let her cool off. But later, he wondered if really she did hate him. He was so preoccupied by making allowances for her sorrow and the strange things it made her do, he assumed that love was buried beneath it all, waiting for the mess to be cleared away to let it breathe again. She was muttering some old nonsense and he pressed his head to the door, desperate for reassurance. There was none.

On the site they were asked to work late for a week to finish a job, and he asked Elizabeth if Millie could stay on for an extra few hours, offering to send her home in a taxi.

'Why waste money on a taxi?' she asked, looking away from him. 'I want to be on my own, anyway. Get a bit of peace, for a change.'

At first he worried about leaving her alone, but every evening he came home late she was asleep in her wheelchair, a cushion supporting her head against the wardrobe. So he relaxed about it. On the Friday evening he was so tired he went for a drink with the other men, and it was later than usual when he caught the tube. There was a lone Teddy boy in the carriage with him, and Hugh idly watched him knock his pointed shoes together for a while as the rocking of the carriage lulled him.

He had been thinking about loving Elizabeth, what it meant. Before he had assumed that it was about give and take, loving and loving back. The thought that she might genuinely hate him had troubled him all week, but now he had decided that if he really loved her, then if she hated him it didn't matter. He would sacrifice his own need for hers, if he could discover what her need was. But thinking about it more brought him even deeper pain when he realized she might still want to die.

Even that? he asked himself. Even that. He would have to grant her even that. He didn't know if he could bear it. The thought whipped up a storm in his head, the back of his scalp crawling, but he braced himself. He forced himself to think it. If he loved her as genuinely as he claimed and discovered that she wanted to end her life, then the logic of that love demanded that he should either kill her, or help her to kill herself. He had thought it, and the storm which he had held back with all his strength, blew up again.

The train stopped at Holloway Road and he got off, alone on the late-night platform apart from a tramp settling for the night. The wind whistled down the stairs, colliding with him and jolting him coldly awake. He forced his weary legs to climb, flight after draining flight, the wind insistent. He stopped half-way up, half believing his soul was adrift in this wind, condemned forever to climb these stairs. Aye, well, he needed to imagine the desolation of it if he had to kill Elizabeth or if she went ahead and killed herself. And yes, it fitted, if there was a hell it would be like this.

Was this what he wanted? Did he want to go to the limits of suffering, if only to know what they were?

He was appalled. What monster had slipped such poison into his head? In turn, he was buffeted by a superstitious fear that by thinking such evil he would bring it about. He ran up the remaining stairs, past a shouting ticket collector, across Holloway Road where the late-night cars swerved to avoid him, horns blaring, along Hornsey Road, his desperate steps echoing under the bridge, and into Citizen Road until he came to number forty-two. His hands were trembling so much he had to steady the right with the left to get the key into the lock, his breath grating against his throat. Drenched in sweat, he blundered into the kitchen, expecting to find her wrists slit, her skirt soaked in blood. When the vision did not materialize, he steadied himself again and got his breath back. It had been a nightmare, somewhere between sleep and waking, that was all. He turned out the light and went to the bedroom, certain now that all was well, but he wasn't calm yet. He eased himself into the room, felt his way along the side of the bed and switched on the bed lamp. He saw that his wife was still in her wheelchair, her head ungracefully lolling on her shoulder, her mouth open, but her breasts were rising and falling and he wept with relief and gratitude.

He pulled back the covers and put her to bed. She stirred but after a moment her breath resumed its steady rhythm. He undressed and carefully lay beside her. He raised himself on an elbow and leaned tenderly towards her, looking closely at her living flesh, from her hairline, right down to where her breasts curved into a hollow at her nightdress. And back again, wanting desperately to touch her, to prove that this was not the other side of his dream, and to give him some class of release. That last of all, the last and first of forces warring in the same man.

When he woke the next morning he was calm and reflective. By allowing himself such dreadful thoughts, by imagining the very worst, he felt that his youth and all its paltry fears had passed, and that now he could face whatever might be in store, without flinching.

At work, he thought of the mountain all morning. When he came home in the afternoon, he looked after Elizabeth's needs, and when she was comfortable he said, 'I thought maybe I should go and see Brendan and Sarah.'

'Suit yourself,' she said evenly.

'It's been far too long.'

'Don't fuss!' she snapped, turning away.

'I'm not fussing,' he said.

She looked at him sharply, surprised.

'Well then, what are you waiting for?'

*

Deirdre was on the street with her coloured friend. He didn't recognize her at first, with her hair in pigtails. But Sarah would never be dead while she was alive. They looked him up and down as he approached, smiling.

'Hello, Deirdre.'

His smile faltered, her brazen stare disturbing him.

'If you're looking for your father and my mother, they're drunk.'

'He's inside, is he?'

'Yes. They're in the basement, drinking their heads off. Go on,' she taunted, 'see if they'll give you some of their smelly old drink.'

Behind all the bravado, she was trying hard not to cry, and her mouth twisted in the effort. He looked doubtfully at the door.

'Go on. It's open.'

'All right.'

He walked slowly down the steps and pushed against the basement door under the stairs. It creaked open. The hallway was dark and cool against the strong sunlight. He turned to look back at Deirdre. She was grinning, keeping up a tough front, like a street kid in a Hollywood film. Her friend was grinning too, though she didn't have her heart in it. How the world had gone sour.

'Go on,' she taunted again.

He stepped in, and knocked at Brendan's door. There was no reply, so he turned the handle and pushed. The room was heavy with cigarette smoke and the smell of whiskey. Sarah sat by the sink, a cup in her hand, staring into her own thoughts. Brendan sat facing him, a cup of the hard stuff in one hand and a cigarette in the other. If he noticed him he showed no sign of it. The scene had a powerful air of familiarity, but Hugh stepped back, closing the door. He stood there for a while, not knowing what to think, and then he left.

Deirdre and her friend were taking turns with a skipping rope. The girls pretended not to notice as he went up the steps but as he approached them they stopped talking. Deirdre faced him, determined to be tough, but she couldn't sustain it and looked away.

'Deirdre . . .'

'Come on, Delly,' she said, tipping Delly on the shoulder, and as one the two girls ran down the street.

*

'Well, how are they?' she asked when he returned.

'Oh, they're mighty. Asking for you, of course.'

'Were they? And what did you tell them?'

'I said you were making progress.'

'Hah.'

'Deirdre's grown up so much you'd hardly recognize her.'

'Deirdre . . .' she murmured.

She was lost in her thoughts for a while. Then she lay her head to one side and looked at him without any trace of emotion that he could see.

'You've changed, Hugh.'

'We've both changed.'

'Yes. Well, maybe it was time.'

It had been months since she'd spoken like that. He felt she was being conciliatory, and encouraged, he reached out and put his hand on her knee. She turned her head as if in irritation, but didn't push his hand away, so he kept it there. It was less an erotic gesture than one of solidarity, of being with her. Insisting on it.

They said nothing for a while. He knew it was a first step, that he couldn't chance going any further for now.

'Right,' he said, standing. 'Would you like a cup of tea?'

'Yes,' she said, subdued. 'I'd love a cup.'

As he made the tea, he knew he had been lying to himself as much as to Elizabeth when he told her about Sarah and Brendan. It had been a stunning five minutes, and he wasn't sure if he hadn't imagined it. But no, he hadn't imagined it. Brendan had drunk heavily when Máire died, and Hugh knew that he was drinking heavily now because of Charlie. And Elizabeth. Oh yes, her too. The grief came up again as he scalded the pot, and he had to stop and take a deep breath before continuing. Sarah and Brendan were all right. It was Deirdre he should worry about. Why should a child have to suffer too, just because adults couldn't handle their broken hearts.

Autumn slipped into winter, and while he worried about Deirdre, the daily grind of work and looking after Elizabeth meant his concern for her slipped to the back of his mind. Elizabeth wasn't aggressive any more, had become reflective, reminding him of an old priest he had seen once, and if only in their tone of voice there was a tenderness between them again. One evening, when Millie had gone and they were eating together, tears spilled onto her cheeks.

'I miss him,' she snuffled. He reached across the table and took her hand in his. 'I know you do too,' she said.

'Very much,' he whispered. 'Very much.'

She stopped crying and looked at him. She looked so tired. They were both so tired, he thought.

Despite the improvement, she made no attempt to leave her wheelchair until one night in the middle of December, he woke as she was getting out of bed. Without realizing the significance of this he was immediately alert. Her body was stiff and her movements mechanical, but she was on her feet, staring at the door. His impulse was to stop and wake her, and he threw back the bedclothes to grab her. She was just beyond reach and he sat back on his heels, seeing that she needed to do this. He worried, watching her take her first, faltering steps, but with an effort he trusted whatever it was that drove her to it. She opened the door and disappeared. Taken by surprise, he gathered his wits and followed her. She paused at the bottom of the stairs as if to take her bearings and then walked up deliberately, it seemed to Hugh, as if she floated slowly upwards.

At the top, she paused, then turned and disappeared. At the foot of the stairs, Hugh was in a quandary as to whether he should follow, but he looked up to see she was there again, staring downwards, through him or past him, teetering dangerously at the edge of the top step.

'O Jesus don't let her fall – don't let her jump,' he heard himself whisper. 'Don't.'

His feet, which had moved involuntarily a moment before, were now rooted to the hall floor. Her head fell forward and he instinctively threw out his arms but in a split second her right foot was on the second step, and her left on the third, as she descended with an unseeing sureness which astounded him. She reached the hall and hesitated. He stood back in case he disrupted the signals he could feel in the air. Then she turned, as if decided, and stood on the spot she had found Charlie. She stared ahead at the centre of the stairs. He watched her as several minutes passed through the silence. Then abruptly, she was satisfied, and turned past him to the bedroom, still staring but obviously seeing nothing except what was in her head. He noticed that he was naked and cold but despite this, he remained where he was, becoming absorbed again in what he had seen until his body protested and he followed Elizabeth to bed. Her eyes were closed, and after he turned out the light he listened to the comforting rise and fall of her breath before falling asleep again.

In the morning she complained of pain in her legs and when he pressed her on it, she decided it was bad circulation from lack of exercise. She genuinely had no idea as to the real reason, as far as he could see. Well, there was no reason to bother her with that, not something so mysterious which was probably taking its own course anyway, and he felt justified when, despite the annoyance of her aching legs, she was relaxed. He got some balsam and handed it to her. She held it there in her outstretched palm, saying nothing but looking him straight in the eye, but all he could say was, 'I'm late.'

That night he kept a vigil until three but nothing happened. When he woke and it was full daylight, Elizabeth was awake too, facing him.

'You're late for work,' she said.

He groaned, made a face and buried it into the pillow.

'What time is it?'

'Half eleven . . .'

'What?'

'. . . But I don't want you to go.'

He lay still for a moment, then raised himself on his elbows and looked at her. It wasn't a demand. Calm and dignified as she looked, it was a plea.

'There's no point now anyway,' he said. 'Do you want to get up?'

She shook her head.

'Will I get you a bedpan?'

'I've already used it. If you're going to the bathroom you can empty it if you like.'

'Right.'

He rolled back the blankets, pulled on his trousers and shoes and walked around to the other side, reaching underneath for the bedpan.

'But come back to bed then,' she said. He looked down at her. 'I want to talk to you.'

When he returned she held back the bedclothes, and still unsure of his ground he undressed and got back into bed. He wanted to take her into his arms, and for the first time in weeks he felt his penis harden, but doubt prevailed and it went flaccid again. They looked at each other in silence for some time before Elizabeth spoke.

'How have you put up with me all this time?'

As if the answer was obvious, he shrugged his shoulders and said, 'I love you.'

She thought about that.

'Even after all I've done and said – and not done and said?'

'I think I love you more than I did. Deeper. Older.' He shrugged again. Surely she knew all this. He was embarrassed, but not for a moment reluctant to tell her. 'We've been through a lot together. I just thought you needed time, and that my place was to give it to you.'

She said nothing to that.

'Is it over, Elizabeth?' He was fighting back hope, the same hope that had sustained him.

'It won't ever be over, Hugh.' She touched away the hair from his eyes. 'I want to walk again – if I can – and I want to be your wife. And something else, though I can't make out what, and the Lord knows I've tried to make it out. Maybe I can do both or all three, if you don't ask too many questions – if being together is enough. Can you accept that?'

'The only answer I need is for you to be well.' He knew this was true, despite wanting to ask many questions, but this was what mattered most.

'You're a good man, Hugh,' she said, her fingers tracing his cheekbone. 'I know how lucky I am.' She closed her eyes and kissed him full on his lips, and he felt his months of loneliness fall away as he gathered her in his arms.

They stayed in bed until mid-afternoon, mostly silent, being together. Making love had been awkward at first, with her weak, aching legs, but oddly enough it had brought them more together, laughing and tender. For once, everything else was forgotten, and they were there for each other, finding their way back.

He asked her if she wanted to practise walking. She looked at him fearfully.

'Now?'

He pulled back the bedclothes, full of the confidence of the healthy and, taking her ankles, dangled her legs over the side of the bed. She looked at him pathetically, and then, in one decisive move, he took her by the waist and stood her up, straight.

'There you are,' he said, delighted and proud, 'you're standing. No bother to you.'

He stood back to admire their achievement, only to see her, with an expression of disbelief, fall forwards as if pole-axed. Only his startled arms prevented her from falling onto her face.

'I told you.' Her wail was muffled in his arms. 'I told you, they're much too weak. I'll never walk again.'

'Of course you will,' he said, shocked and hardly believing it himself. He laid her nervously back on the bed, wondering if he had damaged her. She was trembling and her cheeks were drenched.

'Rest for now. Maybe we went too far, too soon. We'll have to build up the strength in your legs.'

Subdued, he spoke gently, pulling the bedclothes over her again and tucking them under her chin. 'Rest for now.' He brushed back her hair with both his hands, trying to comfort her.

'Rest for now,' he repeated in a whisper and, as he stroked her hair again and again, she fell asleep.

He watched over her, absorbed in the details of her face. He hadn't noticed the wrinkles at the sides of her eyes before, and the lines etched deeply between her eyebrows. She was pale, and her skin had lost its suppleness – soft, but as if it had abandoned hope. This was the woman he loved. How strange . . .

She refused to go to the hospital for physiotherapy. She claimed they would not have her because she'd refused treatment before. He was sceptical, but had no choice but to give in.

*

'Hugh,' Sarah whispered, as if she'd seen a ghost, 'come in.'

'*Hugh!*' Deirdre jumped up from the table when Sarah brought him in and jumped into his arms like a cat.

'Oho, Deirdre!' he shouted, 'It's good to see you again. Let me look at you,' he said, holding her out from him. 'Begod, as soon as I turn my back, you grow another foot.'

'I do *not*,' she protested. 'Sarah, tell him he's dreaming.'

Sarah teased her about her figure when he mentioned sweets. The poor girl was mortified, but Sarah was merciless. She gave as good as she got, mind.

'I suppose you've guessed by now why I'm here,' he said, bursting to tell them and yet wanting to hug the news to himself.

'Is Elizabeth well again?' Deirdre asked.

'She is, love. I mean, she's not walking, but she's come around.'

'That's great news,' Sarah said. 'Here, what am I thinking of – a cup of tea!'

'Ah no, I'm grand. Is the oul' fella out at the pub, or what?'

But no, he was off the drink, they both were, and that was mighty news. Deirdre had heard him come in through the basement, so he went down, sobered by the memory of less pleasant times he had visited this place. He knocked, and it took a minute for Brendan to answer. He was coughing hard.

'Hugh . . .'

No less than Sarah, you'd think he had seen a ghost. It was bloody dark down here.

'Come in, come in!' He switched on the lamp and turned to Hugh. 'Hold on there now till I get my shoes on. Sit down. Sit down!'

Hugh couldn't help but smile, seeing his father like that, shoe in hand.

'Well?' Brendan demanded. 'You look for all the world like Johnny Kavanagh that time three of his sheep had triplets!'

'She's all right. I had her walking this morning.'

'By the Lord God,' Brendan whispered, grinning broadly now. 'You don't say . . . And is she talking to you, so?'

'She is. In a big way.'

'Well, well . . .' Brendan said, examining his shoe from different angles. 'Well, well.'

'Of course, the legs are weak after all this time, don't you know. She'll have to go into training.'

'Hah!' Brendan laughed. 'Get her ready for the sports!'

'Aye!' Hugh said, delighted.

'Would you say she'd be on for the hop, skip and jump?'

'Begod I would!'

'And the hundred yards dash!'

'The marathon, by Christ!'

Brendan couldn't top that, so he put on his shoes.

'Well,' he said, tying his laces, 'you're on the pig's back now.'

'Aye. The pig's back is right . . . Sarah was saying that you're off the drink.'

'I am.'

'That's great. And she was saying you need a start.'

'I do,' Brendan said, rising to his full height.

'Have you got a pen?'

'No, but Sarah has. Maybe we should go up and celebrate.'

*

Sports, how are you! Hugh thought happily on his way back. He kept thinking of Deirdre's face, how it had lit as bright as a new shilling when he told them.

'Brendan can't wait to see you in the hundred yards dash,' he told her merrily. She laughed.

'Dear Brendan. When am I going to see him?'

'Oh, you'll need wild dogs to keep him away.'

'Be a dearie and fetch me a few from the sites, will you?'

They laughed again.

He turned to rummage among the papers on the mantelpiece.

'What are you looking for?'

'That letter from Karl. Oh, here it is.' He opened it and read. 'We should write him a letter and tell him you're better, wouldn't you say?'

'If you must ... Why not phone him? They sent us their phone number, didn't they?'

'Phone him?'

'Yes.'

'But I don't know how to phone.'

'Yes you do,' she laughed.

'No I don't,' he said, suddenly glum. That wiped the smile off her face. 'I've never made a phone call in my life.'

'Oh dear,' she said. 'What about Seán? He'd show you, wouldn't he?'

So he dragged Seán to a phone box and he demonstrated how it was done, even dialling the number for Hugh, and pushing the button when Hugh nodded that there was an answer.

'Yes?' came a loud, exaggerated voice, but it was Karl all right.

'This is my first time using one of these yokes,' Hugh said. 'I had to get Seán to show me how,' he laughed nervously. 'Are you doing all right there, in your grand house?'

'We're doing very well, Hugh. You must come and visit.'

'Oh, surely. Karl ... I've good news. Elizabeth is starting to walk again. She's going to be all right.' Seán mimed that he should lower his voice. Hugh nodded vigorously, but concentrated hard on what Karl was saying.

'Thank God ... thank God,' Karl said, his voice turning natural all of a sudden. 'That is wonderful. That is wonderful, Hugh. We'll come and visit you soon.'

'Well, actually, if you don't mind, maybe we should wait till she's on her feet.'

'Yes. Yes of course. Whatever you think. Well,' he added cheerfully. 'You've got my number!'

'If I don't lose it!'

He heard Karl say, 'Marta, telephones are a wonderful invention,' and then the line went dead.

Hugh grinned as he put the phone back on its cradle.

'Well now,' Seán said. 'That wasn't so bad, was it?'

'No, bedad,' Hugh said. 'It was mighty.'

'That's a pint you owe me,' Seán said.

'Two, by Christ,' laughed Hugh. 'At the minimum.'

A few evenings later he got into conversation with a war veteran in a pub, asking him if he had been wounded.

'Not half. Near blew my leg away, it did. I've no muscle left in the side of my thigh, mate.' He felt his right thigh ruefully. 'Weak as fuck. That's why I need this stick. Can't walk ten steps without it.'

'Did you have physiotherapy?'

'Did I have physio? Did I? If Jerry near half killed me, the physios near finished me off.'

'Why's that?'

And he told him in detail, which was worth another pint.

On his way home, he thought about what he would do. An old leather belt, with padding to protect her legs . . . No, better still, that old canvas bag under the stairs, he could cut it in two, sew up the two halves, fill them with sand – he could steal it from a children's sandpit because the stuff at work was too coarse – and . . . He'd have to think of some way of securing them . . . Of course – take the straps off the original bag and sew them to the ends. Beautiful! A little weight at first, to encourage her, then bit by bit, heavier and heavier . . .

She fought with him, but her legs got stronger, and she got stronger in herself and was in great form when Brendan and Sarah and Deirdre, and then Karl and Marta came to see them for the holiday. At least the exercise had made her hungry again. Although he had got her crutches, she still insisted on going in her wheelchair when they went to Millie's over Christmas. While he and Sam got drunk, and Sam and Millie did everything to make them welcome, Elizabeth admitted that like him she was glad to get home to their own house again.

They had intended spending New Year's Eve alone, but Brendan, Sarah and Deirdre arrived, cheerful as a dog in the woods. It was Deirdre who pulled Sarah's left hand to attention, and the ring sparkled under the light.

'Sarah!' Elizabeth exclaimed. 'That's wonderful. What took you so long, you old rogue,' she grinned at Brendan.

'Sure it took me years to save up for that yoke,' he joked, nodding to the ring.

'It's not a yoke,' Deirdre said. 'It's an engagement ring,' and she examined it, her old lively self again.

They had brought a lot of drink with them, and by midnight even Deirdre was tipsy, and hardly able to stay awake. It was going to be a happy New Year.

It was hard to start after the break, but about a week into the New Year, having worked up to it all week, he finally persuaded her to stand again.

'Don't let me go!' she wailed as she leaned heavily against him, her nails digging into his arms as she clutched them.

'I won't,' he whispered. He was concentrating, wondering how far he should ask her to go. A few steps, maybe. He loosened his grip on her right side and, to his relief, her right leg took the weight. She looked up into his face, startled.

'You can do it,' he whispered again.

'I can't,' she whimpered, even as he drew her left hip towards him, and she took her first step. Her left leg, too, took the weight.

'How do you feel?'

'All right, I suppose.'

'Take a deep breath.'

She obeyed. Gingerly, he took away his support, untangling her reluctant fingers. She stood firm, to his delight and her nervous surprise.

'There you are! What did I tell you? It's just a matter of time now, my love. My dearest love.'

She stared at him for a moment, then burst into tears, though half laughing too.

'I can't,' she blubbered through the terrified happiness of realizing she could. 'You'll have to hold me. You'll have to hold . . .'

Then she took another step. He backed away and, with the

same jerky movement, she took another. He could see the strain was enormous. She took another, then fell into his arms. He expected tears, but instead heard a muffled, weary groan. Her body was limp and heavy against him and, when he lifted her to face him, her head rolled away in exhaustion. The effort had been too much.

He put her to bed and watched her as she slept, trying to be cheerful about her progress. After all, within a few weeks, he told himself, she would be back on her feet. It was like a miracle. Elizabeth, the woman he married, would be restored to him. Or, he corrected himself, simply restored. Yet all he could feel was heaviness, as bad as he had experienced at their lowest point together since Charlie died.

He left her alone, turning at the door to look at her again, baffled by his feelings, and went into the kitchen. Millie busied herself when she saw him, leaving aside her magazine.

'How's our Beth today?' she asked without looking at him.

'She's asleep. I worked her too hard.'

'She's coming on, then?'

'She took a few steps today. On her own.'

Millie looked up at him. He could see the same apprehension in her eyes as he felt himself, Millie's unease if anything increasing his own. He realized that for the first time he shared an emotion with Millie, whatever that emotion was.

'She'll be walking soon, then?'

'Yes.'

'You won't need me for much longer.'

'No. I suppose we won't.'

*

As Elizabeth grew stronger and happier, walking about the house unaided and on the street with crutches, Hugh realized with increasing bafflement that he was faking his own happiness. His jaw ached when he smiled. His body was heavy when he made love. Once, he looked up at her to find Elizabeth staring darkly at him, but she smiled immediately. He wondered then if she too was in despair, or if, beneath everything, she really did hate him, or if maybe it was some dark passion that had taken her unawares. He guessed that if he had asked, she wouldn't have known what he was talking about. Hating himself, he rose and kissed her on an eagerly offered cheek, a Judas kiss.

In late January, she decided to take a taxi to see Millie. It was the surest sign that things were getting back to normal, but that wasn't the only reason he was glad to see her go, taking her crutches with her just in case. They had a laugh when she got confused, not knowing which foot to put forward as she got into the taxi, and she smiled through the window as the taxi turned and left. He sighed in relief as he closed the door behind him. And yet, it had been so long since he had time alone that he didn't know what to do with himself, so despite the cold and damp, he put on his heavy coat and scarf, found his cap and went to Finsbury Park.

He hadn't been here since Charlie was alive. The trees were bare and everything seemed grey. There was a cold drizzle, the type that seems to enter your bones no matter how thick your clothes. The ducks paddled up to him, hopefully, and when he just stared at them they paddled away again. Charlie had been alive and things were different. In tune. He had planned to bring him to the football stadium when he was old enough. Charlie would have been an Arsenal fan. Things were different then.

'*Look, Daddy, look, a fish!*'

He was sure he had heard his voice, clear as a bell.

He turned away from the lake, his body twisting with a grief he could not loosen.

When would it ease; when would this hole in his life close over and let him be? The hole took the shape of Charlie walking by his side. There were holes in the air where Charlie's questions would have hung, unanswered, unanswerable, but full of childish wonder. He walked along the path, imagining Charlie trotting a few steps in front of him, that much bigger and stronger now. A few years more – bigger, taking his rightful place in the world. A few years more – taller, shoulders broadening, his breaking voice out of control and making him blush, cat's hairs sprouting on his lip. Then – a man, making his way. Tall, a strong grip, a steady eye and a love for women, proud and at home with himself, solving his problems as they came upon him.

Hah! More likely he would have turned out like his father, thin and unsure of himself until some woman made him feel he belonged.

Although he walked slowly and darkness fell quickly, Elizabeth was still away when he reached home.

He hesitated, then went up to Karl's old room. It was still much as he had left it, with his books and records. Elizabeth had dusted it now and then, but otherwise never touched it. The dust had settled on the books, on the table, all over the room in the months since summer, and the room smelled a bit damp. He opened the window and the cold, cutting air flowed in. He leafed through some of the books, but nothing caught his fancy. Why Karl had thought they might be of any interest to Charlie was beyond him. In any case, some of them were in German. There was one neatly placed on the table. It attracted him because it had a blue cover, which he thought was unusual. It was a book on astronomy, and a book-marked page fell open at a photo of what must have been a pile of stars in a spiral. Pronouncing the name of it was beyond him, but he looked at it from all sides, and it was for all the world like a white snail. There was another bookmark, and he let it fall open on a passage about Neptune, the newest discovered planet, or so it said. It was invisible to the naked eye, but could be seen with a telescope in the vicinity of Jupiter. Well now, imagine that. He remembered how, especially in summer, when he went outside last thing at night for a piss, the stars over Croghan looked magnificent and even near.

He set the book exactly where he had found it, and browsed through the records. They were 78s with buff covers and purple labels. Karl had brought his gramophone with him but not his records, for reasons best known to himself, and on impulse he chose one and brought it downstairs and put it on Elizabeth's machine. It was Mahler's Second Symphony, the first part, and though initially doubtful, as he listened he realized that whoever wrote this music understood what suffering was. No wonder Karl had played it all the time. Hugh looked up at the ceiling as if Karl were in his room, and believed he now understood a small part of that big man's battered soul.

He hadn't been alone like this in a long time, not since . . .

Everything was, everything had happened before Charlie's death. He suppressed another wave of grief. It was in the past and nothing, nothing would bring him back. He went back to their bedroom and touched Elizabeth's stuff on the dressing table. A tube of lipstick was open. He picked it up and smelled it. Without Elizabeth to lend them normality, so many things were strange and unfamiliar.

A few weeks later, Elizabeth said she was pregnant. The signs had been there but neither of them had the guts to admit them. When she told him, having no choice, he saw fear in her face and knew it was mirrored by his own. It was beginning all over, two forked creatures fooled by joy for a time, long enough for pain to crush them when it was taken away again.

'I'm late,' he said. Then he turned and walked out, slamming the door behind him.

'I want this child!' she called after him. He froze. 'I'm scared too,' she sobbed to herself, 'but I want it and if you don't you can go to hell.'

He gritted his teeth, his eyes clamped shut. Then, as if in a dream, he was standing at the door again, his head bowed.

'I thought you said you were late.'

'No, I've still got time.'

'Oh.' She turned her head away, sniffing and trying to hide her tears.

'We're in this together, aren't we? I mean, there's no turning back now, is there?'

She leapt from her chair and threw her arms around him.

The cliché was true. A weight had lifted from his shoulders. The morning was bright and sunny and there was a clean chill in the air. Her spontaneity had meant everything. He didn't care what happened now. There was one pure moment of truth in his life. There had been others, like when Charlie was born, and maybe there would be more but this was the one that mattered now. He still felt locked in a circle, but, he could see now, there had been advances. His life wasn't unchanging as it had been before Elizabeth. If his son had been taken away, at least he had known a son, what it was like, the love and pain and short temper it had found in him.

There was that – and now the possibilities of new life were unfolding again. The circle was widening. It had a heart, somewhere, a centre. Something eternal lived there. For the moment it was Elizabeth's hug, but that, he felt, was a shorthand.

They kept it to themselves for a while. Karl and Marta visited, flush with the news that Marta was pregnant too, but they didn't mention it. Karl and Marta were tactful, keeping in mind how Elizabeth might feel, no doubt, but there was no mistaking their happiness. It wasn't until she was used to the idea that Elizabeth relented. Without saying it aloud, both of them were almost superstitious about being happy in case they lost it. But when Elizabeth told Millie and Sam, they relaxed.

Deirdre was excited and Sarah delighted but Brendan actually cried when they told him.

'Begob,' he said through his tears, 'that's powerful.'

'Brendan,' Elizabeth said to him softly, her hand on his shoulder. 'If it's a boy we're going to call him after you. You and my brothers. How does that sound?'

'Don't mind me,' he said, looking up to her, his eyes shining, 'I'm only an old fool. And I'd be very honoured if the child was called after me.'

'And if it's a girl, who will you call it after?' Deirdre wanted to know.

'I've promised Millie,' Elizabeth said, which was news to Hugh, 'but how does Mildred Deirdre sound?'

Deirdre blushed with pleasure.

'Very nice,' she said, and never looked more innocent.

Sarah asked Deirdre to help her with the tea and she went happily to the kitchen.

'I'll tell you this, and I'll tell you no more,' Brendan said. 'I only want to live to see that child. I'll be content if I can do that.'

'Nonsense,' Elizabeth said jauntily. 'You're going to live to a ripe old age.' Something in Brendan's eyes chilled Hugh, but he too laughed it off.

Elizabeth became content and absorbed, just as she had with Charlie. She now had no physical trace of her accident, and life settled into an agreeable pattern. At the most unexpected moments, he was still struck hard by Charlie's absence, and he knew that Elizabeth was too, but apart from that, all that niggled at his contentment was Sarah's worry about Brendan's cough, and what Brendan himself had hinted at. But he'd had a smoker's cough for years and, in spite of Sarah's concern, it didn't overly bother Hugh. What did was that occasionally he would still look up and see Elizabeth staring darkly at him, but then she would break into a smile. That dark stare bothered him all right, but he tried to put it to the back of his mind, and count his blessings.

Hugh rang Karl with the news, this time making the call himself. He could feel the relief in Karl's voice as he called Marta to the phone. Marta kept laughing at everything he said, and he supposed that was in relief too.

Sarah and Brendan got married, and while he felt funny being his father's best man, it was a good day, apart from Brendan's cough which put the heart crossways in him. Sarah was right, it was bad, but he told himself that now they were married she could take him in hand. A good rest and the summer sun would see him right, and Hugh made a mental note to find him some easy work in the autumn. The man had worked too hard for long enough and deserved a rest. He was safe enough, and so once again he chose to forget about it.

With a baby due, and Elizabeth getting bigger all the time to remind him, he took a lot of overtime now that summer was at its height. Marta came to see her regularly, and they had become good friends in their shared experience. Elizabeth even went to her house, and sure enough, one Saturday evening he went to see it too, pleased that things had turned out well for Karl. It really was a very fine house, and now it would have a child to run around it, throw a few echoes off the walls.

Out of the blue, Brendan gave them a scare. His cough got

so bad that Sarah dragged him to a specialist, who frightened him off the cigarettes and told him to give up work. Brendan said it was just for a while – till he got his breath back, he joked to Elizabeth, and she laughed – but Sarah said nothing and just looked at the floor.

'He's going to be all right, isn't he?' Elizabeth worried as they walked home.

'Ah, yeh,' he said, trying to be offhand. 'Sure he's as tough as they come.'

She looked doubtful, but they never mentioned it again, and he looked better once he had rested for a week or so.

What preoccupied Hugh was his late shifts, and he wondered if it was worth it. Elizabeth had become restless, and he was sure she was unhappy at him leaving her alone every evening. All this on top of being bone tired, night after night.

He slept late on Sundays, which meant she hardly saw him at all. He tried to make up for it by talking late on Saturday nights. They hadn't talked about Charlie for a while, but now they had to, about the small headstone that Hugh had erected with Sam's help. Elizabeth had refused to go to the grave since Charlie's burial.

When they turned out the light, neither could sleep. Charlie was still in the air about them.

'Hugh? Are you still awake?'

'Yes,' he mumbled.

She turned on the light.

'I want to burn Charlie's things. The teddy bear. You know.'

He said nothing for a while.

'I've been thinking about how he might have been. How he might have turned out,' she added. 'Wouldn't it be good to burn things to do with his growing up, say, a pencil, a book, a ball, and maybe even a photo of a young woman.' He could feel her wringing her hands under the sheets.

'A woman? What's a woman got to do with it?'

'Well, it's likely he would have married a girl some day. Nancy, maybe.'

'O Christ, don't burn a photo of Nancy. God knows what bad luck that'd bring.'

Early the following Sunday morning they made a bonfire in the backyard.

There was hardly any wind, but it created more smoke than they had anticipated, and they could only hope that the neighbours were still in bed.

They burned the objects one by one, beginning with the bear, and saying very little. The years seemed to roll out before them, and to be quieted. It was difficult at first, while Charlie's own things, things that had been made special by his touch and by what he did with them, were burnt away by the flames.

As the fire died, Hugh put his arm around Elizabeth and she leaned into him.

'I want to put the ashes on his grave,' she said.

'Yes. Yes, that's what we'll do.'

When the ashes had cooled, they put them into two biscuit tins, and brought them to Highgate. It was raining lightly and at first they couldn't find it. Elizabeth was shaking.

'I'm going to scream,' she said, but she didn't. Then, to his relief, Hugh spotted it.

CHARLIE KINSELLA
1951–1954

Without a word, Elizabeth laid down the box and began to weed the grass from the gravel over the grave. Hugh made a gesture of helping but let her do most of it herself. Then she ran a finger through the etched letters of his name.

'Maybe we should have put *Beloved son of Hugh and Elizabeth*.'

'There wasn't room,' he said. 'Anyway, sure we know that.'

She looked up at him, saying nothing, but stood up, her knees wet and imprinted by the gravel, and began scattering ash on the grave. He did likewise as the rain at first punctured and then gradually compacted it.

Hugh stared at Charlie's name and wept silently. He wiped his eyes and looked at Elizabeth, and thought that she looked very old, and supposed that he must look old too.

It had stopped raining and the sun broke through, brightening a cluster of weeds beside a nearby grave. Without warning

Elizabeth's face was drenched in tears. Hugh began to cry again, he had only stopped for her sake, and they both cried until they had cried themselves out.

*

During the last few weeks of Elizabeth's time, Millie had taken to staying with her again, while Hugh was at work. She was a week overdue when he came home and found a note from Elizabeth: '*It's wimmin's work.*'

'O Jesus,' he whispered, before assuring himself that it was stupid to worry. They had gone over this often enough. Millie was with her, and he left a note for Millie to say where he would be.

He was having a drink with Seán when Millie came with the flustered news that Elizabeth had had a son, eight pounds two ounces, and was well. He stared at her.

'Good man,' Seán Butler said, pumping his hand, but he looked over his shoulder to Millie asking for Elizabeth, if she was really well. His voice shook. She ignored Seán and put her forearms around his neck, her elbows preventing bodily contact. 'She's well and asking for you.'

'Here you are,' Seán said, pushing a large whiskey into his hand. 'Well done.'

'Sure I didn't do anything,' Hugh said, bemused.

'Hah! Did you hear that, miss, he did nothing! Would you like a drink, miss?'

'A port if you please,' she said, almost standing on her toes. 'After all, I'm an auntie again,' and she laughed nervously.

'A port it is. And I might as well have a large one myself. A celebration is a celebration.'

'I better go and see Elizabeth,' Hugh said, not relishing the drink.

'No point, old son,' Seán said cheerfully from behind the bar. 'They won't let you in till tomorrow.'

'Is that true, Millie?'

'I don't know, I'm sure. George was just gone to Norway when I was confined. And he never did come back.' Her lips trembled on the rim of her glass.

Seán joined them and they raised their glasses. As they did he remembered that Millie had put him off like this the last time, and he was not going to repeat his mistake.

'Listen,' he said, 'I'll go down anyway, and sure if they throw me out, well they throw me out.'

He left Millie home in a taxi. They travelled in silence, but what she had said to him when Charlie was born came back to him, word for word.

'I never saw her smile like that, just staring down at him in her arms. Her face was what you might call transfigured, Hugh. Transfigured. A changed woman, our Beth. She never even heard me when I asked for a peek, not till we were back in the ward. She never heard me.'

He remembered how she had gone quiet then, lost in her thoughts.

'I must have been like that, with little Georgina.'

He touched her arm in sympathy, and she leaned against him.

'You have a fine son, bless all three of you.'

They called him Brendan Daniel Steven, after his grandfather and Elizabeth's brothers killed during the war.

It happened again, Elizabeth soaking him in, all Hugh's old fears and feeling of exclusion, but this time he could take the long view.

Marta gave birth to a daughter and, to Elizabeth's surprise and pleasure, they called her Elizabeth. She said that was Karl's doing, seeing as they had called Charlie after him.

When the children were six weeks old, Marta threw a party to celebrate their birth. Expansively, Karl asked Elizabeth and Hugh to invite their families and friends. Brendan sat on a chair, barely interested in the jollity, barely able to breathe. They seated him beside Elizabeth and young Brendan for the photo, with Hugh behind them, Karl and Marta sitting on the other side with their baby. Karl had hired a professional photographer, but Sam had brought his Kodak, and took the picture that Elizabeth later hung on the wall.

Sam had got a second-hand Morris, and Elizabeth asked Hugh if he would think of buying a car too.

'For Christ's sake,' he said. 'Give us a chance. Sure I've only just learned to use the phone.'

It was obvious now to Hugh that Brendan would never work again. She never said as much but he knew Sarah thought he was going to die. While he couldn't bring himself to face such a thought, he worried about it, and encouraged Elizabeth to visit him with young Brendan, or Dan Stevie, as she was taking to calling him, during the day. Brendan adored the child, as he had Charlie, and Deirdre fussed over him. Despite the worry over Brendan's health, it was a happy period. Hugh had never felt so close to his father, had never felt so much sympathy for him.

He thought a lot about his mother these days too, at last beginning to understand how lonely she must have been on that mountain, away from her people, her husband in a foreign country. She was the real exile, not them. As bad as it was in those early days in London, at least they had the gruff company of each other. She had no one as she snuffed her candle at night, after saying her prayers in Irish. He remembered how she would bring him with her to see the sheep, and look out across the roll of land to the Irish Sea, pointing out the land where Brendan worked. How often must she have gone there alone, when her only son had taken the boat over to a world she had known once, but had often told him he could never imagine, speaking about the lights and shops and cars, as if it was somewhere out of the stories she sometimes told him.

Christmas was more precious than ever to Hugh and Elizabeth. They wept salt tears for their dead son, held each other in desperation, but on Christmas morning they put it behind them as best they could for Dan Stevie's sake. Even if he couldn't understand, they felt they owed it to him, that he was entitled to a happy atmosphere. Sam piled Betty, Millie and Fred into the Morris and arrived laden with presents for Dan Stevie, who bawled when he saw them, but settled down, his head swivelling from one to the other as they adored him in their nonsense language. Sam had too much to drink, and Elizabeth was worried about him driving back, but he claimed the roads were deserted, and the peelers were snoring after their turkey, so she frowned but didn't protest any further as she waved them goodbye on the street. Hugh was holding Dan Stevie.

'Wave goodbye,' he said, waving his son's hand for him. 'I could do with a walk after that,' he said as they went in.

'So could I. Get the pram out, will you?' she asked, taking Dan Stevie from him.

They walked slowly to Tollington Park, which helped them digest the morning's excess, which was just as well, as they had to start over again, Sarah refusing to take no for an answer.

Despite his shortage of breath, Brendan held Dan Stevie in his arms as much as he was let by Deirdre and Sarah, and he looked rapturous, his eyes half closed with pleasure when the child smiled at him. Elizabeth tickled his nose as he lay in his grandfather's arms.

'Bren-Dan,' she laughed at him, and the child yahed his smile back at her. Brendan looked up at Elizabeth, his face shining even as his breath laboured. Hugh noticed that she called him Brendan in his grandfather's presence, never Dan Stevie.

'I think he's a real Kinsella, Brendan,' she said.

'Oh, I don't know,' he said, his obvious pride defeating his attempt to be modest, 'I'd say he has his mother's sense of humour, anyhow.'

Hugh was very moved by the afternoon. Although Dan Stevie lasted longer than they had expected, it seemed the time had gone too quickly when he became cranky and awkward, and so they said their goodbyes. It was dark and cold as they walked home, Dan Stevie asleep in his pram, Hugh lost in thought and a little drunk, wondering if they had to go through all the suffering they had endured to be this happy, to feel this depth of happiness. Nothing could unsettle them now, he thought. He was sure of that.

'Don't pick me up wrong,' Elizabeth said, and he turned to her, more open to her than he had ever been. 'But I love Brendan very much.'

'Ah,' he said, smiling, 'I know what you mean.'

She lifted her face to his, and they kissed.

It was a difficult winter for Brendan, cooped up all day in the house, and Elizabeth visited him regularly with the boy, lifting his depression if only for a few hours. Things improved a little in the spring. At least it wasn't so bloody dark, he said.

He turned grey. Hugh didn't take much notice at first, but by summer he was completely grey, and he had got thin and stooped.

When Sarah let them in one Saturday afternoon near Easter, Hugh stopped dead in the hallway as he heard the creaking strains of the accordion come from the sitting room.

'What's that?' he asked Sarah in astonishment.

'He's teaching the girls.' She kept a straight face.

'Hah!' Hugh laughed, relieved that his father had a purpose. He stayed the women while he listened. 'I don't believe it,' he said to himself, delighted. It was being murdered, but there was no mistaking it. ' "Eibhlín a rún".'

'They love it,' Sarah said to Elizabeth.

'Good for him,' Elizabeth said.

'They?' Hugh whispered.

'Deirdre and Delly,' Sarah whispered back, and this time she allowed herself a smile.

One Sunday in June, Sarah had him sitting out in the back garden, and Hugh joined him while the women prepared a roast.

'That woman insists, insists, mind, that the sun and fresh air will do me good. She thinks that it might even cure me, now that I've given up the fags.' He spoke with difficulty, his breath short, but a glint of humour was in his eye. 'To tell the truth,' he said confidentially, 'it makes it worse. That's a strange one for you now, but it makes it worse. You'd never think it.'

'God, it's a strange one, all right,' Hugh said, looking up at the blue sky and relishing the heat on his flesh. 'You'd think it'd be the opposite.'

'Listen . . .' Brendan faltered. 'Do you remember the last time I went to Croghan?'

'Last January twelve-month,' Hugh said, suddenly alerted by the tone of Brendan's voice.

'Well, I made arrangements with the parish priest, just in case.' He coughed, then looked Hugh in the face. 'I want to be buried with your mother, Hugh. I've talked about it to Sarah and she's agreed. Murphy's in Gorey will look after the details.

Just let them know when the time comes, and they'll look after everything. I have a letter for you inside, all the details are in that.'

The effort of having his say left him wheezing, and he was caught up with getting his breath back as if Hugh wasn't there. Hugh was stunned, then as he pulled himself together he waited until Brendan could relax a little.

'Sure that won't happen for a good while yet,' he said.

'Well, it might, and it might not. I've made my peace now anyhow.' He paused. 'The bit of land is yours and the few bob left over after the funeral belongs to Sarah and Deirdre. I hope that's all right with you.'

'That's fine,' Hugh said quietly. Then Brendan turned to him.

'Croghan is our home. If they'd let me, I'd be buried on the mountain. But as long as I don't have to travel too far, I don't mind,' he grinned. 'Maybe I should've gone back. I've often thought that. But then my life is here.'

He looked away.

'Everyone I love is here, so what do you do? You might love a piece of rock, but it won't love you back. It won't make your dinner for you, that's for sure,' he said as Deirdre called them to eat.

He leaned on the railing with one hand, and on Hugh's arm with the other as they went up the steps at the back. Hugh looked on him with admiration, hoping he would face his own death like that when his time came.

After dinner he found a quiet moment with Sarah and told her what Brendan had told him.

'Well,' she said, looking him in the eye, 'you've got to face up to these things.' She took the tea from the cupboard. 'It's not as bad as you might think. Every moment is precious now. You don't waste it. Oddly enough', she said turning to him again, 'we're very happy.'

'I . . . I'd understand that very well,' he said.

She reached up and kissed him on the cheek, before continuing her preparation of the tea.

On the way home he told Elizabeth about his conversation

with Brendan. She stopped while he was talking and she swallowed hard.

'Poor Brendan,' she said, her voice shaking. 'Just when life got good for him. It's like a bloody roundabout, *life*!' she said, turning angry. Then she calmed and put her hand on his breast, looking at him earnestly. 'But a body has to face up to these things.'

'That's what Sarah said.'

'Yes,' she said, turning to push the pram and leaving him behind. 'What else could she say?'

Bad dreams began to trouble him. At least once a week he woke at night in terror. At first there was only a sickly aftertaste, then, in the third week it stayed with him on waking, in all its clarity.

Out of the mountain peak rose his father's face and shoulders. He had one enormous eye covered by a cataract, yet he knew it could see everything by looking inside. The mouth cried out in anguish as it was covered in cloud. An angel, seven feet tall and dressed in a white robe, descended from the cloud and travelled at high speed. Hugh was forced to follow across the mountain until he was dizzy. He could not see its face, but knew it was the angel of death who had taken his mother. They stopped at one of the streams that fed the river below, and the angel lowered its head to drink. The water turned to blood, and the angel stood to face him, whereupon he woke in a cold sweat, feeling winded. Thankfully, Elizabeth always slept on.

In the last week of August there was a thunderstorm and he knocked off work. It was miserable like this, mud greasing into you everywhere. He had a drink with the others for the sake of drying out enough to knock the mud from his boots and, when he was passable, he took the tube home. Elizabeth was waiting for him, all dressed up and ready to go.

'Oh,' she said, relieved, 'I was hoping you'd knock off early.'

'What's wrong?' He knew, and the blood drained from his head.

'Deirdre was here half an hour ago. Brendan is in the Northern.'

He gripped her arms, wanting to shake her to tell him how he was, but the words wouldn't come.

'It looks bad,' she said. 'Deirdre said to hurry.'

He stared at her, turned on his heel and rooted for clean clothes in the bedroom, then ran upstairs to wash.

'Get a taxi,' he shouted, 'I'll follow you.'

As he stripped in the bathroom, he realized he hadn't shaved that morning. 'Fuck it,' he whispered, looking into the mirror, 'fuck it.' He washed himself as quickly as he could, then looked at his stubble again before giving himself a quick lather. The razor shook in his hand, and only a great act of will steadied it, allowing him to shave with minor cuts. He ran downstairs and found his shoes. The rain had eased so he didn't bother with a coat and, his hands shaking violently, he checked that he had his keys. Fuck it, they were in his old clothes. Fuck it. He got them and slammed the door behind him, running as he had never run. He got to the top of Citizen Road but there was no sign of Elizabeth. He looked up and down Hornsey Road in desperation, and then a black cab came, and she opened the door as it came alongside him and he jumped in. They didn't exchange a word till they reached the hospital and Hugh realized he didn't know what ward he was in, but Deirdre had told Elizabeth and now Elizabeth told him to go ahead, she would catch up. He ran along the corridors, desperately checking the signs.

There was Latin being spoken behind a screen. The sweat on him had gone cold and he felt weak as he eased himself behind it. A priest was giving Brendan extreme unction, the last rites, and Deirdre and Sarah were there, terribly pale. Brendan had an oxygen mask over his face, and the oxygen hissed. Hugh bowed his head and joined his hands as the priest laid on the oils.

When he had finished, the priest whispered some words to Sarah, put his hand on Deirdre's head as a blessing, shook Hugh's hand and left. Hugh embraced Sarah and Deirdre then, holding both of them.

'Where's Elizabeth?' Sarah asked wearily.

'She was on her way up. She's probably outside with young Brendan.'

'Deirdre, get her, will you?' As Deirdre left she glanced at Brendan and Hugh turned to see that Brendan's eyes were open, but expressionless. He was like an alien with the mask on, or a pilot in the war. Sarah went around the bed, stroked his forehead tenderly, and his eyes moved around to her.

'Are you comfortable?' she asked him, but there was no response. 'Blink if you are,' and he blinked. She smiled at him, and he winked, slowly. She laughed at that. 'You old rogue,' she said.

'Take this mask off,' he said, his voice muffled by the oxygen and mask.

'Are you sure?' He nodded lightly, so gingerly she took it away.

'That's better,' he said. 'I'm not dead yet. Do you know something?' he smiled weakly at Hugh. 'That extreme unction does a body a power of good. I'm a new man after it.'

Hugh laughed softly in relief. Maybe he would rally. Just then Deirdre came back with Elizabeth and Dan Stevie. Brendan turned his head slightly, and without a word Elizabeth held out his grandson to him. Dan Stevie laughed in delight at seeing his grandfather and a light of happiness touched Brendan's face. He tried to raise his hands to hold him, but he was too weak, and seeing this, Elizabeth held him closer and the child and man kissed. Tears rolled down each side of Brendan's cheeks, and Hugh realized he was weeping too. Everyone was weeping except Dan Stevie, who wanted to play with his grandfather.

'The hardest thing is to leave you all,' he whispered. 'The hardest thing.' His eyes closed, and they gasped, thinking he was gone. But he opened his eyes and rallied again. 'Hugh,' he whispered, and immediately Hugh leaned forward. 'The mountain, the mountain is our home.' Then his eyes closed again, and his head dropped slightly to the side.

'Maybe we should put back on the mask,' Elizabeth said through her tears.

Sarah put it on, and sure enough, he opened his eyes, but Hugh saw that already he had gone a distance from them. A nurse came in and they stood aside as she excused herself and adjusted the mask properly, before taking his pulse.

'I'll just get the doctor,' she said then. A doctor came within minutes, quickly checking his pulse. He pursed his lips, and then went to Sarah, taking her hand.

'It's only a matter of time, Sarah. I'm very sorry.'

'Thank you, doctor,' Sarah said, and Hugh was struck by her dignity.

The nurse brought them chairs, and they sat around the bed, waiting. His eyes were still open, but now they were sinking back into his skull. He died peacefully at a few minutes past five and, not waiting for the doctor to confirm it, Sarah closed his eyes. As they wept silently together, Hugh, though his heart was breaking, felt consoled that he was there, and in his heart he thanked God for the thunderstorm.

IRELAND

August 1956

Elizabeth's family, and Karl and Marta and their daughter, and Sarah's friends came to the removal from the morgue. Hugh half expected Sam to produce his camera, but no, he was dignified and solemn.

'Our Beth spoke highly of him, Hugh,' he said. 'He was a real toff, by her account.' They shook hands, and the grip was strong.

'It's Hugh, isn't?'

'That's right.'

'I'm Alice, Sarah's friend, and this is my daughter Delly.'

'I'm Deirdre's friend,' Delly said, looking back to her mother for reassurance.

'Sure I remember you well from Sarah's class.'

'That's right!' Alice said, pleased. Then she was serious. 'He was a good man.'

'Thank you. Thank you very much.'

'He sent you to us,' Karl said. 'I will always be grateful to him for that.'

'Yes,' Hugh smiled. 'Yes I suppose he did,' and in a sudden wave of emotion the two men embraced.

They travelled to Euston, following the hearse in a brace of taxis and Sam's Morris. It meant a lot to have family and friends on the station platform, as Brendan's coffin was loaded onto the train. There was a round of goodbyes and embraces, and Hugh came to Millie, her face tear-stained.

'Goodbye, Millie,' he said. 'See you soon.' Then he pulled her into his arms, crushing her to him. 'Thanks for everything,' he whispered, choking back his grief. 'Thanks for everything.' When he released her, she held his face in her hands, her own face knotted with emotion. Then she pulled at both his cheeks before letting him go and turning away. Out of the corner of his eye, Deirdre and Delly hugged their goodbyes, too.

They boarded, found their compartment and put their luggage on the overhead racks, then pulled down the window to say goodbye all over again.

'Goodbye, Delly!' Deirdre called. Delly waved frantically, crying heartily as if she would never see her friend again.

'Good luck,' Millie called, waving as the train pulled out. Karl was the last to raise his hand, towering above them all.

*

Deirdre took the seat by the window and stared at the passing city. As Elizabeth settled with Dan Stevie, Hugh scrutinized the black and white photos of the English countryside over the seats. He glanced at Sarah, whose eyes were downcast, lost in her own thoughts.

Deirdre continued to look out the window long after the city. The green fields and then the canals passed. Hugh noticed large bronze fields where corn had recently been harvested. Deirdre touched Sarah's shoulder to gain her attention. Sarah turned, her eyes heavy as if she had been asleep.

'He was my real father, wasn't he?'

Sarah's lips crumbled as she held out her arms and her daughter fell into them.

'Yes, pet, he was,' she managed before breaking down with Deirdre.

When they reached Holyhead, there were crowds of Irish waiting to take their places on the train. He saw himself in them, all those years ago, trusting his luck in a strange country, but at least he had his father by his side.

Hugh sent the women ahead, while he accompanied Brendan's coffin to the dock and watched as a crane hoisted it onto the foredeck of *Hibernia*. He had seen cattle being hoisted like that, back in the 40s, but never a coffin. He waited for a moment after it disappeared, feeling lost amongst the Welsh of the dockers. The water lapped between the ship and pier, as if to say, *Life goes on, life goes on.*

Right, he thought. Fair enough, and hands in his pockets and head down, he walked around to the gangway and boarded.

The ship was almost empty as it sailed, and that was something to be grateful for. Elizabeth and Sarah got out the flasks and sandwiches and they had some supper. The sea was calm, so when they had finished eating he went to check that the coffin was secure, and then he took Deirdre for a walk on deck.

'Have you ever seen such a greeny blue?' he asked her.

'No. It's lovely.'

They went around to the stern, and watched the wake. The seagulls were still with them.

'What age are you now, Deirdre?'

'Thirteen.'

'Thirteen? God, you're nearly a woman.'

She blushed and smiled shyly at that, as she brushed her long hair from her eyes. The wind blew it back again, and she left it to do as it pleased.

'Have you ever been back to Ireland?'

'No.'

'You're thirteen, and you've never been home?'

'London's my home,' she said, looking at him directly through her windblown hair.

'Oh. Right. True enough.'

They went back inside, and Sarah produced a pack of cards.

'Anyone? It's going to be a long night.'

They settled in and played a few games of twist, but they were all tired and, despite the heave and roll of the ship, they tried to sleep. Dan Stevie woke around two, and Elizabeth fed him milk from a separate flask, and he settled again. Unable to sleep, once dawn broke they went to the foredeck to be with Brendan's coffin. Elizabeth had assumed it would be in some kind of hold, and not exposed on deck like that.

'It's nicer this way, though, isn't it? Prouder, somehow.'

A shaft of light broke through the early morning cloud and

lit the Wicklow mountains. Absorbed, Elizabeth and Hugh watched it as the ferry approached Dún Laoghaire harbour.

'It's a good omen,' Elizabeth whispered as she slipped an arm around his waist. She was nervous about coming to Ireland, but already its beauty touched her. Hugh had painted a bleak picture of it, but he had to admit it was very beautiful.

No less than the sight of Dan Stevie well wrapped in her arms, her hair blowing in the cool wind. He looked south to the mountains.

'One of them yours, love?'

'No, it's further south.'

'Imagine, a mountain called after your name!'

'Ah, when you grow up with something, you take it for granted.'

Sarah and Deirdre came on deck.

'Did you get any sleep at all?' Hugh asked Sarah.

'Oh, an hour maybe.'

Deirdre yawned.

'There you are, pet,' Sarah nodded towards land. 'Ireland.' She glanced at Brendan's coffin.

'It's nice,' Deirdre yawned again.

They huddled together, watching the approaching shore in silence.

It took a while to get the coffin onto the train, but everything worked in the end and after another delay in Westland Row, they set out for Arklow. Brendan had instructed that this part of the journey would be by train, and now Hugh understood why. Much of the route was by the coast, and Elizabeth and Deirdre were enchanted by Killiney Bay.

'I'm impressed,' Sarah said to Hugh. 'I didn't think the east coast was so gorgeous.'

'It's not bad,' he conceded. It was all coming back to him, and it felt strange.

The hearse and a limousine were waiting for them in Arklow. Brendan had arranged a bit of style for his homecoming. Once outside the town, Hugh felt his skin crawling, as he knew he would see Croghan at any moment, and he knew that he had not wanted to come back, that a stern presence on the mountain barred him from it. But Brendan's words about belonging there steadied his nerve. He was back here for his father, and he would never renege on that. The women were chatting quietly among themselves, so that when he saw it he watched it in silence for several minutes before he tipped Elizabeth on the arm and nodded towards it.

'Is that it?' she asked, straining her neck forward as far as Dan Stevie's presence would allow.

'Yep.'

'It's beautiful. It's really beautiful, Hugh.'

Deirdre and Sarah had turned to look at it too, and gazed for some time before Deirdre asked, 'Is that where you were born, Hugh?'

'Aye, Deirdre. With ne'er a doctor, either,' he added, remembering what his mother had told him.

To his surprise, there was a large crowd of cousins and neighbours waiting for them. Five men, all Kinsellas whom he thankfully recognized, joined Hugh to carry the coffin into the church and lay it on a trellis before the altar. They were all very tall. Hugh shook their hands and they told him they were sorry for his trouble. He thanked them, before ushering his family into the front seat on the left of the church. The priest led the rosary and the congregation answered. Then the priest offered his condolences and shook their hands. This was the signal for the congregation to wait their turn to symphatize with Hugh and to gravely shake their hands, one by one, Hugh, Elizabeth, Sarah and Deirdre. In a brief lull, Hugh glanced at the coffin to see that it was covered in Mass cards and flowers.

When it was over, he ushered the women outside, and a crowd was still waiting for them. Several cousins and more neighbours introduced themselves, and Hugh did his best to introduce Elizabeth, Sarah and Deirdre.

'And who's this fine young chap?' a woman he vaguely recognized as a friend of his mother's wanted to know.

'Brendan Kinsella,' Elizabeth said.

'Isn't he a dote?' she smiled, delighted. 'Look, Johnny,' she said, pulling her husband by the sleeve of his jacket, 'Brendan's grandson. He's called after him.'

'Well God bless him,' said the man.

'How're you doing, Hugh?' asked a tall man with a small boy in his arms. 'You don't remember me, but I'm a cousin of yours – we're the Kavanaghs from Cummer.'

'Christ Almighty,' Hugh said, 'how are you? And who's this fine chap?'

'Ah, that's the youngest, Mungo.'

'Good man, young Mungo,' Hugh said, and the boy shyly looked away into his father's chest.

Hugh invited them all for a drink, and they politely agreed to go for one. He knew they had work to do, but knew also, as Brendan had warned him in his letter, that it would be mean not to ask them if they had a mouth on them. The undertakers too. They trooped down the road.

Once at the bar, he turned to them.

'Brendan left me strict instructions to buy a drink for all of you. Now what are you having?'

'He was one decent man,' an old man said, and there was a murmur of agreement.

They had tea in their guest house in Arklow. The woman of the house knew they were in mourning, and showed them deference.

'If Brendan were from Clare,' Deirdre asked, 'would there have been a big crowd like that, shaking your hand and leaving flowers?'

'Yes, there would,' Sarah said, surprised.

'Well, can we go there?'

'Sometime, pet.'

'No. This time, Sarah,' Deirdre insisted, twisting in her chair.

'I'll think about it.'

'Sarah, please . . .'

'I said I'll think about it, Deirdre!'

'Deirdre,' Elizabeth asked, 'would you not like to come with us to Croghan tomorrow?'

Deirdre twisted her fingers, embarrassed but determined.

'I'm sorry, Elizabeth. But I want to go to Clare. I'm sorry, Hugh.'

'That's all right, Deirdre,' he said. 'I understand.'

It took him a long time to sleep that night, and he heard Sarah's muffled weeping next door.

In the morning, there was a blue sky and the clamour of birds. In the bathroom, Hugh looked out the window and caught his breath. There it was, the blue mountain, with not one peak, as he remembered, but two. It seemed so aloof, so distant and beautiful against the blue sky of which it was a part. He wanted to return to London, be anywhere but Ireland, where everywhere there seemed to be a mountain, soft-coloured, beckoning, drawing him towards it, its oldness.

The limousine called for them at ten thirty the next morning and they were in good time for the funeral Mass. Again the church was packed, with more wreaths arranged around the coffin. Sarah and Deirdre started to cry as the Mass ended, but Hugh had no time for emotion as he joined the same five men who had shouldered the coffin with him the previous day, and they carried it to the grave. There, Hugh saw for the first time the Celtic cross which was his mother's memorial.

MÁIRE KINSELLA,
beloved wife of Brendan, mother of Hugh,
went to her rest
January 15, 1943.

There was some Irish underneath that, but Hugh could not remember exactly what it meant. Something about eternal light shining upon her soul.

When the coffin was lowered into the ground, the priest led the rosary again, and was answered by the mourners. When they had finished, Hugh bent down and scooped up some stony earth and, hesitating to take one last look, dropped it onto the coffin. It was only then that Sarah and Deirdre, and then Elizabeth, broke down, and he moved to try and comfort them as the gravediggers started to fill the grave, and then even Dan Stevie started to wail. His neighbours stood back and talked among themselves, but did not leave until Hugh and his family were ready to go, and then some more came up to them and said they were sorry for his trouble, and shook hands with each of them.

There was another round of drinks in the pub, and this time both Elizabeth and Sarah had brandies, and Deirdre had red lemonade, which was on the house.

On the way back to the guest house, Sarah told them that Deirdre and herself would take the afternoon train to Dublin, and the evening train to Limerick. They could get a bus to her family home in Clare the following day.

'Thank you, Sarah,' Deirdre said, looking earnestly into her mother's face and squeezing Sarah's hand.

'It must be very exciting for you,' Elizabeth said.

'It is,' she smiled.

'I was hoping you'd come to Croghan with us,' Hugh said.

'Well,' Sarah said, looking him in the eye, 'you have your inheritance there, Hugh, and Deirdre has hers in Clare.'

'Well, good luck, so.'

The woman in the guest house rang and hired a hackney for them. It was an old but ample green Ford, and when they had seen Sarah and Deirdre off on the afternoon train they asked the driver, one Brian Kennedy, to bring them to Croghan.

'Whereabouts?' Mr Kennedy asked.

'Do you know something, but the name of it's gone clean out of my head . . .'

'It's a big enough place,' Mr Kennedy said doubtfully, but then he rallied. 'But it's not that big.'

'I tell you what,' Hugh said. 'Why don't we stop off in O'Rafferty's in Coolgreany and have a drink, and we can work it out from there.'

'Well now,' Mr Kennedy said, starting out, 'that's the best idea I've heard all day.' They set off at a leisurely pace for Coolgreany, a pleasant breeze ventilating the car, Dan Stevie happy in Elizabeth's arms.

'Are you nervous?' Elizabeth smiled, touching Hugh's hand. She was wearing a lovely polka dot summer dress.

'A bit. It's been a long time.'

'Are you from round these parts?' Mr Kennedy enquired.

Before long, Hugh was placing the names of his neighbours, and where they all lived.

They stopped at O'Rafferty's, glad to be out of the sun's glare in the cool bar. Mr Kennedy came in with them and called the owner.

'Vincey, come down here and serve these good people.'

'Ah the bold Brian,' Vincey called back, 'how're you going on?'

Hugh thought he remembered a shop in the front when he had been as a child, but the prints of the horses and of Robert Emmet in the dock and the laying of the cable to New York and the fireplace were all still there.

'And who have we here?' Vincey asked, drying his hands as he came in from the back.

'I'm Brendan Kinsella's son,' Hugh said. 'I don't know if you remember him.'

'Begob I do,' Vincey said. 'Sure wasn't I at his funeral yesterday.'

'There you go,' Elizabeth whispered.

'And this is Brendan's grandson, I hear,' Vincey said.

Over the drinks, they confirmed the route, and spent a pleasant interlude before setting out again, turning opposite the doctor's house, and driving back up the village before turning left up the steep road on their way to the mountain. Hugh vaguely remembered the way, and in full view of the mountain, the road seemed to travel around it for a long time without coming any closer. Then finally they crossed a bridge over a shallow stream, the mountain looming beyond it, and he knew they were almost there.

Mr Kennedy dropped them and agreed to come back in an hour.

'What a beautiful place,' she said.

'It's hard to think that not so long ago, people died here from famine.'

'Really? How could there be famine in a place like this?'

'My mother told me once, that my great-great-grandmother, I think it was, died of fever in the Gorey workhouse,' he said, speaking quickly in his excitement. 'My great-grandmother was a little girl at the time, and was with her, but she survived, somehow. It's a leather factory now, I think. The workhouse, I mean. That was only in the 1850s. I asked my father about it once, but he said it was all lies. Who knows.'

They continued on, passing some whitewashed, slated houses. Small children played in the front yards, and hens wandered around, clucking. From this side the mountain showed a single, granite peak, with two shoulders sloping away, westward, and eastward towards the sea. Near the centre of its lower reaches was a bog from which sprang a stream. They opened a gate and started out onto the mountain proper. In the pleasant heat, they had no sense of an end to the day, but the long summer twilight had begun.

'Are you going right to the top?'

'Yes,' he said, as if to himself. 'The house is up there, near the top.'

She squinted and cast her eyes around the mountain.

'I don't see any house. Maybe it's been knocked down.'

'It can't be.'

Sweating, they travelled up a narrow lane, past some abandoned granite cottages, and he signalled to Elizabeth to stop. She checked Dan Stevie, who was wakening in her arms.

'This is our house.'

Elizabeth's mouth dropped. She looked the small stone building up and down.

'The window's broken,' she said then.

Hugh tried the door and it creaked open. Rearranging Dan Stevie on her hip, Elizabeth followed him inside. The sunlight streamed through a small back window, dust motes caught in its beam. A layer of dust was everywhere, and the stone which had broken the window was on the floor, the shards of glass arranged as if by design. He picked up the stone and held it out for both of them to examine, then placed it carefully on the table. Brendan had not washed up after him, and a mould had hardened beneath the dust in the blue and white-striped mug.

Hugh went to the open hearth and, leaning down, turned the creaking bellows. A cloud of ash rose in the fireplace.

Elizabeth shifted Dan Stevie again and looked into what had once been Hugh's bedroom.

'Look, Dan Stevie,' she said quietly. 'Is this where you slept?' she asked, turning back to Hugh.

'Yes. My mother used to kneel just here,' he said, indicating the hearth, 'saying her prayers in Irish, and I used peep out from the door there.'

He looked into his parents' bedroom, and the old brass bed was still there, beneath a canopy of cobwebs, the linen crumpled against the bolster. A crucifix hung over the bed, and an oleograph of the Virgin, pointing at her bleeding heart, hung on the side wall. Elizabeth squeezed in beside him with Dan Stevie, who was gurgling away happily. The chamber pot, stained ochre, was still beside the bed. There was a stain on the ceiling where the roof had leaked.

'Well,' he said, letting go his breath.

They went outside and looked in the small outhouses, empty but for a few rusting implements. There were fresh sheep droppings in the lean-to.

'I want to go up the mountain. Do you mind?'

'Can we come?'

'Can you manage?' He touched her arm.

'Let's see how far we can go, shall we?' She smiled. 'Are you going all the way to the top?'

'I want to find an old path up there. A rock.'

They looked up towards the peak.

'People were evicted from cottages like that,' he said out of the blue. 'In the last century. When all this place was owned by one man. All over the mountain, down to Coolgreany. But they fought him. His soldiers, I mean. Men, women and children fought them, for their homes. Some were killed. It was a famous fight. And it was famous for other things too,' he enthused. 'They found gold here, you know. I'm not exactly sure where. Maybe in one of the streams. I'd say you could find it still. I used to look for it as a child . . .' He trailed off.

'I used to think if I found gold,' he said, becoming more reflective, 'we could be rich, and my father could come home from England and there'd be no fighting and we could be together and we could be happy. A child's fairytale.'

'I've never seen you like this,' she said. 'It's good.'

'Well . . .' he said, embarrassed.

Impatient, he hurried ahead. Hampered by the child, Elizabeth could not keep up with him, and let him go.

Panting as he neared where he was sure the path must be, he saw her and waved and, with Dan Stevie in her arms, she returned the wave awkwardly.

He looked below him into the valley and then across the broad sweep of land to the sea. The sea drew him towards the eastern shoulder of the mountain, and he found what he took to be the path. It wasn't quite what he remembered, but he stood on it, looking out to sea, remembering how he used to linger there, sometimes with his mother, looking towards England where Brendan lived. He was sure she used to come here alone when he went to London with his father.

On his way back he saw that the sun was setting beyond Annagh. He took a deep breath of satisfaction as he glanced at the sky to the south-west, above Hollyfort, his eye caught by the waning moon, becoming clearer as light faded. As far as he could make out, Venus had set, and following the sun, faintly, he was almost sure, Jupiter. Nearer the moon, invisible without a telescope, was Neptune. Was that right? Maybe it was the wrong time of year. It depended on things like that. He should have put more effort into reading Karl's books.

He headed for a white rock that he remembered. Below, he could hear Dan Stevie crying. Elizabeth tried to placate him but failed. As a last resort, she took off his clothes, and then, delighted with her idea, decided to bathe him in the stream. 'What could be better, Dan Stevie,' her voice floated up to Hugh, 'than to bathe in your own mountain water?'

Hugh turned at that moment and watched, dumbfounded, as Elizabeth placed Dan Stevie in the stream. Staring, his flesh cold, he saw it as his mother drowning her newborn when Hugh was eight years old. He tried to deny it, to shout that it wasn't true, but only a choking sound came. He ran back up the mountain, and did not stop until his lungs would let him go no further. His trembling worsened until he shook like a machine breaking from its rivets, and a long shout left him. As it was lost over the mountain, he felt a dense energy fall away from his head and body and transform itself into a large male figure which stumbled and then ran away from him down the slope. Weakly, he followed it through clouded eyes and saw that it was his father. Brendan ran awkwardly, without looking back and, as he met the bog, he abruptly slowed, dragging one foot and then the other from the squelching turf. But his effort became more hopeless as his feet were sucked deeper, until suddenly the bog gave way and he plunged vertically under a blue jet of water and disappeared. In a flood of sympathy, Hugh was at one with his father, sinking into the bottomless source as he would when his own time came; and he saw what his father saw as Brendan stared upwards at the blue receding world before he was at peace.

Acknowledgements

Acknowledgements are due to Ciaran Carty who as literary editor of the *Sunday Independent*, Dublin, published *The Mountain*, a short story on which the novel is based; to James Liddy and Creighton University Press for kind permission to quote 'Blue Mountain' © 1964 & 1995 James Liddy; to The Tyrone Guthrie Centre at Annamakerrig, where some of this novel was written; to the editors of *Asylum*, and *Dun Laoghaire–Rathdown Review*, which published excerpts; to Mr Robbie Brennan of the Maritime Museum, Dún Laoghaire, for his maritime information.

A number of books provided inspiration, including *This is London* (subtitled 'From Dawn Till Night') published by Bruno Cassirer, Oxford, distributed by Faber & Faber London, 1953; *Das Gesicht der Hansestadt Hamburg im Wandel der Jahre 1939–1945* (The Features of the Hansestadt Hamburg During the Course of the Years 1939–1945) compiled by F. Werner, Verlag Eckardt & Messdorff, Hamburg; *Mathematics*, Time Life International, 1963, 1965, 1969; *The Stars in Their Courses*, by Sir James Jeans, Cambridge University Press, 1931; *The Wandering Scholars*, by Helen Waddell, Constable & Co Ltd, London, 1927 (from which the verses on page 201 are quoted); *Historic Gorey 3: The famine years* by Michael Fitzpatrick; *An Irish Navvy: The diary of an exile* by Dónall MacAmhlaigh, RTÉ Radio Booktime Series, 1989. 'An Spailpín Fánach' is a traditional poem in Irish. English version by Michael Considine and John Casey.

Personal thanks to friends and family, including Seán and Kay Halford, Michael Considine and Mary Manley for our jaunts around North Wexford, and especially to Croghan Kinsella; to poet Michael Considine, for access to his 1950s newspaper collection, and his critical, witty eye; to Michael Augustin and Hannes Golda for their timely gift of the complete symphonies of Mahler; to James Liddy for his description of Coolgreany circa 1956 and other inspirations; to poet and essayist Thomas Lynch, in whose county Clare cottage some of this novel was written.

Special thanks to artist Veronica Bolay, who kindly loaned me the extraordinary record of her native city of Hamburg, *Das Gesicht der Hansestadt Hamburg im Wandel der Jahre 1939–1945* (cf above), and who spoke to me of that time, to John and Penny Cassidy; to poet Matthew Sweeney and his wife Rosemary; and to novelist Carole Hayman for their hospitality in London while I explored the physical background of the novel; and to Carole, for our trip to Highgate Cemetary, and for the photographs; to poet and dramatist Terry McDonagh, and art historian Ulrike Boskamp for their hospitalities in Hamburg and Berlin, important to the German background of the novel; to nurse and student anthropologist Elaine Clear, for background information on birth; to my brother John Casey, who corrected Irish lines in the novel; to my parents, Annie Cassidy and Patrick Casey, for their generous memories, and to our family, for their constant support over the years; to Lisa Eveleigh, my agent, for her kindness, patience, suggestions and friendship.

Very special thanks to poet and novelist Christine Clear, whose understanding of the difficulties, critical eye, suggestions and constant support and friendship kept the ship afloat.

Thanks to my family, who make cameo, fictional appearances, and also to the family of Vincey O'Rafferty, who plays a cameo, fictional role as his youthful self in the Epilogue. Up to his death on Christmas Eve 1997, Mr O'Rafferty played his piano accordion in his pub in Coolgreany, county Wexford. Apart from these and public events, such as the hangings at Holloway Road prison and the fact that some of the settings are pertinent to the author's childhood, this is entirely a work of fiction.